"Fuck you," I snarl at my sister.

And then I throw a car at her head.

It's not a big car. A little silver Prius. But let me tell you something: if you saw a freaking Prius hurtling through the air towards you, you'd duck too. Chloe and Adam throw themselves to the ground, the car passing feet above their heads with a screech of tortured metal. It crashes into the ambulance, flipping onto its side and skidding away across the broken concrete.

I don't give them a chance to retaliate. I grab yet another Prius, a black one this time, off to our left. I'm not picking Priuses specifically; this is California, and there are ten million of them on the roads. This time, instead of simply throwing it at them with my mind, I swing it in a wide arc. It scrapes paint off the line of cars opposite, rushing at Chloe and Adam with the force of a meteor.

Praise for
Jackson Ford and The Frost Files

Praise for *The Girl Who Could Move Sh*t with Her Mind*

"Furious, frenetic, fun, and 'f★★k you': All equally valid descriptions of this book and its punk rock chef / psychic warrior protagonist. It's like the X-Men, if everybody was sick of each other's sh★t, they had to work manual labor to pay rent, and Professor X was a sociopathic government stooge. A drunken back-alley brawler of a book."
—Robert Brockway, author of *The Unnoticeables*

"Like *Alias* meets *X-Men*. I loved it." —Maria Lewis

"Ford's debut holds nothing back, delivering a sense of absurd fun and high-speed thrills that more than lives up to that amazing title." —*B&N Sci-Fi & Fantasy Blog*

"Teagan is a frank and funny narrator for this wild ride, which starts off with our heroine falling from the 82nd floor of a skyscraper and pretty much never slows down.... A fast-paced, high-adrenaline tale that manages to get into some dark themes without losing its sense of fun." —*Kirkus*

"Ford's breakneck pace keeps the tension high, and the thrills coming the whole way through." —*BookPage*

"The novel unfolds cinematically with loads of breathtaking action, a perfect candidate for film or television adaptation.... [Readers will] want more." —*Booklist*

"Ford's strengths are evident in the taut action sequences and suspenseful pacing." —*Publishers Weekly*

"The writing and storytelling is as clear and fun as the title indicates." —*Locus*

Praise for *Random Sh*t Flying Through the Air*

"A fantastic follow-up.... Readers who enjoyed Teagan's first brush with disaster will be thrilled to see her pushed beyond her limits in this winning sequel." —*Publishers Weekly*

"This second book about psychokinetic superspy Teagan is even more suspenseful than *The Girl Who Could Move Sh*t with Her Mind* (2019). The stakes couldn't be higher.... The suspense, the danger, and the rocket-fueled pace are all turned up to 11 in this more-than-satisfying sequel." —*Kirkus*

"This smart, action-packed novel is tighter than its predecessor, and Ford injects just enough exposition that new readers will be able to pick up here.... Readers will be back for the next entry." —*Booklist*

Praise for *Eye of the Sh*t Storm*

"Fans who've been along for the ride on Teagan's previous two outings know what to expect by now, and this third installment fully delivers, with a breakneck pace, high stakes, and plenty of wisecracks.... The result is gripping, suspenseful, and thoroughly enjoyable. An un-put-down-able, action-packed adventure that packs an emotional punch." —*Kirkus*

"A non-stop adrenaline high. Fans of the series will eagerly await the further adventures of Teagan and her cohorts, and newcomers will quickly fall in love with Jackson's quirky cast of characters, imaginative storytelling, and wry wit."

—*Library Journal*

"Series fans will be pleased to see Jackson's edgy and irreverent tone intact." —*Publishers Weekly*

A SH*TLOAD OF CRAZY POWERS

By Jackson Ford

The Girl Who Could Move Sh★t with Her Mind
Random Sh★t Flying Through the Air
Eye of the Sh★t Storm
A Sh★tload of Crazy Powers

A
SH*TLOAD
OF CRAZY
POWERS

JACKSON FORD

orbitbooks.net

Copyright © 2022 by Rob Boffard
Excerpt from *August Kitko and the Mechas from Space* copyright © 2022 by Alex White
Excerpt from *Shards of Earth* copyright © 2021 by Adrian Czajkowski

Cover images © Shutterstock

Orbit
Hachette Book Group
1290 Avenue of the Americas
New York, NY 10104
orbitbooks.net

First Edition: May 2022
Simultaneously published in Great Britain by Orbit

Orbit is an imprint of Hachette Book Group.
The Orbit name and logo are trademarks of Little, Brown Book Group Limited.

The publisher is not responsible for websites (or their content) that are not owned by the publisher.

The Hachette Speakers Bureau provides a wide range of authors for speaking events. To find out more, go to www.hachettespeakersbureau.com or call (866) 376-6591.

Library of Congress Control Number: 2021950258

ISBNs: 9780316702805 (trade paperback), 9780316702799 (ebook)

Printed in the United States of America

LSC-C

Printing 1, 2022

Dedicated to The Alchemist, Hollywood,
and roast chicken

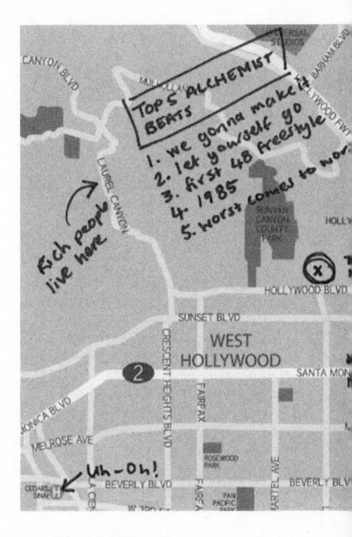

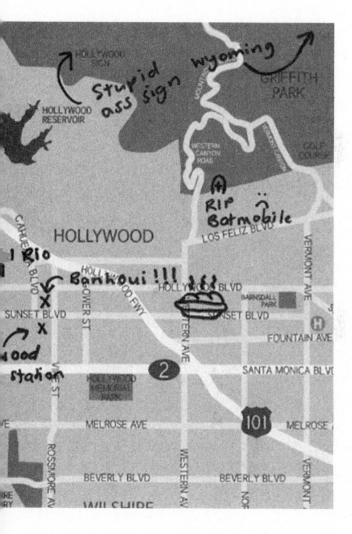

ONE

Teagan

I should have learned kung-fu.

I'm a secret agent working for the US government. I should be able to knock someone out, right?

Because the thing is, people underestimate me. I'm short, not super-fit and I look like I couldn't punch my way out of a wet paper takeout bag. How great would it be to knock someone on their ass with a wild Shaolin axe kick, or whatever they call it? Plus, it would be a tremendous backup for when my psychokinesis (read: my ability to move shit with my mind) goes on the fritz.

Hell, I probably could have gotten Tanner – the terrifying intelligence operative who happens to be my boss – to pay for it.

It definitely would have been useful at this particular moment. Do you know where I fucking am? I am stumbling around in the woods beneath Griffith Observatory, just north of Hollywood. It's muddy, it's cold, it's 5 a.m. and dark as hell. I just survived an enormous car crash, and I have no idea where I'm going. I also happen to be coming down from a crystal meth high, which is a story I really don't have time to get into right now. Oh, and men with guns and helicopters are chasing me.

I can't actually use my psychokinesis – PK, as I call it – on them, because I've used a ton of it tonight already, and I can only use so much before it has to recharge. I have no choice but to run, because if I fight back, I'll get destroyed.

And to make matters worse, my underwear has chosen this moment to ride up right into the crack of my ass.

Angry shouts split the darkness behind me. I'm not in deep forest or anything. It's a regular California scrubland, with lengths of open ground interrupted by boulders and hillocks and sparse groves of birch and eucalyptus. There was a huge storm in Los Angeles last night, so the ground isn't hardpack any more. It's mud – not deep, but sticky, caking my sneakers and pants.

Uphill. That's all I have to do right now. Just keep heading uphill. Uphill is the opposite direction from the road, from the scene of the crash. I have no idea whether it will help me actually lose the people chasing me or not, but it's the closest thing to a goal I've got.

Torchlight flickers on my right, and I actually flinch away from it. That turns out to not be a good idea, because I'm still moving forward, and promptly lose my balance. With a yelp, I throw my hands out in front of me, grabbing hold of a nearby tree trunk. I spin around, going to one knee in the mud.

"Piece of *fuck*," I snarl, forcing myself upright. This would be a lot easier if I didn't have a bum knee. I actually hurt it *before* the crash, and it's currently wrapped in miles of strapping, tight underneath my jeans. It's functional – just – but it hurts like hell. My head feels as if it's trailing three feet behind my body, like it's filled with helium and attached to a string.

Rotor blades roar. A heavy duty searchlight beam splits the

trees, sweeping past no more than six feet away. The blowback from the chopper gusts through the branches, loose leaves flying into my face. I wait, dead-still, until the searchlight moves away from me, then keep going.

The next patch of ground is so steep that I have to use my hands to clamber up it. My lungs burn with the effort, white-hot acid spreading through my torso, searing a wicked stitch in my side. I come over the top of the rise, descending into a small gully. As I do, I get a glimpse of the Observatory through the trees. A blinding-white domed palace on the hill, lit from below by spotlights. If I can just get there, I can . . .

Do what, exactly? How is getting to the Observatory going to help me? If I want to stay hidden, then it's not a great idea to run towards the bright white object at the top of the hill. Problem is, I don't have another solution. I don't have a single clue about where else to go, so I aim myself in the direction of the Observatory, and run like hell.

The stitch eats into my side. Branches whip at my face, scratching at my skin. I'm breathing too fast, and somehow, still not getting enough air into my lungs. The deeper I go, the thicker the mud gets. It goes from foot-deep to ankle-deep, cold and liquid, flooding my shoes. I'm shivering with shock, and a healthy dose of exhaustion. But I have to keep moving. I don't have any other choice. I *cannot* let myself get taken.

No sooner does the thought occur than my foot plunges into a shin-deep hole. I go down, and I go down hard.

I land on my side in the mud, left arm bent awkwardly underneath me, the impact sending up a horrible bark of pain. I cry out, eyes squeezed shut, agonised, frustrated tears leaking out. There's mud everywhere now, on my face, up my nose, in my ears. I roll onto my stomach, a single thought blaring like a fire alarm in my mind. *Get up get up get up.*

I don't get the chance. There are thundering footsteps, and then a knee in my back. White torchlight blinds me. A hand on my head, forcing me into the mud. The panic and anger are like rabid dogs, snarling and foaming. I have to stop him from taking me. I can't let that happen.

It's not hard for me to drain the tank on my PK. After everything that's happened to me tonight, it's not surprising that I'm out of juice. I try to grab as many objects as I can: my captor's weapon, his torch, the zippers on his jacket. All I get back is the barest flicker of dead-static feeling in my brain. It's worse than normal; usually, I can still feel objects around me, but now I can't even do that. I am beyond exhausted, and my PK just isn't listening to me any more.

"Got her!" my captor yells. "She's down!"

The pressure comes off the back of my head. He clamps his hands around my wrists, wrenching them behind me so hard that he almost dislocates both of my shoulders. The cuffs go on with a self-satisfied click, biting deep into my skin.

The man on top of me spits, huffs an exhausted breath. "You have the right—" He breaks off, coughs, tries again. "You have the right to remain silent. Anything you say can and will be used against you in a court of law . . ."

The LAPD helicopter swoops low overhead, the sound of the rotor blades all but obliterating his voice. Not that it matters. Rights or not, I am truly and properly fucked.

And you know what the worst part of all this is?

None of it would have happened if my brother and sister hadn't come back from the dead.

TWO

Teagan

OK, look: if this story is going to make any sense, I need to explain a few things.

I promise I'll be quick. And just so it's worth your while, at the end I'll tell you about a trick to cook the world's best roast chicken. Ready? Here we go.

My parents were brilliant geneticists, and they wanted to create the ultimate soldier. The government wouldn't let them, so they set up shop on a massive ranch in Wyoming. Turns out, it's really hard to put a bunch of superpowers in one person, so they put them in three. Their own children. I got psychokinesis, my sister got the ability to see things in the infrared spectrum and my brother never needed to sleep.

That last one was a mistake, because he ended up going completely, homicidally insane. When I was sixteen, he burned down our house, and killed everyone in our family but me. Then the government discovered what I could do, and locked me up in a scientific facility for four years. When their studies on me hit a dead end, they told me that I had a choice: I could either work for them in LA, or they would cut me open and put my brain in a jar.

I like my brain where it is, thanks, so I went for the first option. Ended up working with a Los Angeles black-bag crew called China Shop. Our jobs involve taking down regular human bad guys, but over the past few months, we've had more than one person with abilities mess with us. We didn't know much about where they were coming from, and fighting them took its toll. The latest little episode put my friend Annie in hospital, in a coma, after she got struck by lightning.

Got all that? Good. Next time you have a chicken, spatchcock it. Cut the spine out with some heavy scissors, and press it flat. Cooks in half the time, is basically impossible to dry out, and you get the world's crispiest, tastiest skin. You're welcome.

Now: let's go back to around forty-five minutes before the LAPD pushes me down into the mud and reads me my rights. I'm in Annie's room at Cedars-Sinai Hospital when my dead brother walks through the door.

I don't recognise him at first. We've tangled multiple times over the past day, but he's been running around with a bandana over his nose and mouth. No bandana now, and even as I grab a bunch of surgical instruments from a nearby tray and bring them into the air between us, my brain is starting to put it together.

When I realise who it is, all I can do is gape.

And that's *before* my dead sister moves out from behind him.

I take a step back, my legs bumping into the chair behind me, sitting down hard. The instruments clatter to the floor.

Outside in the hall, the hospital PA system bleeps, a call for the doctor soaked in static.

"It's good to see you, Emily," my sister Chloe says. "We need to talk."

Emily.

It's been a long time since I used that name. A long time

since I went by anything but *Teagan*. Hearing it makes a cold sweat spring out on my palms.

Seven years since I saw either of them. Seven years since Adam, my brother, broke Chloe's leg and left her to crawl across the floor while he set our home on fire. Seven years they've been alive, and I had no idea.

There's no way. I don't believe it.

But I'm already noticing the details. It starts with the eyes. The Chloe in front of me is older, the willowy teenage figure I remember turned wiry and hard, but she has the same eyes. Deep blue, cold as the Pacific. Seared into my memory. Her hair, which used to blow free around her head, is tied back in a ponytail. The same blonde colour I remember. Faded acne scars pit her skin. She wears a dark green puffer vest over a sleeveless tank and jeans, polished black boots on her feet.

And Adam . . .

He was always big. Huge shoulders, barrel chest, straining at his thick black sweater. He's grown his hair out, a straggly grey-black mane around his head to go with his tangled beard. But like Chloe, his eyes haven't changed. They couldn't belong to anyone else. If Chloe's eyes are the cold, blue surface of the ocean, Adam's are the water a thousand feet down. Blank and empty, filled with monsters you can't see. They are eyes that have never known a second of sleep. That have spent twenty-six years awake, that have been driven somewhere beyond madness.

I open my mouth. Close it again. To my left, Annie lies silent, cocooned in tubes and beeping machines.

She's here because of Adam and Chloe. Because one of their projects escaped: a little kid who could control electricity. Annie got in the way. My friend is in a coma, only barely holding on . . . because of *them*.

Chloe has the good grace to look slightly uncomfortable. She takes a hesitant step towards me. "I know it's been a while—"

I let out a sound that is somewhere between a moan and a sob. My feet skitter on the shiny hospital floor, pushing the chair back, bumping it against the wall.

"Emily—" Chloe says.

"Don't call me that." My voice barely makes it out of my throat.

"Please just listen . . ."

"*Stay the fuck away from me!*"

Chloe puts her hands up. Her palms are grimy, damp from the rain. I have a sudden urge to tell her to go clean herself up. *Doesn't she know she's in a hospital?*

"Emily," Chloe says again. She speaks slowly and carefully. Politely, even. "You're in danger. You need to come with us. Right now."

"I'm not going anywhere with you."

"There's a lot I have to tell you. I should never have let it go on this long. Please, please, just come with me. I'll explain everything."

"*Stay back!*" Cold sweat slicks my skin. My tongue feels like it's twice its normal size.

A strange expression crosses Chloe's face then. Frustration, mixed with the slightest touch of sadness. "I'm sorry about this next part. But we just don't have time."

The icy sweat makes me shiver. Except: the shiver is way too powerful. I'm not just cold: I'm *freezing*, as if my internal organs have frozen solid, blocks of ice around my lungs and heart and stomach.

What the hell?

The shiver is so violent that I almost collapse. I hug myself, my teeth chattering. Chloe tilts her head, and the cold surges. My entire body goes numb. I slip forward off the chair, then collapse forward onto my knees. I roll drunkenly onto my side, my body jackhammering.

And somehow, through the impossible, terrifying cold, I understand.

Our abilities have evolved over the years. Adam can make people dream. I can lift much heavier objects and organic matter, which I never used to be able to move. It's a lot harder, but I can do it. Chloe was always able to see infrared light, which meant she could detect body heat. Apparently, she's learned to manipulate that heat as well. Raise and lower internal temperatures.

If you hadn't figured it out already, Chloe and Adam are bad news. They've been creating more genetically modified kids, like the one that put Annie in a hospital bed. They've killed people, a lot of people – maybe not directly, but through letting those kids loose in the world.

Whatever they want from me, it can't be good.

I hunch into myself, desperate to control the shivering. I can barely move, let alone focus enough to use my PK. The cold is like a living thing, clawing at the inside of my ribcage. Eyes squeezed shut, throat a parched wasteland. I keep thinking that alarms will start to ring, that security guards will come thundering down the corridor. But outside the room, the hospital is silent.

Soft footsteps. Chloe crouches over me, breathing hard. When she speaks, her voice is a little ragged, like she's just run a wind sprint. "Once we're safe, I'll tell you everything, I promise. Just hold on for me."

She gives my shoulder an affectionate squeeze. A sisterly one.

I hunch even deeper, curling into a foetal position, my back to her. Desperately trying to move. To think. I'm numb, burning, shaking so hard that I'm sure my teeth are going to shatter.

I have no idea how Chloe and Adam survived. I have only the barest idea of what's happening here. But I do know this: they aren't the same people I once knew. Deep down, I know – no, I *understand* – that if they take me, they'll never let me go.

Worse than that: what if Annie wakes up . . . and I'm gone?

I don't just mean gone from here. I mean, gone for good. Because if Chloe and Adam take me, I'll vanish. Annie will think I abandoned her. Just plain walked out.

I can't do that to her. I won't.

"Adam," Chloe says.

Back in Wyoming, nobody could control Adam. My mom and dad had to lock him away. That's changed, because he obeys his sister without question. Heavy footfalls approach, a shadow falling over me.

Adam bends down, and gets his gigantic arms underneath my body, forcing them under my shoulders and hips.

No!

But I can't move. Can't speak.

And there's no one coming to save me.

THREE

Teagan

As Adam lifts me up (*my brother, he's here, this is him, it really is*) I twist sideways. There's a moment where I'm hanging half in and half out of his arms, where it looks like he's going to be able to pull me back. Then I wrench my shoulders away, and fall. I land hard, banging my jaw, teeth clacking together, still paralysed with cold.

Not my finest escape attempt.

"Help me," I say. It's barely a whisper. I don't even know who I'm asking for help. Annie, or the doctors, or God, or the fucking flying spaghetti monster. Not that it matters. No one comes. There's no sound but the beeping of the machines, the distant hum of the hospital.

Where the fuck is everyone? I know it's after 4 a.m., but this is a hospital. There must be *some* nurses on the graveyard shift, some junior doc doing the rounds . . .

"We have to move," Chloe tells Adam. He scoops me up, and this time, I'm incapable of resisting.

They hustle me into the corridor, looking left and right to check that it's empty. Adam is breathing hard. His breath smells rank, like something crawled into his throat and died.

I want to tell him to brush his teeth, but I'm still on the edge of freezing to death.

Jesus, can Chloe actually cause hypothermia? If she lowers my core temperature enough, will my organs shut down? The crazy thing is, she doesn't even have to be that powerful to do it. Raise or lower body temperature by even a few degrees, and things start going wrong real fast.

Once again, the disbelief – the sheer unreality of the situation – crashes down on me. Chloe and Adam can't be alive. It's not possible.

"Here," Chloe says, from out of my line of sight. There's the rumble of wheels on vinyl flooring, and then I'm lowered into a chair. A wheelchair. The lights in the corridor are way too bright, and I can't even squeeze my eyes shut to block them out.

I'm shivering so hard that I can barely stay in the chair. I'm pretty sure one of my limbs has fallen off, along with my nose and lips. My head tilts backwards, giving me a glimpse of Chloe. She looks exhausted now, drained. It must be taking a real effort for her to maintain this, the same way it takes it out of me when I push my PK too far. Why doesn't she just let Adam put me in a dream world? Pacify me that way?

It's worked before. Less than twenty-four hours ago, in fact. China Shop had encountered another individual with abilities: a little boy named Leo Nguyen, who could control electricity. He wasn't a bad kid, just scared – and there was no way I was handing him over to Tanner. She would have done the same to him that she did to me: locked him in a facility, alone, to study him. I only had four years of it; Leo would have been in there for a decade. More. No way I was letting that happen.

I dropped off the grid, helping this kid get down the LA River to where his family might be. Annie came to help. So did Nic Delacourt, who may or may not be my boyfriend – it's complicated. Nic made it out OK, but Annie . . .

I don't want to think about Annie now.

Adam chased us, trying to get Leo back. I didn't recognise him; amazingly, when a horrifying, mind-melting bad guy comes after me, my first thought isn't: *Holy crap, it's my long-lost brother.*

So how do I know this isn't a dream?

Because whenever he trapped me in one of his illusions, it was never him I saw. It was other people in my life, twisted, changed in horrifying ways. The fact that I can still see him means that this is real.

Chloe bends down, and then she does the damnedest thing. There's a blanket in her arms – she must have taken it from Annie's room – and as I shiver uncontrollably, she tucks it around me. Then she leans forward and rests her forehead against mine.

"I've missed you so much," she says. She speaks quickly, like she can't wait to get this out. "But that's all going to change. From now on, it's all going to be better." I can't tell if she's trying to reassure me, or herself. "You should see what we've been building, Em. I'm creating a place for us, a *world* for us – people like us, I mean. Where we don't have to be scared, or hide, or try to fit in. A place where you'll be safe."

There has to be somebody who can help me. If the docs and nurses are AWOL, then maybe someone else will come. Where are the rest of China Shop when you need them? Reggie, our hacker – she could see us on the security cams. I could get her to kill the lights, turn on the fire suppression system. Africa, our wheelman, all seven feet of him. Nic . . . he's not part of the team, but he's as close to me as anyone. He should be here. He should—

My sister kisses me on the forehead, then straightens up, nodding to Adam. The three of us proceed down the hallway to the elevator at the far end. Somewhere, very distant, there is the sound of a clanking pipe, catching just at the edge of my hearing. The cold is bone-deep now.

Into an elevator. Chloe's hand on my shoulder, squeezing, Adam hulking just behind me. He reaches over with a meaty arm, hits the button and the doors close smoothly on Annie's floor.

Chloe keeps talking, her voice straining with the effort. "I should have come for you a long time ago. I only found out you were alive after you got to LA, and I wasn't ... I didn't know if you'd want to see us. There's not a day goes by that I don't regret that. But I'm going to do better. I'm going to show you what we've made."

Annie's voice in my head: *Use your voodoo.*

But I can't. It's not going to work this time.

My PK is there, cooking in my veins. But I can't harness it. Whatever Chloe is doing to me has walled it off.

The elevator dings, and the doors slide open. We're in one of the basement parking garages, a dimly lit concrete space with vehicles dotted here and there. An ambulance sits against the wall at the far end, side-on to us, maybe fifty feet away. The rear doors are open, and there's a stretcher parked by the cab. No paramedics that I can see.

"Quickly." Chloe sounds like she's about to pass out. "There's a kit ... in the truck."

A kit. They must be planning on dosing me with something, knocking me out. Quite why they didn't bring it up to Annie's hospital room, I don't know. Maybe Chloe didn't anticipate that keeping me locked down would be this difficult.

We head towards the ambulance – Chloe and Adam must

be parked nearby, in whatever Evil Villain Mobile they arrived in. It's such an odd thought: that these two drove here, that they had to take a ticket and find an open parking spot, that they'll probably have to pay at a machine before they leave—at least, if they want to escape unnoticed. If I wasn't the one they were kidnapping, I'd actually laugh. *All these amazing abilities, and you still gotta find parking.*

As we reach the end of the line of cars, turning right past the ambulance, Adam comes to an abrupt halt. The wheels on my chair squeak against the concrete as he does so.

He giggles. Out of nowhere: this childlike, horrifying little noise. "What will we do about the children?" he whispers. "They're inside the house and its walls go on for ever . . . " He starts laughing again, getting louder and louder.

I know his voice. It's been twisted by the years, mutated. But it's him. It's my big brother. The same one I went ATVing with in the backwoods of our parents' ranch. The brother who put his arm around me when our cat died, held me while I sobbed. The one who would laugh at me when I tried to stay up all night like he could, cackling as the yawns overtook me. The one who always put a blanket over me when I finally fell asleep.

The one who lost his mind.

"Program," Chloe grunts. "Captain. Alpha. Disorder. Zigzag. Zigzag. Zigzag."

Adam's giggle snaps off, silenced.

Control words. Somehow, Chloe has learned how to command him. Pretty sure she didn't know that trick back in Wyoming.

My brother pushes me down the line of cars, and it's then that I realise that one of them is mine. My black Jeep, the Batmobile, is just visible off to the left. The keys are still in my hoodie pouch.

The car may as well be a million miles away.

As we turn right past the ambulance, a voice says "'Scuse me. Hey."

Adam and Chloe stop. They don't turn my chair around, so I can't see the speaker. The voice is male, and sounds like it belongs to someone with a pack-a-day habit. "If she's been discharged, you have to check the chair back into the nurses' station. You can't leave it down here."

"I know," Chloe says. Her words come out in a choked gasp, like she's struggling for air. "I'll bring it . . . back inside in a second."

"You OK?" the man says. "You don't look so hot."

I'm desperate to see over my shoulder, to somehow communicate to whoever this person is that I could use an assist. I'm still locked down by Chloe's ability . . . but even as the thought occurs, I realise that her ability isn't as strong as before. I can actually feel my fingers and toes. As if . . .

As if Chloe is losing her grip.

Behind me, Adam shifts. This time, Chloe all but spits the words out "Program. Captain. Alpha. Disorder. Zigzag. Zigzag. *Zigzag*."

"What the hell does that mean?" the man says. "That some kind of gang thing?"

Footsteps. Then a face appears above me. It's a paramedic, in a short-sleeved white shirt and blue work pants. He's middle-aged, with an untidy splash of stubble. Streaky grey hair hangs down to his shoulders. Despite the early hour, he has a pair of sunglasses, pushed up onto his head.

He frowns at me, then looks up at Chloe. "They discharged her? She looks like she's in shock."

"Voluntary discharge." Chloe has to hiss the words through gritted teeth.

"Bad idea. She should be back inside. Look at her: she's shaking."

He sounds genuinely concerned, which is sweet. But right now, this man is in danger. He is putting himself squarely in harm's way, and he doesn't even realise it. I try to tell him this with my eyes, force words out through my numb lips. But nothing comes.

Still looking at me, the man reaches for his belt, pulls out a walkie. "Donnie, it's Gabe. Can you come back down here for a sec, with the duty nurse? We've got someone—"

Which is when Adam takes two strides towards him, and delivers a crushing blow to his throat.

FOUR

Teagan

It happens fast. One moment, the paramedic is upright, and the next, he's flat on his back. His walkie clatters off the concrete as he clutches at his throat, his larynx crushed, his face drained of blood.

Chloe tries to grab her brother, and stumbles. She goes to one knee, breathing in hot, ragged gasps. I have the strangest urge to wrap my arms around her, pull her to her feet.

My fingers flood with pins and needles, a horrible aching sensation that is the best thing I've felt all day. Guess my dear sister finally ran out of gas.

Which means . . .

I slowly stand, shucking the blanket, pushing the chair away. I'm maybe ten feet from the front of the ambulance. I turn around slowly; they don't notice right away, their attention on the downed paramedic. But the chair wheels squeak against the concrete floor, and Chloe and Adam finally look at me.

I'm wobbly, exhausted, strung out. Last night, I had to ingest crystal meth to stop a flash flood from killing a bunch of people in an LA River storm drain. The drug supercharged my ability, enough to actually grab hold of a tidal wave of debris and rainwater, and push it back. But it utterly wiped me out. By all rights, I should be toast.

Thing is, I am *pissed*.

I don't know what you're supposed to do when your brother and sister come back from the dead, and it turns out they've been the ones fucking with your life and your people for years. Maybe I should be talking to them. Trying to understand. But right now, there's only one emotion I feel, and that's pure, righteous anger.

I have to dig deep to get to my PK. You might think I'd hold back—that I'd never use my PK against my own family. But you know what? No. That shit's not gonna happen.

They may be my brother and sister. But they are also the reason Annie is in a coma. They caused the death of her lover, Paul, buried alive by one of their psycho kids. They kidnapped Reggie, used her against us. They put my friends and my city in danger.

And they abandoned me. They were alive, and they knew I was alive, and they *did nothing*.

I don't know how they survived. I don't know what they're planning. I don't know why they built up the programme that we've heard called the School, and I don't know why they've used our parents' research to develop kids with abilities. I don't know why they decided to reveal themselves to me now, why they want me to come with them. I don't really know how Chloe's ability works, or why Adam isn't using his. I don't have the faintest clue about how I'm going to put my life back together after tonight. But I do know one thing.

An ambulance stretcher to the face will ruin your fucking day.

It's at the front the ambulance, parked near the driver's-side door. I snap my PK out, grab it and send it rocketing

through the air towards them. Adam ducks. Pulls his sister –
our sister – behind the back of the ambulance, around the rear
door. He swings it closed behind him as the two of them take
cover inside.

The stretcher bounces off the concrete floor, but I've already
forgotten it. I grab the ambulance door with my PK, ripping
it out of Adam's hands, then off its hinges, sending it boomer-
anging out and back. I tear off wing mirrors, rip chunks of
concrete out of the ground and ceiling, snap light fixtures to
pieces, a whirlwind of glass and masonry and metal, sending
it all flying at them. The ambulance rocks on its suspension as
my projectiles slam into it.

Take me? Show me what you've built? Let me show you what I've
built, fuckers.

Enough with this wild PK temper tantrum shit. Why am
I bothering to throw things at them from the outside? There
are plenty of objects *inside* that ambulance that are both pointy
and heavy. I send my PK out, reaching it inside the vehicle . . .

And then all at once, the world is burning.

Fire. Everywhere. The concrete ablaze, the cars. Tyres pop,
glass shatters, gasoline catches with horrifying, ghostly *whuffs*.
Scorching smoke chokes me, heat baking onto my face.

It's my worst nightmare come to life. The one thing that
can utterly shut me down. Ever since Adam burned our home,
took away everything I loved, fire has been the one fear that
can paralyse me. It's in my mind, I know it is, a dream world
Adam is trying to trap me in . . . but that doesn't stop the fear.
It doesn't stop my subconscious believing that the fire is real.

But this isn't the first time I've fought my brother. This isn't
the first time he's tried to trap me in a nightmare world. And
as exhausted as I am, I'm expecting it.

I push back. Push past the fire, past the fear. I use my PK, tell it to grab hold of even more objects. The concrete pillars. The vehicle doors. The fluorescent light bars in the ceiling. I'm not even planning to use these things as weapons. I just hold onto them, let them remind me that what I'm seeing is an illusion. The flames aren't real. They can't hurt me.

I send my PK inside the ambulance. My big brother, or whatever the fuck he is, happens to be wearing a belt with a thick metal buckle. Dipshit. Didn't he get the memo?

I grab the buckle, yank it towards me. I don't know if it hurts him, but I'm not going for that yet. I want to slam him against the wall of ambulance, wreck his concentration.

It works. The flames don't go away, but the world wavers, like a TV set on the blink. Like he's losing control.

Right then, the two of them tag team me. Adam makes me see the world burning. But Chloe actually raises my body temperature.

That, combined with the imaginary flames, hammers the danger centre of my brain. There's a moment where I am absolutely convinced, beyond any shadow of a doubt, that I am burning.

The skin on my hands crisps, the fat starting to run. My hair blazes like a torch. I can smell it. I drop to the ground, screaming, rolling, clawing at my face, my worst fears imagined, my body temperature skyrocketing as the flames roll over me.

I don't know how long it is before it stops. Probably no more than a few seconds, but those seconds are a lifetime. Someone is making the worst sound I've ever heard, a kind of mewling whimper. A moment later, I realise it's me. I lie there, shaking, tears streaming down my face. My heart thundering at a million beats a minute. The flames vanish, revealing the destroyed parking garage. The broken pillars and shattered glass.

I look down at my trembling hands, frantically flexing the

fingers. I'm not burned, or blistered. My skin hasn't melted off. There's no damage

A thought, surprisingly clear: Chloe might be able to raise body temperature, but I don't think she can cause blisters. Heatstroke and organ failure, maybe, but she can't cause actual damage to the skin. All the same, it felt so *real* . . .

My sister kneels over me, Adam standing behind her. Gently, she cups the back of my head. "*Please*, Em. I'm trying to help you."

There are so many different emotions pinballing around my head that I can't even move. It's not just anger now. I've missed her so much. I've missed both of them. I didn't even realise it until now.

At the same time, there's disbelief, because there is no way my sister, my *family*, has been the one trying to destroy Los Angeles. There's no way that she could be responsible for so much misery. Not Chloe, not my big sister. Adam I can understand – he's insane, out of his mind. He's a tool – no, a *weapon*. But Chloe . . . she's the one wielding him. She knows exactly what she's doing, and that scares the hell out of me.

It's anger that wins out. Anger that they left me. Anger at what they've done. It's an uncomplicated feeling, straight and direct, blazing bright.

I'm not entirely sure where the surge of power comes from. It might be Chloe messing with my body temperature, or the adrenaline, or the raw, vicious anger. Whatever it is, it taps into a reservoir of PK energy that I didn't know I had. Whatever part of my body and brain produces my ability, it goes into overdrive.

"Fuck you," I snarl at my sister.

And then I throw a car at her head.

It's not a big car. A little silver Prius. But let me tell you something: if you saw a freaking Prius hurtling through the air towards you, you'd duck too. Chloe and Adam throw themselves to the ground, the car passing feet above their heads with a screech of tortured metal. It crashes into the ambulance, flipping onto its side and skidding away across the broken concrete.

I don't give them a chance to retaliate. I grab yet another Prius, a black one this time, off to our left. I'm not picking Priuses specifically; this is California, and there are ten million of them on the roads. This time, instead of simply throwing it at them with my mind, I swing it in a wide arc. It scrapes paint off the line of cars opposite, rushing at Chloe and Adam with the force of a meteor.

They dodge just in time, rolling out of the way. The sound of shredding metal slices through the space as the car bounces away. I have an absurd image of a game of *boules*, beret-wearing Frenchmen trying to knock their opponents' little metal balls out of the way.

Before I can throw a third car, Chloe and Adam retaliate. My brother throws a fireball at me the size of a truck.

It's a huge, roiling boil of flame. I flinch – I can't help it – and even as I tell myself that the fireball is just in my head, that it's not real, Chloe sends my body temperature soaring again.

Flames surround me. I'm at the centre of the sun. Screaming. Burning to ash. And this time, I'm not going to be able to get back up.

And inside my mind, something . . .

Snaps.

I don't mean that I go insane. I mean that something changes. I don't know if I have the words to describe it: it's as if part of my brain *actually* burns away, withering into nothing. It's like a dream where you're flying, where it seems completely natural, and then you wake up and you suddenly realise that it wasn't true. Something that was there before just ... isn't.

And then suddenly, as quickly as the flames appeared, they vanish.

I'm on my back, shaking uncontrollably, whimpering, still half sure that I'm on fire. There's a voice, someone who isn't Chloe, or Adam. Someone shouting.

"*Stop!* Hands on your head, *now!*"

Three silhouettes, sprinting towards us from the elevators. Doctors? Security guards, drawn by the ruckus? All I know is, I've never been so happy to be confronted by multiple shadowy figures.

Slowly, Chloe gets to her feet. She does it gingerly, like she's afraid she'll fall over next to me.

The silhouettes resolve. "Show me your hands," says one of the figures, a burly man in a security guard uniform, pointing a mighty big gun.

There must be cameras in the parking garage. Which means these guys just saw me throw a car. Oh boy. That's going to cause a whole whack of problems later on.

Chloe starts to say something, but at that moment, the big security guard jerks. Like he touched an electric wire. He drops his gun, clutching his head and moaning. To his left, his buddy *shrieks*, a horrible, tortured sound that echoes across the garage. He's wearing a black Raiders fitted cap, and beneath it, his eyes are bulging out of his head. As I watch, he reaches up and scratches at his face, his nails drawing blood.

Adam. Over at my eleven o'clock, grinning like a loon through his bushy beard. Giving these guards a taste of what he can do.

Except: it's not working. At least, not completely. The third guard, the youngest, the only one wearing a tie, still seems like himself. He's not shaking, or screaming. He hasn't lowered his gun.

He keeps snapping his weapon between me, Chloe and Adam. "Donnie?" he shouts, flicking a terrified glance at the big guy, who has fallen to his knees. "Get up, man, come on."

Holy crap. I forgot. One thing about Adam is that he can only affect like two people at a time with his ability. It's the only reason we managed to survive him the last time, when I was transporting Leo down the LA River.

I have my own weaknesses – it's really hard for me to lift organic matter, and although I'm a lot stronger than I used to be, there are still limitations to my range and the amount of stuff I can lift at one time. Chloe and Adam clearly have weaknesses too. *Finally, a break.*

The guard in the Raiders cap is down on his knees now. His face is a red mess, his skin shredded. As I watch, he begins to dig his fingers into his eyes.

"Program," Chloe says. "Captain. Alpha—"

The third security guard, the one that still has at least one foot in the real world, fires.

The bullet goes wide, digging a chunk out of the wall behind us and ricocheting away. The sound drills right into my brain, worming its way through my eardrums. Chloe swears, her gaze darting between Adam, the guard and me. The guard fires again, the report deafening. Another miss, another brain-shattering whine.

Chloe makes a decision. She takes one last look at me, a desperate expression on her face.

Then she turns, and runs. Pulling her brother with her.

For a second, it's impossible to make sense of what I'm seeing. Are they really getting chased off by a couple of security guards? Two of whom they've already disabled?

But then I get it. It's about numbers. Throw two or three people into the mix, and they can handle it. More than that, and they start leaving themselves open. It won't be long before others come down, more guards, maybe even the cops. Chloe and Adam wanted to get me out of here quickly and quietly, and now that it's all gone to shit, they have no choice but to abort mission.

"Get back here." I try to yell the words, but all I can manage is an exhausted, husky whisper.

I raise myself up on my elbows, just in time to spot Chloe and Adam clambering into a dark blue Ford F150 at the far end of the lot. There's a roar as the engine leaps to life, and the pickup truck screams out of its parking spot, pulling a hard right. As it does so, it clips the side of one of the cars I threw, sending it spinning. The impact scrapes a huge chunk of paint off the side of the Ford.

The truck fishtails, Chloe only just managing to keep it straight. She heads for the exit, tyres screeching.

The smart thing would be to let myself get taken into custody. I could tell my handler, Tanner, what happened. Let her take over. Let her use the might of the federal government. Bring in the Marines, the Army, fucking SEAL Team Six. Black helicopters and stealth bombers. Let's see my brother and sister try to run when the sky rains bullets. Let them see what happens if they fuck with us.

That's what I *should* do.

A shadow falls across me. It's the young security guard, his face white as a sheet. "Holy shit," he says. "Are you OK?"

For a second, I'm confused. Shouldn't he be arresting me? Then again, I'm down on the ground already, and I probably look like shit. He thinks I'm just as much a victim as the paramedic Adam killed.

I clamber unsteadily to my feet. "I'll get a doctor," the security guard says.

"I'm good." I jam a hand in my hoodie pocket. My car keys are still there. "Go handle your friends."

He must realise what I'm about to do, because he gawks at me. It probably hasn't crossed his mind that he could restrain me if he wanted. "You can't *leave*."

"Watch me."

My steps are wobbly, uneven. My head is pounding, my skin tingling, soaked in sweat. But that's for later. Right now, there's only one mission: get after that truck.

I want to ask Chloe why she abandoned me.

I want to know if there's any of my brother left.

I want to hug my big sister.

I want to know what she's planning.

I want to beat both of them into the fucking ground.

I want to curl up in a ball and let the world go away for a while.

The security guard puts a hand on my shoulder, but I shrug him off. The Batmobile's lights blink at me as I hit the button on the key fob, sharp and alert. As if it too can't wait to get after Chloe and Adam.

The inside is a mess of takeout wrappers, club flyers and parking tickets. Usually, there's a twinge of guilt every time I get behind the wheel, annoyed with myself that I haven't cleaned up yet. Not this time. This time, I barely notice.

I stab the key at the ignition slot. It takes a couple of tries, but eventually slides home. The beast roars into life, headlights illuminating the parking garage. The other two security guards, the ones Adam went to town on, are just getting to their feet. A little ahead of me, there's the body of the paramedic.

The anger comes back. Raw and red. An open wound, impossible to ignore.

I put the Batmobile into drive. The station I was listening to when I parked here, Power 106, starts up again. "Back on the Scene" by Slaughterhouse is playing. *Fuck-you music.*

Perfect.

"Hey!" The guard shouts. "Stop!"

I hit the gas.

FIVE

,

Teagan

Cedars-Sinai Hospital is in the Beverley Grove neighbourhood. It's an upmarket area: coffee shops, boutique clothing stores, fancy hotels. San Vicente Boulevard, next to the hospital, is usually heavy with traffic, even this early in the morning.

But LA had an earthquake recently. A bad one. The result of Chloe's little experiment, a kid who she sent to wreak havoc with his earth-moving ability. The quake has drastically reduced the traffic. As I come tearing out of the parking lot, smashing through the boom with a giant bang, the dark street is blessedly, amazingly empty.

And it may not be enough.

Chloe and Adam have a head start. A big one. It was at least thirty seconds between their truck driving off and me flooring the gas on the Batmobile, so there's a good chance they are long gone. It doesn't stop me from pushing my little Jeep as hard as it can go.

It's a fifty-fifty chance as to which direction they went, so I go with my gut, twisting the wheel hard left as I come out onto the street. The Batmobile ramps the curb, bucking underneath me, the engine howling.

I tap the brakes slightly as I skid out onto the tarmac, thanking every deity I know that it's my left knee that hurts like hell, and that I never bothered to learn stick. My gaze darts everywhere, frantically looking for a blue pickup truck. Nothing. Not one other vehicle, not a single person out on the streets. I accelerate, roaring north up San Vicente. "Where are you, fuckers?"

I barely notice the red light at Beverly Boulevard. I tap the brake, doing a quick check to make sure that I'm not about to be creamed by an eighteen-wheeler, then accelerate again, exploding into the intersection. Who cares if I'm running red lights now? Just add it to the pile of parking tickets on the floor.

I'm leaving a trail behind me that's a mile wide, which is not good. Chances are, whoever was in the security booth at the hospital saw me throwing those cars. Maybe they don't know that it was me doing it – I wasn't alone, after all – but I'm definitely on their radar. Add that to the little flash flood incident from last night, where I used my ability in front of hundreds and hundreds of eyewitnesses. I'm *pretty* sure they didn't capture that on video; I took the precaution of crunching every camera and phone in a half-mile radius. But that doesn't change the fact that I have been using my ability in front of a lot of people lately. It's one of the big no-nos of my job. I'm not supposed to reveal my PK to anyone.

Fuck it – that's a problem for later. Right now, I am going to find Chloe and Adam. I'm going to stop their truck, pry them out of it and *make* them tell me what's going on.

But I have to find them first. There's nothing ahead of me, and the only vehicle on the left is a garbage truck idling at the curb. But as I look to the right, east up Beverly Boulevard, I spot a few sparse tail lights, most likely early morning commuters; the sun won't even be up for another hour or two, but that doesn't mean the whole city is asleep. Except . . .

Is it my imagination, or is one of those sets of lights weaving a little?

I don't waste time second-guessing myself. I pull a hard right, turning so sharply that I'm pretty sure the Batmobile's tyres on one side leave the ground. I swerve, straighten out, hit the gas.

If only I had Africa with me. He's the team's driver, a seven-foot tall Senegalese immigrant. We haven't always seen eye to eye, but as I accelerate up Beverly Boulevard, I've never needed him so badly. I shouldn't be doing this by myself.

You don't have a choice. Get it done.

And just like that, I spot their truck.

I was right about the swerving lights. The traffic has picked up, just a little, and they're weaving through it, maybe three hundred yards ahead of me. It's possible that there's another dark blue Ford F150 out at this hour . . . but somehow, I don't think so. It's them.

I swerve between other cars, ignoring their frantic hooting, foot flat on the gas. I reach out, crank the volume up on the radio. A new song fills the car, vibrating my stomach and the seat underneath me: "California Love" by Pac and Dre. Hip-hop has always focused me, got me in the game, and I'm going to need it now.

At that moment, they realise I'm behind them. I don't know what gives me away, but the truck accelerates, zipping out in front of a city bus. In the distance, just audible above the music, there is the sound of police sirens.

When I catch them, I'm not going to try and ram them off the road, or get ahead of them and force them to stop. No, I'm going to peel their truck apart with my PK. Open them up like a sardine can, doors, roof, chassis, radio, seats, all of it.

Shit: what if I get in range of the truck, and Adam goes to

town on me? He wouldn't even have to do much. Maybe he
makes me believe there's something in my path – hell, even
an old woman crossing the street would make me swerve, put
me further back, perhaps even crash. And who's to say that
Chloe's power only works on people? What if she overheats
my engine? Leaves me stranded in the middle of the street,
with the cops bearing down on me?

I've got bigger problems to deal with first, though, one of
which is that I'm not getting any closer to their truck. I can *see*
them just fine, zipping in and out of traffic ahead of me. But the
simple fact is that their ride has more power than the Batmobile.
It's kind of amazing that I caught up to them in the first place.

I run another red light, nearly getting T-boned by some
jackass in a Ferrari. The sirens are louder now. I'm barely conscious of what's playing on the radio, focused on nothing but
the twin tail lights of their truck, the Batmobile rocking on its
suspension as I weave through traffic. Rush hour in LA doesn't
really get started until six-thirty or seven a.m., but there are
still enough cars on the road that I have to be careful. You'll
be absolutely staggered to hear that this isn't my first car chase.
And the most annoying thing about car chases is that usually
they aren't over quickly. There are long periods of focused,
silent driving when you're just trying to gain ground. So as I
do my best to keep their truck in sight, as we hit Oakwood
and they hook a left onto North Wilton, I have time to worry.

All at once, the Jeep is suddenly awash in light. Bright
white, coming from above, along with the thrum of rotor
blades. A police chopper has found me. Wonderful. Just fucking wonderful.

This is getting out of hand. Oh, who am I kidding? It got
out of hand twenty minutes ago. I should call someone. Get
the team involved, get Reggie to . . . I don't know, hack the

traffic lights, turn off the police radios, *something*. I claw at my pocket for my phone, but it isn't there. I lost it almost eighteen hours ago, in the storm drains.

There's the piercing *blat* of a truck horn, and a pair of headlights blinds me. With a terrified yelp, I pull the wheel to the left. A massive tractor-trailer shoots by on my left. I swung too close to the opposite lane, and nearly *did* get smushed by an eighteen-wheeler. I will my ride to go even faster, heading up North Wilton even as the traffic builds and builds around me.

There are more palm trees now, shadowy in the street lights. I'm getting closer to the Hollywood Hills. At the place where North Wilton intersects Franklin, the traffic snarls to a halt, a crush of tail lights. *Shit.*

They spot it too. The truck veers hard left, zipping into what looks like an alley between the houses, heading west in the direction of Taft Avenue. I follow, stabbing at the brake pedal, twisting the wheel, turning so hard that my left tyres almost leave the ground. I have *got* to be careful. My Jeep has a high wheelbase, which means a high centre of gravity. And if I roll now . . .

I'm half hoping that the move will help me lose the police chopper. No dice. The light sticks with me as I blaze down the alley, gritting my teeth as too-tight walls rush by on either side. I smash a plastic trash bin aside, garbage spattering across my hood.

If I focus really hard, I could bring down the chopper – and do it in such a way that it *wouldn't* kill everyone on board. It's something I've done before, that one time the cops were chasing the whole of China Shop, after someone framed me for murder. If you kill the fuel pump on a chopper, you can leave the rotor blades spinning, so it can land without crashing. But it's really freaking tough to do, even when I'm at my best.

Ahead of me, Chloe digs in, skids out onto Taft, pointing north towards Hollywood. I push the protesting Batmobile to its limits. The urge to break off the pursuit is growing larger by the second. It's the smart thing to do, I know that. But I'm in the grip of something now, something with teeth. Seven years of grief. Seven years where I thought I was alone.

All at once, we're off the main roads, heading up into Hollywood Dell. This is movie star land now, the rolling terrain below the Hollywood sign: narrow streets bordered by high walls and ornate iron gates, Brad and Angelina territory.

It doesn't make sense. Why would Chloe come in here? The tight streets and switchback turns on the hills aren't going to be friendly to her truck. It's got straight-line speed, sure, but I'm guessing it turns like a pig in mud. Maybe she thinks she can lose me. Wait until I'm out of sight, then zip into a cul-de-sac, ditch the truck, make an escape on foot.

"Not a fucking chance," I mutter, swerving to avoid a dog walker, who gestures at me like I'm crazy. It's a close call – a few feet to the left, and he'd be splattered all over my windshield.

And shit, don't celebrities walk their own dogs sometimes? You see them in paparazzi photos: Johnny Depp wearing sunglasses and looking shifty as his chihuahua takes a dump. That's all I need right now: to run over someone like Keanu Reeves. That would really put a cap on everything.

There's a car backing out of a garage ahead of me. Almost at the moment I see it, the driver spots me too. A woman, with an enormous mane of brown hair and gigantic, owlish glasses, goggling at me in stunned shock.

I suck in a terrified breath, clench my abs, as if I can somehow make myself smaller—

—and shoot past her, making the briefest contact, scraping

a layer of paint off both of our cars. I force the Jeep back under control, swearing, slowing to a maddening crawl as I make my way around a switchback. The lights of Downtown glimmer in the distance.

Is it my imagination, or are there more choppers in the air now? They can't all be police. That means there's probably one or two news networks too. So I'm in a massive car chase, putting celebrities and their staff at risk, and it's all going to end up on KTLA. Right at the time when I should be trying to avoid press exposure, I'm bringing tons of it down on myself. I am laying out a glowing neon trail for every paparazzo and journalist to follow.

I almost quit then. I actually jerk the wheel towards the kerb – if I abandon the Batmobile now, I might have a chance. But the truck is just up ahead, turning around a curve on the tight hillside street. I'm starting to catch them. Again, that confusion: what is she doing? She must have known I'd be faster than her up here.

At that moment, cop cars materialise in my rear-view mirror. And that's when I understand.

"Clever, bitch. Very clever." I'm aware that I'm talking to myself, but I can't seem to find the switch to turn it off. "Maybe you've given up trying to kidnap me. Maybe you're out of juice, you and Adam both, huh? That it? Or maybe you just think it's too risky. Which is a problem, because *Teagan* – not Emily, not any more – Teagan Frost doesn't *quit,* does she?"

The back of the Jeep skids as I accelerate up a short rise, sending a couple of trash bins flying. I barely notice.

"So what do you think? You think, if we can't outrun her, let's slow her down. Let's make it easy for the cops to catch her. After all, she's the one driving reckless, am I right? And why wouldn't she be? Not every day her long lost big *sister* comes back from the fucking *dead*. Take her into the hills, make her fight her way around the turns. Let the cops catch up. Maybe they don't even realise you're there. So I get taken in while you get away."

The cops are almost on my bumper. We're swooping around a long curve, the ground to our left dropping off, showing a spectacular vista all the way to Downtown. A voice comes from behind the Batmobile, amplified and distorted through a loudhailer. *"Pull over. Now."*

I barely notice, barely even blink as the police chopper's spotlight shines directly into my eyes. "Nice try, Chloe. Very nice try. Smart. But you forgot one thing. You might be out of juice, but I'm not. I'm going to hunt you down, rip you out of that pickup, and ... and we can ... "

Dimly, I'm aware that I'm crying, hot tears on my cheeks.

And just like that, the elevation changes. We come round another curve, and suddenly the road drops away. It's a straight shot down to a T-junction, maybe a quarter mile, bordered by scrubland on either side. The pickup is halfway to the bottom of the hill.

Their plan didn't work. The cops didn't catch me in the hills. Now, I'm going to run them off the fucking road.

I roar down the incline, picking up speed. Their brake lights flare as they reach the T-junction, turning left, nearly getting smashed to pieces by a car coming the opposite way.

The cops are still behind me. Their chopper bathes the tarmac and scrubland in white light. I don't care. I block it all out, everything but their truck, peeling away from the intersection.

In desperation, I reach out with my PK, but I can barely get a fix on it. It's like it isn't even there.

Goddammit, what a time to run out of juice.

Fine. Time to smack this bitch up off the road. A hundred yards to the T-junction. Fifty. I hit the brakes, get ready to make the turn.

And right then, I realise I'm going way too fast.

Africa taught me a trick once, where you pump the brakes instead of slamming them, slow the car down gradually. It doesn't help. The intersection fills my windshield. In desperation, I spin the wheel, hoping that maybe, just maybe, I've slowed down enough to make the turn.

The Batmobile skids sideways. I get a split-second glimpse of a single pedestrian watching the action, on the grassy hillside. His dog, a big Alsatian, is barking like crazy. The man has a takeaway cup of coffee, and as I catch sight of him, he drops it. It seems to fall in slow motion.

The Jeep's wheels leave the ground, and the world turns itself upside down. The airbag deploys, snapping my head back, slamming me into the seat.

You already know what happens next.

SIX

Teagan

Yes, Hollywood has a police station.

You'd expect it to be as swanky as fuck. You know, Greek columns, long driveway, maybe a discrete infinity pool for the cops to relax in after a long shift. Nope. You're thinking of the Hollywood Hills, which is different from Hollywood. This police station personifies Hollywood. It's a squat, ugly brick building, apparently airlifted from rural Oklahoma and plunked down in LA.

The only concession is the memorial for fallen officers. It's a walk of fame, with stars set into the sidewalk. Just like they have on Sunset Boulevard. I see it when they bring me in, hustling me through the back for booking. Somehow, no matter what happens today, I know that's a detail that's going to stick with me. A little memory I'll keep coming back to whenever I think of this particular time in my life.

There was a swarm of photographers outside, a buzzing hive of lenses and flashbulbs and incomprehensible, shouted questions. I duck my head, wishing for probably the only time in my life that I wore my hair longer than the short, black, spiky mess it is now. I don't *think* they're here because they've linked me to the flash flood in the storm drain – I'm pretty sure it's because of the car chase. But I can't be sure, and I can't keep the fear and worry away.

Fortunately, the cops aren't bothered about this. They shield me with their bodies, hustling me into the station.

They take my shoelaces. Fingerprint me. Ask a bunch of questions, most of which I ignore. They have a paramedic – does he work here, or was he just passing through? – shine a light in my eyes and take my pulse. I'm alive. Barely.

Good news is, my bad knee didn't get hurt further in the crash. Guess the airbag helped there. But I have a mild concussion, and multiple cuts – I didn't even realise I was bleeding.

The charges wash over me as the duty officer reads them off. Reckless driving. Public endangerment. Property damage. Resisting arrest.

Murder.

That one makes my eyes fly open – holy shit, they must want me for the medic Adam killed. But I don't get a chance to protest. They're already hustling me along, pulling me through corridors with glaring fluorescent lighting and worn vinyl flooring, corridors that smell of old sweat and coffee and cigarette smoke.

"Let her cool off. We'll talk to her later," someone says.

"She got a lawyer coming in?" another voice asks.

"Nah, she ain't said a word so far."

I'm expecting to end up in a drunk tank – the big communal holding cell that most stations have, the ones that are always packed to the gills. I'm already bracing myself for when someone tries to steal my laceless shoes. Instead, they shove me into a cell of my own. A hard cube with no window, a single steel toilet and a concrete sleeping platform. The light is in a thick mesh cage, and the steel door has a tiny plexiglass window set into it. High up. If I wanted to look, I'd have to stand on tiptoe. Not that I care: the second the door shuts behind me, I curl up on the concrete slab pretending to be a bed, put my arms over my head and go still.

I stay there for a very long time.

Someone brings a tray of food at one point, a sandwich and a box of juice. I can't look at it without wanting to retch. I'm shaking, shivering, almost as bad as when Chloe hit me with her ability. Sweat soaks my clothes, and I can't stop my heart hammers in my chest and ears and throat. A combination of the car crash, what Chloe and Adam did to me and the wonderful symptoms you get when you stop using meth.

I could probably bust out of here in a second. Hell, on a good day, I could rip a hole in the wall and just walk out. But even the thought of using my PK right now is enough send my headache soaring.

I have a special talent for fucking things up. It's my real superpower. Usually, I manage to pull it back at the last second. But this time, I may well and truly have gone all the way.

At least I didn't kill Keanu Reeves. That's something.

Even now, after everything just happened, I still can't quite believe that my brother and sister are alive. There is a small part of me that just point-blank rejects it. Because I was in Wyoming, when everything turned to shit. I was there when they died.

Mostly, growing up in Wyoming was awesome. You wouldn't think it. My life sounds like a horror story: created by geneticist parents, given abilities against my will, hidden from the world. But I wasn't kept in a vat. I wasn't brainwashed. My parents may have been … let's go with *unusual*, but they loved me. Me, and my brother and sister. And when you're eight years old and you have amazing abilities and acres and acres of perfect Wyoming wilderness to explore, you're not exactly unhappy.

The problem was, kids don't stay kids for ever. They become teenagers. And when our abilities combined with our adolescent hormones, things got a little weird. Especially for Adam. As he got older, his ability to go without sleep started to change him. He lost touch with reality, and became convinced that Mom and Dad were trying to hurt him. Instead, it was my mom who got hurt first. Adam broke her arm.

Chloe hated the fact that her twin couldn't be free any more, that the only solution anyone had was to lock him in a cell in the barn. Perhaps it was worse for her: she could, after all, see his body heat through the thin walls, see him pacing, crouching, whirling his arms and cringing from imaginary monsters. She could never pretend that he didn't exist.

She had screaming matches with our parents, insisting that she had found a way to control him, that she knew he would listen. To this day, I don't know how Adam got out, but it's a good bet that Chloe just got tired of waiting.

I'd taken the ATV out onto the property to haul back some logs that Chloe and my dad had cut down the day before – logs to refresh our woodpile. I smelt the fire before I saw it, the thick tang of smoke on the breeze. All the same, I didn't really register what was happening until I came off the forest track onto our driveway.

Our big ranch house was on fire. The woodshed next to it had already collapsed in a pile of embers, the dry cords going up in smoke. The barn, where my parents had their lab, where the three of us – me, Adam, Chloe – had our abilities tested, was a blackened, burning husk.

And coming from inside the house: screams.

I don't remember jumping off the ATV and entering the house. It's entirely possible that I just blocked it out. That's what the government psychologists told me later.

My parents were dead. Lying in bloody, crumpled heaps. Chloe was still alive, but her leg was broken. She was crawling across the floor, grimacing in pain. And Adam ...

He was standing in the middle of the room, a cackling demon, eyes horribly bright. When he looked at me ...

I ran. I didn't have a choice. My body moved of its own accord. Maybe I could have taken Adam down with my PK, but I was sixteen, and scared out of my mind. In a few seconds after I popped out the door, the whole house collapsed. When the people from the fire department arrived, they couldn't find anyone left inside: just ash and bone. Same for the government, when they showed up. The general consensus was that I was the last person in my family, the only one left. And in the past seven years, I've seen absolutely zero evidence to change that.

Before today.

A thought occurs, one that makes my eyes fly open. If my brother and sister are still alive, does that mean ... does that mean my parents could be as well? What if ... ?

No. When I went into that house, and saw my parents, they were dead. No question. I saw their bodies, saw what Adam had done to them. He and Chloe might be alive, even if I don't have the faintest idea how that's possible. But I don't think my mom and dad are out there.

I spent four years in custody at a black site in Waco, Texas, while the government tried to find out what made me tick. And I've spent almost three years here in LA, as an indentured servant of the same government. All this time, Chloe and Adam were out there.

I'm desperate to sleep, but I can't. Every time I get to the edge of it, the thoughts rocketing around my brain pull me back. In the end, the only thing I can do is just lie very, very still.

I don't know how much time passes, but at some point, I become aware of voices outside my cell. Two – no, three people are having an argument. I can't make out what the voices are saying, but I swear that at least one of them is familiar.

Even then, I don't move. Not when I hear the key jangling in the lock, or the clanking shudder of the door opening. I don't move when footsteps enter the room. It's probably not worth it anyway. They're probably coming to tell me that my court-appointed lawyer has arrived, and I need to go and have my two-minute conversation with them where they advise me to plead guilty and accept a reduced sentence, or some shit.

The door slams closed. The footsteps come to a stop by the concrete slab. There's something about them that I don't like. They aren't cop footsteps, which I've come to realise are heavy, almost dragging. These footsteps are precise and clean. Crisp.

And then a bitterly cold voice says, "Good afternoon, Ms Frost."

Slowly, I turn around, and find myself looking up at Moira Tanner.

SEVEN

Teagan

I have not, shall we say, been an easy employee for Moira Tanner to work with.

The deal she offered me, all those years ago, was simple. Work for her, as part of a black bag crew in Los Angeles, or have a bunch of government scientists vivisect me to see what I'm made of.

So when I say I haven't been an easy employee, I'm not apologising for it. I didn't like the choice I had to make. Over the past few years, I have walked a very thin line with Moira Tanner. Most the time, it's only luck that has stopped me from crossing that line completely.

Tanner's eyes tell me that my luck has just run out.

I sigh. Slowly lever myself to a sitting position, swinging my laceless shoes off the bed. "So, funny story . . ."

"Do you know there is a corporation that has offered the government five billion dollars for your hippocampus?" she says. Her voice is breathy, elegant, the New England accent faded but still there.

" . . . What?"

"Five billion. Just for that one small part of your brain. They aren't even interested in the rest. They don't actually know if that's where your psychokinesis resides; they just have a theory."

All I can do is blink at her.

"In the time since you've been in Los Angeles," she continues, "we have stopped five different snatch squads working for foreign powers, all of whom infiltrated the country with the sole intent of bringing you out. Two Russian, two Chinese and one Israeli. I have lost count of the number of online conspiracy theorists who have tried to expose you and your team's activities. There are people in prison, right now, who will never see a courtroom. All so you can walk around free, in this city, and continue to do your work."

Her voice hasn't risen, not even a little. It's as smooth and even as thin ice over a dark lake.

"I have stood between you and these people as a shield because I do not believe it is fair for you to tackle them on your own. I believe it's my job to protect you from those threats. And all I asked of you was that you keep a low profile. That you be a little circumspect."

"Look," I say. "I know I screwed up."

"Screwed up." It sounds as if she's pronouncing the name of a hideous disease. "You've jeopardised everything."

The apologetic note in my voice gives way to irritation. "What was I supposed to do? In case you hadn't noticed, I was kind of being kidnapped."

"Don't misunderstand me. I don't blame you for fighting back. That could be understood, if not condoned. But I reviewed the security camera footage, and it is very clear to me that your assailants were leaving the scene. You *chose* to follow, and in doing so, you brought attention to yourself at precisely the time when you need to be as invisible as possible. After the flagrant use of your ability on the LA River last night—"

"Those people were going to die if I didn't do something."

"There is *video*, Ms Frost. And unlike the security footage from the hospital, it made its way out into the world before we could stop it."

"But . . ." I squeeze my eyes shut. "No. That can't be right. I crunched all the phones and security cameras. No one should have been able to . . ."

"You are very fortunate that it doesn't show your face," Tanner says slowly. "But the sharks are circling."

At that point, the elephant in the room reaches out with its trunk and knocks me sideways. "Holy shit – Adam and Chloe. Did you find them? If there was footage at the hospital, then you saw their truck, right?"

Somehow, I manage to stand up. Get on my feet, without wobbling too much. "I can help. I know what they look like. I mean, I know you do too, probably, because of the security video, but I was *right there*."

Tanner watches, expressionless. Like I'm an animal in a zoo.

"Come on," I say, stumbling towards the door. A head rush hits me, making me woozy – stood up too fast, I guess. "We have to get moving."

"I don't think so." Tanner says. Her lips barely move.

"Uh, do I really need to explain this? My *brother* and *sister* are *alive,* and they are here in LA. Why the hell are we standing around talking? We gotta move!"

"You are not owed an explanation. You should consider yourself lucky you are still alive."

"What the fuck does that have to do with—?"

"We are aware of the identities of the people who attacked you. It changes nothing."

I gape at her. "*Changes nothing?*"

"We now know that they have abilities. We know that they

were intent on leaving with you. But it does not change our current operations, beyond narrowing our focus slightly."

"They're my—"

"The fact that they are related to you is utterly irrelevant. Despite what you may think, you don't bring any particularly useful skills to the table here. Hunting down fugitives is not your strength. We will find them, we will catch them, and none of that requires your assistance."

The wooziness isn't going away. I have to put a hand on the wall to steady myself. "I grew up with them. I know how they think."

"I doubt that."

"And you're not the least bit curious about how they managed to stay alive all this time?"

"Obviously. But that does not require your input or assistance." She sniffs delicately. "You are a liability."

"Eat shit, lady. You're not leaving me on the bench."

That's when my balance fails me completely. I slump against the wall, then slide down it. I'm about to get to my feet again, when my stomach gives a nasty growl, a growl that is actually painful. I let it pass, eyes squeezed shut. Tanner says nothing.

"Wait." I raise a finger, like I'm making a point of order. "How are you here?"

"Whatever do you mean?"

"Yesterday you were in Washington. You wouldn't have come out here just to tear me a new asshole. I'm pretty sure I haven't been in here more than a few hours anyway, so you wouldn't have had the time."

A strange look crosses her face. "Of course. You wouldn't be aware."

"Aware of what?"

"I've taken over the running of China Shop. I'll be handling the day-to-day operations."

"*What?* What about Reggie?"

"She's been dismissed, effective immediately."

I goggle at her. "Have you lost your fucking mind?"

"Not that I have to explain myself to you, but Ms McCormick disobeyed several orders yesterday. She is no longer a part of our operation. I dismissed her in the early hours of this morning, then flew out from Hyde Field in DC." The very slightest smirk flickers across her face, and it makes me want to reach up and slap her. "You were very low on my priority list today."

"Oh, fuck you."

She doesn't respond to that. There's another uncomfortable silence as she looks around the cell. She seems to be evaluating it, taking in the walls and the steel toilet. I desperately want to stand up, but my body ignores me. I don't have the energy to get my legs underneath me.

"So what," I say, "am I supposed to just sit at home? Catch up on Netflix?"

"No." She sounds bored. "You're going to stay right here."

For a second, I'm sure I misheard her. I don't know if I ever had control of this conversation, but if I did, I've lost it completely. "You can't be serious."

"I have a lot of things to do today, Ms Frost. Things that are far more important than deciding how to proceed with your employment status."

Employment status. Isn't that a fun way to put it.

"I don't trust you to stay in one place," she goes on. "So no: you will not be sitting at home. You will be sitting right here, in this cell. It is safe, secure and away from prying eyes. Furthermore, if your brother and sister do decide to try and reach you again, they will have a much harder job doing it if you are in here, rather than in your home."

"I'll bust out," I snarl at her, jerking a thumb at the wall behind me. "I'll rip a hole in the concrete and just walk away. You can't stop me."

Probably not true. If she was so inclined, she could get me shot full of tranquilizers and put into a coma. *Just like Annie's.*

"Ms Frost, I am well aware of the extent and strength of your ability. Given your recent ... antics ... my guess is that you won't be strong enough to do that for some time. And even if you were, I would not try and stop you."

She raises a finger to stop me interrupting. "But consider this. If you attempt to leave the cell, you will not only have to deal with our special forces teams, but you will have every police officer in Los Angeles County looking for you. They tend to take a dim view of escaped prisoners."

"You think I can't outrun the fucking *LAPD*?" I decide not to mention the fact that a few hours ago I proved that I quite literally couldn't outrun the fucking LAPD.

"Then let me put it in a way you can understand. If you leave this cell, I will issue orders to terminate you as an asset. No negotiation. No ambiguity. You will be put down."

"Oh," I say, trying not to let my voice shake. "And if I stay here, we're cool? You'll just let me out and we'll go back to normal. OK."

"Ms Frost, you are at the bottom of a very deep hole. Are you really sure you wish to keep digging?"

"You can't just ... just leave me here."

"I can. I am doing exactly that."

She turns and heads for the door, clearly thinking this conversation is over. Well, I think differently. I grab hold of my loose shoe, intending to bean her in the back of the head.

My hand wavers, then drops. I so badly want to convince her, make her put me back in the fight. But I don't have a clue what else to say.

As she raps on the door to signal the guard, another question comes to my mind – one I've been a little scared to ask. "Tanner – have you seen Annie? Is she . . . ?"

The guard opens the door, but Tanner doesn't step through immediately.

"As far as I know," she says, without turning around, "her condition is unchanged."

And then she's gone.

The slam of the closing door kicks me into gear. A sudden, manic energy fills me, a wild swing away from the lethargy I felt before. I scramble to my feet, seething, screaming Tanner's name. I hammer on the door, which of course gets me absolutely nothing.

OK. All right, bitch. You wanna lock me up? *Keep me in one place?* While my freaking brother and sister are wandering around scot-free and very much alive? That's cute. No, that's *adorable.* I'm getting out of here, and just to spit in her face, I'm going do it exactly like I said. I'm going to punch a hole in the concrete wall.

Concrete looks solid, But it's actually quite uneven: a mess of particulates and air pockets. If it's not perfectly mixed – and most isn't – it has a ton of weak spots. Weak spots I can easily bust through, even when I'm not at my best.

Apparently I'm somewhere south of that, because nothing happens. And I mean *nothing.* This time, there's not even a little fizzle of that dead-static feeling. I cannot get a single bit of feedback from my PK.

I'm gritting my teeth, and have to force myself to relax. Fine. Clearly the fight hit me harder than I thought. Not a problem: I might not have enough strength to bust through a wall, but a lock on a door is going to be no trouble. I don't even know why I bothered waiting. I should have got my ass up and got the hell out of here ages ago.

Better late than never. I focus on the lock, thinking about wrapping my PK energy around the internal mechanism.

Nothing.

I blink, focus as hard as I can. I know what it's like to drain the tank on my PK, but this time it's different. This isn't just low PK energy. It's like . . .

Like it isn't even there.

I step back from the door as if it stung me, suddenly panicked. I've never felt this . . . this absence. Even when I'm completely spent, which has happened a couple times in the past, there's still a sense that something is there. It's the equivalent of trying to lift your arms after a massive gym session. You might not be able to, but you're still aware that there are muscles attempting to get it done. What I'm feeling now is as if the muscles have simply vanished.

I take another step back, and my foot bumps against the dinner tray left here by the guards. I yelp, stumble backwards, sitting down heavily on the bed. I need something small that I can wrap my PK around. I need something unquestionably inorganic, so simple to lift that I could have done it when I was four.

The plastic tray. I focus on it, doing my best to block out everything else. If I can lift it, just the tiniest bit, or even nudge it . . .

Nothing.

The fight with Chloe and Adam. When they tag-teamed me, made me believe I really was burning alive. I felt something then, didn't I, as if . . . as if something in my head had burned away to nothing. I didn't think about it at the time, and I didn't get a chance to use my PK again, because they bolted right after.

But in a way I don't quite understand, their abilities inter-acting with mine *changed* something. It's as if they cancelled out my PK, turned off those particular synapses in my brain. I try again, desperately hoping that I've got it wrong, but I still can't move a damn thing.

For the first time in my life, I have no psychokinesis at all. And I have absolutely no idea what to do next.

EIGHT

Teagan

Sleep.

If you can call it that.

It's light and uneven, a stone skipping across the top of the water. I don't know how long it lasts. I lie on the concrete slab, shivering, doing everything I can to focus on my breathing and pleading with myself to go back to sleep, please, just sleep.

Every time I wake up, I can't tell how long I was out for. There's no window in the cell. The light above my head never goes out; I don't know if that's an oversight, or just the cops being their usual sadistic selves. I don't care.

I eat, or try to. One time, they send in a doctor. A bald guy shorter than me, with drooping shoulders and a skinny moustache. He gives me Adderall, which helps with the meth comedown, and refuses to speak in anything but two word sentences.

"Any pain?"

"Take two."

"BP Normal."

"Eat shit."

Fine, I made up that last one. But from the look in his eyes, he may as well have said it.

I have had bad days before, OK? I've always prided myself on not letting them get me down, which is a trick I learned in the facility in Waco, in the aftermath of my parents' murder. If I focused on the things that mattered to me, then there was nothing I couldn't do. Sure, it sounds cheap and trite; well, it actually sounds like something you'd read on one of those god-awful motivational posters. But that doesn't stop it from being true.

Except now, with Chloe and Adam still alive … with my PK gone …

I don't know.

A couple of times, as I'm lying there, I test my ability. Find something in the cell that I could lift, even a little. No dice. My PK is gone. Like it was never there in the first place.

Maybe this is what happens when people with abilities use them on each other – or at least, abilities like Chloe and Adam have. It doesn't happen all at once, but over time, the more the abilities get used, the pressure builds. Until …

Snap.

There's a chance it could be the meth I took. I had to ingest a pretty large amount on the LA River, when that flash flood was about to wipe out that camp of homeless people. The meth supercharged my ability; it's just possible that it broke my brain.

But the thing is, I still had a sense of my ability for *hours* afterwards. I was wiped out, running very low on energy, but I could still feel things. And I was still able to use my PK to fight off Adam and Chloe. It was only after they both tag-teamed me that it went away.

I can't know for sure that it was them, and not the meth. All I have is a hunch. And to be honest, it doesn't matter. Gone is gone.

I have absolutely no idea how to feel about all of this.

I've had my psychokinesis for my whole life. It has never *not* been there, even when it hasn't been very strong. Its absence is so huge, so impossible, that I genuinely can't get past it.

One of two things is going to happen here. Option A: Tanner stands aside and let the government take me, shipping me off to a classified facility and cutting me open to see if they can pull anything useful out of me. They'll probably call it something boring and bland, like *salvaging the asset*. Nothing but a line in a black budget somewhere. Hey, just because you're an off-the-books government agency doing weird experiments on human beings doesn't mean you can neglect basic accounting.

Option B: Tanner lets me go. Does me one last solid, and releases me from her service. Considering that this would deprive the government of asset salvaging, the chances of it happening are about as good as a time-travelling ninja unicorn from the twelfth dimension teleporting in and saving me, busting us out of here with its wild martial arts skills.

The weird thing is, fantasising about the second option is the only thing that keeps me sane, in those long hours when sleep won't come. Not fantasising about the ninja unicorn, cool as that might be. No, I'm talking about the fantasy of living without my ability.

If there really was a way to walk away from my role as government stooge without consequences, I would do it. Wouldn't even think about it. I'd stay in LA, for sure – I like it here. Maybe move to a nicer apartment than the one I'm currently in, although that might not be possible at first because hey, you know, no job. Fortunately, I could take care of that one real quick. I'd just hit up every restaurant I could find until someone was willing to give me a job washing dishes or running prep.

Work for the government as a super-powered secret agent,

or spend twelve hours a day doing nothing but debearding mussels and cleaning grease traps? That's not even a question for me. Because every mussel is a step towards what I really want: working the line. Becoming a chef.

Opening my own place.

And maybe I get lucky. Maybe I get to go and work for one of those amazing, up-and-coming LA chefs like Bricia Lopez at Guelaguetza or Ria Dolly Barbosa at Petite Peso. Hell, maybe I get *really* lucky and end up in the kitchen at N/Naka, working with Niki Nakayama, who is basically God, only a much better cook. To be honest, I wouldn't even care where I ended up. As long as I could be somewhere noisy and hot, filled with knives and fire and boiling liquids.

The long hours would suck, but Nic would understand. And I really would do my best to make us work. I don't know if what I have with him is love exactly. I don't think we've reached that stage yet. But I like him. A lot. He's seen sides of me that aren't very pleasant, and I've seen the same with him. Somehow, we're still cool with each other. That kind of acceptance is rare. But the idea of having an approximately normal relationship, being able to have sex . . . my goodness, being able to have sex without my PK going insane and trashing everything around me! What an incredible idea. It helps that Nic is hot, too. Imagine a younger Chadwick Boseman with a shaved head. Plus some serious muscle – Nic is a dedicated rock climber, when he's not surfing or snowboarding.

You know what I'd also like? A middle name. I've never had one.

Before LA, I was Emily Jameson. When I got here, I picked the name Teagan Frost – Robert Frost is my favourite poet, and the name Teagan, in Ireland, means Little Poet; I liked that, even though I don't have a drop of Irish in me. Middle name, though? Nope. Never considered it, for no real reason. If I am truly done with China Shop, why not pick one? Make a new start?

I should pick one that weirds people the fuck out. Like Tequila Peaches. It's actually one of my favourite deserts: halved peaches grilled with tequila, cream and cinnamon sugar. It would make a *badass* middle name. Teagan "Tequila Peaches" Frost.

On second thought, maybe not. I sound like a stripper. Nothing against strippers, but that's not really the vibe I'm going for.

Working for China Shop has meant that I'm not allowed to leave LA. At all. Going on vacations outside the city – *finally* – would be epic, too. My new job would be insane, but surely I could take a weekend or two here and there, right? Get on a plane? Jesus, Mexico is less than two hours away. A whole different country I've never been to, with some of the greatest food on the planet. Fish tacos and *mole poblano* and *menudo* and . . . fuck it, tequila peaches too, why not, and—

Stop it, just stop it, don't do this to yourself.

But oh, it's an island in this horrible, sick, stormy sea, and I cling to it with everything I have. Imagining lazy mornings on my days off with Nic, drinking coffee in bed. Getting a dog – fuck it, two dogs; I don't even care what kind, as long as I can roll around in the park with them and get them to chase things.

And Annie. I could finally come to some kind of understanding with Annie.

The last words we said to each other were . . . not good. She was already grieving the loss of her boyfriend Paul, and as it turns out, Annie doesn't deal with grief well. When I decided that I was going to try and save the homeless camp from the flash flood, she told me she never wanted to see me again, for the deeply fucked-up reason that I was her only friend and I kept putting myself in danger.

On the one hand, I get it. If I'd just lost someone close to me, I wouldn't want to lose a friend either. But I also wouldn't do what Annie did, which was treat me like dirt.

Bottom line: she and I have a few issues to work out. But it's not hard to imagine us being friends again, with me in a situation where I'm genuinely not trying to save people with my ability. I can't exactly see us going on coffee dates – she's not what I'd call a coffee-date kind of person – but getting a drink together? Going to a show? Doing a barbecue at her mom's house in Watts?

Yeah. I can see that.

Which is the worst thing of all.

At some point, the door to my cell clunks open. I'm curled on the slab, facing the wall, shivering and grinding my teeth. Hands squeezed between my thighs.

Heavy footsteps cross the concrete floor. They come from someone too big to be the doc, but I'm honestly too strung out to care.

The footsteps come to a stop by the slab. "Rise and shine, Frost."

My eyes open. I know that voice. It belongs to possibly my least favourite person in the world outside of Moira Tanner.

Slowly, I roll over and look up into the wolf-like, moustachioed face of Kyle Burr.

He's special forces, although he's not in uniform today. He wears a well-cut dark suit, white shirt and navy tie, with aviators pushed up on his buzzcut. He's grinning the evil, sarcastic grin that I have come to know as the Kyle Burr Special.

We've tangled before. The first time, he tried to take me down, and I responded by breaking his finger (PK plus wedding ring equals ouch). The second time, we actually worked together, helping stop an evil little kid with earth-moving abilities from causing a massive quake. We might have been on the same side then, but I can't say it made me like him any more. I was kind of hoping to see him again some time after the heat death of the universe.

Burr, appearing right now, while I'm imprisoned in a concrete cell with my future hanging in the balance, is not funny. This isn't God playing a joke. This is God being a gigantic douche-nozzle.

"The fuck are you doing here?"

That's what I try to say. What actually happens is that I get three words in, then lean forward and vomit all over the floor.

It comes out of nowhere. A tidal wave of nausea that squeezes my stomach in a vice, forcing everything inside to come out. Burr dances backwards with a most un-soldierly yelp, although he can't stop the upchuck from splattering all over his fancy leather shoes. "Jesus *Christ*," he says.

It's the meth, I think. Whether or not it has anything to do with me losing my ability, the comedown is brutal. PSA: don't ever do that shit. It's not worth it. Like, at all.

I cough weakly, wiping my mouth, enjoying the tiny little spurt of adrenaline bouncing around my poor brain. "Howdy."

"That's disgusting."

"Hey, I didn't ask you to come stand next to my bed. What are you even doing here?"

"Jesus Christ," he says again, putting a hand over his mouth and nose. Kind of an odd behaviour for a hardened special forces operative. "All right, come on. Let's go."

I stare up at him. So this is how it happens. This is how Tanner hands me off to the government scientists.

She didn't even have the spine to come and do it herself. She had to send her errand boy. I'm actually kind of surprised that I haven't had a black bag pulled over my head yet.

OK. If this is how it's going to be, then I'm not going down without a fight. I reach out with my PK, before remembering that I can't reach out with my PK because it's not there any more. Fine. I can still fight. I've got fists and feet and teeth. And if he really wants to take me, then he'll lose an ear or an eye doing it. Swear to God.

Except ... I'm pretty sure Tanner didn't know about my sudden lack of PK. She wouldn't have just sent Burr in cold like this, would she? If she thought I could fight back, she'd send more than Kyle Burr in a fancy suit.

I try to keep the desperation off my face, try not to think of Nic and Annie, of Reggie and Africa, of everything that is about to be snatched away from me. "I'm not going anywhere with you," I tell him. But there's no conviction in my words.

"I will pick you up and carry you out of here if I have to," he says, lacking conviction himself. That seals it for me. He must think I still have some PK, and he doesn't want to get on the wrong side of it. I have no intention of telling him otherwise. Not until I know what the hell is going on here.

"You're alone." I raise an eyebrow. "That's brave."

His eyes narrow in confusion, but then understanding dawns. "Would you relax? The boss hasn't decided what to do with you yet. We got some other shit to take care of first, so she sent me to get you."

"*Other shit?* Burr, why are you here? Why are you even in Los Angeles?"

He grins. "Well, Tanner's my boss, but now that I'm her number two, I guess that makes me *your* boss."

"*What?*"

"So get your ass up. We gotta go."

"What about ..." My mind scrambles, remembering that Reggie is no longer with China Shop. "What about Africa?"

"The big guy? Guess I'm his boss too." He yawns, as if bored by the whole thing. "I was down in Coronado with the SEAL boys a couple days ago – putting the new class through the BUD/S course, you know? – when I got the call. Tanner said she needed someone to run the day-to-day."

And of course, she picked Burr. Her go-to guy for difficult jobs involving people with abilities. Perfect. Just fucking perfect.

"Wait, hold on." I squeeze my eyes shut, running his words back in my head. The adrenaline is starting to fade, leaving me weak and shaky. "A couple days ago? But I just saw Tanner this morning ..." Is that even true? I know time has passed, but I don't have the faintest clue how much.

He gives me a strange look. "Tanner ain't been back here since Tuesday. It's Thursday now."

I just stare at him, completely stunned. Thursday. That means it's been two days since my dawn car chase. Two days since Adam and Chloe walked back into my life.

Burr pinches his nose. "Look, man. You've clearly got some shit going on, but right now, I don't care. I'm supposed to come get you, and bring you back to HQ."

"But *why*? Tanner told me she was going to leave me in here." Understanding dawns. "Oh, I get it. Need-to-know basis. And I don't need to know ... or wait, maybe she hasn't told you either."

"Please," he drawls. "Of course I know why she's pulling you out of here. I just don't feel like explaining in a cell that stinks of puke." He claps his hands. "So come on. Up and at 'em."

The way he sounds the words makes them come out as

Adam. A little shiver sneaks up my spine. "What about . . . I don't know, the charges? All the arrest paperwork? Won't the cops—?"

He gives me a look. "They're the LAPD. They'll do what I fucking tell them. Now, get your ass up. I don't want to have to drag you out of here."

NINE

Teagan

It's around 7 a.m. when we get to the China Shop office. It's a long way from Hollywood, in Torrance, a non-descript suburb just north of Long Beach. No business park or skyscraper for us; our place of work is an apartment in an anonymous new build block on a quiet street. Well, quiet outside. I can hear Tanner shouting from the far end of the hall once we reach our floor.

And I have never heard Moira Tanner raise her voice. Not once. Not in the entire time I've known her.

I know *why* she's shouting. Or at least, I have an idea: Burr did actually kind-of-sort-of explain on the way over. Tanner is in charge of China Shop, sure, but we are a government agency and she is a government employee. As powerful and as scary as she is, she doesn't operate in a vacuum. There are people above her. Not many, but still a few. People with advanced security clearances, people who are able to take a red pen to black budgets. People who she actually has to pay attention to.

And it appears that one of them has suddenly decided that they want a closer look at me.

The person in question happens to be a senator – Burr told me his name, but I admit, I don't remember it. Apparently, he's in town for some sort of convention or conference. He's been getting death threats, and has specifically requested that I provide security for him.

Yeah, I thought the timing was suspect as hell too. But the conference has been in the works for months now, and it looks like it was just bad luck that it happened to fall right when my entire world came crashing down. Even then, he only started getting the threats a couple of weeks ago, and clearly made an executive decision.

"I think it's bullshit," Burr told me during the drive. "I think he's been authorising Tanner's operations for years, and he wants a closer look at the merchandise."

Which explains the shouting.

There's that lovely German word: *schadenfreude*. Pleasure at another's misfortune. It's nice to hear someone else giving Moira Tanner orders for once. And I admit: I'm curious to see how this plays out. It's a stay of execution, for a little while at least, and I'm feeling better than I have in days. OK, I still feel like warmed up ass-cakes, but the little spurt of adrenaline from throwing up, and actually getting some early-morning sunlight on the ride over, has smoothed me out a little.

I grin at Burr. It's obviously not a pleasant expression, because he actually winces. "Shall we?"

No sooner has he opened the door than a giant tidal wave sweeps me off my feet. I'm squeezed so hard that my ribs creak. A voice booms right next to my ear. "*Teggan!*"

My left arm is still free, and I pat our wheelman on the back. "Hey ... bud," I manage to squeak out.

One final squeeze later, and he puts me down. The only reason I don't fall over is because of the enormous hands on

my shoulders. From two feet above my head, Idriss Kouamé –
Africa – inspects me. He obviously doesn't like what he sees,
because he whirls, jabbing a finger at Burr. "What did you do
to her? Huh? You bloody *toubab*, do you know what she has
been through?"

"You think *I* put her in jail?"

"She was in *jail*? Teggan, what did you do? Do you need a
lawyer? I know one, very good, he helped when I was accused
of laundering money, the time when I have the friend who was
maybe Russian mafia, you remember? He—"

"Woah, hold on. Dude . . . how did you not know where I
was? Didn't they tell you?"

"They tell me about your brother and sister, yes. I am not
sure I believe it, but it makes sense, after everything that
happen to us. They say your brother and sister attack you at the
hospital, and then after, they say, Teggan is at a secure location.
I think, *yaaw*, they are looking after you, maybe you hurt too,
but now you say you were in *prison*?"

Before I can say anything, he rounds on Burr. "Now listen
here. Mrs Tanner put me in charge after she said no more
Reggie. I know you have taken over now, but you cannot
just keep me in the dark, huh? I have been here far longer
than you."

"And doing a great job," Burr says, deadpan.

I butt in. "You tell him about what went down at the hospital, but not the car crash? Or where I was? That's fucked up.
What's wrong with you?"

"*There was a car crash?*"

"Excuse me," Tanner mutters into the phone. She is over by
the floor-to-ceiling windows, dressed identically to the way
she was when she visited me in jail. "All of you, quiet. That's
an order."

Africa simmers down, but only a little. "Do you know what she did?" he says to Burr. "She put herself in danger, to save all those people in the storm drain. She did not have to do that. And you ... you could never ... *you bloody toubab*."

Abruptly, he puts a hand on my shoulder again, spinning us around so that our backs are to Burr. "Teggan, I want you to know: when I was trying to find you in the storm drains, when you have the electricity boy, I was just ... there was nothing that would ..."

I squeeze his hand. "It's cool. We're good."

I don't really know if that's true. He's being friendly now, for sure, but I can't quite forget the fact that just three days ago, I was technically on the run from him. He thought we should turn Leo – the boy with the electricity powers – over to Tanner and the government. I disagreed, so we went on the run, with Africa chasing us. It wasn't especially fun to avoid someone who you thought was a friend.

Then again, nothing about today makes sense. An hour ago, I was locked in a cell, awaiting shipment to a government black site. Now, I'm standing in our sunlit office, back on my feet, feeling ... well, if not exactly chipper, then better than I was before.

I don't know who the senator is, the one who wants me on bodyguard duty. But when we meet, I should give him a high five. And hey: maybe he can stop Tanner shipping me off to a black site if I'm extra nice to him. And if someone does make an attempt on his life, and I do detect it, and save him ...

Oh yeah. Sure. That'll go really well, especially since I don't actually have my ability any more.

One thing at a time.

I step past Africa, into the apartment proper. We're in the massive open-plan living room, the kitchen off to our right.

Over by the floor-to-ceiling windows is the giant whiteboard which we use to plot out missions. The coffee table, I can't help but notice, is clean of paper for maybe the first time ever. The last time I was here, the place was a mess, with invoices and coffee cups everywhere.

I rest a hand on the kitchen counter, which is raised to accommodate Reggie's wheelchair. The thought makes me look over at Africa. "Hey – is Reggie here?"

He shakes his head, a dark look flickering in his eyes. "Mrs Tanner said she can stay here, even though she is not with the China Shop any more. But she left yesterday. I don't know where."

I grimace. I could really have used Reggie right now. She has a calming presence on the people around her, always has. If anybody could talk sense into Tanner . . .

Except Tanner was the one who fired her. I have to remember that. Nothing is the same any more.

Africa keeps talking, his voice low. "After Annie is put in hospital, and Reggie . . . after Reggie no longer works at the China Shop, Mrs Tanner says to me: Africa, you are in charge. But then she and him –" He jerks a thumb at Burr, who is ignoring us, rummaging around in the kitchen. " – come down and take over. They say to me, thank you, but no more. We will take it from here. And then they say, no, Teggan will not be joining us either. So it is just me. Even when I work as an undercover policeman in Australia, doing very dangerous things with the gangs down there, I was not treated like this. I remember one time, there was this small town in the out-back, and we—"

"When the hell was . . . did you say *Australia*?"

"Of course! I was there for three years. You not believe me?" He clears his throat. "Crikey, mate."

You have not lived until you've heard a seven-foot-tall Senegalese gentleman try and do an Australian accent. Not to mention trying to picture him going *undercover* successfully.

Tanner is still holding an angry conversation with whoever is on the other end of the line. I'm guessing she probably wouldn't yell at the senator herself, so she must be having a conversation with an aide. Burr is still busy rummaging around in the kitchen cupboards, pulling out a couple of mugs. "I'll take a coffee too," I tell him. "Africa, you want one?"

"No coffee," Burr says, without turning around. "Threw it out. Herbal tea only."

"I . . . excuse me?"

"Coffee is a stimulant. Pure poison."

I stare at the back of his head, too stunned to speak.

He looks over a shoulder at us. The little grin on his face makes me wonder if he's fucking with me, but then I remember that it's his default expression.

"You can't not have coffee," I say, a little too desperately.

"Human body hasn't adapted to caffeine yet. It's a crutch. That's not how we do things."

"Now this again," Africa says darkly.

"You . . . " I gawp at Burr, unable to come up with an insult that accurately conveys just how disgusted I am with him. "You *monster*."

He sighs, fishes two teabags out of a box. "We got chamomile, Meyer lemon and . . . " He squints at the box. "Raspberry Refresher."

"Dude, you're a soldier. You go into war zones and shit. How in the hell do you survive without coffee?"

"Because I treat my body right. I don't put anything into

it that disrupts my equilibrium." He glances at me, looks me up and down. "Sounds like it would be good advice for you, too."

"OK, *Kyle*. Let's get one thing straight here. You're the new fish. The rookie. We –" I gesture at myself and Africa. "– have been doing this a lot longer than you. And we need coffee."

"Did you really just call me a rookie?" He sounds amused.

"At all this shit, yeah. And even if that wasn't true, you can't just come into peoples' workspaces and start rearranging them to fit your own psychotic beliefs."

"*Ya.*" Africa wags a finger, looking absurdly like Dikembe Mutombo, a basketball player who used to do the same whenever he blocked a shot. "I have been reading, *yaaw*? Marie Kondo, she is very good, and now what you have to understand is that coffee sparks joy, not just for Teggan, but for me too, and for Annie, even though she likes cappuccinos." His brow furrows. "Although I am thinking, maybe the ones in hospital are not so good."

Hearing Annie's name doesn't make me feel any better. I'm about to ask Africa if he's had any news when Tanner speaks, making me jump. I didn't hear her end the call, or walk over to the other side of the kitchen counter. "All right. We've got our orders. Staff Sergeant Burr, could you please—"

"Hi." I give her a little wave. "Concerned sister here. Any progress in tracking down my long-lost family?"

Tanner barely glances in my direction. "We have several of our top teams on high alert for them. Discreet enquiries are being made."

"*Discreet enquiries?* Do you have any idea how dangerous these people are? Or have you been asleep for the past year?"

"The last thing we want is to draw the attention of the

media. Our best operators are searching for them as we speak, and right now, that's all you need to know."

"Yeah, so, this *need to know* shit has got to stop." I point at Africa. "You're telling your own team only half the story. He didn't know where I was? What kind of bullshit is that?"

"Watch it," Burr says.

"I wasn't talking to you, Kyle!"

"*Enough*," Tanner snaps. I swear the room grows ten degrees cooler.

After a few moments of silence, she says, "We have an assignment, and unfortunately, that's our priority right now."

Africa clears his throat. "Who is this person that Teggan must guard the body for?" he asks hesitantly.

I can't help but smile. "Yeah, good point. Whose body am I guarding?"

"Arthur Weiss."

"Cool. Cool cool cool. Who's Arthur Weiss again?"

"Republican Senator for North Dakota," says Burr.

"And is he ... like, does he know about what happened in the storm drain? And about ..." *My brother and sister.* Even now, talking about them feels wrong. Like they won't actually be real unless I say they are.

"He's one of my immediate superiors," Tanner says, talking over me.

"Thought you were the boss."

"I'm a civil servant," she says primly. "I answer to the executive branch, and Senator Weiss is who I report to directly. Well, he and two others – they form a committee, of sorts, and they oversee this project."

"China Shop? Me?"

"Indeed. They are responsible for providing the budget and mandate for the China Shop programme, alongside other top-secret projects." Tanner leans forward. "It would be in your best interest to perform well today. He flies back to Washington at 8 p.m. tonight, and until then, he will be in your care. I have told his staff repeatedly that I do not consider this a good idea, but he is insistent."

Jesus. Even I can read between the lines there. Be a good soldier, and maybe this Arthur Weiss person keeps me in the field, with all my essential organs inside me. Cause problems, or let him get hurt . . .

This should be a good thing. Under normal circumstances, it would be. Except for the small fact that I have no PK at all – for the first time in my life, my ability has completely and utterly vanished. If whoever is making death threats against the senator tries to follow through, I am going to have a massive problem.

I tell myself to relax. Making death threats is easy; you can't go two clicks into the internet without falling over a dozen of them. Actually putting your money where your mouth is is a different story. Chances are, nothing will happen. I don't even have to do anything. Stand around, looking pretty.

I can do that. I'm very pretty.

And then I can go see Annie. And then I can go hug Nic. And then I can sleep in a real bed, eat some real food and work out how the rest of my life is going to go.

"So where is this Arthur White?"

"Weiss."

"Right. Him."

"The Del Rio."

"Which is . . . ?

Tanner gives me a strange look. "It's a hotel," she says slowly. "The Del Rio Hotel, in Hollywood. You must have heard of it."

"Oh, of course. Because I stay at hotels in the city I live in all the time. Why would I have heard of it?"

"Buster Keaton used to stay there." She sounds vaguely offended. "And Clara Bow."

"Old actors from silent movies, back in the '20s," Burr says.

"I know who they are, dipshit," I tell him. Not that I'd be able to identify Buster Keaton if he came back from the dead and slapped me, but I'm not going to give Burr the satisfaction.

"Admittedly, I was hoping to visit under better circumstances," Tanner says, more to herself than to me. She exhales, short and sharp, then says: "At any rate, the senator is due there this morning. It's our job to protect him."

"Mrs Tanner," Africa is saying. "As your colleague, I do not think this is a good idea. We are not security people, *yaaw*? And Teggan is—"

"I am aware," Tanner says, clipped and sharp. "We don't have a choice."

"But—"

"It's OK." I put my hand on his arm. "I got this."

He looks desperately worried, but gives me a tight nod.

Burr gives a final slurp of his tea, puts the mug heavily down on the counter. "We can do a full brief on the way. Let's go."

"Nope," I say. "First, I—"

"Ms Frost." Tanner draws out my name, burying it under a glacier. "This isn't a request. This is not something that is up for debate. I am giving you a direct order, and you *will* do what I tell you to. There is no wiggle room here, not this time. Have I made myself clear?"

I raise an eyebrow. "First," I say, "I need to take a shower."

"We don't have time for—"

"Unless you want your boss's boss's boss's boss or whoever he is to meet me when I haven't showered for two days and I smell like dinosaur carcass and have puke on my shoes? I mean, hey, if you think that's cool, I don't mind, but I just feel like we all might give a better impression if I don't stink."

"... Fifteen minutes. That's it."

"Thank you," I sing, squeezing past them and heading for the apartment's bathroom.

TEN

Annie

Annie Cruz comes out of her coma so suddenly that it's like getting hit by lightning all over again.

Her entire body jerks, every single muscle fibre wire-tight. Her eyes fly open, a hacking cough bursting out of her chest. The machines connected to her body register her increased heart rate and blood pressure, and welcome her with a dawn chorus of frantic beeping. There is so much input, so much sensory information, that all she can do is gasp and shudder like a dying fish.

It's not just her iron-tight muscles screaming at her. It's the horrible, itching-burning pain along the left side of her chest and torso. It's the lights above her bed, bright as a thousand suns. It's the insane sound of the machines, although she can only hear them through her right ear. Her left is cold and silent.

A confused procession of images blink on and off in her brain like neon signs. *Teagan lightning Reggie storm drain Nic lightning hit bright hit—*

"Oh my God."

A face appears above her. A young woman, thick black

locks tied up under a headband. Her eyes are wide with shock. They look like baseballs, huge white baseballs hanging in the summer sun, midway between pitcher and home plate. "Miss, just stay calm. You're in the hospital. You—"

Annie's back spasms, completely out of her control. The idea of baseballs sticks in her mind, blocking out everything else. It puts her right back on the mound, hearing the sparse crowd of parents shouting at their daughters, her father yelling her name; smelling the sweat and sun cream. Cleats digging into the earth under her feet.

Running footsteps. Someone yelling, "Find Dr Rajkumar, stat!"

Annie barely notices. She can't look away from the ball, and all at once it's ball lightning, burning bright, crackling as it swings back towards her. It's going to hit her, burn her to a crisp. She twists sideways, retching up a thin stream of gruel along the side of the bed.

It's good to see you, Emily. We need to talk.

It's as if the words have unblocked a clogged sump. A lightning strike, right next to her. She was unconscious, deep in the dark. But there were times when she *could* hear what was happening around her. She couldn't see, or move, but she remembers her mother speaking with a doctor. Someone telling a joke, another person – a nurse, perhaps? – cracking up laughing. Every time she became aware of her surroundings, she would slowly sink back into the dark.

She remembers Teagan. Talking to her. Shouting at her. And then . . .

Teagan was talking to someone else.

Someone who called her *Emily*.

Someone who called her by her old name.

How many people would ever call Teagan by her old name?

Even Moira Tanner doesn't do it any more. There's only one person it could be.

The thought is as cold and hard and true as a bullet. Teagan's sister is alive ... and she's taken Teagan. Annie heard it all. Deep in her coma, she heard everything.

"Nnnnnnnnn," Annie says. "Nnnnno. Nuh. Nuh."

"Ms Cruz?" Another voice, urgent. "Annie? Can you hear me?"

"*Nnnnnnnnnnnnnnn.*"

A face swims into view: a tired middle-aged man, dressed in medical scrubs. "Annie, just stay calm. You've been in an accident."

She can't move her legs. Why can't she move her legs?

And then all at once, she can. A connection, a synapse firing as it should, sending spasms of electricity across her thighs and shins. Driven by pure, urgent need, she swings her legs sideways. She needs to get up, she needs to go, she needs to stop Teagan's sister—

"Ms Cruz!"

The movement of her legs rolls her off the side of the bed. Hands snatch at her, a millisecond too late.

She falls. It seems to take for ever. Wires and IV lines rip from her nose and arms.

Annie lands hard on the hospital floor. The impact sends her down a very dark tunnel. Time elongates, twists into strange shapes.

"—was in a coma, how could she—"

"—not unheard of, get me fifty CCs of—"

"—crash cart? Is she coding?"

"Annie? Annie, you're OK, just breathe."

Her eyes hurt. Someone is shining a very bright light into them. She twists away, but can't escape it. "Nnnnnnnno. We have to. Stop. We have stop. Sister. Sister is—"

"Easy. Easy!"

Annie's legs piston out. She skitters backwards like an injured spider, pushing up against the wall. Her head feels ten times its normal size, and she can't slow her breathing, can't even conceive of how to do so.

"Doctor, we need to—"

"Christ, first all that chaos downstairs, and now this? What is it with this damn room?" The man with the light leans in. "Annie? Look at me. Look at me, OK? Right here."

Annie doesn't want to look at them; all she wants to do is get up, get out. But she finds herself doing it anyway. Slowly, her twitching legs begin to settle.

"Sssssssister," she says. "Her sister. She's got Teagan. We have to harp her. She needs harp."

She blinks, knowing she said something wrong, but unable to sort through the tangle of words.

The man with the calm eyes moves forwards onto his knees. He reaches for her, takes her hand in his.

"Do you remember what happened?" he says quietly.

"Th . . . the . . .the . . . "

"There was a lightning strike, Annie," the doctor says quietly. "You were in a coma. You came out of it really suddenly, a lot faster than we were expecting."

"Nnnn." God, Why can't she speak right? She wants to tell him to let her go, but she can't bring the words together.

"Do you remember anything? Anything at all?"

She swallows. She can feel every muscle in her throat working individually. Every neuron responsible for the movement, firing in sequence.

"Can you understand what I'm saying?"

Somehow, she manages to nod. Jerky, spasmodic.

The man smiles, just a little. "Good. That's good. Nurse

Williams and I are going to get you back into bed, OK? Will you let us do that?"

She can't control her time. It changes speed every few seconds. Some movements take an aeon, while others pass faster than she can register. She is desperate to leave, desperate to find Teagan. But her legs won't listen to her, and in a few moments, she is back on the bed. Sweat drenches the sheets and pillows underneath her, soaking right through her hospital gown. The pain in her torso and left arm is unbelievable.

"Should we sedate her?" the nurse asks.

"Are you kidding me? She's 13 or 14 on the GCS. Verbal probably isn't there yet but still." He leans in close to her, the smell of sweat and cologne invading her nostrils. "We're going to need to dress the burns again. And get me neurology. I want them down here yesterday."

The nurse jogs away, and the doctor shines the light in Annie's eyes again. It's not as bad this time, even though an enormous headache has started to hammer at the back of her skull.

"Sssss . . . side. Hurts."

"Yep." He pulls the stethoscope from around his neck. "You've got burns all the way down that side, although I don't want you to worry about those. We'll give you something for the pain, and I promise they'll heal up just fine."

He puts the stethoscope above her left breast, holding up a hand to silence her protests. After a few moments, he nods, satisfied. "I'm going to ask you some questions. Do the best you can. Do you know what year it is?"

They go through the questions, and although she knows the answers, she finds that sometimes the words won't come. When they do, she has a sense that she said the wrong thing, although she doesn't know what.

The doctor leaves briefly, comes back with a glass of water, a straw floating in it. To her surprise, Annie is able to drink without assistance. The water is wonderful.

Water. It was raining when the world went white, then black. She was wet. They were in the park, with Nic and Reggie, and Leo, the boy who could control electricity. Teagan was—

All at once there is that desperate need to move, the uncontrollable urge to get out as fast as she can. Christ, she has to tell someone, she has to tell someone *right now.*

The doctor is examining her chart at the end of the bed. His eyes widen, and he springs forward, gripping her shoulders and holding her in place. "Easy."

"You don't understand. Don't. You. Her sister is allowed. *Allowed.* I have to go to Shop China." Again it's all wrong. The words are in her mind, but by the time they get to her mouth they've changed in subtle ways. It's like one of those spot-the-difference puzzles she used to play when she was a kid. Her dad would never play with her, but her mom would, lying on the ratty mattress in their living room with her, helping her find the differences.

The doctor frowns. "Looks like the old language processing centre took a hit. You just need to stay still right now, OK? You've been in a coma for two days, and you came out of it faster than just about anyone I've ever seen. Your body is still adjusting, and it's probably going to be a while before you're back to your old self. The more you fight it now, the longer it will take, you feel me?"

Annie can't stop thinking about her mom. Can't stop picturing her face. It takes a second to realise that her mom really is there. Standing in the doorway. Her mom's greying hair has come loose from its bun, frizzing out from around her head.

Her blue eyes are wide, and although she's only fifty-five, she seems a decade older.

"Mmmmmmmmmmom."

Sandra-May Cruz makes a sound that is halfway between a moan and scream, exploding into the room. Annie has never seen her move that fast. She has emphysema, has had it for years. There's a cannula in her nostrils, piping attached to a small tank, pulled behind her on a wheeled cart. Today, it doesn't slow her down.

The doctor tries to step in front of her, but she shoves him out of the way. She all but leaps at the hospital bed, wrapping her daughter in a powerful hug, squeezing so hard that Annie's side flares in agony. She doesn't care. Her mom is here. *Her mom is here.*

"I was getting some food," her mother says, her voice muffled. "I should have been here, I'm so sorry, baby, they said they'd call me if there were any changes, but they didn't, they said you were in a coma, they ... it was ... "

The words trail off as she sobs into her daughter's hair.

There are more people in the room now. The nurse has returned, bringing two other doctors with her. The first one, the middle-aged doc, stops trying to pull Annie's mother away. He huddles with the other doctors, talking in low voices about the Glasgow Scale and responsiveness and cardiac arrest.

"It's going to be OK," Sandra-May says eventually. She kisses Annie on the forehead. "You're going to be OK."

"Mmmmmom." With a real effort, Annie makes herself speak the right words, the words in her head. It's like trying to shift a boulder. She has to take it slowly, forcing each word through gritted teeth. "Teagan ... in ... trouble. Have ... to find ... Reggie. Now."

Annie has never told her mom what China Shop Movers

really is, and Sandra-May has never questioned it. Annie has always thought that was because it was, on the surface, a legitimate job: after years of watching her daughter continually fall back into the street life, it was a relief to see her at a job with an office and co-workers and a van with a logo on the side. She doesn't know the truth about what China Shop does, or that her daughter works for the government, or anything about Teagan's ability.

At least, that's what Annie thought. But looking into her mom's eyes, seeing the expression on her face now, she wonders if that's true.

"OK, baby," her mom whispers, hugging Annie close. "Tell me what you need."

ELEVEN

Teagan

So the Del Rio Hotel is dope.

To be fair, LA specialises in amazing hotels. There's the Cecil Hotel on Main Street, which has a little problem with suicide and violent death – they even found a body in the water tank there one time. The company that owns the Cecil now has renamed it; tried to do a big glitzy rebrand, but everyone in LA still calls it the Cecil Hotel. There's the Millennium Biltmore in DTLA, an architectural wonderland where they used to host the Oscars. And of course, there's the Château Marmont on Sunset Boulevard. Say what you like about the hotels you've stayed in, but I bet none of them have had Jim Morrison climbing around on the outside of the building while high off his tits. Apparently, the dumbass slipped and fell like ten storeys.

The Del Rio is just off Hollywood Boulevard, at the top of a hill, with a long, curving driveway sweeping up to it. Ornate, wrought-iron gates separate the hotel from the street, along with a ten-foot stone wall. The gates match the hotel itself. It's seven storeys tall, a wonderful, ridiculous mess of Gothic spires and protruding windows and pointed towers. The only concession to modern life, as far as I can tell, is the helipad on the roof; I can just spot the rotor blade of a chopper up there.

It doesn't look like the hotel was too badly damaged in the earthquake: a few cracks to the outside, one or two spots where a turret or a chunk of stone has fallen off the edge of the roof, but that's it. Makes sense. The older buildings in LA were better built, generally. And a building like this would *definitely* not have been able to get away without earthquake-proofing. The city would have sued them into the next century.

It's a little embarrassing that I've never really heard of it. No doubt Annie has. If she were here, she'd be telling us all about it, being boring about its history and who used to live there and how they bulldozed a mom-and-pop store to make way for it and—

God, I wish she was here. I would give anything to blow this off and go visit her. But as much as I hate to admit it, Tanner is right: there's not a lot I can do for her that the docs aren't doing already.

We're in Burr's SUV; him and Tanner in the front, me and Africa in the back. When Burr got behind the wheel, there was almost an argument, Africa insisting that he was the team's driver. Tanner had to tell him to back off. He hasn't said a word since we left the office.

At least we've eaten. I insisted we stop for food, and I was a little surprised when Tanner said yes. Guess she wants me at peak performance, which is going to be hilarious if she finds out my PK is dead. And by hilarious, I mean terrifying. Anyway, we stopped at Banh Oui on North Cahuenga Boulevard for Vietnamese pork belly subs. I've never been to Vietnam, but if the subs there are any better than Banh Oui's, I think my head might explode.

Tanner and Burr, of course, said no, although Burr definitely hesitated.

As we approach the hotel gates, we have to slow to a crawl. There are people, lots of them. Milling around on the sidewalk, spilling onto the street. The bottom drops out of my stomach.

Press.

Photographers and TV crews. Lights and vans. Satellite dishes.

I've exposed my ability more than once over the past few days, and if the press has worked out who I am, then nothing is going to save me from a one-way trip to a black site.

Burr nearly runs over a photographer. The dude jumps in front of the car, camera rig up, snapping wildly. Africa curses in Wolof. Tanner sucks in a breath as Burr slams on the brakes, only just managing to stop before he creams the photographer. The man doesn't move, just keeps taking pictures.

Burr leans on the horn, gestures wildly. The photographer looks up from his camera, takes a closer look into the car. His gaze flicks between each of us in turn, and his face sours. He mutters something to himself, turning away, rejoining the other photographers and TV crew clustered around the gate, the hotel's security frantically trying to push them back.

I let out the breath I didn't realise I was holding. It's not just the media here. There's a small knot of protestors across the street, waving signs, someone shouting nonsense through a bullhorn. I squint out the window at what's written on the cardboard signs: NO TO WEAPONS OF WAR; WHEN DOES IT END???; GENEVA CONVENTION FOR A REASON!!

"I don't get it," I say, my voice still a little shaky. "They brought out the paps for a bunch of arms guys?"

"These are major players," Burr says.

"Dude, this is LA. We have Scarlett Johansson. Who gives a fuck about a group of suits in a hotel?"

Maybe it's because it's so exclusive. As Tanner said in the

briefing, after my shower, the conference Arthur Weiss is attending isn't your regular conference. It's more like a meeting of the world's most powerful arms manufacturers. CEOs whose companies build M-16s for armies. Fighter jets and smart bombs. Aircraft carriers. The event is called the Strategy and Defence Conference; nobody laughed when I asked if they referred to it as SADCON.

You can't buy a ticket. It's invite-only. They've booked out the entire building, maybe fifty people in all plus a few aides and assistants. No other guests. They're here to talk shop, shake hands, tell middle-aged-white-people jokes, discuss the business of killing for cash.

Weiss isn't involved in the arms trade, but one of the companies here is looking for a location to build their new factory, and it would be just dandy for the senator if they'd pick South Dakota. Whoever organises SADCON is letting him deliver the keynote address this morning. I've never met the guy, but I'm starting to get a picture of him in my mind. And it's not a very flattering one.

Burr has a hushed conversation with the security guard, showing him something on his phone. The man waves us through, yelling at the paparazzi to get back, the gates swinging wide.

"Is there secure parking?" Tanner murmurs as we make our way up the sweeping driveway.

"Yes, ma'am. Underground lot."

"And is it everything you ever dreamed of?" I ask her. "The hotel, I mean. Not the parking."

To my surprise, a very small smile flickers on her face. It's probably there for no more than half a second.

"It's very attractive," she says, gazing up at the building.

"You like the silent films, huh?" Africa asks.

"I do, yes." She pauses, as if she's not sure how much she wants to admit. "Keaton. Bow. Pickford. Chaplin, of course. Greta Garbo. There've always been these rumours that she used to sneak John Gilbert – her lover – through a secret passage from the basement. Apparently it went all the way up to the rooftop bar."

"Maybe they'll give you a tour," I say. "The manager's gotta be around, right?"

She looks over her shoulder at me, diamond-tipped eyes boring into mine. "This is not a vacation, Ms Frost."

"I didn't mean—"

"We are here to work. Keep that at the front of your mind."

Africa and I exchange a look. *Wow*, I mouth, and he nods back. I swear, even Burr gives his boss a puzzled glance.

"I just . . . didn't know you were into that stuff, is all," I say. "Do you . . . like, do you have a favourite movie?"

"I did my dissertation on DeMille. This must be it, staff sergeant – on the right."

We pull into a gap on the hillside, and Burr has yet another quiet discussion with a man in a security booth. From there, we head into a surprisingly cavernous parking garage, jam-packed with other cars.

Africa has a thin gold chain around his neck, just visible above the collar of his shirt. I focus on it, licking my dry lips, trying to pick up that familiar pull of mental energy. Nada. Not a damn thing.

Relax. Nothing is going to happen today. Hang around, look scary, everyone goes home.

We step out into the echoey parking garage. At the far end is a gleaming silver elevator, a metal detector sitting in front of it, and nearby is something that makes me convinced I'm hallucinating.

It's an ice sculpture of an assault rifle. Six feet tall, beautifully carved, sitting behind velvet ropes. The sculpture is slowly melting, standing in a growing puddle on the concrete floor.

I lick my lips. "Well, that's . . . unexpected."

Burr glances at the sculpture. "Fucking California," he mutters under his breath.

"Hey, question: if this is such a VIP party, why are they holding it in the middle of LA? Don't they usually hold these things on, like, a ranch in Texas? Or up in the mountains? Somewhere where the paparazzi can't go?"

"I don't like it either," he says, "but it is what it is."

There's a metal detector to the left of the sculpture, attended by a bored-looking security guard. Two people are about to go through it. One of them is an Asian woman, middle-aged, with bangs clearly styled by a laser cutter. I'm going to go out on a limb and say she's one of the CEOs. I'd be surprised as hell if her companion was. His shoulders are so wide he must have to turn sideways to go through doors.

The giant is talking to the security guard as we come up, and he is *not* happy. " . . . have to secure my principal," he's saying, voice like a tectonic plate shifting.

"Sorry." The security guard is a weedy dude in a clip-on tie, wearing dark glasses despite being inside. All the same, he's stony-faced as the two confront him. "Only event security can have weapons. You can't bring them in from outside."

"I am not surrendering my firearm," the giant says. "My company has a reputation for—"

The Asian woman puts a hand on his forearm, mutters something inaudible. After a long moment, the bodyguard pulls out his handgun and unloads it. The security guy locks the gun and ammo in a portable safe, then has the grumbling monster sign for it. They slip through the metal detector into the elevator, the woman giving me a baleful glance as the doors close.

The guard gravely checks Burr's credentials a second time. He insists on having Burr turn in his sidearm too, which makes our friendly staff sergeant lose his ever-present smile. "I'm not comfortable with this, ma'am," he mutters.

"Noted," Tanner replies.

We file into the elevator. All of us staring straight ahead. My gaze lands on Tanner's tight bun. It's still hard to believe that she's actually here, even though she's standing right in front of me. Ever since I've known her, she's mostly been this distant, malevolent presence: an angry God, who could be watching at any moment without my knowledge. Having her here sets my teeth on edge.

I can't believe she fired Reggie. I still haven't wrapped my head around it. I'm sure Reggie is OK, wherever she is, but the thought of operating without her is insane.

Actually: why am I keeping quiet about this? Right now, we're not even doing anything, just standing around. I clear my throat, but before I can say anything, the elevator dings, and the doors slide open on the sixth floor.

If you ever want to know how wealthy a landlord or owner is, look at the transition areas in their buildings. The corridors, elevators, stairs. The Del Rio's elevators are nice enough, but the corridor we're looking at right now? Damn. Wooden floorboards, strewn almost casually with Persian rugs. Acres of marble on the walls. Each light fixture looks like it should be on the prow of a ship; even the glow from the bulbs seems expensive. Every few feet, there's a discreet wooden table, with a vase of flowers that looks like it costs more than my Jeep. That's definitely true now that the Batmobile is a heap of metal in a scrapyard somewhere. Goddammit. I loved that car.

Tanner leads us through the twisting corridors. She stops in front of a door, with a brass sign on it reading 6016.

"All right," she says, straightening her jacket. "I do the talking. Clear?"

"We copy," Africa tells her. She glances at me, eyebrow raised.

"Crystal," I say, straightening my own shirt. Not that it makes much difference. I still had some clothes at the office, including the vaguely professional blue button-down I have on, the sleeves rolled up to my elbows. But it's wrinkled to shit, as are the jeans. Even my shoes – scuffed black Timberlands – are old and worn. I look like someone attending a job interview at a Starbucks. At least I'm clean, with fresh bra and panties. The shower was probably the first truly good thing to happen to me today.

For the first time since I discovered my ability was gone, it really feels like it's missing. It was a part of me for so long, and I didn't realise how unconsciously I'd absorb the feedback it gave on the world around me. I got used to sensing objects in space, and now that it's gone . . .

Well, let's just say all the Vietnamese subs in the world aren't going to fill that hole.

For the thousandth time, I catch myself fantasising. I could own a Vietnamese restaurant! Make banh mi! OK, white girl making Vietnamese food – appropriation much? Then again, wasn't there that Jewish guy who went to Japan and learned how to make ramen and then opened up his own noodle shop in New York and it's like one of the best in the world and—

Stop.

Tanner gives me a quick up-and-down look. I can tell

what she's thinking. She's wishing that she'd made me dress
up a little more, forced me into a stiff suit or something,
just like her.

Why the hell are we here? In the midst of everything, with
Chloe and Adam running free, some jackass politician decides
he needs *me* as a bodyguard? And he needs me here, in this
ultra-secure hotel? What the hell is he scared of? Does he think
the protestors are going to scale the wall?

But this isn't just about Tanner impressing her boss. This is
about me impressing her boss, too. If this senator likes me, if
I can get through today pretending that I kept him safe, then
he'll help keep *me* safe. It will give me breathing room, give me
space to find a way forward with my ability gone. Let me see
Annie. Find Chloe and Adam. Make some sense of the mess.

Tanner knocks, and the door opens. There's a bodyguard,
strikingly similar to the big one from downstairs. Beyond him,
down a short entrance hall, there's a luxurious hotel room,
with plush couches and tasteful art on the walls. The backs
of heads, belonging to people on couches, are just visible, and
there's the soft murmur of voices.

The bodyguard checks our credentials again, and ushers
us through.

It's a suite, with a bedroom off the main living area. Bright
sunbeams kiss the thick carpet. A full wet bar sits next to the
bedroom door, and the glass-and-granite coffee table in front
of the enormous couches is strewn with papers and iPads.
Two more bodyguards occupy the room, standing silently in
individual corners, eyeing us.

The couches form an L shape, the long side facing the windows. Sitting on one end is a smartly dressed woman about
my age, tapping away at a tablet. She looks up at us, nodding
at Tanner, holding up a hand for us to wait.

I crane my head around Africa, and get my first look at Arthur Weiss.

You know those character creation screens in video games? You can dial in your race and sex and change the length of your nose and give your character a gigantic green afro and hideous facial tattoos, which is what I always do. Arthur Weiss looks like someone created a preset called *Washington Insider*. White hair? Check. Dark pinstripe suit and power tie? Check. Onyx cufflinks, hanging jowls and paunch from too many long lunches? Checkaroni.

He's deep in conversation with the two other people on the couch: an older Latinx woman, and a teenage boy who looks like her son. The woman is talking in rapid Spanish. Weiss is nodding, laughing, asking questions in fluent Spanish of his own.

He glances up at us, his eyes landing on me. I'm expecting them to be like Tanner's eyes: cold, sharp as icicles. But I'm surprised at the warmth in them, the brightness. And there's no momentary confusion, no slight puzzlement as he tries to remember who we are and what we are doing there. He just raises his chin a little, mouthing *two minutes* at me.

He turns back to the couple on the couch next to him, listening in rapt attention. Right then, just as I'm feeling a little smug that he communicated with me and not with Tanner, another wave of nausea hits me. I grunt, turning away slightly and holding my stomach.

I'm going to throw up again. Right here, in this fancy hotel room. Right in front of the senator.

Africa's harsh whisper in my ear "Hey, Teggan, you OK?"

Oh God, it's coming. I can't stop this. I'm about to spray Vietnamese sub all over this nice hotel suite.

There's a hand on my shoulder. Burr, bending close. "Frost, look at me," he says quietly. "Hey: eyes up. Right here."

Then he does the damnedest thing. Without breaking eye contact, he starts singing. "Dashing through the snow . . ." His voice is low, almost a murmur, but there's no mistaking it: Kyle Burr is singing to me. "In a one-horse open sleigh, over the fields we go . . ." He trails off, peering closely at me. Then he nods, clapping me on the shoulder.

I open my mouth to ask him what the hell just happened – and realise that he's right. The nausea has passed.

"You distract her," Africa says. "S'good."

At that moment, the meeting on the couch comes to an end. The senator and his guests stand. He shakes both their hands, continuing to talk in perfect Spanish. Everyone is all smiles, and it turns to surprised laughter when the senator wraps both the woman and the boy in a huge hug.

After they've left, Arthur Weiss finally turns to us, still smiling. "Forgive me. Hi. Thank you all so much for coming." His voice is surprisingly soft, almost melodic. "Moira – it's always such a pleasure."

Tanner mutters a response, giving the senator's hand a quick pump. Burr introduces himself, then turns to do the same for Africa. Weiss stops him. "I know who this is. Mr Kouamé – I've been getting good reports about your work. It's great to finally meet you."

Africa looks as stunned as I feel, enveloping the senator's hand in both of his own. And finally, those bright eyes turn to me.

"The famous Teagan Frost." His hand is warm and dry, the grip just the right side of firm. "The name on everybody's lips in Washington. Well, those with security clearance anyway."

I don't quite know what to say to that, so I settle for a small nod.

Weiss looks up at his staff. "Would you give us the room please?"

The guards glance at each other, then nod. "We'll be right outside, sir."

They head out, followed by the aide, who still hasn't said a word. At that moment, Tanner's phone vibrates, startlingly loud in the sudden quiet. She glances at it, apologises to the senator, telling him she has to take this.

As she moves over to the window, Weiss turns back to me. "I saw the video from the storm drain," he says gravely. "What made you do it?"

Everyone is looking at me now. Even Tanner, who is still on the phone over by the window. It occurs to me that, this whole time, she never once asked *why* I actually did what I did. Why I used my ability to stop the flash flood.

Fuck it. I refuse to be embarrassed about this. I'm not going to apologise. "If I hadn't, people would have died."

"Go on."

"I don't really know what else to say. I was there, and the flood was coming, and I . . . I had to do something."

"You realise the dilemma you put us all in," he says. "My colleagues and I."

I lift my chin. "I wouldn't do it any different if it happened again."

I'm expecting him to get angry. For the cold steel to creep into his eyes, like it was there all along. Instead, he says quietly, "That must have been a difficult decision."

For the second time in as many minutes, I don't quite know what to say. The silence stretches out, long enough to make me squirm. The senator doesn't look uncomfortable, though. It's as if the whole room has shrunk to just him and me.

"For what it's worth," he says slowly, putting his hands in his pockets and rocking on his heels, "you did the right thing. I don't know if I could have made that decision, and I think *you* know that there will be consequences no matter what, but ... " He breaks my gaze, looking out the window. "But I bet there are a few hundred people in LA who got down on their knees and thanked God that you showed up."

He claps me on the shoulder, his face breaking out in a giant grin. "Against all that, you probably don't need a Nervous Nellie like me asking for your help. It's not that I don't trust my security to get the job done, but the death threats have been ... a little worrying. More than the usual, if you get my drift."

He fumbles in his suit pocket. "Even took to carrying this dratted thing around."

"What thing?" I ask, which is when he pulls out a Taser. Bright yellow with a black trigger and trigger guard, like he's holding an angry wasp. It's the kind of Taser that fires twin barbs attached to wires, as opposed to the kind you have to jam into someone yourself.

I don't like Tasers. I've been hit with them before, and it sucks.

"Senator, that really isn't necessary." Tanner is done with her phone call. She takes a step towards him, as if she actually wants to confiscate the weapon.

"Don't I know it," says Weiss, putting the Taser back in his pocket. "Alina – that's my wife – insisted. Said she'd feel a lot safer if I had one with me. Frankly, I'm astounded I haven't electrocuted myself yet. You would not *believe* how hard it was to clear it with the event security team."

"You won't have to use that, sir," Burr says. "We're at your service. And if I might say so, we're a little more effective than a Taser."

"Ya," Africa echoes, nodding.

"And I'm grateful, believe me." The senator's eyes suddenly widen. "What a numbskull I am. Do any of you folks want some coffee?" He bounds over to the wet bar, which has a Nespresso machine propped at one end.

"I'd love some," I say, giving Burr a look that reads: *If you say anything about stimulants and poison I will punch you in the dick.* Wisely, he doesn't object.

"I'm only here until about, oh, six o'clock I think," Weiss says, rooting through a container of coffee pods "so I shouldn't take up too much of your time. Black or white?"

"Sorry?" I say.

"The coffee."

"Oh. Black, please. No sugar."

"A woman after my own heart. Moira? Staff sergeant? No? How about you, Mr Kouamé?"

"Yes please," Africa says. "Also is there the Ristretto? If not, a Lungo would be—"

"Uh-huh, yep, got Ristretto right here," the senator says without turning around. "Anyway, like I said, the death threats ... " His voice drops in pitch, becoming almost a growl. "I don't rattle easy, but for some reason, these ones have gotten to me. They mention my family."

"Senator," Tanner says, suddenly alert. "Your wife isn't—?"

"What? Oh, no. No no. She's back in Washington, and I have a few contacts at the secret service who can provide extra security there." He hands Africa and me our coffees. "It's here I'm worried about. This hotel. I'm sure they've taken all the necessary precautions, but ... well, let's just say there are clearly people who don't want me to put out my stall here today. I'm, ah, trying to get Steiner Group to pick South Dakota as a site for their new facility, you know, and I guess there are some folks who don't feel too happy about that. I wish I could make them understand how many jobs it'll bring."

I picture the protestors outside. Their angry, desperate faces and handmade signs.

He turns the machine on, speaks over it. "From the intelligence reports I've been reading – thank you for those, by the way, Moira – it appears your own family has been at the front of your mind too, Ms Frost."

"You could say that," I reply.

"I know you're probably champing at the bit to join the hunt yourself, but I hope you understand when I say that you need to stay out of it for now."

Just like Tanner said. And yet, strangely, I'm not angry about it. I'm not quite all the way to agreeing with it either, but at the very least, I don't want to throw my coffee in Weiss's face. Not that I would do that, because I *needs it, precious.*

"Hey," Weiss says, brightening. "Can I ask you a favour?"

"Sure?" I say, taking a sip of my espresso. *God, that's good.*

He rubs his chin. "I've seen plenty of footage of your skills, of course. Everybody on the committee has reviewed the testing you underwent. But I've never . . . well, this is the first time we've actually met, and I have to say I'm a little curious."

Oh no.

"Would you mind showing me what you could do?" he says. "I know, I know, you're not a performing monkey, and it's wrong of me to treat you like one. But chances are nothing is going to happen today, and I'd kick myself if I didn't at least ask. How about it? Humour a curious old guy?"

I glance at Tanner. She'll save me, surely. *Come on. Come on, you heinous bitch. Tell him it's not appropriate. Tell him that you've banned me from using my ability until I'm court-martialled, or whatever. Tell him I have a cold. Come on!*

But Tanner just nods. "Go ahead," she says, without looking at me.

I genuinely don't know what else to say. There's not a single thing I can do. I can't even dive out the window; the glass is probably reinforced.

The seconds tick by. I look left and right, up and down, as if trying to settle on an object to move.

I glance at Tanner, and now she looks back at me. Really looks. As if seeing something for the first time.

"Ms Frost." Her voice is even softer than normal. "You heard the senator. Do it."

TWELVE

Annie

It took so long for the doctors to find Annie a pair of shoes that she almost marched out of there barefoot. Only a sharp look from her mom prevented her from doing so. In the end, all they could find for her were rubbery clogs that are a size too small.

By then, the doctor had enlisted two neurologists *and* two nurses to get her to stay, to impress on her that she needed rehab, more tests, observation. Annie ignored them all. They'd criticised her mother for not pushing Annie to stay, which was absolutely the wrong thing to do; Sandra-May had been wavering up until that point, but when they started in on her, she insisted on taking her daughter home. In the end, they made Annie sign a DAMA – a Discharge Against Medical Advice – and let her go.

The shoes turn out not to matter, because they won't let her leave under her own steam. They insist that she uses a wheelchair. The one they find for her has a squeaky bearing, the sound setting off a cascade of cluster headaches. She grits her teeth as they approach the elevator leading to the hospital's parking garage, trying to ignore it. The fact that she's wearing a flimsy, paper-thin set of old scrubs doesn't help matters. Still, better than leaving in a backless hospital gown.

How much time have they wasted already? By now, Adam and Chloe could have taken Teagan anywhere. Has she been missed? And beyond that what if Reggie – or even Tanner herself – left a standing order for the hospital to call them if Annie's condition changed? She didn't see anyone making that call, but . . .

It's getting harder and harder to keep a thought in her head. The headache isn't going away, and there are strange little dots at the edge of her vision. She can't remember the damn numbers for Africa, or Reggie, or even Teagan herself. It's the kind of thing she can usually recall with no trouble, but that's out the window. She gets part of them, two or three digits at most, but it's not enough. Sandra-May has the China Shop office number stored in her phone for emergencies, but that goes straight to voicemail when they try it.

Annie's own phone is long gone. Probably lying in the grassy park east of the LA River where she got struck by lightning, a hunk of fried circuitry. Right now, she may be the only person who knows what happened in her hospital room. The only one who knows about Teagan, and that her brother and sister are still alive, and she can get hold of precisely no one. She's got to get out of here, and she's got to get out of here now.

They stop in front of the elevator doors. Sandra-May hobbles over to the button, presses it with an arthritic finger. As she does so, Annie's whole body jerks. She twists in the chair, her face contorting, what feels like every muscle she has clenching all at once, every neuron firing. A moan hisses out from between her gritted teeth.

"Annie?" Her mom's hand is on her shoulder.

And all at once, the spasms are gone. As if they were never there in the first place. Annie forces her eyes open, looking back at her mom, tears doubling her vision. "I'm . . . OK."

"No, you're not." Sandra-May shakes her head. "This was a bad idea. I can't believe I let you talk me into this." She steps behind the chair. "I'm taking you back. The doctors were right; you—"

"Remember San Pedro," Annie says.

She wishes she didn't have to do this. She has promised herself, over and over, that she'd never say those words to her mother. But she has no choice.

The effect on Sandra-May Cruz is immediate. Her mouth snaps shut, her eyes narrowing as she stares hard at her daughter.

"San." Annie licks her lips. "Pedro. *Por favor, má.*"

All at once, Sandra-May darts forward, gripping her daughter by the shoulder, talking in a harsh whisper. "You want me to trust you? Is that what you're trying to tell me right now?"

"San P-Ped . . . "

"*Stop saying that.*"

Slowly, Annie turns to look at her mother, at her tight, hardened face, the face of someone getting ready to throw a punch. But the eyes tell a different story. The anguish in them takes Annie's breath away.

With real effort, Sandra-May gets herself under control. She lets go of her daughter's shoulder, drops her head.

"I'm going to take you home," she says. "Just like you asked."

"We can't go—"

"And then you are going to rest, OK? And so help me, if I decide that you are not improving, or if it gets worse, I'm going to bring you right back here."

Ahead of them, the elevator dings softly. Annie is barely

aware of it. "Mmmmmmom, we can't go ho ... home yet. We need to go to the office."

Sandra-May is about to speak when she's interrupted by a voice from the elevator. "Oh shit – *Annie!*"

Annie looks up, and Nic Delacourt is striding towards her. Before she can react, he bends down and envelops her in a massive bear hug.

What the hell is he doing here?

Nic is Teagan's friend – or boyfriend, Annie hasn't quite worked that out yet. More than once over the past eighteen months, he's gotten involved in China Shop's operations. Usually against his will; Teagan has a nasty habit of roping him into things.

He was there when Annie got struck by lightning. He had helped transport Leo, the kid who could control electricity, down the LA River.

He's in bad shape. He looks exhausted, and his nose is swollen and bruised, taped, a very faint crust of blood under the nostrils. With his height and his broad shoulders, it makes him look a little like a football player after a tough game.

His clothes are clean, an old-school Death Row hoodie and jeans over black Timbs, and Annie catches the fresh, woody smell of body spray as he pulls away from her. But he can't disguise the bags under his eyes, or the haggard, almost haunted look on his face.

Annie doesn't mind Nic. He's a good dude, smart as hell. He used to work as a lawyer in the District Attorney's office, but gave it up to help with earthquake relief. There was no denying that he helped them out with the whole Leo thing, too. And he's a fucking saint for putting up with Teagan. All the same, right now, she doesn't have time for this.

"They told me you were in a—" Nic stops, as if he's worried

about offending her. His voice is slightly nasal from the broken nose. "You know. They said you probably wouldn't wake up for a while."

Annie forces a smile. "I'm very hard to kiss."

"Uh ..."

"Kill. *Kill.* Kill."

He tilts his head. "OK?"

"I'm sorry, Annie, who is this?" Sandra-May asks.

"Oh. I'm Nic. Nic Delacourt." He extends his hand. Annie's mom shakes it warily, glancing between Nic and her daughter. "From the looks of things," Nic continues, "I'm guessing you're Annie's mom?"

"Sandra-May Cruz. How do you two know each other exactly?"

Even in her current state, Annie can't help but smile. After all, what is he supposed to say? *Yeah, so Mrs Cruz, I recently helped your daughter move a superpowered child across the city to help them escape from two more superpowered people. Yeah, no, it was great!*

Nic looks past her, down the corridor. "Hey, is Teagan here? She isn't answering her phone. I don't know where she's living now, or I would have gone over, so I thought I'd come see if she was with you. Is she around?"

Nick doesn't know about Adam and Chloe yet, does he? He has no idea they're related to Teagan. Shit – does he even know that Teagan is gone?

She chews her lower lip, desperately forcing her thoughts into order. If she tells him about Teagan, he'll try to help. He'll insist on coming with her. And he's not part of China Shop. He's still a civilian. If Annie tells him what's going on and he ends up getting hurt, for real this time ...

Teagan will never forgive you.

The wave of shame that sweeps over Annie in that moment almost knocks the breath from her lungs. When Teagan risked her life to save those people in the storm drain, Annie told her she never wanted to see her again. Even as she was doing it, even as the words were coming out of her mouth, she knew what was behind it. Teagan is one of the most exasperating, irritating and confusing people that Annie has ever met . . . but she is also her friend. Maybe her only real friend.

If Annie gets her back, she can save that friendship. Rebuild it. But if Nic is hurt in the process, or killed . . .

No way she's going to let that happen.

There is so much about this situation that she can't control. But the one thing she can do is make sure she keeps the people her friend cares about well out of the firing line.

"She was . . . here earlier," Annie says, hoping that the grain of truth will help sweeten the lie. "I heard her when I was asleep. Unca. Unca . . . Unconscious, *fuck*." She forces a smile on her face. Makes herself meet Nic's eyes. "I thhhought she might be with you."

He frowns. "Are you . . . OK?"

"Not really, yo. But if I gotta get well somewhere, it may as well be at h-h-h-home. They said I could go if I wanted." Christ, her side is killing her. It's like a rabid dog gnawing at her ribcage. Did they get painkillers from the doc? Did she ask, or her mom? She can't remember.

"Anyway," she says. "We're gonna h-head out. If you see Teagan, tell her I'll call her tomorrow. If I'm, you know. Feeling OK."

Nic says nothing as they slip past him, rolling into the elevator. But as her mom turns her around, he speaks. "So you haven't seen her? Or like, gotten a text or anything? Since you woke up?"

Annie is breathing hard now, as if she's just sprinted a hundred yards. "Pretty sure my phone is toast, so I don't know."

"Right. Of course. Well, if you hear from her . . ."

"It was good to meet you," Sandra-May says, just as the doors close.

With a thump, the elevator starts to drop. After a few seconds, Annie's mom says, "Why did you lie to him?"

"I—"

"I don't like this, *mi hija*. I don't like this at all. I want you to tell me what's going on. All of it."

"I will, Mama, I promise."

"Why did these people take Teagan? What kind of trouble is she in? Is this a drug thing? I thought you worked for a house moving compa—"

"*Má.*" A wave of pain rolls up from Annie's side, burying deep into her jaw. Has she ever been in as much pain in her entire life? "It's not a drug thing. I don't do that any more. You know that."

When her mother speaks again, there's a coldness in her voice that wasn't there before. "Do I?"

"Just get me out of here, Má. Get me to the office first. Then I promise, you can take me home."

THIRTEEN

Teagan

Einstein tells us that time is relative. I've never actually tried to understand it before – why would I spend time studying physics when there were taco stands in LA I hadn't tried yet? But I get it now, because everyone is looking at me and each second lasts a thousand years.

In the end, I do the only thing I can think of: I fake it. It's a terrible idea, but it's also the only one I've got.

"OK!" I clap my hands. "That's the demo over, and we can get on with our day."

Silence. The senator's eyes narrow in confusion. "What do you mean?"

"You didn't see me move it?"

"Move what?" I swear, Tanner hasn't blinked in about two minutes.

"Eh, Teggan, what did you move?" Africa is actually looking around, like he's going to spot something hovering in the air.

"The ... the thing." I force a smile. "Sorry. Um. Not really doing the words today. The. You know. The, ah. The ..."
I put a hand to my forehead, digging as deep inside me as I

possibly can, willing even the tiniest bit of PK to be there. But there's nothing.

"Is there a problem, Ms Frost?" Tanner says. Voice very quiet, and very even.

I laugh, which comes out as more of a cackle. "What? No. No problem. I can't help it if you missed it."

"I'm not sure—" the senator starts, and then there's a noise from the suite's entrance hall. Raised voices in the corridor.

Burr reacts immediately, stepping in front of the senator. Tanner joins him. I want to collapse with relief. *Yes, let them come in here. Let them stay. Let them move in permanently. Oh, these are the people who made death threats against the senator? Fuck it, don't care, come one come all. We'll figure out the details later.*

"Sir." Outside in the corridor, one of the bodyguards, his voice dangerous. "Step back from the door immediately."

"Don't be ridiculous," comes the muffled response. "The senator knows who I am."

The accent is male, German, cultured. It's an accent I know. It's a *voice* I know.

"Arthur," the speaker shouts. "Are you in there? We must discuss—"

"Sir!" one of the bodyguards yells.

"Who is that?" Weiss says. "Is that Jonas?"

"Step back please, senator," Burr says. He reaches in his jacket for his gun, then rips his hand away, cursing. Guess he forgot about handing in his weapon.

"Oh, for God's sake." Weiss squeezes between Tanner and Burr, strides out of sight into the hall.

I stare at where he went, more stunned than I want to admit. There is no possible way the person in the corridor can be who I think it is.

There's a long moment of confusion, of raised voices and shouted questions.

"Apologies, sir." Weiss's young assistant sounds furious. "I told him you were in a meeting ..."

"Are you kidding?" Weiss asks. "Jonas, I'm so sorry—"

"It is quite all right," the visitor says. "But if I could just—"

"Of course, of course! Come in."

"Do you know this person, senator?" says one of the bodyguards.

"Damn right I know him! I'm amazed you don't. Marla – you should have let me know immediately."

Soft footsteps on the carpet, inside the suite's entryway. Tanner and Burr are standing stock-still. From where they are, they can see into the corridor; I tell myself to go and join them, but I can't seem to move my legs.

And then Jonas Schmidt walks into the room.

No freaking way.

Here are a few pertinent facts about Jonas Schmidt. He is German. He is young. He has intense, piercing blue eyes and a gently messy mop of blond hair. He is a billionaire, with interests in tech, manufacturing and finance. He is into some seriously kinky shit, which I know because I once broke into his private plane on a China Shop mission, and discovered the bondage sex swing he had installed in the aircraft's bedroom. And here's another little factoid: despite the fact that I'm not really into bondage sex swings, I have a major crush on him.

It's kind of hard not to. It's not just that he is rich and hot; he's actually a decent dude. Shortly after he discovered me breaking into the safe on the plane, a massive earthquake hit the city. A psychotic little four-year-old with abilities was the cause, although we didn't know that at the time. We were already in the air, and Jonas would have been well within his rights to get the hell out of California and find somewhere a little more seismically stable. Instead, he turned the plane around, taking it back to Van Nuys Airport so he could provide assistance on the ground. It was a horribly dangerous move – have *you* tried landing a plane during an earthquake? – but his pilot knew what he was doing, and we all made it out OK.

Later on, when Reggie and I were frantically trying to reach Tanner, he welcomed us onto his grounded plane and let us use his satellite phone. This was despite the fact that we were actually working against him, trying to stop him from acquiring a list of American operatives overseas. As it turns out, he wasn't planning to distribute it. It was an insurance policy, in case the US government ever tried to assassinate him.

I never thought I'd see him again. Why would I? Our worlds may have briefly intersected, but they moved apart pretty quickly. Except: here he is, right now. I didn't even realise he was *in* the arms trade. Then again, his companies have fingers in so many pies, it's hardly a shock.

I met him because of my ability, and the path it led me down. It's the reason I was on his plane in the first place. It's the only reason we crossed paths. Christ, I can't get a handle on this. There must be a hundred times in the past when I've wished I never had my ability, where I imagined leading a normal life. Now my ability's gone, and Jonas is here, and I have absolutely no idea how to feel about any of it.

There's a friendly smile on his face as he takes us in. Tanner, Burr ... then me.

He pauses for a moment, his eyes showing the barest hint of surprise, a very slight widening. They get even wider when he notices Africa, but then his face clears. In less than a second, the surprise is gone.

He wears a clean, blue V-neck T-Shirt under a lightweight linen suit, thin gold chain just visible. On his feet are leather loafers that look handmade. He's with his bodyguard, Gerhard, a giant with hands that could swallow my whole head. We've met before, too. It didn't go especially well. He's in a dark suit, carrying an oversized briefcase that looks like it contains the nuclear codes.

There's someone else too: a woman, coming down the hall behind Jonas and Gerhard.

She must be his assistant. She has the same poised, efficient look as Weiss's aide. But there's something in her eyes that says otherwise. They're cool, observant, as if she's cataloguing everything she sees. She's in her early thirties, Asian, her black hair pulled back in a neat ponytail. She wears a tight, black pencil skirt and a purple silk blouse. There's a bright red, gleaming stud in her nose, which is at odds with her professional appearance.

"Jonas," the senator says. "It's good to see you. I didn't know you'd arrived yet." His eyes flick to the woman. There's a note of barely concealed alarm in his voice as he says "But you brought a journalist with you? I don't know if—"

"She's writing a profile on me," Jonas says smoothly. "For the *New Yorker*."

The woman steps forward, a wide smile on her face, holding out a hand. "Michiko Kanehara, Senator. It's a pleasure." She has a deep, even voice that makes me think of peanut butter. The kind you see in commercials, covering sandwich bread in a way that is just a little too smooth and perfect.

"I know who you are, Miss Kanehara," Weiss says evenly. He pauses for a moment, then takes her hand. "Forgive me, but . . . I'm not sure I appreciate—"

"And I absolutely wouldn't have barged in like this if Jonas here –" Kanehara gives him a playful poke on the shoulder. " – had told me where we were going. But you know him, he tends to do things spur-of-the-moment."

Jonas laughs, dramatically shying away from Kanehara's finger.

"I promise," she continues. "The story is about Jonas, senator. And it's not a political profile. I probably won't even need to mention you."

Weiss relaxes, ever so slightly. "Oh, you can mention me. It's no secret that I'm here. As long as you report that I'm better-looking than him!"

He gestures at Jonas, and the three of them laugh. I would very much love to say that it's a fake circle-jerk type of laugh, the kind that says, *we all hate each other's guts, really, but none of us are going to admit that.* Problem is, the laughter sounds genuine.

As it trails off, Jonas smiles serenely at the senator, with the rich person's assurance that no door is truly closed to him. It makes look both adorable, and badly need of a slap.

Weiss glances at me, the faintest hint of regret in his eyes. Looks like he really wanted that demo … but he also *really* wants to be friends with Jonas Schmidt. He seemed happy to let him inside, no matter who happened to be in the room.

Weiss claps his visitor on the shoulder, glancing at Tanner. "Jonas here is an old friend."

"An old friend with connections to the Steiner Group," Jonas says mildly.

And there it is. Steiner. The company looking for a spot to build their new factory.

"Oh come on." Weiss turns to us. "He and I were in Washington during that big storm, maybe five years back – Moira, you must remember *that* one. Neither of us could leave the airport, and it turned out that my German friend here is a half-decent poker player … "

"Only in comparison to you, Arthur."

Weiss rolls his eyes. "Probably true. I'm frankly amazed that I kept talking to him after how much money I lost. Jonas, I want you to meet Moira Tanner, an associate from Washington."

Tanner reluctantly shakes Jonas's hand. Burr mutters a hello.

"My staff." Tanner gestures at us.

Jonas looks over at me again. The next second stretches out for an eternity. At any second, I'm expecting him to accuse me. He's going to stick out his finger and say something like "Hey, you're the bitch that robbed my plane!"

Instead, he nods pleasantly. His face is a perfect, showing none of the recognition from before. "Hello."

Have you ever had days where you simply don't know what to think? When you get some really good news followed by some really bad news, one after the other? Like, at midday you find out you're getting a promotion, and at 12:15, your wife calls to tell you she's leaving you for her tennis instructor? And your head is left spinning so fast that you can barely tell which way is up?

That's kind of how I feel right now. It doesn't help that Gerhard is staring at me like I insulted his mother. His boss might know how to be diplomatic, but he clearly missed that class.

"Forgive me, Mr Schmidt," Tanner says. "I didn't realise you were involved in the arms trade."

"My company has partnered with Steiner to develop components for supersonic fighters. I admit, even I was surprised to be invited today." He nudges Arthur. "Good for you though, yes?"

Kanehara is looking at me, her eyes very slightly narrowed. The stud in her nose catches the light, gleaming red. Heat sneaks up my neck, trying to force its way onto my cheeks.

She knows who you are. She recognises you. She's a journalist, she's seen the video from the storm drain, she must have done, and she knows about the hospital, and she's going to expose you.

I have to tell myself, very firmly, to calm the fuck down.

My face wasn't in the video. It was shaky, and unclear. It may have captured me using my ability, but there's no possible way she could know who I am. Of course, that doesn't stop me almost gasping with relief that I don't actually have my ability right now. If I did, and I'd been floating something through the air when she and Jonas barged in . . .

Of course. *That's* why there were so many paparazzi here. They were all trying to get a photo of the German Tony Stark. Come to think of it, how did we not know he was going to be here? How did Tanner not know?

"Madam," Jonas says, addressing Tanner. "I am truly sorry to interrupt, but I must steal Arthur away for a few moments."

The senator winces, very slightly, then nods. "Sorry, folks," he says to us. "Herr Schmidt here is on the money. We're going to have to cut this short."

"Senator." Tanner steps close, turning away from the two visitors. "We really should stay. If you want us to deal with the threats you've received."

"Oh, I'll be fine up here, Moira. It's downstairs I'm concerned about, during the conference. Why don't you head down, and I'll see you in the ballroom?"

"Any objections if I stick around?" Kanehara says. "Strictly off the record. This is all just background colour."

Weiss chews his cheek. "Well . . ."

"I can bribe everyone with lattes." Kanehara crosses over to the wet bar, slipping her phone into her purse. "I worked as a barista for a year or two, when I was trying to break into the industry."

For a moment, I think we'll be expected to stay too. Hoping for it, in fact, because it would mean that I wouldn't have to explain myself to Tanner. No such luck. She murmurs an apology to the senator, saying she's going to go downstairs and check on security.

Handshakes all round, and Tanner gestures at us to follow her out. As we file past him, Weiss pulls me aside. "I really would love a demo. Would you mind if I grabbed you for a minute before I leave today?"

I'm kind of amazed that I manage a confident smile. "Of course."

"Attagirl." He winces. "Sorry. I'm trying to be better, get rid of expressions like that. Old habit."

As we head out into the corridor, another emotion joins the ones yo-yoing through my body: guilt. That man is counting on me to keep him safe. He's going out there, despite death threats, with the genuine belief that I'm going to have his back. What if something happens and I can't help? What if . . . Jesus, what if he actually does get shot? Or stabbed? And I'm right there, and I can't stop it?

"*Yaaw*," Africa says to me out the side of his mouth. "Mister Germany, huh? That was surprising. I don't think he recognised us."

"All right," Tanner says. "We may as well do this properly. Staff sergeant, I want a visual sweep of the ballroom. Get Mr Kouamé to help you."

"Roger that."

"We'll see you down there. Ms Frost, a word."

I stare at Africa's retreating back, as if he's somehow going to turn around and save the day. After a few moments, Tanner and I are alone in the corridor. Unless you count my desperation, which is so strong it's like a third person standing with us.

Tanner looms over me. She pulls a cell phone out of a holster on her belt, a thick black slab that doesn't look like something you could buy from T-Mobile. "Lift this."

"In a public place?" I raise an eyebrow, an expression which doesn't even convince me. "Not a good idea."

"There's no one else in this hallway. I'm blocking the security camera on the ceiling behind me." She reseats the phone in her hand. "I'm giving permiss— no, I am giving you a *direct order* to lift this phone. Lift it an inch, hold it, drop it back down. Now, please."

I swallow, trying and failing to control the anxiety clawing its way up my throat. "What are we even doing here? I—"

"*Now*, Ms Frost."

I look down at the phone. Back up at her. Back at the phone. Try, once again, to martial some PK energy, even though I already know what's going to happen.

After a long moment of nothing, Tanner pockets the phone. She doesn't even look at me. Just turns, and heads for the elevators.

Fuck.

FOURTEEN

Teagan

There's not a lot that would take my mind off the gigantic clusterfuck that has become my life, but the lobby of the Del Rio Hotel almost does it.

If 2Pac came back from the dead, this place is probably where the party would be. It's a gigantic expanse of warm wooden flooring, dominated by a sweeping marble staircase that is wider than my entire apartment. The staircase climbs up to a luxurious mezzanine level. Enormous gold pillars hold up the balconies, the colour picked up and elevated by the discrete blood-red carpets, almost casually strewn across the floor. At the far end, on the other side of the stairs, is the hotel's reception desk. It's an actual desk, an expanse of mahogany that looks like it belongs in the Oval Office.

And then there's the chandelier.

It's bigger than my car, and as much as I loved the Batmobile, it's much better-looking. It's a glimmering kaleidoscope, picking up the room's colours and refracting them, then shining back with its own. It looks like a fractal: an infinitely complex, never-ending pattern of crystal. If I had my PK and wrapped it around the chandelier, it would feel like a handful of freshly fallen snow.

If I had my PK.

"*Yaaw,*" Africa breathes. I puff out a breath of my own. This place is *dope.*

Well, it would be, if wasn't for the big crowd of rich people milling around. They're clustered in small groups across the lobby, most of them congregating around a set of double doors on the far side, another large space just visible beyond. Like most crowds of rich people, it's a mostly white, mostly male demographic. But no matter what ethnicity or gender they are, they all have the same expression: mildly impatient, slightly stuck-up, and very bored. One or two of them glance in our direction, but since we clearly don't own our own private jets, we don't hold much interest. That's just how it is at SADCON.

Well, mostly. A few of the people look in my direction for a little longer than is polite. I can feel their eyes on me, even though I keep my gaze firmly locked on the floor. Guess they aren't used to seeing someone my age in a setting like this – or at least, someone not serving them drinks.

It's only just before 11 a.m., but the booze has already started flowing. Bow-tied waiters move through the crowd, distributing champagne and canapés, like this was the freaking Met Gala. Here and there, antsy bodyguards stand with arms folded, trying to look everywhere at once, clearly uncomfortable without their weapons. And there's event security, too: five – no, six burly dudes.

Burr walks slightly ahead of us, eyes sweeping left and right, alert for threats. He hasn't said a word to me since we left the hotel suite; I have no idea if he suspects that my ability is gone. Africa definitely does. As we head towards the doors at the far end of the lobby, I catch him giving me the oddest look.

I've tried to catch Tanner's eyes more than once, but she

just marches ahead, utterly ignoring me. The little bit of wonder at the Del Rio's amazing lobby has drained away, leaving behind a light head and a dry mouth. I tap Africa on the elbow. "Hey – you have any water? Like a bottle of water or something?" My voice is a croak.

He turns his head to look at me, and for a horrible second, it's like he doesn't know who I am. Like I'm some random who just walked up to him.

Then his eyes clear. He gives himself a little shake of the head. "Water. Ya, good idea. I will get us some." He glances at Tanner, who gives him a distracted nod, and he lumbers off towards the big wooden desk. There's a slim counter running along the wall behind it, lined with glasses, along with big crystal pitchers of lemon-spiked water. I hadn't seen it before – maybe that's why he gave me a strange look. Like I was asking him to do something I could have done myself.

Burr stops in the middle of the floor. "All right, ma'am," he says to Tanner. "Should be pretty straightforward. When the senator arrives, we have Frost join his entourage. They can find a seat close to the stage. The rest of us can take up positions in a wide circle, back of the ballroom. For the rest of the day, we can—"

He falls silent as Tanner puts a hand on his shoulder, pulling him to one side and murmuring in his ear. It's no more than a few seconds before he looks over at me.

Perfect. Now two people know that my ability is gone.

I close my eyes, make myself count slowly to five. *Just make it through the day. That's all you need to do. Sit there quietly and look like you know what you're doing. Everything else is out of your control.*

Someone bumps me from behind, and I nearly scream. It's a large man in a string tie, booming an opinion to his buddy about "that bitch in Tampa", whoever the hell that is. *One. Breathe in. Two. Out. Three.*

"Here." Africa's giant hand appears in front of my face, holding a glass of water.

It's impossible to miss the little glance he gives Tanner as he says it. She doesn't notice. She's still in conversation with Burr.

There's a slight change in the noise. Senator Weiss emerges from the elevator, Jonas walking next to him. It would be wrong to say that every pair of eyes in the room turns towards them, but plenty of people notice. Gerhard hovers behind them, along with the senator's aide, and his own security crew. Kanehara is there, too, slim notebook tucked under her arm. She's tapping on her phone, thumbs moving rapidly. Probably tweeting. More theories about the Saviour of the Storm Drains. Or just casually mentioning that she's on the job with everyone's favourite hot German billionaire, getting up close and personal.

I squeeze my eyes shut, open them again. I have no idea where these thoughts are coming from, but they are going to stop, right now. If Jonas wants to bang this woman, he's more than welcome. It's got nothing to do with me. I very clearly and very firmly push her out of my mind.

Jonas and Weiss move through the crowd, shaking hands, slapping backs. This might be the senator's territory, but there's no question that Jonas owns this room. He probably – scratch that, *definitely* – owns any room he walks into. Will I actually get a chance to talk to him? What am I even going to say?

I look back at Kanehara, without really wanting to. As I do so, she frowns at her phone, then raises it into the air, doing that ridiculous thing people do when there's no signal.

Oh, is the Wi-Fi malfunctioning? Are you cut off from your Twitter feed? Too bad.

"Ladies and gentlemen," booms a voice, making me jump. The speaker wears a sharp tailored suit over a white shirt and red power tie. He has one of those faces that could make him thirty or fifty, and a military-style buzzcut. Hell, with the way he has his shoulders back and his chin up, he could be a drill sergeant on shore leave. Or whatever the Army term for time off is. He must be the manager, or at least someone high up in the hotel staff; there's a silver name tag on his lapel. "Welcome to the Strategic and Defence Conference, and to the Del Rio Hotel. The opening remarks will begin in five minutes. Please make your way into the ballroom."

Jonas and Weiss start heading over, then Jonas stops. Pats his pockets, like he forgot something. Exchanges a quick few words with the senator. He taps Kanehara on the arm, speaks to her too. Then the two of them, along with Gerhard, hustle away in the opposite direction from the ballroom.

Oh, my imagination can be a dick sometimes.

Tanner and Burr have gone silent, both of them staring at me. Tanner sets her mouth, and walks back in towards me and Africa. I take a sip of the water, reminding myself to stay calm.

The water is warm. No, the water is actually *hot*. Like it was being stored next to an oven. It's somehow thick inside my mouth, viscous, coating my teeth and tongue. When I swallow, my throat almost rejects it, spewing it all the way back up.

"Ms Frost." Tanner folds her arms. "Here's how this is going to unfold."

"I can't do this."

"Excuse me?"

I move away from them, first at a walk, then at a trot, then a jog. The only reason I don't go into a full-on sprint is because the crowd is too thick. They're hemming me in, way too close, a sea of business suits and strong cologne. I force my way past them, ignoring the snarled exclamations, ignoring Tanner and Burr shouting at me to stop.

I don't pay attention to where I'm going. Truthfully, I don't actually care. I just need to get away, away from people, away from China Shop, away from my entire life.

"I need to think," I mutter to myself, over and over again, saying it every time my feet impact the wood floor. My jog becomes a drunken stumble, and more than once, I nearly smash headlong into a marble wall, pulling out my hands just in time. I can't raise my head, don't want to, so all I can see is the floor, the occasional foot, the edge of the carpet. I just keep going. It's all I can do.

I head down a passage off the lobby, not caring where it goes or what's down there. At some point, I run out of energy. I come to shaky stop, and stand for a moment, rocking gently. Then I tilt sideways. *Going down.*

Fortunately, I've come to a stop next to a wall. I slump against it, then slide to a cock-eyed sitting position. Then I put my head between my knees, and breathe, just breathe, just breathe and everything will be fine . . .

I won't cry. I'm not crying for this bullshit. I'm not crying for losing my ability: an ability I never asked for, and which has brought me more pain and frustration than anything else in my life. I won't cry. I *won't.*

"And you will be hated by all for my name's sake, but the one who endures to the end will be saved."

Slowly, I raise my head.

It's the hotel manager, from before. The one who looks ex-military, in the sharp suit and red tie. He stands over me, arms clasped behind his back, head very slightly tilted. The passage we're in is marbled, like the lobby, lit by discrete spotlights in the ceiling. To our left, there's an equally discrete door with a brass plaque that reads STAFF ONLY.

"... What?" I say. My voice is barely there.

"Matthew 10:22. Not my favourite, but appropriate in your case, I think."

Before I can respond to this, he crouches down, dropping onto his haunches. His eyes are a piercing green, and his skin holds the kind of tan you need a little more than a Californian beach to achieve. Again, I get a sense of that discipline, that control. It's in the way he sets his shoulders, the way he barely blinks. His name tag, I notice, is gone.

"I like the following verse too, actually," he says, speaking as if we were two friends shooting the breeze over coffee. "*When they persecute you in one town, flee to the next, for truly, I say to you, you will not have gone through all the towns of Israel before the Son of Man comes.*"

"Not really a Bible person," I mutter.

"No? Because I have to say, if there's anybody who looks in need of a little salvation, it's you."

I can't help but laugh at that – or at least, make a noise that might be a laugh under better circumstances. "Buddy, this is not the time."

I'm expecting an argument, or maybe for him to reach into his little book of quotations he keeps in his head and pull out one about how a woman's work is never done in the eyes of the Lord, or something like that. Instead, he reaches out, and grips my shoulder. My first instinct is to start away, but there's something about his grip that holds me. It's firm, intense ... but not unpleasant.

"You can do this," he says quietly, eyes never leaving mine.

I don't know how to explain to him what I'm supposed to

be doing, and I get the feeling he wouldn't believe me anyway. "... I can't."

"Yes, you can."

"You don't even know me." What the hell is this? Who is this guy? "Why are you trying to—?"

"Because —" The grip gets a little tighter. " — you ain't got another town to flee to." The faintest hint of an accent there: Arkansas, maybe, or Tennessee. "You've got to stay here, no matter how much they hate you. That means you have one choice, and one choice only: you need to endure. Do your job, no matter what the cost."

"*Teggan!*"

Tanner and Burr, and Africa. Heading down the passage towards me. The exasperation on Tanner's face – the disgust – brings a fresh wave of fear.

Abruptly, the hotel manager stand, and give me a final, grave nod. "Remember what I said," he murmurs. Then, louder: "She's all right. A little shaken, that's all." Before the others can respond, he strides past them, looking like a man who has a long to-do list. They barely notice him.

"Are you OK?" Africa says, reaching down.

I'm still trying to wrap my melting brain around the conversation I just had, but despite that, Africa's question hits me right in the gut.

"I'm sorry." I don't know if I'm speaking to him, or to Tanner. I told myself I wouldn't cry, but with Africa here, I can't stop the tears coming. "I didn't want this to happen. I was just trying to help people, and it all went wrong. I never meant to ..." A sob bursts out of me, like an animal clawing its way through my chest and my throat. "Please don't send me back. Please don't send me to Waco. I'm so ... I'm so sorry ... "

Did I really think that lying on the concrete slab in the

Hollywood police station was my lowest point? That was barely a stepping stone. I would give anything to be back on that slab, right in the middle of a meth crash. Because at least, when I was there, I could kid myself that there might be another future for me. I could tell myself a nice little story. But here, sitting up against cold marble with tears streaming down my face, it's impossible to lie to myself. Not even a bunch of motivational Bible verses from a strangely intense hotel manager can help.

And I hate this. Begging for mercy? From *Tanner*? It's the worst thing I can imagine.

Especially since I know she won't give it.

"Frost." Burr crouches down. "I want you to take a breath. Just one breath, in and out. You can do it."

"I've had enough of this," Tanner says. She is still standing over me, And as I watch, she turns and starts to walk away.

"Ma'am, just hold on a second," Burr says, holding up a hand. Is it my imagination, or is there the slightest touch of annoyance in his voice?

"No, staff sergeant. This has gone far enough. I'm bringing an end to it."

Africa sprints to his feet, jogging to catch up, stepping into Tanner's path. She has her back to me, so I can't see the expression on her face. But if it matches the venom in her voice, then Africa should be very, very scared. "Move, Mr Kouamé."

"Mrs Tanner, no." He holds up his hands. "I cannot let you do this."

She doesn't even bother responding, just side-steps around him.

He talks quickly. "I know what happened is not good. I know she is not herself. But I have been in charge of China Shop before. This is not the way to treat a team member. We have to listen to her. We have to—"

Tanner rounds on Africa. "Mr Kouamé, you were acting head of this outfit for less than twenty-four hours, and you were only in that position because there was no one else. Your input here is not required. Am I clear?"

It's like she slapped him. He actually takes a step back. "I did not mean ... "

Even before the words out are of his mouth, Tanner is walking away.

"Goddammit, Frost." I can't tell if Burr is pissed at me, or pissed at Tanner. He heads off after her, leaving Africa and me behind.

Africa comes back. He crouches down, gripping my shoulders. I collapse into his arms, sobbing uncontrollably. Burying my face in his chest.

Right now, I want Nic. I *need* him, and it's a primal need that has nothing to do with physical touch. I need someone who isn't going to judge me. Which sounds strange, because Nic has done plenty of that in the past. But recently we agreed we'd start over, see if we could go on actual date, find a way to be with one another. I want him to wrap his arms around me. I want the scent of his skin, earthy and alive. I want to hear his voice in my ear.

Or is it Jonas Schmidt you want? He's never judged you, either. Not once.

I want Annie, too. Which is crazy, because lately, she's been doing nothing *but* judging me. The last conversation we had was not good. She accused me of being selfish, told me I was going to get myself killed by helping out the people in the storm drain, begged me to come with her. I want her because I want us to get past that.

You know what I really want? When you get down to it?

I want my fucking life back.

"Everything is going to be fine," Africa says, patting my back. There's no disguising how unsure he sounds. "I will talk to Mrs Tanner. She will understand."

I almost snap at him, but I just don't have the energy. And really, what difference does it make? Who cares whether he believes me or not?

"I will talk to Mrs Tanner," he says again. Like a mantra.

"I don't know." I pull away from him, wiping at my face. "Do you speak asshole?"

He raises his chin, his expression solemn. "Teggan: I speak English, French, Wolof, Swahili, Zulu, Italian and some Spanish. I am very good with languages."

I stare at him. A second later, his face cracks in an awkward smile.

I'll tell you one thing: it beats any stupid Bible verse. It straight-up smites that shit.

"Now come," he says, pulling me to my feet. "We go one step at a time, huh? One step. That is all you need."

FIFTEEN

Annie

China Shop is one of the most top-secret government teams ever created. Its existence is privileged information, and you can count the number of people who know about the team and their real work on a single hand.

Moira Tanner kept them secret by hiding them in plain sight. Black-bag crews don't usually moonlight as house-moving companies, or have their bases in new-build apartment blocks in Torrance.

Their premises do not have particularly heavy security, no laser grids or turrets that pop out to riddle foes with depleted uranium rounds. They have no more barriers to entry than the other apartments in the block. There is a code to get through the building front door, and a code to get into the office itself, and Annie can remember neither of them.

She could swear it's 1921, but it didn't work when she tried it. Then she remembered that that was the code for her locker in high school: 1-9-21. She concentrates hard, doing everything she can to ignore the blossoming headache. She knows it's in there. It has to be. This is her own office, for fuck's sake, one she's entered a hundred times before. Why can't she remember?

Sandra-May hasn't said much since they left hospital, but now she clears her throat. "Baby, maybe we should just—?"

Annie gives up, hammering at the buzzer for the office. At any moment, she's going to hear Reggie, or Africa: *Who on earth is ringing the bell so much, yaaw?*

But there's nothing.

Tanner would have left word at the hospital to call her if Annie woke up, so where is she? Surely she would have made contact by now, or asked one of the team to do so?

Annie jams her finger onto the button, sagging against the wall. One hand pressed to her burning side. *Come on, assholes, one of you has to be there.*

Gently, Sandra-May puts a hand on top of her daughter's, pulls her finger away from the button. "I don't think they're home."

Maybe she can break in. The offices are on the third floor, sure, but it wouldn't take much to climb up there.

Right. OK. Climb up there when you can barely stand. Somehow get through the window, then do what, exactly? Hang around an empty office waiting for them to come back? And let's not forget, you're dressed like you escaped from an asylum.

"Tell me what you need," Sandra-May says. She does her best to make her voice calm and even, but there's no mistaking the ragged edge to it.

There's got to be someone she could call. One of her contacts. That's the whole reason she's on the team in the first place. Her massive, multi-layered network of contacts that stretch across the city. Annie's Army, Teagan calls them. A seemingly never-ending collection of janitors, line cooks, minor politicians, cops, vagrants and gangsters who owe her a favour. An army she built from years on the streets, years running the streets.

She needs to go home to her tiny apartment in Firestone Park. Her iPad is there. She won't even *need* a password: hasn't she got it set to log on automatically on trusted Wi-Fi? Hasn't Reggie given her endless hell about that?

Except . . . her iPad isn't at home. It's upstairs, in the office. Sitting on the kitchen counter.

A howl of rage starts to build inside Annie's chest. She clamps down on it, willing it to stay put. "Just take me home," she murmurs.

She isn't referring to her apartment. When it comes to the Cruz family, there's only one home.

"Finally, she sees sense. Careful now, I've got you. That's it."

Sandra-May's house is in Watts, twenty minutes to the north-east of Torrance. Annie barely registers the drive there, slumped against the window, staring out at the bright LA streets and trying to figure out what the hell she can do next. Trying not to rub and scratch at her burning side.

The house is on East 107th Street, a neat bungalow set back from the road behind a waist-high chain link fence and a scraggly garden. It's directly opposite the enormous Watts Towers, a set of spiralling concrete artworks. The bits of broken pottery and glass embedded in the concrete glimmer in the sunshine as Sandra-May pulls her Chevy Spark to the curb. It's mid-morning, but the block around them is silent, save for the ever-present hum of traffic.

It takes Annie more than one try to wrap her hand around the door handle. When she finally pops the mechanism and clambers out of the car, her right leg turns to jelly underneath her. Her knee gives way, and she crashes to all fours on the dusty tarmac, skinning her palms. Her mother is saying something, but she can't hear the words over the horrid ringing in her ears.

Her mom swims into view, hand gripping her shoulder. Hard enough to hurt. "That's it. I'm taking you back to the hospital, no arguments."

"I'm fine." There's barely any strength behind the words, and for the first time, she wonders if she's really up to this.

There's a long moment where her mother just looks at her, slowly shaking her head. After a few moments, her shoulders sag. "You're gonna have to help me. I can't lift you up on your own. Or, wait, hold on, I'll call Del from next door, he's usually around. He can help."

Annie is about to tell her to stop, when another explosion goes off inside her mind. Another burst of blinding clarity. It's the word *Del* that does it. It makes her think of a computer, a *Dell*, that peculiar angular logo visible in her mind. The logo sets off a whole chain of thoughts and images, like firecrackers going off, one after the other, until—

"I remember," she breathes.

". . . What?"

"My password. I remember." The feeling of triumph is enough to propel her to her feet, sends her stumbling towards the house, pushing through the chain-link gate.

Rocko, her mom's gigantic Rottweiler, comes exploding from around the side of the house, skidding to a delighted halt when he sees who it is, barking and whimpering in pleasure. The scratch behind the ears Annie gives him is automatic. She barely slows as she hits the stairs to the porch. It's a bad move: her right foot catches the edge of the top step, almost sends her sprawling. She only manages to avoid it by slamming into the front door, barked palms screaming at her.

"*Jesu Christo.*" Sandra-May moves her aside. "*Me vas a dar un infarto si no lo paras!*" She unlocks the door, arthritic hands moving slowly.

The inside of Sandra-May Cruz's house is absolutely spot-less: not a speck of dirt on the countertops, not a chair or rug out of place. Her emphysema means that she struggles with even the smallest amount of dust. The China Shop salary isn't spectacular, but it's enough for Annie to have arranged for a team of cleaners to regularly visit the property. Every two days, a pair of cheerful Filipino ladies scrub and vacuum the house from top to bottom, including any hair Rocko has shed. Admittedly, it doesn't take long: front to back, the house is per-haps seven hundred square feet, with a small living and dining room leading to a kitchen at the back, a tiny yard beyond. The back wall of the kitchen doesn't match the rest of the house: the earthquake from a few months ago destroyed it, and it had to be rebuilt from scratch.

Annie finds some clothes, old ones she hasn't gotten around to removing from her mom's spare closet. A black BornXRaised tank top, a pair of old jeans. A set of sneakers she last wore back in high school, a hole in the right toe.

Shortly afterwards, she's on the couch, her mother's ancient laptop in front of her. It's an Asus, not a Dell, but that hardly matters: it has Wi-Fi, which means she can get online.

Reggie has them use a special dark web database to store all their contacts and messages, and Annie accesses it now: csmbksctvenice.site. It's a reference to the old China Shop Movers offices, on Brooks Court in Venice Beach. Annie once asked Reggie if it wouldn't be better for them to have some-thing on the dark web, and Reggie had just rolled her eyes.

She punches in the password: *!Zambran086!*. When Annie was a kid, her favourite player was Carlos Zambrano, a Venezuelan pitcher for the Cubs. Annie had his glove, his name stitched on the inner, and in permanent marker underneath, she'd written the number she wore on the back of her shirt: 86.

As she types the password, she gets another mental image of that baseball, hanging in the air against the blue sky. *You're not ready*, her dad whispers in her ear. *You haven't practised enough*

For a moment, she just sits there, paralysed by the bright, bitter taste of the memory. It's broken when her mother puts down a glass of water on the table next to her, ice cubes floating on the top.

"Thanks," Annie mutters, forcing the memories to the back of her mind. It's only then that she realises how truly haggard her mother looks. It's not just the exhaustion, or the ordeal she's gone through as her daughter lay in a coma. It's being outside the house for this long, in a world of dust and pollen and pollution.

Sandra-May collapses on the couch, clearing her throat with a sound like gravel shifting under truck tyres. She won't sleep tonight, maybe not even tomorrow night, lying in the dark and concentrating on each breath.

Annie doesn't apologise, despite the guilt. She'd just earn herself an earful. You only went down that route once with Sandra-May Cruz.

She goes to work, digging out her contacts list. She already has her mother's phone, and with a shaking hand, she taps in Teagan's number.

"Hello," says a neutral voice. "You have reached the voicemail of—"

Teagan's crackly voice comes over the line. "Angelina Jolie."

"Please leave a detailed message after the—"

"Stupid bitch," Annie murmurs, without any real conviction.

"What's that, honey?" her mom says.

"Nothing."

Annie doesn't have a direct number for Tanner – the

woman isn't exactly a fan of conversations she doesn't initiate. She tries Reggie next, but the phone just rings and rings. Tiny bolts of electricity shoot up and down Annie's arms, from the tips of her fingers to the base of her jaw and back, as if some of the lightning is still trapped inside her. It's a new symptom, and not a welcome one. Outside, a car drives past, blasting music so loud that the bass rattles the front window of the house.

With shaking fingers, Annie punches in Africa's number, aware that if this doesn't work, she doesn't have a backup plan. But as she is about to dial, another call comes in.

Annie's breath catches in her throat. The number isn't saved in her mother's phone, but she swears it's familiar. *Don't get your hopes up. It could be anybody. It could be a cable company cold call.*

With a shaking finger, she answers. "Hello?"

"Who is this?" Reggie's Louisiana accent is unmistakable. She sounds exhausted.

"R . . . Rrrrrreggie?"

" . . . Annie? Is that you?"

Which is when the dam breaks.

All at once, Annie is gasping, the trauma boiling out of her. The lightning strike, the coma, lying there and hearing them take Teagan without being able to do a thing about it. It's as if someone is punching her in the chest, again and again. It's all she can do not to let go of the phone. Her mom is hugging her, frail arms wrapped around her daughter shoulders. There's even more shame then: shame that she broke down in front of her mom, instead of one of her colleagues.

"I tried," Annie says, barely able to get the words out. "They took her, Reggie. They took. Adam and Chrissie. *Chloe.* And nobody was at the office and even Turner, *Tanner*, Tanner, she wasn't . . . she didn't . . . "

"Annie, are you safe? Are you still at the hospital?"

"No . . . I'm in Watts. At my mom's place."

Silence. Then, cautiously: "They discharged you? So soon?"

The tears have shaken something loose inside Annie, unclogged her mind, just a little. The words come easier now. "Reggie, they took Teagan. Her brother and sister are alive, and they came to the hospital, and they took her."

"*What?*"

"Those people from before who were ch-ch-chasing us? They're Teagan's fam. They've got abilities too. And, Reggie, they took her, right out of the hospital room . . . "

Reggie breathes, long and slow, as if she has to calm herself down. "Well, this is a lot," she murmurs.

"Where are you?" Annie says. The tingling in her arms and fingers has gotten worse. She reaches out, grips her mother's hand. "Why was there no one at the office? Where is everybody?"

"Annie, I need you to stay calm right now, OK?"

"Don't tell me to stay calm. I'm not a . . . " This time, she loses the word entirely. She can picture what she's trying to say – a small adult, a little person – but the word simply won't come. It's as if the lightning bolt reached into her brain and plucked the word away.

"Listen, we've got a lot to talk about," Reggie says. "I'm going to take a cab over to Watts."

"There's no time. Teagan is—"

"Annie." It's been years since Reggie was in the Army – the regular one, rather than Annie's collection of contacts – but she still has the ability to call up the steel in her voice. "You're not yourself. Stay put, and I'll come to you."

SIXTEEN

Teagan

Look, I'm not saying I like rich people. I definitely don't like rich people from this particular era, who tend to take the whole "Entitled Giant Asshole" thing to an entirely new level. But I will say this: rich people in the 1920s had style. Those fuckers knew how to party.

It's impossible to see the ballroom of the Del Rio Hotel without thinking about the soirées you could throw there. It's magnificent, which is not a word I use lightly. For a few seconds after we walk in, I'm not thinking about what I'm going to do, or the conversations I just had. I'm just busy gawking.

It's smaller than the lobby, but doesn't feel that way. Alternating diamonds of pale gold and deep blue make up the parquet floor, the colours amazingly rich, almost glowing. The wood is very slightly scuffed and worn, as if they're still holding nightly dances here. For all I know, maybe they are. The walls are light grey marble, tastefully patterned; and then there's the ceiling. Goodness gracious, is that a ceiling. It looks like it was stolen from a Renaissance palace: a gleaming, golden dome edged with intricate white plasterwork. The panels around the dome are a light blue, each with a miniature version of the lobby's chandelier hanging down.

Circular tables pack the dancefloor, each loaded with pitchers of water, vases of flowers, even more champagne. The great and good of the arms industry mill around, casting glances towards a raised wooden dais at the far end of the room.

This place is way too good for an event named SADCON.

Senator Weiss is in conversation with a group of officials at the back of the dais, lots of laughing and backslapping going on. Behind them, there is a pull-down screen, and on the screen is about the only thing that looks out of place in the room. These people represent the cutting-edge of weapons technology – smart bombs and radar guided missiles and (I'm assuming) space death rays – so why are they still using PowerPoint presentations? How can they talk about the future using technology from the 1990s?

The first slide is up already. It reads: *Teamwork & Innovation in the Armaments Industry: A New Legislative Paradigm. Senator Arthur T. Weiss (R/SD). Keynote Address.*

Come to think of it, maybe I understand the PowerPoint thing. Half these idiots look like they came up in the 1990s themselves.

Africa and I come in the left-hand set of double doors. Tanner is walking towards the dais, Burr close behind. I should do something to stop her, but what? Even if I catch up, or Africa does, she'll just ignore us. And somehow, I don't think tackling her to the ground is going to have the desired result.

And then I can't do anything, because Tanner catches the senator's eye. He waves her over, putting a hand on the shoulder of one of his buddies, as if he can't wait to introduce them.

"What now?" I murmur at Africa.

After a long moment, he says, "I don't know."

Tanner mounts the stage, bending in to speak with the senator, Burr lingering at the base of the dais. Weiss's face shows puzzlement, then a flash of irritation. He glances up at me, our eyes meeting for a split-second.

I can't help but look away. I stare down at my feet, but then find myself looking around the ballroom, everywhere except the dais.

It doesn't help that this time, plenty of people really are looking at me. The kind of searching, almost distant glances that you give someone who doesn't belong. I catch sight of the Asian woman from the parking garage, the one with the laser-cut bangs. She's not even trying to disguise her stare. Jesus Christ, am I that much of a mess? Do I really look that out of place?

Fuck them. I am having one hell of a day. I don't have time for a bunch of judgy business people right now.

Jonas is nowhere to be seen. Neither is that journalist, Kanehara. Which makes my mind go to places I'd rather not visit. I tell myself that I'm just overreacting, but it doesn't help.

Something catches the corner of my eye. The hotel manager stands against the back wall, arms folded, surveying the scene – checking to make sure that everything is shipshape and Bristol fashion, or whatever people in the service industry call it. I can't help but think back to our strange little conversation, and the Bible quotes he threw at me. The way he seemed to know who I was ...

Then again: I might be overthinking this. Maybe he was just trying to help, in his own strange way. People are weird.

Tanner comes down off the dais. She moves towards us slowly, pushing past people making their way to their seats, never taking her eyes off me.

I lick my lips. *OK. Calm. Just be calm.*

Tanner stops in front of me. "I've spoken to the senator. I've told him that—"

"Ladies and gentlemen," booms a voice, blocking out her words. She looks over her shoulder, annoyed. There's a man behind the big wooden lectern, a self-satisfied looking dude with thousand-watt white hair and a bulbous nose. "Please take your seats, as the keynote presentation is about to begin."

I'm expecting him to step back, for Tanner to resume what she was saying. But whoever this guy is, he's obviously been jacking off over this moment for days, because he just launches right into it. "I want to say thanks to y'all for coming out today, which is probably the only time of the year we get to have a drink and call it work, am I right?"

A whine of feedback accompanies the joke, and it's hard to tell if there are any laughs among the loud groan that accompanies it. Behind the speaker, Weiss waits with a slightly embarrassed smile on his face, hands folded at his waist.

"As most of you know, my name is Daniel DiSantos," the man continues. "You'll probably be sick of my face by the end of the weekend. But right now, what I'd like to do is thank a few people for their help with putting this little meet-and-greet together . . ."

Tanner tries to speak to me again as Daniel DiSantos reels off names. But between his voice and the sporadic applause, I barely hear her. Seeing my blank look, she gives up, raising a hand to tell me to wait. As she does so, the hotel manager shifts position. A bunch of his staff have just come in: the same bow-tied waiters from before, filing through the doors and spreading across the room. One of them shares a meaningful look with a member of the hotel security team.

Something's wrong.

"Hey," I say to Africa. "You see that guy over there?"

"Huh?" He can't hear me.

"OK!" DiSantos claps his hands. It's a bad idea, because it sounds like a gunshot as the mic amplifies it. Next to me, Africa flinches. "Now I know everyone's expecting a big speech from me, but really, I just wanted to thank everybody, and welcome you all to the show today. I think you'll be relieved to hear that in a moment, I plan to step aside, and hand the floor over to our keynote speaker, someone who we're all excited to hear from."

More scattered applause.

"So please, give a warm California welcome to the senator from the great state of South Dakota, Arthur T. Weiss, presenting today on . . . " DiSantos actually turns and reads the words on the PowerPoint. "*Teamwork & Innovation in the Armaments Industry: A New Legislative Paradigm.*"

Weiss steps forward, pumping DiSantos's hand. As he steps to the lectern, the hotel manager pushes off the wall, making his way towards the dais.

"Thank you." Weiss clearly has experience with unwieldy mics, because his voice comes across crisp and clear. "Thank you very much for that enthusiastic welcome."

There are a few genuine laughs from the audience. The hairs on the back of my neck are standing at attention. I dart forward, bypassing Tanner and grabbing Burr's arm. "Dude. That guy?"

"What?" Burr hisses.

"Him." I point.

"What about him?"

Weiss's voice swells out over the room. "I may not win many fans today, but I hope to at least win some. I want to present to you a new way of looking at things. Because let's face it: we're all tired of hearing about gun control. My good friend Daniel, who would rather give up his left arm than hand over his rifle –" More polite laughter; behind Weiss, DiSantos grins. " – regularly informs me that I'm a tiresome old fool. He's probably right, but what I *can* speak to is this . . . "

The manager reaches into his jacket, and pulls out a gun. He does it slowly, almost absently. Next to me, Burr goes very still.

Get down! is what I want to yell. But my voice catches in my throat.

The man points the gun at DiSantos, holding it in both hands, legs wide, and pulls the trigger.

Pistols aren't the most accurate firearms around, and the man is at least thirty feet from the dais, aiming at an upward angle. But he knows how to shoot. A neat red hole appears in the middle of DiSantos's forehead, dead centre. Behind and slightly above him, the screen showing the *Teamwork & Innovation in the Armaments Industry* slide is suddenly spattered with red.

SEVENTEEN

Teagan

Everything freezes.

DiSantos's body, mid-fall, an expression of mild surprise on his face.

Weiss, looking at the gunman. There's a faintly quizzical expression on his face; like he's just seen something he doesn't quite understand.

The entire audience, making a sound like every single one of them got punched in the stomach.

Then the screaming starts, and things go from frozen to fast-forward real fucking quick.

Africa yanks me backwards as people scramble away from the gunman, pushing each other and knocking over chairs in their terror. Burr steps forward, reaching for his own gun, cursing when it isn't there. Tanner gets in front of us, shielding us with her body, arms out.

In the split-second before I fall on my ass, I catch sight of the hotel manager. He calmly lifts his pistol into the air, and fires, once, twice, a third time. Somebody tries to rush him, and he turns and puts them down.

And the waiters . . .

They've got guns too. They pulled them from nowhere. Pistols and Uzis. Firing into the air, taking down anybody trying to rush them. The five hotel security people join them, guns out, hunting for targets. I don't know how many hostiles there are – ten, maybe, fifteen, shit—

"Teggan, *down!*" Africa rolls on top of me.

Let me tell you: if there is one thing you don't want, it's Africa rolling on top of you, whether it's in aid of a good cause or not.

And *still*, I try to reach out with my PK. Still, I try to grab the guns, shut them down, rip them away from their owners. And of course, I get absolutely nothing.

"The doors." Tanner pulls Africa off me. "Get out of here."

"We cannot leave!" Africa says.

On the dais, one of the attackers – a woman – has grabbed Weiss. She forces him to his knees, gun to his head.

Tanner ignores Africa. She lunges forward, yanking me to my feet, all but hurling me towards the nearest double doors. Even as she does so, a man with a gun steps in front of us. A short, squat dude with a rat-like face, bow tie askew. His gigantic gun dwarfs his amazingly tiny hands. As I stumble towards him, he lifts it and points it right at me.

Oh, fu—

Burr comes out of nowhere, delivers a flying elbow right into the man's throat. Rat Face gives a shocked squawk, collapses to the floor. As he goes down, Burr snatches the gun out of his hands.

I may not like Burr very much. Most of the time, he is complete and utter douche-nozzle. But boy, am I glad he's on our side now. *OK, assholes, guess what? I may not have my voodoo any more, but I have Staff Sergeant Kyle Burr, soldier boy extraordinaire. He came to kick ass and chew bubblegum, and he left his bubblegum in the car.*

Except: soldier boy extraordinaire doesn't charge back in. Soldier boy extraordinaire grabs me by the collar and yanks me out of the ballroom, hustling me through the double doors. Gunshots ring out, bullets whistling past us. "Move," Burr spits.

"What about—"

"Run!" Tanner bellows. I don't think she's ever bellowed in her entire life. And that's when I start to get really scared.

I hate it when people misuse the word "literally". It's a cliché, I know, but that doesn't stop it from being annoying. No, you did not literally fall over after your little jog around the block. There is not literally a ton of people inside that stadium. But this? This is *literally* my worst nightmare. A chain of events that will send me directly back to a government black site as an experimental subject. An attack that I can do nothing to prevent. It's happening in front of me, right now, and there's not a single thing I can do about it. I don't even think kung-fu would help here.

Burr keeps a hand on the back of my head as we sprint into the lobby, pushing me down. Tanner on my right, elegant pumps pounding the marble floor. The entrance to the hotel is to our left: big glass doors leading out to a covered portico with an actual red carpet, the driveway just beyond. Thank Christ. If we can get the hell out of here, then maybe—

Africa shouts something, his words obliterated by the noise of the gunfire, and Burr yanks me to a halt. I squawk – yes, that is the actual sound I make – as he spins me around, hustling me towards the stairs. "What the *fuck*?" I yell.

I have never felt so useless. Never felt this loss of control. Take away my PK and what do I have left? Nothing. I am a piece of driftwood, swept down a roaring river, heading straight for a waterfall.

In seconds, we're thundering up the marble staircase. A

bullet digs a wide chunk out of one of the steps ahead of us, showering me with marble shards. The mezzanine, a chest-high wall on my left. My feet tangling up in themselves, almost sending me flying. Africa's panicked face. Tanner yelling. We hit the top of the staircase, turn hard left, marble giving way to carpet, running along the mezzanine level. Passing through a set of double doors.

Burr lets go of me. We're in a gym. An expensive one, by the looks of it. There are racks of pristine weights, gleaming machines, lines of exercise balls on rails. Tall stacks of neatly folded towels sit lined up against floor-to-ceiling windows at the far end, windows that look out onto the back part of the hotel property, the view taking in a manicured garden.

Thudding and swearing from behind me. I turn, somehow managing not to fall over. Burr and Africa are holding the double doors shut, leaning against them. Tanner is pulling a rack of weights towards them, sweat popping out on the corded muscles of her neck.

"What the fuck?" I say again. I'm eloquent when I'm running from bad guys.

The irony is, if I had my PK, then I could utterly wreck anybody who stepped foot in this room. It's full of very heavy metal, things that would seriously ruin your day if they got thrown at you at speed. It would be incredibly, *ridiculously* satisfying to destroy these assholes with a tornado of dumbbells and steel bars. Of course, if I still had my PK, they wouldn't have even made it into the ballroom. I would have picked up their guns almost instantly.

As Tanner gets the weights in place, a muffled shot rings out, shattering the lock on the door. Burr and Africa jump backwards, splintered wood digging a cut in Africa's cheek. Tanner snaps a finger at me. "Get to cover."

"But—"

"Hide, Ms Frost. *Now.* Mr Kouamé, go with her."

I'm too stunned to do anything but obey. I stumble into the gym, casting around for a hiding place as another gunshot rings out behind me. What the hell am I supposed to do? Hide behind a squat rack? I have had way too many pieces of Korean fried chicken in my life to pull that off.

Africa grabs my hand, pulls me sideways towards another set of doors. Before I can ask what he's thinking, we pop out into another room: one with a pool. An Olympic-sized swimming pool, lit from above by gleaming spotlights, the floor slippery tile under my Timbs.

There are more gunshots from the gym, more muffled shouts. I have to stop. If I don't stop now I'm going to fall over. I put my hands on my knees, sucking great gulps of air into my chest.

"Teggan, we must take cover."

"Yeah, bro ... one ... second."

"Over there. There are changing rooms, I think."

"Get on the fucking ground!"

That last one comes from our left. We whirl, and my eyes go wide.

One of the waiters is heading right towards us, no more than twenty feet away. It's a woman, one of the security guards, wearing a dark suit over a white shirt. Her long blonde hair is pulled back in a ponytail, and there's a gigantic gun in her hands. Pointed right at us.

She didn't come in from the gym. There must be another entrance.

Before I can process this, or decide what to do about it, she points the gun at Africa and pulls the trigger.

But the floor here is very slightly slippery, and she's firing while moving, her balance not quite what it should be. The bullet goes wide, ricocheting off the tiles. In the same instant, Africa charges.

Here's the thing about my dear friend Idriss Kouamé. He's a decent driver, tells entertaining stories and is a good person to have on your side. He's great at making friends and contacts. He is also the most overconfident person I have ever met. You could ask him to pilot the space shuttle, and he'd not only say yes straightaway, he'd start telling you about how his cousin's brother's best friend's plumber once fixed a pipe at Neil Armstrong's house.

That overconfidence, unfortunately, extends to fighting. Africa may be big, but he can't fight for shit.

He swings a wild punch on the run, clearly trying to channel his momentum and put this woman down. She doesn't even flinch, and she doesn't risk a shot at a moving target. Instead, she sidesteps, then sweeps her leg out and trips Africa up. He goes sprawling, slamming onto the tiled floor. Whereupon she brings the gun around, and aims it at the middle of his back.

Clear shot.

EIGHTEEN

Teagan

People underestimate me.

My job means I've had to negotiate with scary people more often than I'd like, and they always think I'm a pushover. It's something I've come to accept, but it's still annoying.

But sometimes, it helps. Like, for example, when a woman with a gun completely forgets about me while she tries to take out my friend. Maybe she expects me to stand there and wail for help.

Thing is, I don't care how big a gun you're holding, or how scared I really am. You try to shoot my friend, and I will ruin your day. If I can't do it by taking the gun away and smashing it into your face a few hundred times, then I will knock you the fuck over.

I don't bother throwing a punch. I don't go for subtlety. I just charge into her from behind, wrapping my arms around her midsection. She tumbles over my back, yelling in surprise. I get a split-second glimpse of the gun flying through the air—

—and then we crash into the pool.

I have no idea how it happened. The pool was on our right. Either she slipped, or I slipped, or the universe decided to make me wet and cold as well as underpowered, because suddenly I'm underwater, my limbs tangled in hers, both of us flailing. For a second, we move apart, and I instinctively break for the surface.

But the woman won't let me.

She grabs me around the neck, puts a knee in my torso. It must be absolute hell for her to keep her head above water, but it doesn't matter, because it's impossible for me. I thrash and kick, lungs already starting to burn, push her off. No dice.

Panic, real panic, sets in. Normally, when that happens, my PK goes into overdrive. I can lift heavier objects at much greater ranges, and lately, I've even been able to lift organic matter. If I were my usual self, I could throw this woman into the middle of next week. But once again: if I had my PK, I wouldn't be here. It's like I'm stuck in one of those Chinese finger traps. The more I struggle, the worse it gets.

The woman won't budge. Every time I think I'm about to make it to the surface, she twists me around, forcing me back. Every time I think natural buoyancy is going to help, she stops it. Bubbles everywhere, the water freezing, my throat and lungs screaming at me to open my mouth and inhale.

And then all at once, the pressure vanishes. The woman's hands come off my neck.

I don't wait around to find out why. With a strained sound through clenched teeth, I get my hands underneath me, and push upwards. The woman rolls off me, suddenly slack. A second later, I break the surface, inhaling a choked, desperate grasp of air.

I'm facing away from the gym, looking towards the changing rooms. I flounder, slapping at the surface with hands that feel like chunks of numb meat. There's water dripping into my eyes, my hair plastered to my skull. I shake my head, snorting like a buffalo, sending a spray of droplets outwards. Which is when I realise the water around me is turning crimson.

What . . . ?

I turn around, and see three things.

The body of the terrorist who attacked us, floating face down, the water around her dark red.

Africa, standing poolside, holding the woman's gun in trembling hands. Eyes as big as baseballs.

Tanner and Burr coming out of the gym, walking quickly over to us.

"Are you OK?" Burr asks us. Before we can respond, he takes the gun out of Africa's shaking hands.

"I . . . Teggan was in the pool . . . the woman, she . . . "

"There'll be more of them soon," Tanner snaps. "They're spread thin right now, but that won't last, and I don't believe this place is defensible. Staff sergeant?"

"Affirmative." Burr checks the gun's magazine, slams it back home, loading a bullet into the chamber before slipping it into his empty shoulder holster. "If we move fast, we can make it to the stairs. It'll take a while for them to check the rooms, and if we get far enough away from the ballroom—"

"Copy." She snaps a finger at me. "Are you hurt?"

For a strange moment, I think she's asking if I'm offended – as in, hurt feelings. I don't even know how to begin to answer. *Well, my ability is gone and the person I needed to protect is probably dead and some random woman just tried to drown me, but other than that I'm doing OK.*

Fortunately, I don't say that. "No . . . I don't think so."

"Search her pockets."

" . . . I'm sorry, what?"

"Ms Frost, time is of the essence. She may have something we can use."

I'm too stunned to disobey, too fired with adrenaline to get squicked out. I swim over to the floating body, turning it awkwardly towards me so I can put my hands in the pants pockets. Distantly thinking: *What the hell are you even doing?*

Let's just say that when I woke up this morning, I didn't think I'd be searching a body while paddling in a swimming pool in the middle of a terrorist attack.

There's a cheap pen, a couple of coins – one of them slips out of my fingers, sinking to the bottom of the pool. There's a walkie on her belt, which gives no response when I turn it on. Fried by the water, I'm guessing. She's also got a wallet – one of those slimline ones with the lever you pull to pop the cards out.

"Get out of there," Tanner says, as I'm about to look at the contents. "We have to move."

No kidding. I put the wallet in my pocket, and haul ass out of the water.

NINETEEN

Annie

"Oh, this is some *bullshit*," Annie says, for perhaps the fifth time.

Despite her trembling legs, and the horrible burning itch in her side, Annie is on her feet, pacing her mom's living room, fingers linked behind her head. By the window, Reggie sips her tea, calmly watching Annie from her wheelchair. Rocko snores under the coffee table.

From the couch, Sandra-May watches her daughter. She hasn't said a word since Reggie began telling the story of what's happened to China Shop in the past forty-eight hours.

"What the h ... the *he* ... the *hell*, Reggie? She fires you, and puts A-A-A-Africa in charge? I love the guy but that's insane."

"Only temporarily. She's assumed direct control of China Shop."

"Oh, this is some—"

"I am aware. She said I could stay in the apartment until I found my own place, but I got the hell out of there as soon as I could. I've been staying with a friend." She lifts the tea to her lips again, but doesn't take a sip, staring into the distance. "Clearing my head."

Sandra-May shifts on her seat.

"So where are they?" Annie asks, her right leg turning to jelly again. She only just makes it to the couch, perching on the arm. "Do they know about Teagan? About her brother and sister?"

While she waited for Reggie to arrive, Annie checked out the local news sites, and couldn't believe what she found. *Murderous Rampage at Hospital Leads to Car Chase*, reads one headline. A paramedic and a security guard dead. Possibly gang-related. A car chase all the way into Hollywood which led to a crash in the hills, followed by a foot pursuit and an arrest of a twenty-three-year-old woman. No name.

Teagan.

"I don't know," Reggie says.

"Why the fuck not?"

Sandra-May's head snaps towards her daughter. "Annabeth Ramona Cruz, You will start watching your language in this house. *Ya no lo toleraré.*" She points at Reggie. "Especially when you are speaking to her. She can't walk over there and slap some sense into you, but I can."

Reggie raises an eyebrow, but says nothing.

Annie makes herself take a couple of deep breaths. "I tried to call them. Nobody's picking up."

"Same here, honey," Reggie tells her.

"What about your ashes. *Access.* Could you maybe look on our system?"

"Well, you know, when you get fired, the law says you get to retain all your login details and can jump into your company's computers any time, so—"

"Shut up, you know what I mean. You're telling me you couldn't hack your way inside?"

Reggie sighs. "That's the problem with being at my skill

level. I made it really, really difficult for anybody to penetrate
our systems."

"And you never put in a ... a back door?"

Reggie looks away, and for the first time, Annie registers
how exhausted she is. When she came into the house, and
Annie wrapped her arms around her, the tension in Reggie's
shoulders was unbelievable.

"Never thought I'd have to," Reggie says, more to herself
than to Annie.

Annie is about to reply when Sandra-May cuts in. "I don't
understand any of this," she says slowly. "Annie, you work in
a removals company, *si*? Why does a removals company need
a computer hacker?" Her eyes bore into her daughter. "What
are you into?"

Annie's eyes meet Reggie's, both of them realising the same
thing at the same moment. Sandra-May Cruz is a civilian, and
she not only has no idea about Teagan and her abilities, but she
has no idea about what her daughter actually does for a living.
One of the conditions of their employment is that they never
discuss their true work with anybody outside the team. That's
part of the reason they have the front as a removals company,
so that they have a legit cover if anybody asks.

"Mom," Annie says slowly. "It's not what you th ... what
you thi ... *think*."

"Then what is it?" Sandra-May folds her arms. "I have a
right to know."

"It ... it's ... "

"Annie, if you say it's complicated, I am going to ... "
Sandra-May's fingers hook into claws. She raises them to her
throat, as if about to tear it out, her hands shaking. The fingers
clench into fists, which she lowers to her lap.

From outside, the sound of children playing slips through

the windows: a group of kids in the park by the Towers, bliss-fully unaware of what's happening just across the street.

Reggie's voice is gentle. "Mrs Cruz, I can promise you, we are not involved in anything to be ashamed of."

"Then tell me."

"... I'm afraid we can't do that."

Sandra-May shakes her head, then reaches down and grabs hold of her oxygen tank, pushing herself to her feet. *"Me tratas así en mi propia casa,"* she mutters as she walks away. Rocko springs to his feet and follows, casting a doleful look at Annie. *"Mi propia hija."*

"Mom—"

"How many times, Annie?" Sandra-May wheezes. "How many times are you going to lie to me? Every time, you say you're finished with it, it's done, no more. And every time, you go right back. I cannot do this again, Annie. I cannot sit here and wait for a phone call to tell me that you are back in prison, or ..."

Another of those hooked claw motions, not looking at her daughter. Without another word, Annie's mother stalks from the room, her dog padding at her heels. A few seconds later, a door slams.

Annie stares after her. She wants to call her mother back, plead with her to stay, yell at her for not trusting her daughter. The number of choices crowds her brain, turning her pain up to eleven. She hunches over, desperate to rub at her burning side, knowing it would only make it worse. Her heart is beating too fast, her pulse thudding in her ears.

"Just breathe." A note of urgency creeps into Reggie's voice. "Just breathe, Annie."

Her mind slips its tracks, flashing up the image of that baseball hanging in the air. Huge, white, rocketing towards her. *You can't aim that fastball. You haven't practised enough.* She's breathing too fast, way too fast, she's going to pass out—

"OK then – tell me about baseball," Reggie says, her wheelchair squeaking on the worn wooden floorboards as she wheels herself over.

It's such an odd request that it momentarily jerks Annie out of her own mind. "What?"

"You were saying the word *baseball* just now," Reggie tells her.

When Annie gapes at her, her frozen shoulders give an approximation of a shrug. "Trust me, I've been through enough trauma to know how this works. Get it out. It will help."

"We don't have time. Teagan—"

"Two minutes Annie. Take two minutes, and tell me the story. After that, I promise we'll go after Teagan."

Annie is about to tell her *no.* Instead, the words that come out of her mouth are: "I used to play baseball."

The corners of Reggie's mouth quirk upwards. "I figured."

"My dad used to play himself, in one of the minor-league teams. When he was younger."

"Go on."

"He used to coach me, you know? I couldn't have been more than ten, but he was really hard on me. I was a pitcher on a team out in Compton, just Little League stuff, but . . ." Amazingly, she finds herself smiling. "I was pretty good, I think.

"There was this one game, though, out in Reseda. I was talking to my friends the whole time, and wasn't playing too well. The, ah, the other team had this hitter that I couldn't handle. He read all my fastballs like they were moving at ten miles an hour. Home-run city, except for one time he bunted for a base hit. And on the way home . . ."

She almost stops herself. Almost shuts it down. Speaks anyway.

"My mom and dad were driving me home, and he kept saying how disappointed he was, how I wasn't ready, that I needed to practise more. And I'm sitting in the back seat, and my mom is telling him to lighten up, because I'm just a kid, you know? And were at the lights and my dad just . . ."

Annie swallows. "He just hits her. Straight reaches across the car and cold-cocks her. She goes down, and he does it again, and I'm just sitting there staring at him."

"Oh, Annie."

"And then the light goes green and he drives off. Like nothing happened." Is she really telling Reggie this? It's something she's never told anyone. She once mentioned to Teagan that her dad was abusive, but she never went into the specifics, and Teagan never asked.

"Did he ever hit you?" Reggie says quietly.

"Uh-uh. Always my mom. Never touched me, only her."

"He's not around any more, is he?"

"What? Oh, no. Son of a bitch got himself killed in a car crash, back in '03."

"I'd say I'm sorry to hear it, but I don't think I am. I'll tell you one thing though."

"What's that?"

"You haven't stuttered or missed a word once since you started talking."

Annie opens her mouth to protest – then blinks. Reggie is right. And amazingly, the pain in her side has dialled down. There are still electric shocks zipping up and down her arms, and she's still nauseous and lightheaded, but . . .

Reggie taps her chair. "That's one thing I learned early on. You hold that stuff inside, honey, it eats away at you. You feel better?"

More than that, Annie wants to keep talking. She wants to tell Reggie how she started spending less time at home, and more time with her friends. Or people she thought were her friends. She wants to talk about how she went from keeping lookout to moving packages to making sales herself. About how it helped her build her Army, her huge network of contacts across Los Angeles. The contacts that help to make a name for herself in Watts and then Compton and then North Hollywood and East LA and Skid Row. Crips and Bloods, MS 13, Black Dragons, Vatos Locos, Hells Angels.

She wants – *needs* – Reggie to understand that the reason her mom is angry at her is also the reason she is so damn good at her job. She never wants to go back to prison again, but if she can't convince her mom that isn't going to happen, then maybe she can convince Reggie. At the very least, she can do that.

Except: the words won't come.

"Listen," Reggie says gently. "Your mom might be right."

"Oh, come on . . . "

"No, hear me out. I'm not saying we should involve her, not at all, but . . . what are we doing here?"

"What do you mean?"

"We need to consider the possibility that Moira is ahead of us on this. She may already be following up what happened in your hospital room. If we do this, we could end up causing more problems than we solve. And if Moira finds out that I'm involved, I might be risking a little more than just a slap on the wrist. China Shop is still top-level classified, in case you've forgotten, and she's revoked *all* my clearances."

"Are you sssss-seriously suggesting we back off?"

"I didn't say that."

"What are you saying, Reggie? Because it sure as hell

sounds to me like you're saying we should sit here and twiddle our g-g-goddamn thumbs."

Anger flashes in Reggie's eyes. "I said nothing of the sort."

"These people? Teagan's brother and sister? They fucked with us. They ran us r-r-ragged all over LA, almost got us killed a dozen times. Jesus, Reggie, they took you hostage. Do you not remember that? And yet here you are, telling me we should hang back, let the authorities handle it, stay out of everyone's way. After everything they did to you"

"I am *not*—"

Reggie's looks away. When she next speaks, there's a coldness to her voice that wasn't there before.

"You know what Teagan's sister did? Around the time she was chasing you down the LA River? I was still at the office, trying to figure out what the hell was going on, and she called me."

"She *what*?"

"I didn't know it was her at the time. She said she was an agent."

"Like . . . like an agent for actors?"

In her spare time, Reggie is a theatre actor, performing in a troupe made up of people with disabilities. Annie has been to her shows once or twice, at a playhouse in Anaheim.

"Somehow, she knew," Reggie says. "She wanted to take me out of the picture, and she knew exactly how to get in my head. She told me that she thought I might be good for a part in a movie, and I have to admit, she was pretty convincing. I think part of me always knew it was a lie, but I was . . . distracted. Not performing at my best."

She looked out the window. "The acting I do? The performances? That's personal. It's *mine*. And she used it to mess with me. One way or another, she's going to pay."

Annie finds she can't look at her friend. It sounds like such a small thing: almost mischievous. Pretending to be an agent, offering Reggie a part, making her think another path was open to her. But it's not small. The cruelty of it almost takes Annie's breath away.

"I don't understand," she says eventually. "They did all this shit to you – to *us*. And you *don't* want us to go after them?"

"I can't go after them if Moira throws me in prison for compromising her investigation. Or whisks both of us off to a black site."

"So what—?"

"We have to do this smart. We dig up as much intel as we can, *from here*, and we wait. Eventually, someone from the team is going to make contact, and when that happens, you – not me – can tell them what we learned." She makes an amused huffing sound. "After all, you're still part of the team, even if I'm not."

"I don't like this."

"Well, I'm not such a big fan of the whole situation either, but—"

"No, I mean . . ." The clarity she felt from Reggie's impromptu therapy session is starting to fade. The pain is coming back, the electric shocks, and she has to push past them. "This doesn't feel right. Tanner would have left word at the hospital for them to call her if I woke up. She would have wanted to talk to me about what happened, right? So why hasn't she gotten in touch? And even if she didn't, what about Africa? You're telling me he wouldn't have reached out?"

"You're jumping at shadows," Reggie says. But she sounds unsure.

"Nobody at the office. Nobody answering their phones. No contact whatsoever. Something is *wrong*, Reggie. And didn't you think it was weird that T-T-Teagan didn't reach out? Try call you or whatever?"

"Last time I saw her, she looked like she was going to pass out. I have never known anybody who needed a hot and a cot as much as that girl. Honestly, I thought she could use a couple of days to get her head together." She chews the inside of her cheek. "Look: we're going round in circles. We don't even know if it really was Teagan who got arrested."

"Massive car chase through the middle of LA ending in a huge crash and police custody and you're telling me that it's *not* Teagan?"

Reggie smirks. "I guess not."

Sandra-May has shut herself in her bedroom, but her laptop is on the kitchen counter. Reggie can't use it with her disability, lacking enough fine control in her hands to work the touchpad and keyboard. Annie drives, working at her friend's direction to find her way into the servers of the Los Angeles Department of Transportation. The city has thousands of cameras installed at intersections, which only trigger if someone runs a red light. *Hard to have a car chase without that happening.*

It's not long before they find Teagan's black Jeep, speeding through an intersection. This time, Annie can't help smiling.

"Look," Reggie murmurs. "Her Jeep wasn't the first car to activate the camera. If you go back . . . "

With a little prompting, Annie does so. A few seconds before Teagan's Jeep appears, there's a Ford pickup truck, blasting straight through the intersection. Annie can't get a clear view of the occupants – the camera resolution just isn't that good. But she can pick up the plate: 8JGO957. There's a massive scratch down the side of the car, a huge slash of scraped-off paint

"Has to be them," says Reggie. Next, she has Annie jump

onto the LAPD systems. But here, they hit a dead end. There *is* an arrest report for Teagan, and a record of the crash . . . but 8JGO957 isn't on their systems.

Annie is tired now, fatigue building behind her eyes and in her numb fingers. In contrast, Reggie sounds more alive than she has since she got to Watts. "This is the LAPD we're talking about. Maybe they haven't gotten around to logging it – it might just be on some detective's notepad still. But it doesn't matter; we still got 'em."

"Plate ain't real."

"Guaranteed. And chances are they'd have ditched that vehicle by now."

Annie clenches her fingers. "Which leaves us nowhere."

"Not necessarily. There are some systems we can access that might—"

"If the cops didn't arrest them and they got away, they won't be triggering any more cameras. Who knows where they could be?"

"We don't know. But if I can look at traffic patterns, maybe cross-reference with their direction and what we know already . . . "

"Better idea." Annie sets the laptop down, looks around. "Where the hell is my phone?" Too late, she remembers that it's still lying in the park where they fought Chloe and Adam.

"I think you lost it. What are you doing?"

"I need to make some calls."

Ever since she popped awake in that hospital bed, Annie has felt like she's been playing catch-up. Like events are happening too fast for her to keep track of. It's starting to piss her off.

The anger is something to hold on to, an ice floe in the dark ocean. And if she's going to do something about it, she can't just sit here and be Reggie's hands. She'll go insane.

"I'ma find these assholes," she tells Reggie, snagging her mom's phone. She pulls up her contact list on the laptop, the familiar names jumping out at her. Old friends. Old enemies. "Time to put the word out. If they're still in LA, they don't get to leave."

TWENTY

Teagan

I admit, I lose track of things after we leave the pool.

Maybe it's the adrenaline pumping around my system. Maybe it's the fact that I'm soaking wet and shivering, hair plastered to my scalp. Or maybe it's the fact that my knee hurts like hell, because Tanner and Burr make us move crouched over in a stupid roadie run position. Either way, I don't pay much attention to where I'm going.

At some point, we climb a set of dimly lit fire stairs, the concrete beneath our feet cracked and mouldy, the air smelling of dirt and cigarette smoke. We don't run into any more terrorists, which is good, I guess, but ...

Terrorists. Is that what they are? It's such a loaded term, one that I don't know if I'm comfortable with. Problem is, I don't have a better one. I can't call them *hostage-takers*, because for all I know, they may have murdered everyone in that ballroom. *Criminals* doesn't seem quite forceful enough. *Evil-doers*? Too comic book. I could probably get away with *assholes*, but it doesn't seem right somehow. After all, Tanner is kind of an asshole herself. So is Burr. So am I sometimes.

Assholes or not, Tanner and Burr keep us safe. At some

point, they lead us out onto the third floor. As far as I can tell, they picked it out more or less at random. More soft lighting, more frothy vases. Plush carpet underfoot. And it's quiet, with no screams and gunshots at all. We could be in another world.

"Clear," Tanner murmurs.

"Hold," Burr replies, pointing. There's a T-junction ahead. He sidles up to the corner, gun held low, then sneaks a peek. "No hostiles. One body."

Behind me, Africa lets out a low, shaky breath. He hasn't said a word since we left the pool.

Once we're around the corner, I don't really want to go near the body, but Tanner and Bur lead us there anyway. And when I get close, I let out a low, shaky breath of my own.

It's Gerhard.

Jonas Schmidt's bodyguard.

He's sitting against the wall, head on his chest. His blood soaks the hotel carpet.

My mouth has gone very dry. "That's . . . "

"Yes," Tanner says quietly.

"He was with Mister Germany," says Africa quietly.

"Yes," she says again.

I swallow, which does nothing to relieve my dry mouth. "Does that mean that Jonas . . . ?"

No. I won't even consider it. He was probably taken back down to the auditorium. Or . . .

"We need to keep moving," Burr says.

"Hold." Tanner kneels, and begins going through Gerhard's pockets, pulling out a slim black key card from his jacket. "Try one of these rooms," she mutters, handing it to Burr.

Burr complies, and the third door he tries beeps. Within half a second of the light going green, he kicks the door in. Enters with gun up, sweeping left and right, moving in that hunched-over stance that special forces use. Tanner comes up behind him, staying just as low.

It's another suite, although definitely not as nice as the senator's. It's smaller, for one thing, and there isn't as much art on the walls. There's no wet bar, just a regular minibar fridge and a Nespresso machine. It looks more like the kind of suite you'd find in chain hotels; there's even an adjoining door to the next room over.

If Gerhard had the key card, was this his room? It must have been, with Jonas the next one over – Gerhard would want to be close to his principal, after all. It's nice enough, but someone like Jonas Schmidt wouldn't settle for *nice enough*. He'd be in the Emperor's Suite, or whatever they call the penthouse in this place.

As Tanner and Burr check the bedroom and the en suite bathroom, I wander around the living area, not quite sure what to do. It's neat, with nothing but a slim laptop on the coffee table and a neat stack of papers with a fountain pen lying on top. Not a single piece of furniture is out of place.

Tanner and Burr re-emerge, and soldier boy extraordinaire pops the adjoining door to the next suite over. He doesn't go in, just sweeps his gun left and right. Guess he figures it isn't worth it. "Clear," he says.

Africa and I sit next to each other on the couch as Tanner pulls the drapes on the windows closed. She hasn't turned on the lights, leaving the suite in semi-darkness.

"POA?" she says over her shoulder.

"Comms." Burr opens the drapes a crack, peers out. "No phones."

"Jammed?"

"Yes."

"Land lines?"

"Cut. You saw the blast blocks?"

"I did. Go or stay?"

"Go."

"How?"

"Um, hi?" I say.

Tanner ignores me. "Us two. They can't guard all—"

"*Hey*."

Burr glances at me. "Not now."

"If you two don't stop talking in single syllables, I'm going to push you out that window."

A pause. Tanner rubs the bridge of her nose. "Something on your mind, Ms Frost?"

"Oh, you know, the usual. Just thinking about the massive gunfight. Basically just a regular Thursday morning for me."

I'm expecting Africa to tell me to calm down. He doesn't. He's a million miles away, lost in his own thoughts.

"We are currently formulating a strategy for that." Tanner turns away.

"Does it involve saving the people in that ballroom? Because I gotta admit, it didn't go so well the first time."

"That was—"

"We fucking *ran*." I jab a finger at Burr. Now that I've had the chance to actually sit down, the full horror of what we just went through is finally settling in. "You're special forces, and you just . . . left. We were supposed to protect the senator, weren't we?"

"And what, exactly, do you think we could have done?" Tanner says, folding her arms.

"OK, you know what? Fine. I couldn't have done shit. My ability is K-O. There. I said it. But last time I checked, you –" I point at Tanner. "– have plenty of field experience, and *you* –" My finger swivels to Burr, shaking only a little. "– are one of the hardest motherfuckers this country has ever produced, unless that Ranger creed of yours is bullshit."

"I'm a SEAL."

"Whatever. Both of you just *left*."

It occurs to me that I didn't include Africa in this little tirade, but honestly, I'm not sure what he was supposed to do either. As we've already established, he can't fight for shit.

Tanner looks at the ceiling, like she's asking God why she has to put up with this. "Ms Frost, you can't possibly understand—"

"Ma'am," Burr says. "If I may."

Tanner rolls her tongue around her mouth, then sighs. Nods. Waves a desultory hand at me.

With a sigh of his own, Burr lumbers over to us. Sits down on an ottoman, resting the gun on his lap. "Hi," he says.

"So what were you—?"

He lifts a finger. "No, this is where you shut the fuck up and listen. I'm going to spend exactly two minutes explaining this, and not a second more. The only reason I'm doing it is because I don't want you asking stupid questions and getting in the way. How many hostiles were there?"

"What?"

"Two minutes. Tick tock. In the ballroom: how many people with guns?"

"I don't know. Shit. A lot."

"Seven left, eight right, three more down by the dais. Military or ex-military, by the way they moved."

"Exactly. A lot, like I said. What's your point?"

"My point," Burr says, "is that while you were standing there with your jaw waving in the breeze, I was counting. There were at least eighteen hostiles, waiters and security detail, all heavily armed. For all we know, they got their weapons from that lockbox in the parking garage. On our side, we have myself, Mrs Tanner and my man Africa here, who at least knows how to act fast."

"And me," I mutter.

"No, we don't have you, because you apparently have no powers any more, for whatever damn reason."

"I got hit by my sister's—"

"I don't care. You were and are an absolute non-factor. There's just the three of us. You're seriously suggesting we start a firefight with these guys? In an environment filled with panicked civilians? The only reason we are still standing is because we've been lucky so far. We've only had to face them one-on-one, in situations where we outnumber them."

My chest, about to burst. Blood in the water. Africa holding the gun; the shocked, disbelieving look in his eyes.

I frown, replaying the encounter in my head. There was something strange about it, something . . . off. It's like a word that is just on the tip of the tongue, one that doesn't sound quite right no matter how many times you turn it over.

Burr snaps me out of my thoughts. "It's called a tactical retreat."

"Oh, give me a fucking break."

Burr sounds bored. "Most likely, they're all hostages. My guess is anyone who didn't try and be a hero is just fine."

That strange sense of unreality again. Like none of this is actually happening. "Pretty sure I saw the host get shot in the face." I tap the centre of my forehead instinctively, and shudder.

"Classic method of crowd control. Instil fear, seize all the power in the room, establish firm hierarchy. It's exactly what I would have done."

"It really does worry me that you've thought about this."

He ignores my jab. "You probably didn't notice after the initial shot, but the most of the other bullets went into the ceiling. They locked the place down with minimal casualties, and now they have a highly defensible position with a large number of hostages. They've even secured the hotel entrance with blast blocks."

"With ... what?"

"C4 packages, across the lobby doors. They'll trigger if they're tampered with, or if the door opens. That is some *serious* tech, and I'm guessing they've locked down the other exits too."

"Are you not even remotely worried about the fact that the senator is still—"

"If they wanted to kill him," Tanner says, not turning away from the window, "they would have shot him instead of DiSantos. He's more valuable as a bargaining chip."

"And now," says Burr, getting to his feet, "we have a defensible position of our own, with a natural bottleneck." He nods towards the hallway. "We also have two weapons. We are in a far better situation than we would have been in if we'd stayed, where we'd all either be dead or hostages." He taps his watch, which he hasn't looked at once. "One hundred and twenty seconds done. Now: sit tight, shut the fuck up and let the grown-ups figure out the plan, which we will do in as many or as few syllables as we want. Is that OK with you?"

He doesn't wait to find out if it's OK with me or not. Just turns and stalks back to the window.

"Dick," I murmur. But that's the thing about dicks. They usually have a point.

I sit back, slumping on the plush couch, running the events of the past few minutes through my head. Not really wanting to, but not really having a choice. The manager, the guy quoting scripture at me. He was part of it . . . no, fuck that, he was *running* it. Why did he talk to me before? Did he . . . Jesus, did he know what I was supposed to do? Does he know about my ability?

As if reading my mind, Tanner appears at my shoulder. "Ms Frost, the man we found you with – what did he want?"

When I tell them, they're silent for a few moments. "Anyone you know?" Tanner asks Burr.

"No, ma'am. Plenty of religious nuts in the armed forces, but I don't know this one."

"I see. Nothing actionable, then. We'll put that aside."

Maybe she can. I can still hear his voice. *And you will be hated by all for my name's sake, but the one who endures to the end will be saved.*

"What about the wallet?" Tanner says to me, holding her hand out.

"What?"

"The one you took from the woman in the pool."

"Oh! Shit. Yeah." I pull the waterlogged wallet out of my pocket, trying not to think about the fact that the woman who owned it is now floating face down in a pool of bloody water. I pop the cards out, ignoring Tanner's outstretched hand. "Miss Frost," she says, snapping her fingers at me.

"Hold on." There's an Amex credit card and a Kentucky driver's licence. Both in the name of Randi Metzger. An address in Lexington, and a photo of the woman, looking way too innocent and normal for someone who tried to drown me. What kind of asshole brings ID to a hostage situation?

One who doesn't plan on getting caught.

Tanner snaps her fingers again, and I have to restrain the urge to bite them off. I pass the cards over, and she and Burr study them. "Real?" Burr asks.

"Unknown."

"Name ring any bells?"

Tanner purses her lips. "Metzger . . . no. I haven't seen it on any watchlists."

There's something else in the wallet: a homemade, laminated piece of paper the size of a credit card, words written on it neat, looping handwriting. *For every house is builded by some man; but he that built all things is God. Hebrews 3:4.* The edges of the lamination are worn and frayed, as if it's been pulled out and put back many times over.

"Check it out," I say, passing the card to Burr.

He and Tanner take a look. "So there's definitely a religious angle," he murmurs.

"A few groups could have pulled this off." Tanner looks at the licence again, flicks it with a manicured nail. "Kentucky. That means a group like the Believers, or Lambs of the Father."

"Oath Keepers, maybe?" Burr asks.

"Not their style." She straightens up. "This gets us nowhere. We can work out *who* they are later."

Through all of this, Africa has sat perfectly still, elbows on his knees. Staring at nothing. As Tanner and Burr go back to planning their movements, I look over at him. "You doing OK, big guy?"

His response is a barely audible grunt.

I huff an exhausted laugh. "Me too."

This time, he doesn't make a sound. Just reaches up, scratches the back of his neck.

"You should be over there," I say, nodding to Burr and Tanner at the window. "They could probably use the help."

Jesus. Not even I am convinced by that. All the same, his stillness worries me.

"I killed her," he murmurs.

"Um . . . yeah, I mean . . . "

"I never thought I would ever . . . I am the driver. That is all. I do not . . . guns are not what I . . . "

"OK." Burr steps back from the window. "You two." He points at me and Africa. "Stay here."

"What are you going to do?" I ask.

"Find an exit."

"You're leaving us here?"

"Yup. They've locked down the main exits with those blast blocks, but not even they can cover every point. Our phones are dead, which means they must be employing a jammer somewhere. We get out, find the authorities, report on the situation inside."

"Why not just . . . I don't know, find whatever is blocking the cell phone signals and smash it?"

"Not worth the risk. We don't have enough intel. We don't know where the jammers would be located, how many there are, whether or not they overlap. We can't waste time hunting for them. We'll find an exit somewhere else, take out anyone who gets in our way."

"Well, good for you, John McClane. What about us?"

"Like I said. Stay put."

"And if the men with guns come looking?"

"Hide," Tanner says.

"That's it? That's your plan?"

"Indeed," she says. "After we leave, both of you need to find a place to hide in this room. If you are caught, do not put up a fight. Do whatever you are told. Because for as long as this situation goes on, I do not want either of you involved. Neither of you have the training to handle armed assailants."

I flatter myself that I can read between the lines on that one: *Maybe you would have been useful once, but right now, you're just a waste of oxygen.*

"Don't worry." Burr claps me on the shoulder. "We'll be back before you know it." He leans in, whispers: "Yippee-ki-yay, motherf—"

"Get out."

He smirks, drops me a wink. Then he and Tanner are gone.

TWENTY-ONE

Teagan

Whenever I catch a Lakers basketball game, I always wonder about the injured players on the sidelines. There they are, on the bench, in street clothes. Putting themselves in front of a court they can no longer play on, just to support the team.

Now imagine telling the player he *can't* watch the game. *Back to the locker room with you. You're a liability just by being here.*

Crappy metaphor. I'm not on a court; I'm in a hotel patrolled by murderous terro ... crimi ... fuck it, I'm just going to go with *hostage-takers* because I can't think of anything else. There is absolutely nothing I can do right now that Tanner and Burr can't do themselves.

Africa and I sit in silence. I'm half listening for sounds from the hall, gunfire or heavy footsteps. We should really hide ourselves pre-emptively, like Tanner said, but I just don't have the energy right now.

"Hey," I say eventually. "You want some coffee?"

"Huh?"

"Coffee. Wake-up juice. Yes? No?"

"I'm fine."

I lever myself up, stagger over to the minibar. Halfway there, I decide the coffee isn't actually what I want. What I want is a beer. Yes, day drinking is bad, blah blah blah, I don't care. The only beer there is Budweiser, which is disappointing, but the bottles are ice-cold. I crack one, taking a good few slugs. Is it possible to be both disgusted with yourself and ridiculously satisfied? Fuck it. I'll take it.

I grab another bottle to keep the first one company, then crash back on the couch. What happened to me in the pool feels like a distant dream, like something that happened twenty years ago, not twenty minutes. It's not the first time someone has tried to kill me, and it certainly won't be the last. I'm still here, and while I'm tired and stressed out, I'm not going to let a little thing like almost dying fuck up my *chi*. That's just not how I'm wired.

Taking a life, though ... that messes you up bad. I've only had to do it once before, and it's one of the worst things I've ever gone through. And yet weirdly, looking at Africa, I find myself trying to make excuses. *He didn't know the woman who was trying to drown me. She was actively trying to kill us. It was her or me, and he saved my life anyway, so—*

I rub my face, irritated. None of that is going to help. Africa is deep inside his own head, and presenting him with those reasons, valid though they may be, would be like trying to break a rock in half by grimacing at it.

I reach out a hand, squeeze his knee. For a long moment, he doesn't react. Then, slowly, he puts his hand over mine.

"Do you want to talk about it?" I say quietly.

His voice sounds like a mutter coming from inside a deep cave: "I don't know."

"Like, for what it's worth," I tell him, "neither of us should have been in that situation. Tanner should have figured out that there were other ways in. We got caught with our pants down."

Honestly, I don't know if this is true. Tactically, it may have been the best option to focus on securing that one entrance to the gym, and having us hide. But sometimes, you have to tell a little white lie or two.

"And by the way," I say, "we shouldn't even be here. We're not bodyguards. I'm not a bodyguard. This whole situation is—"

"Do not talk about her that way."

"—messed up and . . . Talk about who?"

"Mrs Tanner. She is doing the best she can."

I force a smile. "We're hiding in a hotel room drinking Budweiser in the middle of a hostage crisis, and she's the one who put us here."

It's meant as a joke, and it fails. Dismally. He gives me a sharp, ugly look, then turns back to gazing out the window.

I should leave this alone. This is a jagged, zigzagging conversation that neither of us are equipped to have.

"Hey." I hold the second Bud out to Africa.

"No, I'm good, *yaaw*."

"Yeah but, like . . . come on. Have a drink with me. Matter of fact, you know what? I propose a toast. To us."

He looks at me like I've gone crazy.

"It's bad luck to drink a toast by yourself." Suddenly, it seems very important to get him to clink beers with me. "Africa, come on. This might be the last time we do a mission together. I want to raise a glass to us, you know?"

"Don't be crazy," he says.

"What's crazy about a toast?"

"No, not that. Stop talking crazy about last mission and what-what."

I blink at him. "OK?"

"This is difficult, this one, but we will be fine. And then we will keep doing missions together. We will find your brother and your sister and—"

"Uh, dude?" I put the beers down on the table. The clink of glass on glass sounds far too loud. "You do know Tanner is probably going to send me back to Waco, right?"

"No, she's not. Don't say those things."

I squint at him. He can't be serious. "My ability is gone. It's toast. There's no way she's keeping me on the team."

"Ya, she will. And even if she doesn't, she is still going to keep you in Los Angeles, *yaaw?*"

"Are you insane? They're going to fill me full of drugs, take me to an underground facility somewhere and cut me open."

I get he's been through a lot, but he isn't stupid. He must know that this is the threat I've lived with for the past three years. Why the hell is he brushing it off?

He mutters something to himself, not looking at me. For some reason, that *really* pisses me off. The anger chases away the hollow feeling in my stomach, pushes back against the dizziness.

"Listen man," I say. "I am Done-zo Washington. Finito. No PK. No more moving shit with my mind. What do you think Tanner is going to do after this is all over? Huh? What—?"

"*No.*" He slaps the couch, his palm cracking on the leather with a sound like a gunshot. "Teggan, I am sorry, but I am not going to listen to this. We are in a difficult situation here, and all you are doing is making it worse. The only way we are going to make it out of here is if we trust Mrs Tanner."

"This again." I stand abruptly, interlacing my fingers behind my head. A sliver of sunlight sneaks past the drapes, stabbing me in the eye, making me wince. "What about Tanner makes you think she gives the tiniest shit about me now? Or you, actually?"

"She put me in charge of the China Shop."

"*For less than a day!* You know how stupid that is?"

"It is not stupid to have me in charge." Now he's angry, genuinely curious, his voice rumbling like a volcano.

I groan. "Of course not. But if she was coming to take charge of the crew anyway, then why even put that in front of you? Why put you in the top spot only to take it away twenty-four hours later?"

"It was a test," he says, although not even he sounds completely convinced.

"Please. She acts like she's this omniscient super-spy, but when it comes to managing people, she hasn't got a fucking clue. Do I have to remind you that she fired Reggie? Like, the most competent person on this entire team? Stop defending Tanner. She doesn't give a shit about you, or me, or anyone. We are *nothing* to her."

Africa sweeps his enormous arm sideways. He smashes the beers off the table, along with the papers, the coffee mug and the computer. Everything goes flying, beer spilling across the carpet, the laptop thumping the floor, the mug flying through the air and smashing against the table. He rockets to his feet, towering over me.

I take a step back, heart beating a little faster. You would too, if a seven-foot-tall-man looked at you like Africa is looking at me. But it's only a single step. I don't scare easy.

I open my mouth to tell him to back off. To apologise. To ask *him* to apologise. Instead, what comes out is: "Crikey, mate."

He tilts his head. "Huh?"

"Because of . . . you know, that . . . that story you told this morning. When you were in Australia."

"Yes, I know, but you have the worst accent I have ever heard."

I goggle at him. "*I* have a bad Australian accent?"

"Very bad."

"Are you *serious*?"

"Of course. I spent three years there. I know how they speak."

I snort-laugh. I can't help it. He says nothing, and for a long moment, the two of us just stare at each other.

"I know what it's like," I say quietly. "I've been where you are now. And I wouldn't be standing here if you hadn't taken that shot."

I trail off, and he looks away. Then, slowly, he says, "I think I will have that beer with you. Ya."

Which is when there's a soft sound from the suite's front door.

Like someone tapping a key card against the lock.

We both freeze. And I can tell we are both thinking the same two things.

One: that probably isn't Tanner, or Burr. They haven't been gone for nearly long enough.

Two: we were told to hide, and we're standing right out in the open.

Crap.

I will give Africa this: he can move really fast when he wants to. He grabs me by the hand, and hustles me over to the door leading to the bedroom. He moves lightly, feet barely making a sound as they impact the soft carpet, dodging around the edge of the couch even as I bump against it, hissing a soft swear word.

Halfway there, a better idea pops into my head. I grab Africa's forearm, pointing at the door to the adjoining suite.

If they're coming in here, then I don't want to be in this room, period.

We slip through the door as the key card reader beeps, Africa quickly and silently closing the door behind us. Half of me wants to pretend that it really is Tanner, that she forgot her secret-agent encrypted cell phone or something. The other half tells me not to be so stupid. We need to find a hiding place. Like, now.

It's a lot messier in this room. There are half-full cardboard coffee cups on the table, a slim MacBook Pro next to them. I barely have time to register these, as Africa hustles me along towards the bedroom.

Unmade bed, room service tray, dishes crusted with half-eaten food. Drawn curtains, a lone beam of sunlight picking up motes of dust. There's a nightstand on the far end of the bed, clustered with pill bottles and at least three half-full glasses – two with water, one with what looks like whiskey. An open suitcase disgorges shirts and pants across the floor.

"What do we do?" I hiss at Africa.

"Bathroom," he murmurs. We pad across to it, slipping inside as soft footsteps reach us from the living area. It's almost as much of a mess as the bedroom, as if someone didn't just unpack a toiletry bag, but decided to swing it around their head a few times to spread the contents as far and wide as possible.

It's a small room, mostly off-white marble. There's a sink to our left, a claw-foot tub to the right. Ahead of us, on the far side of the sink, there's a wall rising almost all the way to the ceiling. A metal pipe is visible through the gap, along with the tip of what must be a showerhead.

I point, and Africa nods. He closes the door softly, then

moves past the wall to the shower – and stops dead. A second later, as I come up behind him, I see why.

The shower area is behind a glass door. It looks pretty dope, with multiple jets and a bunch of steel knobs on one wall. It also happens to have Jonas Schmidt and Michiko Kanehara standing inside, gazing at us in shock.

TWENTY-TWO

Teagan

Look, I'm not gonna kid myself here. I have a crush on Jonas. I've had one since the moment I met him. But it never felt like a real thing. It was like having a crush on Idris Elba, or Bradley Cooper. Jonas is a multibillionaire technology investor who moves in very different circles to the ones I hang out in.

Of course, that doesn't make the crush go away. You can't help what you feel.

And yes, I did fantasise, OK? Not just about getting into bed with him. Before our awkward encounter in the senator's suite, I'd fantasised about how we might cross paths again. A low-lit bar, cocktails, the soft murmur of conversation, me in a slinky little black number. My fantasies didn't include armed guys with guns running around,; and they definitely didn't include discovering him hiding in a shower with another woman.

For what feels like an age, we all gawp at each other. Jonas is the complete opposite of the confident, smooth businessman from before. His shoulders are tense, his skin somehow pale despite his tan. Kanehara looks terrified. Her hair is way less perfect than it was before – and is it my imagination, or does she have one or two more blouse buttons undone than when

we first met? Come to think of it, how long have they been
hiding here?

Africa gets over the surprise first. He pulls the door open,
and shoves me inside.

I only just manage to suppress a squeak, before I'm slammed
face-first against Jonas, my face pushed into his neck, my
hand on his nose, my other hand on what I'm pretty sure is
Kanehara's right boob.

Would it be so bad if the hostage-takers shot me? Right
now? Just put a bullet in my head?

Instead, before I can even shift to get more comfortable, or take my hand off Kanehara's breast, Africa steps into
the shower.

All seven feet and three hundred pounds of him.

The shower area is fine for one person, maybe even two if
you want to get romantic. But four? Jonas and Kanehara and
I are all different sizes and body shapes, but we all manage to
make exactly the same hissing, groaning squeal. Africa pulls
the door closed behind him.

This is how I die. Not heroically. Not saving people from
the flash flood, or fighting my evil siblings, or dying in my
sleep after a Michelin-starred meal. I'm about to be crushed
to death in a shower.

Somehow, we reach a kind of equilibrium, the four of us
squashed together. I know they're doing the same thing as I
am. Listening intently, waiting for the moment when whoever
it is enters the bathroom. Sure, you can't see the shower area
from the door, but they'll only have to take a few steps inside
to spot us.

The footsteps are closer now, in the bedroom itself.

Maybe it's Tanner, or Burr. Maybe I'll just end up horribly
embarrassed instead of dead. But that can't be true, can it?

Because if they came back, they'd call out for us, wouldn't they? No, it's the hostage-takers. Clearing the rooms, checking for stragglers . . . hell, planting more blast blocks for all I know. Just what we need right now: a little C4 to spice things up.

If they killed Gerhard already, why are they back?

I don't have an answer for that one. Maybe they didn't check the rooms the first time. Maybe they're looking for something.

Maybe this is all a nightmare.

I start counting the seconds, because if I don't, I'm going to go insane. Five. Ten. Twenty.

The footsteps are right by the door.

There's another sound. A shout, the words inaudible.

"You think so?" says whoever is on the other sound of the bathroom door. Male, gravelly voice.

Another inaudible response. Closer now, not shouted.

"Fuck you, Shane," says the speaker on the other side of the door. "You got a problem with this, go tell the Reverend."

"Don't let him hear you call him that. He gets mad." Whoever it is has a Southern accent, one that reminds me of Reggie's Louisiana twang.

The door opens.

Footsteps on tiled floor.

I close my eyes. I swear, my heart is going to punch through my chest wall.

"I'll call him whatever I want, 'long as I get my share." The first speaker, Not-Shane, sounds like he's right on top of us. "He creeps me the fuck out anyway."

"Me too," says Shane. "Him and his buddies."

The footsteps move away, then stop, as if Not-Shane is just standing in the doorway. "Reminds me of those imams, out in Helmand. You know the ones I'm talkin' 'bout?"

"Amen, brother."

They both laugh at that.

I don't get it. The Reverend – the guy pretending to be the hotel manager, I'm guessing – is obviously a Jesus freak, and so was that woman Randi. And clearly they're part of *some* religious group – I've come across way more than the usual number of Bible verses today, and it'd be crazy to think they aren't connected. But these guys don't sound like they're part of it.

Shane sighs, and there's the creak of bedsprings. "Let's just get out of here, man. I already did this place this morning."

"I'm just sayin'," Shane continues. "I didn't sign up for this shit to be on patrol detail."

"With the money we're making, I'll do as much patrol as they want me to. You head on out if you want. Come visit me down in Tulum after."

"Fuckin' Tulum," Shane mutters.

"You ain't seen the beaches down there. They got this—"

"Brandon, can we just get out of here already? Please?"

Not-Shane – Brandon – shifts, shoes squeaking on tile. This is it. This is where he peaks behind the wall, and we all die.

A few seconds tick by. A few more.

"Fuck it." There's a creak, and then the bathroom door slams shut.

"Right on," says Shane, voice muffled.

I don't move. I don't even dare breathe. Not that I'm able to. One of Kanehara's hairs is tickling my nose; if I sneeze, right now . . .

The footsteps fade into silence. A few seconds later, there's a sound that might just be my imagination: the distant click of a door closing.

Silence.

None of us move for a good minute. Then another. That hair is still tickling me, just touching the inside of my nostril.

"I think they are gone," Africa whispers.

I manage a thin, weak, wheezing noise. And unfortunately, that little exhalation of air makes me sneeze, loud and proud, showering my crush with moist droplets of snot.

Yep. One bullet in the head, please. Now would be good. Thanks.

TWENTY-THREE

Annie

Annie realised early on that most drug dealers were dumb as rocks.

Moving weight seemed simple enough. When you were selling a highly illegal substance, you wanted to make transactions straightforward, with as few unknowns as possible. You wanted to *reduce* complexity, because complexity could get you arrested. Or shot. But they just didn't get it.

When Annie was sixteen, she worked for this obese dude from Compton named Marathon. He'd acquired a major new connect from across the border, and it got him eighty kilos of very pure, very fine blow. She still remembers the expression on his face when it came in. He'd actually started giggling, the fat on his neck almost vibrating. "We big time now, baby," he kept saying, waddling around the bricks on the table. Annie had said nothing, scuffing the toe of her Converse sneakers into the concrete floor. It was major weight, sure, and she knew they'd be able to shift it, no problem ... so why couldn't she help feeling that something was off?

That feeling solidified when Marathon stepped on it and started to flood the streets, expanding his dealer network to do so. He'd been using seven people up until then, including Annie, all of whom had been with him for a couple of years. Except suddenly there were new faces around. People Annie didn't know. *Cholos* from North Hollywood and 'roided-out white boys from the Valley, dudes from Inglewood with their locks and fake-ass Jamaican accents. Lots of new faces hanging out at Marathon's crib in Watts, and all of them trusted with a brick apiece, two bricks. Way too much.

Annie took the uncharacteristic step of asking Marathon about it. Wouldn't it be better, she said, to move the weight slowly? Use people they trusted, watch the money trickle in without attracting too much attention? He looked at her like she was crazy, his baby face cracking in a smirk, then erupting in a belly laugh. "Someone getting scared over here," he told the room, packed with faces she didn't know. Faces smiling back at her, pleasantly, almost indulgently. She'd stalked from the room, Marathon's laughter following her down the passage.

Turns out one of those faces didn't like the idea of sharing the profits with Marathon. Marathon didn't like that very much, and it resulted in a burst of drive-by shootings which the LA Times called a *horrific spate*, and which ended up with Marathon and at least three of Annie's fellow dealers dead. Annie was lucky to avoid it herself, and she couldn't help but think how none of it had to happen. What a waste.

Annie got a second reminder of this when one of her own deals went to hell a year later. She'd been working for a dude with MS-13 connections named Blanca, and he ended up wearing a wire. Annie had copped two-to-five in Chowchilla, and had been lucky not to get more. When she got out on good behaviour after a year and a half, she understood two things.

One: prison sucked. Two: both the Marathon and the Blanca situations could have been avoided.

Even before her dad died, Annie had been a quiet kid. Introverted. She forced herself to change that. Instead of spending her time hanging with the same dudes on the same block, or getting high by herself in the tiny apartment she was renting, she started talking to people. Anybody and everybody, whether they were in the game or not. Just shooting the shit. Talking about their families, their kids, the music they were making, their jobs (or lack of them). Having conversations without a goal, without wanting to get an edge on someone.

Annie made friends with postal workers and bus drivers, ConEd repairmen and secretaries, firefighters, groundskeepers, even a few cops. There were plenty of areas in the city she couldn't go into, areas where anyone from Watts risked a beatdown, or worse. But she found a way in, making friends with the people who lived in those neighbourhoods while they were at work. She made herself a familiar face. Someone people would holler at when she walked past, cross the street to fist bump. She'd buy ice creams for groups of little kids, talking to them about their lives, their parents, their schools, hanging out on the courts playing HORSE.

And she'd help. If someone needed a connection made, she'd do the introductions. If someone needed cash for a new engine, or bail money, or a book bag, she'd help them figure it out.

She was still in the drug game, in a low-key sort of way, and there was no way that what happened to Marathon was going to happen to her. When she did end up doing time again, it had nothing to do with any sort of betrayal; just bad luck, a neighbour seeing something he shouldn't have and calling the cops. Back to Chowchilla, except this time, half the ladies on the block knew who she was already.

This time, prison sucked considerably less.

She can't remember who came up with the term Annie's Army first. Did it exist before China Shop? Maybe not – it sounds like something Teagan would have coined. All the same, it's the reason Moira Tanner hired her. She doesn't know how she got onto Tanner's radar, but she did, and then suddenly she was in a room with this scary government woman who was offering her a choice. Stay in the drug game, and risk a third prison sentence – one that wouldn't be as short or as comfortable. Or go and work for her. Put the Army to good use.

Annie took the deal. And not just because Tanner scared her, a little. It was because of all the people she knew, there was one she'd never quite been able to get a handle on: her mom. There'd been a distance between them since her dad died, and Annie rather liked the idea of trying to close that gap. Going legit – or at the very least, having a legit front – was a start.

Less than two hours after she first puts the word out, one of her Army comes through. A part-time actor and full-time line repairman named Elijah Copeland. Two kids, one of them at Cornell on a scholarship. Wife who once had a little problem with blow, which was how Annie came into the picture. Carlita Copeland was being harassed by her dealer over unpaid debt, so Annie stepped in to straighten him out. Told him to wait like a good little boy for his money. Elijah and Carlita bought her a drink, and she got herself two new recruits for her Army.

Annie had spoken to Jah's supervisor Cynthia earlier, asked her to spread the word around. Looks like she came through.

"What it do, Annie?" His voice on the phone is even more

gravelly than she remembers. *He must be back up to a pack a day.* "You still out in Watts?"

"Yessir." She is burning with the need to ask him if he's seen anything, but sometimes, you can't rush it. "You good?"

"Yeah. You should come by the crib some time. Marley been asking 'bout you."

"How is she?"

"Sixteen and already turning heads." He chuckles.

Annie smiles, despite herself. "I'll be round your way soon. You got anything for me?"

Silence over the line. For a moment, Annie is sure she's lost him, but then he says, "Dark blue pickup, right?"

"Uh-huh." She licks her lips, trying not to get her hopes up. She's already had three calls since she put the word out, all of them reporting sightings of dark blue pickups. None of them had the big scrape down the side. There's no reason this should be any different.

"I'm out in Laurel Canyon," Jah murmurs. "Fixing some lines from the storm the other night. They got these wild houses out here, millionaire stuff. I just seen your truck pull into one of them."

"Jah, that's cool and all, and I appreciate it, but can you tell me—?"

"If it's got the scrape down the side?" She can hear the smugness in his voice. "Cynthia told me to watch out for that. Saw it myself. Something took the paint right off."

Annie's heart starts to beat a little faster. Her body position must change, because Reggie looks up sharply. "Can you see it now?"

"Nah. Came down off the rig to make the call. I'm in my truck. But it's still there. I even saw who got out of it, although I don't know if that helps . . ."

"Tell me." *Don't get your hopes up, It might be a false alarm, they can't have the only truck in LA with a fucked-up side . . .*

"Some white girl was driving. Nothing special about her, but the other guy . . . he's big, man. And hairy. Looks like a fuckin' animal, you know what I mean?"

Very carefully, Annie transfers the phone from her right ear to her left, her free hand hunting for a pen. "You're sure? Did you take any photos?"

"The hell I take photos for, you think I want that animal-looking dude coming out, asking why I'm Instagramming his crib? But look: I know what I saw, OK?"

"Anybody else watching the place? Any other cars?"

"Nope. Empty street except my truck."

"No moving vans?" *If the team is there . . .*

Jah sounds amused. "What you mean, moving vans? Like I said, nobody up here but us chickens."

Annie's hand finds a pen on the edge of the table. Her fingers lose control of it, and it clatters to the floor. She lunges forward, snatching at it, doing her best to ignore the snarl of pain in her burned side. "Give me the address."

Jah does. Somehow, Annie manages to write it down, scrawling it in big, shaky capitals on the back of an electricity bill sitting on the coffee table. When she tells him to stay put until she gets there, Reggie goes very still.

Laurel Canyon. It's a half-hour's drive away, north-west of Hollywood. An expanse of hills and canyons cut through with sweeping roads, and killer views from the mansions dotted across the rocky cliffs. A land of actors and executives, CEOs and movie stars. Annie ends the call and gets to her feet, shoving the electricity bill into her pocket. *Got you, motherfuckers.*

"Don't even think about it," Reggie says.

"Ain't got a choice." She can't drive herself, doesn't quite trust her fine motor skills yet. But she can Uber over there, no problem, or get someone to drop her off . . .

"Need I remind you that a few hours ago you were in a coma? Lying in hospital? And now you want to go tearing off on some wild goose chase?"

Christ, she's thirsty. Water, that's what she needs. Maybe there's a bottle in the kitchen she can take with her. She stumbles through the door beyond the living room, mind racing. If Jah is wrong . . . and there's a good chance he is, because there's no way these assholes are still in town . . .

"Listen to me," Reggie says from the doorway.

"Why they still here, Reggie?" Annie says over her shoulder. "Why didn't they get the fuck outta town?"

"It doesn't matter," Reggie snaps. "You are not in a state to go into the field, and as your superior, I expressly forbid—"

"You aren't my superior any more. You got fired remember?"

It pops out of her before she can stop it, and she instantly regrets it. A flicker of shock flares on Reggie's face, just for a moment, and then the shutter comes down.

Annie wants to say sorry, wants it more than anything. But the words won't come. After a moment, she gives up, returning to her hunt for a water bottle. "Just keep trying to contact the time. The *team*," Annie says.

"If you head out there—"

Another lucid moment, another connection, and Annie takes advantage of it. "We got lucky. By now, they should have skipped town, but they're still here. I don't know how long that's going to last, so if we don't get up there now, we might lose our opportunity. And we can't just assume that Tanner and Teagan and whoever is on top of this. We don't know what happened to them. And I'm not just gonna sit here and let this chance slip away."

"So you're just going to go out there on your own? Annie, these people have abilities too."

Annie finds a water bottle, fills it. Pointedly not looking at Reggie. When she steps past, the woman puts a hand out to stop her. "Dammit, Annie, *please.*"

Annie says nothing. And a thought, unwelcome and intruding, swims to the top of her mind. *If you go, Reggie will have no one to be her fingers. She won't be able to do anything. She has just as much reason to hate these people as you do, and with you gone, she won't be able to do anything about it.*

In that moment, she almost takes it back. Almost agrees to stay. Almost.

But then Reggie speaks again. "Just ... just promise me you won't engage them. Observe from a distance, stay hidden, then come right back here. Will you at least promise me that?"

Speechless, Annie nods.

"You'd better take a phone," Reggie tells her. "To call an Uber for yourself, if nothing else. I'd offer mine, but I want to be available in case Moira tries to get in touch. Do you think your mother would let you use hers? Or maybe she's got a spare one?"

Sandra-May's phone is on the coffee table. Annie picks it up, is about to pocket it, then weighs it in her hand. She can't stop herself glancing towards the other side of the house, and her mother's closed bedroom door.

Reggie catches the gaze. "Don't worry," she murmurs, unable to keep the regret and frustration out of her voice. "I'll square it with her."

Annie still can't speak. Doesn't trust herself to. She squeezes Reggie's shoulder, then turns to go.

"Annie?"

Reggie's voice has regained some of its former steel. "Observe *only*," she says. "Don't get anywhere near these people. Are we clear?"

"Clear," Annie says.

TWENTY-FOUR

Teagan

So turns out, the room we hid in actually *does* belong to Jonas.

I know this because when we finally climb our squashed asses out of the shower, he turns to me and says, "What are you doing in my room?"

Which leads to a discussion about how we even got in here, and I tell him we had a key, and he asks where I got it from, and I have to tell him about Gerhard and . . .

Yeah.

He insists on seeing the body. Won't listen to me when I ask him not to. Just heads out into the corridor, not even bothering to check whether any bad guys are there or not.

When we get to him, he's standing over Gerhard's body, face white. Absolutely still.

"Help me carry him," he says after a few moments.

Africa steps past me, grabs Gerhard's ankles. Jonas takes his bodyguard under the arms. Grunting, they bring him in past Kanehara, who stands with one hand over her mouth, hugging herself with her free arm.

They bring Gerhard into the bedroom of his own suite, place him carefully on the unmade bed. Unlike other bodies

I've seen – and sadly, I've seen plenty – he does not seem like he's sleeping. They haven't closed his eyes yet. I get one look at them, and turn away. Can't do it.

"I want to be alone with him." Jonas's voice is horribly steady.

None of us argue. We leave him sitting on the bed, elbows on his knees, staring at nothing.

The main living area of Gerhard's suite is no longer spick-and-span, thanks to Africa sweeping everything off the table. I want to ask why Jonas picked such low-key rooms for them to stay in, but in the light of everything else, it doesn't seem like the most pressing question. Haltingly, Kanehara tells us what happened. Turns out, Gerhard made them hide in the shower when the hostage-takers started doing their thing. They heard voices from Gerhard's suite, after we arrived, but they didn't know it was us, and they sure as hell weren't going to check.

When she finishes, there's a long moment of awkward silence.

"All right," I say, when it gets too much. "Guess we got lucky."

"Not sure Gerhard would call it luck," Kanehara murmurs.

"I mean, yeah, obviously not. Obviously. But what I'm saying is they won't be back. We can just hide out here."

"At least until Mrs Tanner returns," Africa says.

"Look, I'm sorry." Kanehara spreads her hands. Her voice is a little stronger now. "Who are you guys, exactly? You were with the senator before, but you're definitely not staff."

She doesn't need to know. The thought is petty, spiteful, and makes me feel about five years old.

Africa clears his throat. "I am Idriss Kouamé," he says. "This is my associate, Teggan Frost. We are with the intelligence services."

Hearing him introduce us makes me think of the middle name thing. Maybe something long and floral would be fun. *Teagan Hortensia Eleanora Frost*. Maybe I should introduce myself that way now, just to fuck with Kanehara.

I rub my eyes. Some thoughts are just too weird to entertain. The journalist looks me up and down. *"You're* with US intelligence?"

"Like you would know," I mutter.

"I would, actually," she says, without missing a beat. "Are you here because of the shooting? But no—" She shakes her head, as if she's struggling to get her thoughts in order. "You were here before. What agency are you with?"

We're saved from having to answer when Jonas Schmidt comes out of the bedroom, closing the door softly behind him. He's still ashen, but there's a steel in his eyes that wasn't there before.

"Jonas." Kanehara gets to her feet. "Do you know who these people are?" He doesn't respond, so she keeps talking. "The other one, what was her name, Tanner? I'd say NSA, or Homeland, but these two don't fit the profile."

"Better question," I say, trying to get a handle on this increasingly fucked situation. "Why were *you* guys up here? Everybody else was in the ballroom when it all . . . you know, when shit went south."

But of course, I know what they were doing up here. Or at least, I have a pretty good goddamn suspicion.

Kanehara gives an exasperated shrug. "Jonas forgot his phone, and I wasn't getting any signal down there anyway, so we decided to skip the opening speech."

I have to bite off my sarcastic reply.

"What the hell happened down there?" she asks. "Who are these people?"

Much as I want there to be a reason not to talk to her, it doesn't seem fair to keep her and Jonas in the dark about this. They listen silently as we tell them about the ballroom. When I mention that DiSantos got shot, Kanehara swallows, and Jonas mutters an ugly-sounding word in German.

"Have they made any demands?" the journalist asks. "Anything?"

"Probably. But they didn't exactly yell them out while they were shooting up the place."

Jonas has moved over to the window, staring out the gap in the curtains, arms folded. I want to tell him to hide, but let's be real: wherever the hostage-takers are, it's unlikely they're *outside* the hotel.

But now, with Jonas back in the mix . . .

"What about DiSantos? Perhaps he was the real target?" Kanehara bites her lip. "No, never mind, that doesn't make sense."

"Ya," Africa says. "If you want to shoot this DiSantos person, then why follow up with taking everyone as prisoners? And why kill him in public like this?"

Nobody answers.

"Anyway," I say, when the silence gets too much. "I think we're pretty safe here. We lock the door, hold out, wait for my boss to come back. And it's not like we're short of beer. We can probably just get hammered and chill." As much as I don't like the idea of being on the bench, staying put and having a drink really does seem like the safest option. It's not as if the hostage-takers are going to come back and check this room again, and as long as we're here, no one will be shooting at us. Sure, we're trapped with an inquisitive journalist, but . . .

"Ya," Africa says, interrupting my thoughts. "Mister Germany looked after us last time, with the plane."

Kanehara frowns. "What plane?"

Africa either doesn't hear, or decides not to answer. "So maybe he will help us again, huh?"

"What is that you call me?" Jonas says.

"Mister Germany. I am sorry, it is just—"

"That is not my name," Jonas snaps.

I stare at him. *What the hell was that?*

Africa and Jonas have met before, back when we broke into his plane. Africa called *Mister Germany* then, and he didn't appear to give a shit. I get that we're in a tough spot, but why he's acting like an asshole?

Before I can ask him what the hell his problem is, he says, "If they have taken hostages, then where are the police?"

The abrupt change of topic startles Africa "They must be here. Someone must have phoned the 911."

"Apparently not."

"What do you mean?" I say.

He beckons us over to the window. The intense sunlight blinds me for a second, and I have to put up a hand to shield my eyes.

"See the gate?" Jonas says.

The room we are in looks out over the hillside, the winding driveway in view, along with the wrought-iron gates at the bottom. One or two of the paparazzi and TV crews are still there, and there is traffic rolling past on the road outside the hotel.

You know what isn't there, though? Cops. Any sort of police presence. Not a single black-and-white. No choppers in the sky. Not even a patrolman strolling past.

That's . . . odd.

The LAPD might not give a tin shit if there is a shooting in a place like Watts or Compton, but at a swanky hotel in

Hollywood? Come on. The place would be crawling with detectives.

Africa peers over the top of my head. "Maybe the police are trying not to antagonise these people. Maybe they think, *yaaw*, we keep our distance, we not risk more people getting shot."

"Or maybe they're around the back?" I jerk my thumb behind me. Unfortunately, Jonas happens to be standing there, and I almost poke him in the eye. *Smooth.*

"Doesn't seem likely," Kanehara says. "It's all wild – the hotel grounds, I mean. The nearest road is some way away. Not a good place for police observation."

Jonas points down towards the gates. "Even if they are on the other side of the hotel, or were told to keep their distance, they would have closed the road to traffic. Dispersed the media. Why hasn't that happened yet?"

The four of us fall silent, eyes on the remaining journalists and photographers at the bottom of the hill. Two of them appear to be arguing about something, gesticulating back and forth. A few of them are looking up at the hotel, but as far as I can tell from this distance, their expressions are ones of boredom. Nobody looks like they are urgently reporting on a hostage crisis.

Kanehara has pulled out her phone, started tapping at it. "I still can't get a signal," she says to Jonas, ignoring me.

Jonas glares down at his own phone. "No cell data, no wireless."

"They are using a jammer," Africa says.

I know a little bit about jammers, and how they work. They block all signals. That means that not only have the hostage-takers stopped any of their hostages making calls, they can't, either. Tanner and Burr said the landlines were out of commission, too.

Maybe they called the police with their demands *before* they activated the jammer ... but it still doesn't explain why there are no cops on the road. Or why it isn't closed to traffic. If the police or the FBI or whoever knew what was happening here, we'd be seeing *something*, surely?

None of this makes sense. What's the point of taking hostages if you're not going to communicate your demands?

"What do they want?" Kanehara says, echoing my thoughts. "The ... terrorists, or whatever we should call them. The guys who came in were talking about some reverend?"

"Yeah," I say slowly. "I met him. Not a fan."

Jonas and Kanehara listen as I tell them about my little encounter with the Reverend, and Randi Metzger. When I'm done, Kanehara shakes her head. "But the guys in the bathroom didn't sound religious."

"Nope," I say.

"OK, so they are not part of it," Africa says. "The religion, I mean to say. They are, what do you call, mercenaries. Guns for hire."

"Makes sense." Kanehara bites her lip. "Fundamentalist groups in the US make a lot of noise, but not many of them could pull this off. They'd need manpower. *Trained* manpower."

Ugh. This situation doesn't even have the good grace to be your average hostage drama. We have this kind-of-sort-of-maybe religious angle, and then there's the lack of cops. What is—?

All at once, the nausea comes back. It's like an ice pick through my stomach, a horrible, boiling cramp. I stagger away from the window, clutching at my torso. Willing myself not to throw up.

"Teggan." Africa reaches for me, massive hands on my

shoulders. I jerk away, desperately not wanting human contact right now. I cough once, twice, squeeze my eyes shut, cold tears forcing their way out.

I stumble on over to the couch. As I sit down, Jonas and Kanehara are staring at me. Jonas's expression, in particular, makes the bottom drop out of my stomach. It's an expression of pity. Like he expected more of me.

"Even if... *huuuurrrmm*... even if there is something weird about the cops, it doesn't matter," I tell them. "You know my boss, from earlier? The scary lady with the man bun? She's already on the case."

"On the case?" Jonas frowns. "I am not understanding."

"She and her ... what assistant? Aide? Toy boy? I don't know. Either way, they got themselves some weapons, and they headed out a while ago. They probably had the same thought you did. About the cops, I mean. So yeah, I get that it's weird and all, but it's not like we can do anything about it."

"Oh, and who are you now?" Africa asks. "I will tell you who you are. You are the person who was saying, no, we cannot trust Mrs Tanner, and now you are saying yes, we must trust her?"

"Dude. She is a horrible, evil old bat – no, shut up, you know she is. But she also happens to be a government operative, and she's rolling with a hardcore special forces motherfucker. And OK, fine, I gave her shit about leaving the people in the ballroom behind, but she was right about that. I admit it. And when you get down to it, I would rather she take the lead here, since she probably has the best chance of actually turning this around. Do *not* write that down."

Kanehara is still tapping at her phone. She glances up at me, annoyed, then back at the device. "Little constitutional amendment you might not be aware of."

Africa starts to clear up the mess he made, placing the beer bottles and coffee mugs back onto the table. Kanehara notices, and strides forward, gracefully dropping to her knees to assist. Far more gracefully than I could have done if my skirt was that tight. "Let me help with that," she murmurs.

Africa grunts his thanks.

"I didn't introduce myself before," Kanehara says. "I'm Michiko. I'm a reporter with—"

"Yes, the *New Yorker*," Africa rumbles. He centres a stack of papers – Jonas's papers, I guess – on the coffee table, tapping them so the edges line up. "I have read your work before. Your article about the refugees in Guyana."

"Oh, great!" Her smile doesn't quite reach her eyes. "And you must be . . . Senegalese, right? Judging by the accent?" She leans closer. "If you're intelligence, then you must be with the Gendarmerie, correct? Is there a West African element to all this? Is that why you're here?"

"*Hey!*" I don't intend to raise my voice, but oh well. "You don't get ask him shit."

This time, she utterly ignores me. I don't want her reporting anything. In the aftermath of the storm drain, and the hospital, I don't want a journalist anywhere near me. If Kanehara realises who I am, if she publishes, or puts it on her Twitter feed, then it's over. There's no going back.

Then again, what am I supposed to do, tie her up and lock her in the bathroom? That won't be suspicious *at all*. Besides, Jonas is the one with the bondage sex swing on his plane, so she might just be into that kind of thing.

All the same, I need to shut this shit down. "This is not just a . . . a . . . a profile you're writing any more. This is real life. We don't have time for you to interview—"

Which is when Jonas strides past us, heading for the suite's entryway.

Africa and I exchange a look. Then we both move at the same time, taking off after him. "Um, Jonas?" I say. "What are you up to there, bud?"

"I am finished with hiding," he says, as he pulls the suite's door open with a soft hiss of hinges.

"This is not a good idea," Africa snaps.

"Jonas?" Kanehara says from behind us.

"Yeah, woah, OK, no." I push myself out the door, into the corridor. "Jonas!" I hiss, trying to shout and whisper at the same time.

He's striding down the hall to my left, and he doesn't even look my way. I take off after him, sure that at any moment I'm going to get a bullet in the back from an unseen attacker.

Somehow, I manage to catch up to him, grabbing his shoulder. "Have you lost your fucking mind?"

"Let go of me."

"Yeah, no. I'm not having you take on an entire hotel's worth of bad guys by yourself. You're German, but you're not the fucking Terminator."

"Arnold is Austrian. I said, let *go*."

He jerks away from me. Behind us, Africa and Kanehara have emerged, both of them clearly as freaked out as I am. At last, Jonas appears to realise that he can't just run off without any explanation. He runs a hand through his hair. "I'm not going to *take on* anyone. I'm going to destroy one of the jammers."

"For real? We don't know where the jammers are, or what they look like, or how many there might be. Or how many people with guns are standing in front of them."

"I hold controlling interests in several large European telecommunications companies."

"... Um, good for you? What does that have to do with—?"

"It is a very boring business. But I have attended more than a few conferences when I was seriously considering whether it was a sector I should invest in or not. I once attended a presentation that explored if it was ethical to install jammers in hotels, in order to force the guests to pay for a dedicated wireless connection."

"You are saying the hotel might already have jammers inside it?" Africa says.

"What is more likely? That our hostage-takers somehow smuggled in enough jammers to cover the entirety of the building, or they simply used ones that were already installed?" A strange smile sneaks onto his face. "It would never have worked in Europe. There are laws. And we respect our customers enough to—"

"Oh my God, we get it," I say. "America bad, capitalism nasty. Jesus."

The disconnect is tripping me out here. Is this the same Jonas who put himself in harm's way during an earthquake to save others? Who gave us shelter when we needed it? Then again, I spent barely any time with him at all. Crushes develop fast – I think mine came on in about 0.6 seconds -- but they don't give you a sense of who a person truly is. And Jonas, lest we forget, is a fucking billionaire. You don't make that much money without betting big on yourself, and apparently, that includes being arrogant enough to play lone hero in a hostage crisis.

Is it weird to both have a crush on someone and want to punch them really hard in the face? This seems to be a theme for me. I've had a crush on Nic for a long time, and there are several things he has done and said in the past that have made me want to beat him to a bloody pulp.

"So you'd know what a jammer looks like," Kanehara says, almost to herself. "And where they'd put one."

"Yes."

"So where would they be?"

He seems to almost physically bite down on his frustration. "It will be a larger, desktop-type model. Two-hundred-metre range, blocking 3G to 5G signals, as well as GSM. For optimal coverage, they would ..."

He looks at his shoes, then at the ceiling. "There are several scenarios. I would place two jammers. One on the ground floor, one near the top. Although I admit that it is possible for there to be only one, with a much stronger signal. In that case ... yes, I would place it at roof level. So: I know what they look like, and I believe I can find them. If you will excuse me ..."

"I'm coming with you," says Kanehara.

"No, you're not. Don't be stupid." I tell her.

The look she gives me could curdle milk. "Two years out of college, I was embedded with the Marine Corp in Kandahar. Then I got tapped by Reuters to cover Eastern Europe, just in time for the violence in Budapest when Orbán came to power. I'm not letting this story happen without me."

"I will go too," Africa says.

"Are you *serious*?"

"Mrs Tanner is always trying to save lives. That is her philosophy. If I let these people go off and do this, without trying to help them ..."

"*Then you'll get shot just like they will.*"

He stops me with a look. Takes a long, slow breath, in and out through his nose. Never once taking his eyes off me.

"No one else dies," he says. "Not as long as I am here, and I can help."

"Please, dude. Don't—"

"I'm sorry, Teggan. I have made up my mind."

I stare at them as they go. Trying to process the last twenty minutes, trying to figure out why I am suddenly the only sane person in this entire hotel. The only person who thinks charging wildly into a place crawling with gun-toting psychopaths is a bad idea.

Fuck it. They want to be stupid about this? Let 'em. They're counting on their pride and their egos to protect them from bullets. You've done what you could. Go back to the hotel room, have another beer, curl up on the couch. Sleep.

I turn to go.

Then I make a disgusted snarling noise, not sure if I'm directing it at me, or the idiots I've been saddled with. Wincing as my injured knee barks, I take off down the corridor after them.

TWENTY-FIVE

Annie

Ride-share drivers don't come to Watts. Same for pizza delivery guys. Too many carjackings, robberies, shootings. Annie hates it more than she can say, although she wasn't surprised when it started to happen. When you herd people into the inner cities, as the racist fucks who ran LA back in the 1920s did, when you gate them off from economic opportunities with clever zoning . . . well, you get crime. Lots of it. Nowadays, ride-shares won't even do drop-offs at the Towers, which are a legitimate tourist attraction.

Where they *do* make pickups is Martin Luther King Jr. Memorial Hospital, a fifteen-minute walk away, south of the 105. Annie has her mom's phone, and there's an Uber app on it. And Lyft. Her mom will have a five-star rating on both.

The light-headedness ratchets up she pushes out the gate onto East 107th Street, and hot on its heels, the pain from her burning side. She leans on the chain-link fence, her left arm pushing tight against her body, and breathes hard through her nose. Counts very slowly to ten. Then does it again. And again. On the fourth time, she loses count completely, the number that comes after six deserting her. She almost laughs at the absurdity of it. Here she is, heading off on her own mission, and she's forgotten how numbers work.

She rolls her tongue around her mouth, spits onto the cracked sidewalk. It couldn't hurt to turn around, go back inside, grab some of the painkillers in the—

Annie lifts her head. Looks down the block, to the point where 107th intersects Willowbrook Avenue.

It's around midday, barely a shadow on the street, not even from the Towers. Baking hot, and unusually quiet. The kids have long since left the park, and even the traffic sound has dropped a little. There are no people on the corner. No people at all, in fact. Nobody in the gardens in front of the rundown houses. Even that loud-ass barking dog from three doors down is asleep, sprawled out next to the fence. There are barely any cars parked on the street. Del's truck, one wheel up on the curb outside his house. Jamal's busted old '70s Chevrolet, up on bricks in its usual spot.

And a black Corolla, parked around fifty yards away, the rear facing her. A car she hasn't seen before.

It's them. They found you. They found you, and your mom, and Reggie, and any second now they're going to—

A voice reaches her from the other end of the block. Someone singing, melodic and unbothered. Annie turns to look.

The park that holds the Towers is a cockeyed triangle running alongside Santa Ana Boulevard. The source of the voice is just crossing the eastern tip of the park, and it's somebody Annie knows. Candice Jensen, a short woman with colourful box braids who she was in high school with. Unlike Annie, Candice graduated, and last time she checked, the woman worked at a Starbucks on 103rd. She's singing "Rim Shot" by Erykah Badu, her voice surprisingly sweet.

The plan is there instantly, fully formed. Keeping one eye

on the Corolla, Annie strides across to Candice, slipping into her field of view. Candice's face cracks in a surprise smile, and she pops her AirPods out. "Look who it is," she says, pulling Annie in for a hug. "Where you been, girl?"

"Just working, you know?"

"I ain't seen you round the building in a while. Y'all should come down." Candice grins, dimpling her cheeks and making her look even younger than her thirty-some-odd years. "You still with that Navy boy? The bald one?"

"Not any more. Listen: you strapped?"

Candice's expression shifts, a coldness coming into her eyes. The smile falls away. "What's going on?"

"Yo, let me hold that."

The woman looks around briefly, then lifts her shirt to reveal a .38 tucked in the waistband of her jeans. Annie looks left and right herself, then takes the gun, shielding the exchange from the car behind her with her body. All six cylinders are full.

"My mans are two blocks over," Candice says quietly, pulling her phone out of her jacket. "We got you. Just let me know what's going down."

Candice Jensen happens to run with the Bounty Hunter Bloods out of the Nickerson Gardens projects, a few blocks to the south. The Bounty Hunters have an on-again-off-again beef with the Grape Street Watts Crips, a beef Annie has had to mediate more than once. While there is an appeal to the idea of bringing a whole squad of Bloods down on whoever happens to be in that Corolla, Annie shakes her head. If it does turn out to be Chloe and Adam, then there'll be major collateral damage. She needs to handle this on her own, even though she wants to run like hell.

"See the black car?" she says, avoiding the urge to jerk her head at the vehicle.

"Yeah, I see it."

"Got a bad feeling. I'ma roll up on 'em. Stay back here for a minute."

"Let me go with you." Candice's voice is as cold as her eyes. "This motherfucker wanna start shit at the Towers?"

"I said, I got it. Just let me hold the piece. If it starts popping off, get the fuck out."

"I ain't running."

"And I ain't asking."

Candice tilts her head, taking a closer look at Annie. "Yo, you OK? You don't look so good."

"Fine." Annie slips the gun into her own pocket, then turns and walks away. Candice does not follow.

Annie takes her time, strolling down the middle of the street, tapping at her mom's phone while keeping an eye on the Corolla. She flicks a glance upwards as she gets within twenty yards: one person in the driver's seat, facing forward.

Annie has driven more Corollas than she can count. This one is an older model, without that ugly-ass rear bumper guard the new ones have. An older model means no blind-spot detectors. Annie slips into the gap, sprinting forwards, raising the .38. The driver scrambles, twisting around in the seat as he loses sight of her in his wing mirror. Just as she planned. By the time he spots her again, she's at the door, gun up and pointed right at him. "Aight, motherfucker, hands on the—"

Nic Delacourt blinks up at her, eyes wide, mouth a shocked O. Moving very slowly, he puts his hands on the wheel, ten and two.

For a long moment, they just stare at each other. Then Annie lowers the gun, dropping her head to her chest and muttering something very dark and ugly in Spanish.

Nic rolls down the window. "Hi. So, here's the thing . . . "

"Get out of the fucking car, man."

He gets out of the fucking car.

"How long have you been out here? How would you even know where I live? Did you f . . . ffffollow us home from the hospital?"

"Kind of. I mean, no, I didn't follow you. Teagan told me you lived next to the Towers, so I figured I'd spot you sooner or later."

"I could have shot you. Do you get that? You understand what I'm saying?" And arriving on the heels of her words, a guilty thought: if she had shot Nic, then Teagan would never have forgiven her. It's a sickening, almost nauseating thought.

"Yeah . . . " Nic raises his hands. "I totally get that. But—"

"And what if it wasn't me? You roll up to a hood you're not from in a car nobody knows, posting up like you the opps or some shit. How long you think it'd be before one of the homies sees you? You think they gonna call the cops on you? Police don't come round here, and if they did, they wouldn't be reading you your fucking rights first, you know what I mean?"

She's sweating. Drips of it rolling down her forehead, slicking her palms. Quickly, she puts the gun away before she drops it.

Nic takes a deep breath. "OK, I get it. Not super-smart."

"You think?"

"It's just . . . I can tell something is wrong. With Teagan, I mean. She's dropped completely off the map, not even a text message, and then when I saw you at the hospital . . . " He rubs the back of his shaven head.

"So, what, you thought I'd lead you right to her? What am I, a . . . a . . . ?"

She can't find the word she wants to say. The dog with the supersensitive smell, the one they use to track escaped prisoners in old movies. But she can't get the word from her mind to her tongue.

"I wasn't gonna follow you the whole time. I wanted to talk to you. I was just waiting for the right moment." He looks up and down the street. Annie glances to her right, spots Candice making her way over. The woman is still on alert, shoulders tense, but at least she doesn't look like she's about to call up her Bounty Hunters.

"I know I'm not part of China Shop," Nic says. "But I've been hanging around you guys for a while now. I know how things work. I can tell that you're worried about Teagan, and I'm guessing you don't know where she is either." He lowers his voice. "You care about her. I do too. I don't wanna just sit around and do nothing if she's in trouble."

"Annie." Candice leans against the trunk, looking Nic up and down. "We good?"

Annie chews the inside of her cheek, then steps towards Nic. "Look, man. You did OK with that LA River shit, aight? No question there. I'm not gonna sit here and pretend you didn't help. But right now, you need to go home. I'm getting into some major shit, and I don't have time to watch your back."

He can barely hide his irritation. "I can handle myself."

"Like I give a fuck." She passes the gun back to Candice. "C, do me a favour? Don't let him leave before I do. He tries anything, take care of it."

"No doubt." Candice lifts the gun one-handed, pointing right at Nic's chest. Startled, Nic takes a step back, bumping his hip against the car's hood.

"I mean his tyres," Annie says. "Shoot his tyres out if he tries to follow me. God."

"Oh yeah, for sure," says Candice, lowering the gun reluctantly.

"Annie." Nic raises his voice as she walks away, heading for a gap between the two houses opposite the Corolla. "Annie, hold up!"

But Annie's already gone.

TWENTY-SIX

Teagan

We don't dare take the elevator. That's the equivalent of running naked through the corridors screaming "Over here! Hello! Murder us please!"

Instead, we take the fire stairs. All of us try to be as quiet as possible, all of us on edge, alert for the slightest hint that there is anybody in our vicinity. But there's not a sound. The stairs are echoey and quiet.

They're also even dirtier, if that's possible. When we made our way up from the pool to the third floor, the stairs were grimy, but still serviceable. But judging by the cracked and gouged concrete, it's clear nobody's given this place a refurb since the days of Greta Garbo and Buster Keaton. There are cobwebs everywhere, and more than one landing where the lights are completely gone. It's an odd contrast to the glamorous rooms, the lobby with its gigantic chandelier and plush carpets, the opulent ballroom. Kanehara gets one particularly big cobweb stuck in her hair, and I have to bite my lip to stop myself laughing as she frantically claws at it.

Jonas leads the way, and doesn't bother to disguise his irritation that we came with him. We are close to each other on the stairs, and more than once, Africa stands on the back of his heels. The second time it happens, Jonas looks ready to knock him down a couple of flights. I'm about to intervene – that's all we need right now, a fist fight between the good guys – when he visibly calms himself, turns around and keeps climbing.

At the top, there's a set of double doors labelled ROOF ACCESS in big stencilled letters. There's also an explosive device attached to them, so yeah, we're not going there. Guess they don't want people heading to the roof and signalling passing choppers for help.

"What if that's where the jammer is?" Kanehara asks.

"They would not put a jammer somewhere they could not get to," Jonas says, although he doesn't sound sure.

We head back down to the seventh floor. Jonas pauses at the access door, ear close to it, listening.

I put my hands on my knees, trying to suck air into my burning chest. It's ridiculous; we only went up five floors. How the hell were there so many stairs? Africa and Kanehara, of course, have barely broken a sweat. The former gives me a confused look, and I have to stop myself from flipping him the bird. *Fine, I get it, message received loud and clear. I'll lay off the salted caramel ice cream. Buy some running shoes. Download a fitness app.*

"OK," Jonas says softly, pushing open the door. Amazingly, given the condition of the stairwell, the hinges don't creak at all. He peers out, then slips through. The rest of us follow. Well, Africa and Kanehara follow. I have to take another moment to catch my breath.

The seventh floor is identical to the one the senator's room is on. Gleaming wooden floors, Persian rugs. It's the top floor, unless you count the rooftop bar and helipad. It's actually kind of amazing that somewhere this luxurious can exist right next to the gankiest stairs I've ever climbed.

I start to speak, and Jonas holds up a hand, cocking his head. Listening.

Silence. We're alone.

I think.

There are fewer rooms on this floor than on the ones below – which makes sense, I guess, given that it's the penthouse. Jonas leads us to one labelled PRIVATE, displayed on the same brass plaque as the room numbers on the other doors.

A thought occurs to me, one I probably should have had a few floors back. "You seem awfully sure about where we're going," I say, my voice still wheezy from the climb.

"I have stayed here before," Jonas says, distracted. He's put his ear to the door again. "I know the manager."

"And what, this is his office?"

"On the top floor?" Africa whispers. "In the hotels I work at before, the offices are always in the basement." He nudges me. "When I work at the Four Seasons in Budapest, the manager did not even have an office. He had a tiny desk in one of the food storerooms, and—"

Then Jonas pops the door to the office, and Africa stops speaking.

"Guess we do things a little different to Budapest," I murmur.

If I had this kind of office, I don't think I'd have a house. I just put a double bed in a corner here, live out of this place. I could do it, too, because it's enormous. Six hundred square feet, at least, a rectangular space leading to a gigantic arched window, skylights letting in even more light from above. The furniture is the kind of stuff you see in high-end design magazines, and the desk looks like it came from the timber of a Navy warship. The view is magnificent, looking west towards the Pacific, just visible as a bright blue band on the horizon.

"Well, this is something," Kanehara says.

Jonas seems to be the only one who takes the surroundings in his stride. He marches over to the desk – which, now that I take a second look at it, is pretty damn messy. There are papers and laptops everywhere, textbooks on hotel management stacked haphazardly, as if whoever occupied this office was still boning up on the finer points of running this place. A pot of coffee sits half full, and when I touch it, it's stone-cold.

A chill sneaks up my spine. Where is the *real* manager? The one my little Bible-quoting, gun-toting nemesis replaced? Is he even still alive?

"Why here?" I ask Jonas.

"What?" He's rifling through the drawers of the gigantic desk.

"Why put the jammer here?" I find myself hissing the words, as if speaking any louder will bring all hell raining down on us – which, in fairness, it might. "Does it give, like, optimal coverage, or . . . ?"

"The jammer isn't here."

I wait for him to continue. He doesn't. "Sorry, I thought there was more to that. Let me rephrase. If the jammer isn't here, then what the fuck are we doing?"

"Found you," he says.

The device he pulls out of the drawer looks like a supermarket checkout scanner, the handheld type. With his other hand, he puts a stack of rubber-banded key cards on the desk.

"You want master access," Kanehara says. She sounds impressed.

"That *is* clever," says Africa. He notices my confused expression. "They are for the staff, so they can get into the rooms to clean. Those cards are blank, but you can use the reader to put the code on them."

"The jammer—" Jonas frowns as the reader beeps a

rejection at him. He tries again, and this time, gets the result he wants. "It is either on this floor, or somewhere on the roof. We can start here."

He stops, looks up at us. "I can do this on my own. It will be far safer if there is just one of us."

I'm still really annoyed that this turned into a big group expedition. "We're here now, aren't we?"

The four of us fall silent as Jonas scans multiple cards. The office's location may be epic, but now that we're standing in it, it reminds me of the stairwell. There are fewer cobwebs, sure, but it could use a refurb. The furniture looks a little tired, and there are at least two spots on the walls where paintings used to hang that are now just blank spaces, a little paler than the rest of the wall.

Jonas dishes out the rewritten key cards to each of us. "There are four or five suites on this floor," he says. "We each take one. The cards should let you in now."

"What are we looking for?" Kanehara says.

"It will be a black box with multiple antennas on it. Chances are it will be hidden, in a closet or under a bed. When you find it, pull the plug."

"What about if it is on a battery?" Africa asks. Jonas ignores him, hitting his key card against the reader on the nearest door. When it opens, he slips through without a second glance.

I bite my lip. I can't keep my thoughts straight. It's as if there's a pervasive background noise, a hum that I can't shake. A feeling of *wrongness*. The lack of police, the fact that the person I thought was a hotel manager clearly wasn't. And there's something else, too, something pulling at the edges of my mind. Something I missed. Every time I get a fix on it, it darts just out of range.

We each take a room. Mine is 7002. At any moment, I'm

expecting thundering footsteps, shouting, very big guns shoved under my nose. But there's nothing. Wherever the bad guys are, whatever they're doing, it's not happening on the seventh floor. All the same, it doesn't stop me from being hyper-alert.

The layout of the room is the same as Senator Weiss's, with only a few differences. The wet bar has a marble counter and an actual drinks rack, built into an ornate mirror. There's a little private gym, with an exercise bike and weights and a killer view over LA. A projector and a pulldown screen in the living room, instead of a TV. You know what there isn't? A black box. Nothing under the bed, or in the wardrobes. The hotel safe hangs open, empty. I even check in the bathroom cabinet, and behind the weight racks in the gym. Nada.

The bedroom has signs of someone staying here; there's a laptop and some papers stacked on the ornate wooden desk by the window, along with a half-full glass of water, lone lemon wedge floating. Certainly nothing that looks like a jammer. I sit down on the edge of the bed, relishing the chance to stay still for a minute. Would it be so bad if I curled up here and just went to sleep? How often am I going to get a swanky hotel bedroom to myself? *Probably never again.*

It's an ugly thought, and I push it away, like I've tasted something poisonous. Fuck it – at the very least, I can raid the minibar for snacks. The one in here is pretty big, and I can feel what might be cookies, the foil wrapping around the plastic trays, so—

Wait. Wait one damn minute.

I can feel them.

I can't see them, or even the fridge, which is under a counter in the living area. So how, exactly, do I know about the cookie packaging?

My PK is back.

I spring off the bed, scarcely daring to believe it – and then it's gone. As if paying attention to it made it vanish. I concentrate, actually squeezing my eyes shut, but it doesn't come back.

All the same, it was definitely there, no question. For a split-second, I was back to normal. I think. Maybe. I don't know. I should confirm things by checking that the cookies really are there, though. If they are, I can reward myself by having one. Two at the most. No more than three. I head out the bedroom door, crossing over to the fridge under the bar counter.

"Anything in here?" Africa says, making me jump. He's just coming in the front door of the suite. For some reason, I feel absurdly guilty, like I've been caught doing something I shouldn't be.

I shake it off, irritated with myself. "Nah. Place is clean." I crouch down, rummaging in the fridge. I may or may not give a little squeak of joy when I find an unopened packet of mini chocolate chip cookies.

"Same same." Africa spreads his hands on the bar, raising an eyebrow as I rip open the packet. "Maybe Mister Ger— I mean, Jonas, maybe he will have more luck."

"*Nein.*" Mister Germany himself appears, shoulders slumped, closely followed by Kanehara. "Nothing. I am guessing you did not find anything here, Teagan?"

I shrug. "Sorry, dude. Zip." I celebrate my failure by tossing a cookie into my mouth.

Jonas spreads his hands on the bar. He drops his head, muttering to himself. Then, like a striking snake, he grabs a nearby glass, and in one movement hurls it into the wall next to the bar. "*Scheiße!*"

"*Jesus.*" I drop the cookie, jumping backwards. Africa and Kanehara, too, take a startled step back.

"What is wrong with you?" Africa hisses.

I can't stop myself glancing towards the suite's entryway. If one of the bad guys is nearby, and they heard that . . .

Jonas turns away from us, hands laced behind his head. "I am sorry," he says carefully. Then he says, almost to himself, "*Alles ist ruiniert*. Fucked."

"OK," I whisper-shout. "I don't know what that means, but how about a little warning next time?"

"I am sorry," he says again. Thankfully, at a lower volume.

"We'll find the jammer. We just need to—"

"Fuck the jammer." He turns to face us. "I don't care about the . . . " He trails off, staring at Kanehara. The journalist has her phone up, staring at the screen. "Are you *filming me?*"

A guilty look crosses her face, almost immediately replaced by an expression of defiance. "I've been filming everything," she says.

"Have you lost your mind?" He takes a step towards her. "Give me that."

Startled, Kanehara turns sideways, pulling the phone in close to herself. "I'm just doing my job."

"You are being unprofessional."

The effect is immediate. Kanehara's expression goes from shock to disbelief to pure, venomous anger, all in the space of a second. She turns to face Jonas, bringing the phone up like a shield, camera pointed right at him. "You're saying I shouldn't document this? Everything that's happening? I shouldn't do the thing that is *literally* my job?"

Jonas points a finger at her. "I don't care. Delete it all. Now."

She gives him a thin smile. "No, I don't think I will."

"Keep your voices down," I hiss at them. "Jesus fucking Christ, really? We're doing this now?"

Jonas makes a grab for the phone. He actually gets hold of

it for a second – and then Kanehara's surprise wears off. She grabs his wrist with her free hand, digs her thumb in, and I guess she must have taken a few self-defense classes because Jonas yelps and backs the fuck away real quick.

"Don't even *think* about it," she says.

Jonas glares at her, hands balled into fists at his sides, then turns away, a disgusted look on his face. On the one hand, I get that he's angry – this whole situation is a mess, and I'm not wild about a journalist filming it either. On the other, he seriously needs to calm the fuck down.

I puff out my cheeks. Maybe I was wrong about the two of them sleeping together. I don't know. My brain hurts.

Africa throws up his hands in disgust. "Teggan, did you check the bedroom?" He doesn't wait for a response, heading over to the door.

Jonas barely notices, and he does not keep his voice down. "I do not want to be shown on camera having an outburst that—"

"You think this is all about *you*?" Kanehara sweeps her hand out, gesturing to the rest of the hotel. "Jonas, we are in the middle of an historic event. People are going to want to know what happened here."

There's a small, very guilty part of me that is delighted to see Jonas fighting with Kanehara. But we don't have time for this. As much as I'm amazed to be the responsible one, I can't have these two acting like children. Not to mention making enough noise to bring every bad guy in a ten mile radius down on our heads.

Kanehara is still in full flow. "I have a duty—"

"*Hey.*" I hiss through gritted teeth, slapping my hand on the bar, partially crushing the bag of cookies. I point at Kanehara. "You – stop filming." My finger flips to Jonas. "You – stop acting like an asshat."

Jonas turns. Looks me up and down, the same way he did with Africa downstairs. It's a look that says: *Why should I have to listen to you?*

You know what it reminds me of, actually? The same look I saw on the faces of the crowd downstairs, before everything went to shit. Arrogant. Entitled. The look of a billionaire who is used to getting what he wants.

The Jonas I'm seeing today is not the same Jonas I saw back during the earthquake. Back then, he was ... well, I don't know if I'd use the words *good guy*, but at least he was acting like one. Today, it's like he's a different person. And looking at him, I think I know why.

Jonas Schmidt gets what he wants – that's why he's a billionaire. During the earthquake, he wanted to help, and I really do think it was genuine. But it was also easy: he didn't need permission to land his plane, provide communications and power and food for those who needed it. But now he's in a situation he can't influence. He can't schmooze his way to a solution, or make a deal. He's made it this far in life by believing in himself, and today, that just isn't cutting it. He wants to help ... and he can't. It's bringing out a side of him that is distinctly un-sexy.

I don't get a chance to respond, because that's when Kanehara turns the camera on me. "And what are you doing here, exactly? Who are you to give me orders?"

"I'm—"

"You're what? Intelligence services? Military? Come on. Tell me. Prove you have some authority. Show me some credentials, and I'll stop filming."

My instinct is to brick her phone. I *should* brick her phone. Just reach inside and crunch the internals. But even if I could – and I don't know if my PK is strong enough yet – it's not the smart play. *Yes, let's make her phone completely stop working right at this very instant. She won't suspect a thing.*

She keeps going, the stress of the past couple of hours boiling up and out, her voice getting louder and louder. "I mean, even if you are US intelligence, which I highly doubt, by the way, what are you doing here? Am I really supposed to believe that the intelligence services are in this hotel right before a hostage crisis, and it's a coincidence?"

All at once, the fight goes out of her. Her shoulders slump, and she runs a hand through her hair. Strands of it have come loose from her ponytail. She lowers the phone.

"Give it to me," Jonas says again. The journalist ignores him.

"It's always the same," she mutters, turning away. "Don't do my job perfectly, I'm a little girl out of my depth. If I *do* do it perfectly, I'm a cold bitch."

"Teggan," Africa says from behind me.

"Just a sec, dude." I hold up a hand. "Look ... Michiko, right? I get it. This is all fucked up. But there's a—"

"Teggan."

"—time and a place for filming, and we're all kind of stretched thin right now, and—"

"*Teggan.*"

"Jesus, dude, *what?*" This time, even I can't stop myself shouting. I turn to face him – and my mouth falls open.

Africa is standing in the door to the bedroom, holding up a piece of paper. Blocks of text, in a foreign language. There's a photo taking up the top left quarter of the page.

A photo of me.

TWENTY-SEVEN

Teagan

For a long moment, no one says anything. We all just stare at the photo. Dimly, I'm aware that the inside of my mouth has gone completely dry.

Kanehara speaks first. "I don't get it."

I take two strides towards Africa, and snatch the paper out of his hands. Staring at it in disbelief. I have no idea exactly when the photo was taken, but it looks to be from a few years ago. The photo shows my head and shoulders, in profile; I obviously know whoever took the photo, because I'm smiling slightly, as if caught in the act of doing something I shouldn't. I look maybe nineteen or twenty, which means the photo was taken while I was locked up in the government facility in Waco. The background is blurred, so I don't know exactly where I was when the photo was snapped.

There are a lot of things that are still a mystery to me, but one thing I am certain of is that I should never appear on a piece of paper in some random person's hotel room.

"Bullshit," I breathe, shifting my attention to the blocks of text filling the rest of the page. There are two words in English: my name, written in slightly larger font at the top.

The rest of the text is smaller, and although the letters are familiar, it's in a language I don't recognise.

"That's Vietnamese," Jonas says, as if I'd asked the question out loud. He is right next to me when he speaks, making me jump.

"Where did you get this?" Kanehara asks Africa.

"Just in the bedroom. I was taking another look for the jammer, and I see the papers on the desk. Teggan is the one on top."

"Phan Duc Hong," she says.

I swivel my head towards Kanehara. It seems to take a really long time. "What?"

"Not what. Who. She's the CEO of InterArm."

"Cool," I say. "And InterArm is . . . ?"

Africa snaps his fingers. "Of course. I saw the name in *The Economist*. They make weapons also."

"Largest arms manufacturer in Asia," Kanehara says. "Headquartered in Saigon."

My eyes go wide. "Phan Duc Hong . . . about fifty? Super-scary looking? With bangs?"

Kanehara nods.

Holy crap. The woman from the parking garage. The one who eyeballed me like she knew who I was. "This is her room?"

"It has to be." There is a little bit more energy back in Jonas's voice now. "As far as I know, she is the only Vietnamese at this conference. And she is old school. She prefers printed notes to digital ones." I look at him, and he shrugs. "You get to know people."

"I don't understand." Kanehara takes the page herself. "Why does she have a photo of you?"

Damn good question.

"There are more," Africa says. He ducks back into the bed-room, returns with a thicker sheaf of papers. We spread them out on the bar, and as I look at them, my stomach twists itself into a knot.

One of the pages shows Moira Tanner: a file photo, severe and unsmiling. There are others I don't recognise, men and women I haven't seen before. I spot the two dudes who nearly found us in the bathroom – Shane, last name DuBois, and Brandon, last name Evans. I've never seen their faces, but their names are right there. Shane is bearded, heavily built, the photo showing him in wraparound shades and carrying an assault rifle, somewhere hot and dusty. Brandon, in contrast is smiling – the photo looks like it was taken at a barbecue.

And then: Randi Metzger. Like Shane, she's in military uniform, glaring at the camera. And on the piece of paper next to her:

The Reverend.

The Bible-quoting guy I met downstairs. In the photo, he wears a neat suit, virtually identical to what he was wearing when I met him. He's standing behind a lectern of some kind – the photo has caught him in mid-gesture. His name, like the others, is at the top of the sheet: Vincent Earl Dyson.

"Got you, fucker," I murmur.

His sheet is a little different from the others. There are notes scribbled in the margin. Most of them look to be in Vietnamese as well, but there are numbers, too. *100? 150?*

What does that mean? A hundred million? Is that how much Phan paid Dyson, or wanted to offer him? Is that how much he was going to pay her? What the hell are we looking at here?

"Don't suppose anybody reads Vietnamese?" I ask. Nobody responds. I look at Africa, who is bent over the papers at the other end of the bar, tight-lipped. I catch his eye, and he shakes his head.

"What are the Children of Solomon?" Jonas says.

I look over. "Huh?"

He taps Randi's sheet. "It is written here. The only other English words I can see."

I can't believe I didn't see it before, but there it is. *Children of Solomon.* It's on Dyson's sheet too.

"I know that name." Kanehara chews her lip. "I've seen it on watchlists."

"Who are they?" Africa asks.

"I don't know the details." I can feel her looking at me. What the hell is going on here? Why did Phan have freaking *notes* on me? On the people who took all the hostages? She must be a part of this somehow . . . but . . .

"It doesn't make sense," I say, straightening up. "She was in the ballroom downstairs. I saw her. She got guns pointed at her like the rest of us."

"And yet she obviously knew this was going to happen." Kanehara folds her arms.

"What do you want me to say? Up until today, I'd never even heard of her."

"Well, she'd heard of you."

"Could she be responsible for . . . for all of this?" Africa rumbles.

"She must be," Jonas says. "In some capacity, at least."

But how? And *why*? None of the puzzle pieces in front of us fit together. At all. We have a religious group who are clearly up to no good, but they've hired mercenaries as well. We have them taking hostages in a hotel, but not calling the cops. And now, we find that one of those hostages knew about the whole thing beforehand – and that somehow, she knew about *me*. She knew I'd be here. I don't know if the Vietnamese writing on the sheets mentions my ability or not, but it doesn't matter. I was on this woman's radar. So was Tanner.

What am I missing?

Kanehara lifts her phone, starts taking photos of the sheets of paper. Jonas opens his mouth, and she holds up a warning finger. "This is a lot bigger than we realised," she says, continuing to take photos.

"So what do we do now?" Jonas sounds sullen.

I open my mouth to tell him I have absolutely no idea, but Africa gets there first. "The same as before. We must find the jammer."

He taps the sheet with my photo on it. "This is for later, *yaaw*? It does not help us now. There are still hostages, and we are still stuck here, and the only way we can change that is if we find this phone jammer."

"We already searched everywhere," Kanehara says. "It's probably on the roof, right?"

"Not good." Africa folds his arms. "There is C4 on the doors going up there. Could we maybe find an elevator? If we move quickly . . . "

"No. They've almost certainly shut the elevators down anyway."

They go back and forth, debating what to do next. My thoughts drift, tumbling in a whirlwind of questions and theories and worries. But Africa's right: whatever the fuck is going on with Phan Duc Hong and the Children of Solomon – which sounds like the title of an adventure story, if I'm being honest – it doesn't help us *now*.

My PK coming back, though . . .

There's a lamp on the end-table, next to one of the couches. It looks like a piece of impenetrable modern art, but it's made of metal. Slowly, cautiously, I move my focus over to it. Grip it with my mind. Feel the cold texture of the surface, the plastic of the recessed switch, the brass accents.

My PK might not be back to normal. I have to remember that. Just because I can feel objects and their position in space does *not* mean I can lift a car. But it's definitely returning, trickling back in. I don't know whether it came back naturally, or whether I did something to kick it into gear. Don't know, don't care. God knows, I fantasise about life without my PK, but I'm more than happy to see it now. *Welcome to the party, pal.*

Should I test it out? Try to lift something? Probably ... but definitely not with a journalist present. That's the last thing I need.

I push my range out. I'm not sensing anything beyond about fifty feet, so I'm not completely my old self, but it'll come. Best believe, it will come. And when it does, I am going to shut these assholes down. March back downstairs and right into that fucking ballroom. Let's see how scary these dudes are when their guns don't work.

Not right away, though. My PK is like a chef's knife – one that's been in use for years. The cook holding it knows its shape intimately. They know how it feels in the hand, the resistance it gives against various ingredients, the spots on the blade that are likely to be sharper or blunter than others. If there is a tiny burr or divot on the grip, they'll know. I have the same type of knowledge with my PK. And right now, I'm getting a strong sense that my grip on it is tenuous. The longer I leave it, the more control I might have.

What does the return of my ability mean for my relationship with Tanner? China Shop? Do I get a reprieve, if my powers are back to normal? A written warning? Having my PK come flickering back to life was like shaking the hand of an old friend, but . . .

It means my chances of a normal life go out the window. It's not like those chances were high to begin with, but it's impossible not to feel a little cheated. I shouldn't be ungrateful, I know that. But you try having a fantasy snatched away from you.

Jonas walks over to the window as Africa and Kanehara go back and forth. He stands with his back to us, staring out over the city. I follow his gaze. If I was a regular superhero, I'd have flight powers. I could just zip on up and out of here. Of course, I'd also probably have laser vision and super-strength, so I wouldn't need to *zip* out of here, but—

"Guys," I say. "Hold up. I've got an idea."

They all turn to look at me. I'm still staring out the window. Thinking hard. Remembering what the building looked like, as we were coming up the driveway.

And for the first time, I'm glad that Annie isn't here. She's terrified of heights.

Which means she would absolutely hate what I'm about to suggest.

TWENTY-EIGHT

Annie

Annie has met enough millionaires to know that she isn't a big fan. She even knows a billionaire, if you count that idiot Jonas Schmidt.

She is no stranger to wealthy spots like Pacific Palisades and San Marino; shit, she went to some of those places with Marathon long before she began working for China Shop. But she hasn't spent a lot of time in Laurel Canyon. It's nestled between Hollywood in the south and the Valley in the north, a land of sweeping roads that cut through rocky, wooded hills, dotted with mansions half glimpsed between the switchbacks.

She already has the address from Jah, her line repairman contact. The gates of the property open up onto Laurel Canyon Drive, the main artery through the hills. Annie has her Uber driver drop her at the corner of Elrita Drive, which dog-legs off the main drag a few hundred yards to the north of her quarry.

Ride services like Uber and Lyft are a gift to Annie. Every time she's taken one, she usually finds a potential recruit to her Army. The drivers aren't as gossipy with each other as traditional cabs, but they still hear things, and they've proved very useful in the past. This time, however, she makes as little conversation as possible, and the driver – a taciturn Sikh – seems happy to oblige.

She steps out of the Prius, muttering a thank you to the driver, who gives an answering grunt. It's around one o'clock, the air baking in syrupy, almost liquid heat from the hills. Chic bungalows crowd in from all sides, bracketed by tall eucalyptus and scrubby chaparral. Somewhere, there's the *tsk-tsk* sound of a hummingbird.

Annie takes a long slug of water. She can't remember ever feeling this awful. The sunlight sears her eyes, and the air seems to press in on her, constricting her chest and throat. Her head is pounding, as if it's ten times its normal size, the thoughts bouncing around the cavernous interior space, ricocheting off one another. Her gut is a roaring hollow, and her side . . .

Best not to think about her side.

There's a moment where she almost quits. Where she wants to get back on her phone, pull up Uber, bring the Sikh back to her location.

The moment passes. She allows herself another sip of water, and starts trudging up Elrita Drive.

The road isn't steep, but by the time she reaches the dead end at the top, she's pouring with sweat. The houses here are more opulent, with swanky cars out front, even some of those ridiculous Greek columns put in place by people who should really know better. Over a small stone wall at the end of the road, a dirt path leads through the chaparral bushes, winding its way across the hillside. In moments, the brush swallows her.

She stops in the shade of a eucalyptus, takes more water. Is it her imagination, or does her head hurt a little less? For the first time, there's a tiny prickle of excitement. However much pain she is in, however messed up, this is better. It's better to be out here doing something than sitting around and waiting for others to do it for you.

San Pedro . . .

Despite the heat, Annie shivers. "Shut the fuck up," she murmurs to herself, resuming her march.

A few minutes later, she crests a rise, the scrub opening up, and she gets one of the best views of her life.

The hills roll out beneath her, leading down to Runyon Canyon Park the shimmering mass of Hollywood beyond it. A few landmarks poke above the grey sprawl, including the gothic Del Rio Hotel. It's perched at the top of its own hill, lording it over the streets below. In the distance, just visible in the smoggy haze, are the skyscrapers of Downtown – those that survived the earthquake, anyway – thrusting up into a sky that is so blue it hurts to look at. As views go, Annie has definitely seen worse. *No wonder people pay to live around here.*

She lets her gaze track downwards. And there, just visible through the trees on the hillside, not two hundred yards from her position, is her target.

She's got a surprisingly good view of the property. The house is enormous, shaped like an uneven U. Two storeys, at least, with a sizeable garage attached to one wing. The steeply-gabled roof juts out over multiple smaller balconies, curtains blowing through open doors. The garden on the house's west side is just visible, a huge pool and attached deck in the centre, surrounded by carefully manicured landscaping. A man in overalls prunes a tree, his back to her, standing on a tall ladder. A wheelbarrow full of tools sits nearby.

The garden runs down to a sheer cliff, the edge sealed off behind sturdy fencing. Annie can't tell from here how far the drop is, but it doesn't matter. *Not going in that way, that's for damn sure.*

On the east side of the house, there's a winding gravel driveway. And there, parked a little way off from the front entrance . . .

Got you.

Annie eyes the dark blue truck with the gigantic scrape down the side. Sure, this could be a wild goose chase. It might just be a coincidence, some millionaire's daughter who took a corner badly, scraped up her ride. But something tells her that isn't the case. She's found them.

Shit – she should have asked Reggie to look up who owns the house. Then again, that's something she may not need her co-worker for – hell, she could have done it herself, in the car, if she'd been thinking straight. She pulls out her mom's phone, crouching down behind a shrub. Her headache is back, insistent and pounding, but she ignores it. House this big, someone must have written something about who lives there . . .

It doesn't take her long. The owner is James Wilcox, a thirty-something hedge fund billionaire who seems to like New Era fitted hats and pink golf shirts. Made his money by shorting stocks, as far as she can tell. Is he working with Chloe and Adam? Did they take the house from him? More importantly, why are they still here? After everything that happened, *why are they still in LA?*

Should she call Reggie? Tell her what she's found? Only . . . what *has* she found? So far, all she's done is confirm what Jah saw with her own eyes. It proves absolutely nothing.

Well, she told Reggie she was going to observe, so that's exactly what she needs to do. She casts around, eventually settling on a spot that allows her to lie in the dirt, shrubs and shade covering her. From here, she has a clear view of the property below, and it would take the most eagle-eyed watcher imaginable to spot her. She rewards herself with another swig of water, trying not to pay attention to the pang of hunger in her stomach. Should have brought something to eat. Not a problem Teagan would have had; the woman has a food radar that is second to none.

There's no question that a lot of what Teagan does is annoying as hell. She has zero strategic skills, no filter, a constant ability to screw up even the best-laid plans. She can be ungrateful and whiny, and she takes sarcasm to an Olympic level. Annie hated her at first – and, just FYI, with good reason.

But it's awfully hard to hate someone who gives as much of a shit as Teagan does. Who absolutely point-blank refuses to quit on people, even when they give her a very good reason to.

She picked up very early on that Annie wasn't her biggest fan – a feeling which was entirely mutual, thanks very much. And yet, Annie was never shut out. To Teagan, Annie was a member of the team, another person under Tanner's thumb, and so the girl genuinely made an effort. Bitch probably didn't even realise she was doing it – she's always been oblivious.

And Teagan may have been sarcastic, but she was never mean about it. Her sarcasm never devolved into *snark*: the kind of vicious, bitter put-downs that Annie had heard from others time and time again. You could accuse Teagan of a lot of things, but not that. Never that.

When Annie stumbled – when Paul died – it was Teagan who helped catch her.

Maybe it was because she'd been there when he died. She'd tried to save him, done everything she could to dig him out of the earth he'd been buried in. Or maybe it was because that was just who she was. It was Teagan who kept checking in, who wouldn't let Annie dwell on her pain, who kept coming back no matter how often Annie pushed her away.

At some point, Annie started to need that. She started to rely on this wild, uncontrolled, ridiculous white girl. It was why she couldn't bear it when Teagan kept putting herself in danger to help others.

Annie is not used to people giving as much of a crap about her – and everyone else – as Teagan does. Paul did, but he isn't around any more, and Annie is not about to let down one of the only true friends she has left.

She shifts her body, trying to find a position that doesn't set off her burned side. The gardener finishes up, heading into the house, and that's the last movement she sees on the property. Nobody emerges from the doors out front. Nobody steps out for some air on the balconies. The water is long gone, her throat a parched wasteland.

"Come on, man," she says. She's unsure if she's giving herself a pep talk, or urging Teagan's psycho sister to show herself. Hell, right now, she'd settle for the nut-sack tech bro who owns the house.

This is bullshit. She's getting nothing from up here. She could wait for hours more, and still get nothing. She needs to get closer.

In the back of her mind, Reggie's words whisper at her: *Just promise me you won't engage them. Observe from a distance, stay hidden, then come right back here.*

Well, OK. Let's just look at that. Observing from a distance isn't getting her anywhere, but getting a little closer might. If she does, she may be able to see things that she can't spot from here, even if it's just a sense of movement from inside, a glimpse of who might be on the property right now. She's not going to engage, she's going to stay hidden, and when she's done she'll head right back to Watts. She'll go down the hill, past the houses with the ridiculous Greek columns, and call herself up an Uber like before.

She leaves the empty water bottle where it is and begins to scramble down the hillside, keeping one eye on the property below her. It's steeper than she thought, and harder going. She has to use the shrubs as leverage, and in under a minute, her body is rebelling. Nausea and pain, a nasty little cocktail in the shaker of her guts, eating into her side. At one point, her hand slips off a branch, and she has to slam it into the slope to steady herself. The pain nearly makes her black out, and she has to stay very still for a few moments, breathing slowly and deliberately.

This was a bad idea.

And yet, she keeps going, sticking to the cover of the chaparral. Her plan is to stop at around the level of the top floor of the compound; from this distance, she should be able to at least see inside.

There are three rooms visible from her spot on the hillside. Two have their curtains closed, and the third one – a set of French doors opening out onto a balcony edged with wrought-iron railings – has no movement in it. There's the edge of a bed, a dresser, something that might be a suitcase . . . but that's it. Sweet fuck-all.

A nasty thought brings her up short. Chloe, Teagan's sister . . . her ability was infrared detection, wasn't it? She could track people using their heat signatures. If she happens to be looking Annie's way . . .

Then again: so what? Just because she can see a heat signature doesn't mean she knows who Annie is. This is public land – or at least, land that isn't fenced off – and Annie has every right to be here. All the same, if Chloe decides to send someone to take a look, or comes herself, she'll have to run. *That's going to be fun.*

A few minutes later, she is at the bottom of the slope, close to the north wall of the property. She catches her breath, blinking hard, then takes a good long look at the perimeter. No cameras that she can see, and no razor wire. It's true that there might be a silent alarm system, motion-activated perhaps, or . . .

She should regroup, get additional intel. *And by the time we do that, Chloe and Adam might be gone. How much trace will they leave behind? They don't seem like the kind of people to drop a trail of breadcrumbs for us to follow.*

"Losing my damn mind," she says to herself.

The thought of coming away from this little adventure with nothing sticks in her gut. Because it's not just about gathering intel, is it? Chloe and Adam exploded into her life, took the most precious thing in the world from her. Paul. Buried under seven feet of dirt by a monster *they* unleashed.

They weren't the reason for the lightning strike and the coma that followed, but it would never have happened if they hadn't been out there causing havoc. She wants . . . no, she *needs* to hit back. To invade their space, prove to herself that they aren't invincible. And if she has to do it while at something less than peak physical capacity, then that's exactly what the fuck she's going to do.

Which is going to be a problem, because there is no way in hell she's climbing this wall.

Even in peak condition, she'd struggle. It's twelve feet high, and although there's no razor wire on top, it's a sure bet there are cameras and motion sensors. Getting over undetected? Hell, getting over *at all*? No chance. Bitterly, Annie remembers the ladder that the gardener was using – a ladder that just so happens to be on the wrong side of the wall. There certainly aren't any convenient trees close by; everything that might help someone jump the wall has long since been cut back. Oh, and lest we forget: Chloe might not react to a heat signature on this side of the wall, but she'll sure as hell take notice if that signature comes inside.

The walls end at the cliff face, bracketing it on either side. Annie couldn't slip round the edge, even if she somehow managed to psych herself up to hang out over the drop. The owner clearly anticipated someone trying this, and has ended each wall with a nest of spiked fencing, extending a good six feet out into open air. Annie saw the fencing from the cliff; it looked pleasant enough at a distance, but would be murder to get round.

At the edges of Annie's mind, an idea starts to form. It's a long shot, a hell of a long shot, but maybe . . .

She starts walking, moving parallel to the wall, heading away from the cliff. It's hard going – the closer she gets to Laurel Canyon Drive, the more she has to battle through uncut chaparral, scratching up her bare arms. Twice, she has to clamber over concrete gullies, built to handle rainwater run-off. By the time she reaches the street, a hundred yards or so to the north of the property gates, she is bloody and exhausted, on the verge of passing out.

She spots a shady area a little way up the street, in the shadow of a wall. She can rest there, catch her breath.

"Yo!"

Annie turns.

A figure is walking up the street, in her direction. She has to shade her eyes against the blinding sun, and even then, all she can see is a black silhouette. But of course, she knows who it is.

Unbe-fucking-lievable.

"Don't blame Candice, all right?" Nic Delacourt says, holding his palms out as he walks closer. "She waited till you were gone, then said she'd shoot out my tyres and make me walk if I didn't get the hell out of there. But listen, you think I don't know Uber drivers don't come to the hood? And I figured you were getting a ride-share, because there was no way you were in a state to drive a car. I don't know Watts all that well, but I know MLK Hospital."

Annie walks towards him, the sun beating down on her. There's a thin whistling noise in her ears, as if her head is a steam kettle, on the verge of blowing its lid.

"I actually got there before you, if you can believe it. Even then, I almost didn't spot you. Kind of a lucky break. Come on, Teagan wasn't answering her phone, and you're telling me to stay out of something major? No way. There was *no way* you were leaving me on the bench. I'm in way too deep for that. I— Woah, *hey!*"

Annie tries to shove him to the tarmac. Problem is, her feet aren't really listening to her any more. When she leans forward, they tangle up. She goes down hard, ripping the skin off her palms on the hot surface.

She rolls over, her side screaming at her. Nic appears in her field of vision, down on one knee. She takes an awkward swing at him, not even sure what she's doing any more. He grabs her wrist. "Jesus Christ, Annie, come on. Enough."

His voice sounds like it's coming from the end of a long tunnel. Hot. Has she ever been this hot? Nic's face drifts in and out of focus and the blue sky above him gets brighter and brighter until the only thing she can do is close her eyes.

TWENTY-NINE

Teagan

Usually, hotels seal off the windows on their upper floors. Especially in LA. You can only have so many down-on-their-luck movie producers splatting themselves across Rodeo Drive before you finally decide to do something about it.

But this is the Del Rio, a place where actresses had secret passages so they could meet their lovers, and the chandeliers cost more than my annual coffee budget. So yes, the windows open.

And here's the thing about this hotel. It used to be a house. A house with lots of gables and balconies and towers and battlements. Which are useful features if, say, you want to move up a floor without using the stairs or the elevator. It's kind of amazing that our little group of hostage-takers forgot about this; either that, or they didn't have enough C4. Rookie error, guys. Always have more plastic explosive than you actually need.

It's nice to get ahead of these assholes, even if it's only by a little. I don't know what Phan is plotting, or how the hell she and Dyson knew about me. But for the first time today, I actually have a plan.

I swing my legs out over the sill, and drop down onto the little balcony beyond. Blinding sunlight forces my eyes shut for a second, and I have to open them slowly, adjusting to the glare. The penthouse suite we were in may be immaculate, but it's pretty clear that no one has been on this balcony – if you can call it that – for a very long time. It's dirty as hell, covered with puddles of stagnant water despite the bright sunshine. There are even drifts of leaves here, which confuses the hell out of me. Where did *they* come from? This hotel is the tallest structure for miles around.

Behind me, Africa sticks his head out the window. Jonas and Kanehara are just visible behind him, staring at me in confusion.

I beckon Africa out the window. He clambers out with infuriating ease, the drop proving no obstacle for him.

"Dude." I pull him in close. "PK's back."

His brow knots in confusion – then his eyes go wide. "You OK?"

"Seems like it." I send it out, testing my range. I'm up to about seventy feet now.

Africa's face cracks in an evil grin. "Now they will find out the true power of your powers."

That's a weird way of putting it. Whatever. I can't help grinning back.

"What are you two doing?" Kanehara says from inside.

I point upwards. "Let's take out that jammer." I won't even have to get close to it. I'm pretty sure I can find a jammer-shaped object once I'm on the roof, and I can crush it to pieces without even seeing it. Or give it a hell of an old college try, anyway.

"And call the police?" Africa licks his lips. "Maybe not a good idea. The Solomon Children could start killing hostages . . ."

"Which is why we're not gonna call the cops." I'm actually

really proud of myself for thinking this through. *Gold star, Teagan. Have a cookie. Gee, thanks Teagan, don't mind if I do.* "We'll call Tanner. Let her know we've taken care of the jammer. *She* can decide whether to call the cops or not."

"What if she is downstairs? And there is another jammer?"

My grin falters. "Fine, good point. If we can't get hold of her, you and I can figure out what to do."

He nods slowly. And for the first time since he had to shoot the hostage-taker trying to drown me, he looks like his old self. "It is a good idea," he says.

"Um, hi?" Kanehara leans out of the window frame, one knee on the sill. "Care to share with the class?"

"Not really," I reply. "You and Jonas stay put. We'll take it from here."

"No thanks." She finishes clambering out the window, almost but not quite falling over.

"I'm serious. We are about to go do some major secret agent shit, so—"

"*Major secret agent shit?* Whatever – I'm coming too."

"I said no."

"Try and stop me."

Jonas is at the window now, clearly trying to decide what to do about all this. Kanehara spots him, and gestures impatiently. "You too, OK?"

"What?" I put out my hands. "This is not a group field trip. You *really* need to stay here. Hunker down."

Kanehara locks eyes with me. "If you think I'm abandoning this story, you're out of your mind. And if I start filming something, don't you dare tell me to stop."

"Miss Kanehara," Africa says. "You must—"

"We're a lot safer out here than we are in there, right? And unless you plan on locking us inside . . . "

God, that's tempting. I would very much like to be away from these two for a while. And I *really* don't want to use my PK while Kanehara is hanging around. Then again, it's not like she's going to *see* me use it; I don't fire laser beams out of my ass. The energy is invisible. I can crunch the jammer before we even get close.

And as much as both of them need to back the fuck off, she's right. The outside of the building is maybe the one spot the hostage-takers won't actually be.

"OK," I tell them. "But you stay way back. And we are not gonna be able to grab you if you slip and fall, so be damn careful, yeah?"

To be fair, that's not really a problem at first. The balcony is narrow but walkable, and continues for twenty feet. We move single-file around a short tower, and that's when the balcony abruptly dead-ends at a stone wall. There's a flat section seven or eight feet above and in line with it, but it's going to be murder getting up there. The wall to my right is way too steep to climb.

Africa solves the problem. He uses his height and reach to lever himself up there, even if his thrashing legs almost knock me off the side. Then he spins around, and reaches out for me, pulling me up. I flop onto the patch of flat roof, and get to my knees. There's no railing here, nothing to stop any of us from dropping right off the edge if we get too close.

It occurs to me – a little too late – that we could just leave Jonas and Kanehara. Just *not* help them up. Unfortunately, Africa has a bigger, less shrivelled heart than I do. He's already helping Kanehara.

Shakily, I get to my feet, suddenly realising just how high we are. I know, I know, probably should have clocked that *before* we went on this insane mission.

We're on the west side of the building, out of sight of the driveway and the paparazzi. The view is immense, looking west past UCLA and Santa Monica to the Pacific, all of it under the dome of a perfect Californian sky. High above us, a jet tracks a contrail against a few scudding clouds. There's almost no sound up here except the odd gust of wind; the city's traffic, already at low levels thanks to the quake, is all but inaudible. It's peaceful – or as peaceful as it's likely to get for us today, anyway.

And as I look out over this view, another puzzle piece clicks into place inside my head.

Burr's words, echoing in my mind: *There were at least eighteen hostiles, all heavily armed.*

Eighteen.

To take fifty people prisoner.

I'm not so good at math, but that's nearly one hostage-taker for every three people. Three *unarmed* people, most of whom are slow and soft and middle-aged and probably scared out their minds. You could control the whole group with three or four armed bad guys, tops. Why the overkill? Why go to the trouble of having even more people masquerade as waiters, just so they could help?

Why did Dyson and these Children of Solomon people hire so many people, then? Is it just for safety? In case something goes wrong? I guess the numbers would help you cover the whole hotel, if you need to, but that's iffy as shit. And besides, if you're doing this for money, which I assume is the case, wouldn't you want *fewer* people involved? Why split the payout eighteen ways?

When is a hostage situation not a hostage situation?

The question comes to the front my mind unasked, awkward and heavy.

"How do we get to the top?" Kanehara's voice jolts me out

of my thoughts. She's pointing to the roof, the edge of which is just visible ten feet above us. Problem is, it's at the top of that steep part of the roof. No way we're getting up there.

I reach out with my PK, but my range isn't quite there yet. I get plenty of objects on the roof – air conditioning units, metal railings around the helipad – but nothing useful. Weirdly, I don't feel the helicopter I saw earlier. It must have taken off at some point, maybe to refuel at Burbank Airport, which isn't far.

"We need to keep going," Africa says.

There's another gothic tower ahead of us – maybe if we get around it, we can find a way up to the roof. Problem is, the little flat section we're on gets a lot narrower before it reaches the tower. We have to flatten ourselves against the wall behind us, crab-shuffle along. I'm no longer enjoying the view. Christ, maybe Jim Morrison had the right idea: get high off your face *before* you go clambering around the outside of a building.

I take the lead, Africa following, then Kanehara, then Jonas. The last two have started to bicker again, talking in low, ugly voices. Africa hisses at them to can it. He's finding it tougher going than the rest of us; heights don't scare him, but his centre of gravity is a lot higher than ours. Sweat stands out on his forehead in large drops.

The tower once had windows, but they're bricked up. God knows why; I would have thought a tower hotel room would be a pretty sweet place to stay. I collapse against it, resting my aching thighs and lower back. Raising my head, I take in the path round the tower. If anything, the ledge is even narrower than the one we just handled. How the fuck are we supposed to get around that? It'll only take one error, one little slip . . .

"Hey, Africa," I say. "Can we get onto the roof from here?"

"We must go round the tower."

"Yeah, I kind of meant *without* doing that."

"It is too steep here. Come come: go round."

"You know what, now that I think about it, you have longer arms than I do, so it's probably best if you do it."

"We do not have time for this."

"No, seriously, I really think is more in your wheelhouse than mine—"

"Could one of you please just *go*?" Kanehara hisses.

"Maybe we should head back," I say.

Africa glares at me. "This was your idea."

"It's kind of a work-in-progress thing?"

"Oh my God, just move." Kanehara tries to get past Africa, but the ledge is too narrow. She and Africa end up in a tangle of limbs, muttering at each other, going nowhere. Either we all go forward, or we all go backwards. *Crap.*

Jonas clears his throat loudly. He has to do it a couple of times before we all look at him. "*What?*" Kanehara snaps.

"There's another way."

He points. "See where the tower meets the wall? Africa, if you boost Teagan up . . ."

I crane my neck. As much as I hate to admit it, he's right. The tower joins the sloping wall maybe four feet above my head. The joined section looks narrow . . . but it should be enough to stand on. From there, I might be able to reach the edge of the roof. Emphasis on *might.*

"Not bad, Mister Germany," Africa says.

"Do not call me that."

I look at the ledge leading around the tower, then up at the joined section, then back at the ledge. "No. Nope. Noooo. This is a shitty idea. Let's go back and rethink this."

That's what I try to say. What actually comes out is: "Fuck it, OK, why not?"

Being boosted onto a ledge is tricky business at the best of times. Doing it while seven storeys off the ground is ... let's go with *ambitious*. Africa links his fingers together to make a foothold, and with an inward curse at myself for attempting something so stupid, I manage to get my right foot onto it. This positions us awkwardly on the ledge, with my ass hanging out over the edge, Africa half bent over. *Please work.*

With a grunt, Africa propels me upwards. There's a horrible half-second where I'm in motion, knees threatening to buckle. But it works. I grab the edge of the joined section clearly. "OK, push, push, push—"

Which is when a pigeon attacks me.

The moment I get my head over the edge, the world explodes in a mess of squawking feathers. The damn thing was perched on the ledge, just out of sight. Claws brush my fingers as it slams into my face, and I jerk back reflexively—

—and let go of the ledge, toppling backwards.

THIRTY

Teagan

Not for the first time, Africa saves my ass.

I use the word deliberately. When he catches me, it's ass-first, his big hands cupping my butt. Normally that's the kind of behaviour that would earn you a flying object to the windpipe, but in this case, I'll give him a pass.

I don't know he keeps his balance. He turns me, letting me drop into his arms, like a husband carrying his bride across the threshold.

With an undignified flapping, the pigeon shoots past above us. I stare up at Africa, so stunned I can barely speak.

"Jesus Christ," Kanehara says.

"You OK?" Africa says. I'm amazed at how calm he is, as if I merely missed the last step on a flight of stairs and came down a little hard.

"Fine," I manage to squeak. And it really is a squeak. *Fuck me. Let's do not that again.*

But of course, there's no choice. Somehow, we manage to get me standing, and this time, Africa manages to push me all the way up onto the ledge.

The joined section is about a foot wide, just enough for me

to kneel on. I have to make myself stop shaking, quiet the alarm bells in my head.

"Can you get up from there?" Kanehara calls up.

Be an awful goddamn shame if I can't.

The edge of the roof is actually surprisingly close. I have to stretch a little to reach it, and I'm worried that I won't be able to pull myself up, but that turns out not be a problem. The lip is narrow enough for me to get my fingers around. It takes a few seconds of grunting and flailing and awkward mantling, but I manage to pull myself up and over.

And I really do mean over. The lip and the surface of the roof aren't on the same level – the surface is a few feet below. When I roll over into open air, I do a little undignified flapping of my own, landing hard on my forearms.

God, I hope I'm alone up here. This is the least stealthy entrance of all time.

Getting to my knees, I finally get a look at the Del Rio's roof.

I'm in a narrow trench that borders the back of the helipad, running end to end across the roof. It must have something to do with maintenance, or wind control. For all I know, it's where the celebs stash their coke. It's maybe four feet deep, and the metal surface under my knees is damp and grimy, soaking through my pants. Bulky air conditioning units line the roof to my left and right, spaced at intervals, fans whirring quietly.

Waist-high metal railings ring the helipad above me. I sneak a peek over the edge: as expected, the pad itself is empty, no chopper. The bar is a squat structure at the far end of the roof, maybe a hundred feet from the big H, a patio surrounding it. Glass barriers enclose the patio – can't have the stench of helicopter fuel killing the vibe, I guess, or gusts of propeller blowback ruining actresses' hair.

The bar itself is dark and silent, but it must be fun when it's pumping. It's not hard to imagine the bar at night, an ocean of light in twinkling darkness, packed with movie stars and celebrities. Don't get me wrong, celebrities are mostly dipshits, but there's no denying that the Del Rio's rooftop bar is rad. *Especially since there may or may not be a secret passage inside it, don't forget that.*

Movement from above me. I turn, and help Kanehara over the lip. She drops into a crouch. "Thanks. Anybody else up here?"

"Not that I can tell." My PK certainly isn't picking up anything jammer-shaped. Then again, the bar is probably out of range from here.

Jonas is next. I'm a little worried about how Africa is going to manage, but he puts his height to good use, although it takes him a little longer to get onto the joined section, with a lot of grunting. Eventually, though, all four of us are in the trench, peering over the lip of the helipad.

"OK," I say, glancing at Africa. "I'll get a little closer." *And get in range with my PK.*

"That's crazy," Kanehara says. "What if you get caught?"

"There's nobody there."

"We can barely see into the bar. How do you know?"

"I did not just climb the outside of a building to sit here and do nothing." A better idea pops into my head. "We'll split up. Africa, you go with her round that side. Jonas, you come with me round this side. We can watch each other's backs, and if we do get caught, at least there are two of us in each group."

They all look at each other, weighing up my plan. One by one, they nod — because if I do say so myself, it's pretty solid. And it has a few unexpected bonuses. I might be able to crush the jammer without anyone knowing, but this puts Kanehara on the other side of the roof from me, which is like an extra layer of safety. She'll be with Africa, who has some idea of what's going on. And she won't be with Jonas, which is good, because otherwise they'd probably end up killing each other before the hostage-takers even got to them.

"Take care," Africa says, giving me a fist bump. He gestures to Kanehara, and the two of them head off to the right.

I turn to Jonas, and the son of a bitch is already moving. A gust of wind tousles his perfect hair, blond strands blowing around his face. "This way," he says, his voice low.

"Jonas!" I head after him, moving in an awkward bent-over run.

He hops up onto the ledge next to the nearest blocky AC unit. It's as tall as he is, and he ducks behind it quickly, staying out of sight. I follow, a gust of hot, stale air hitting me as I climb up.

We move from unit to unit in quick bursts, but stop way short of our goal – there's a big, open concrete apron between the bar and the helipad, taking up most of the roof. We're not going to be able to get all the way to the bar in cover, which is fine: my PK is in range, and working just as it should.

Keeping out of sight, I reach out with my ability, hunting for anything jammer-shaped. I pick up glasses, bottles, plastic tap spigots, knives, forks . . . but nothing that could be a jammer. *Shit.*

We're maybe thirty feet from the bar now. I force myself to keep searching – and freeze.

Gun.

Assault rifle.

I risk a peek over the edge of the trench. There: emerging from behind a support strut inside the bar. Dark suit, heavy weaponry, mirror shades.

There's no sign of Africa, or Kanehara. Hopefully they have

the good sense to stay hidden. *Goddammit.* I was really hoping this was going to be easier.

Jonas spots him too, mutters a soft *"Scheiße"*. Then, before I can reply, he lunges for me.

For an absurd moment, I think he's trying to hit me. Instead, he grabs me, pulling me back behind the nearest AC.

"What the hell?" I snarl at him.

"More," he says, his lips barely moving.

Fuck, he's right. My PK just picked them up. Two of them, both of them holding assault rifles. Slowly, I take another peek.

It's a hostage-taker I don't recognise: a muscular woman with a thin, hawk-like face. And with her: Vincent Dyson. *The Reverend.* Same suit, same military haircut. As unruffled and clean as a preening bird.

There's someone else with them. Someone the woman is dragging, pulling onto the patio.

Senator Arthur Weiss.

Beside me, Jonas goes very still.

The two of them drag the senator out onto the concrete apron. He clearly doesn't want to be there, his face red with fear and fury. His mouth is moving, but I can't quite hear what he's saying. His tie is askew, and he looks like he's aged ten years in three hours. And this was a guy who was pretty old to begin with.

What the hell is he doing up here? What do they want with him?

Weiss says something to Dyson. Something that has the words "wouldn't dare" in it. Dyson smirks, scratching at his pointed chin. He raises his eyes towards the woman, who calmly reaches round and punches Weiss in the gut.

Jonas makes a very soft hissing noise as Weiss goes to his knees, coughing, shoulders shaking. I have to force myself to relax my clenched fists.

Weiss lifts his face, blinking, and Dyson socks him across the jaw, snapping his head sideways.

It doesn't matter that Arthur Weiss is a senator right now. It doesn't matter that he's one of the most powerful men in the country, or that he technically holds my fate in his hands. Right now, he's an unarmed old man, getting the shit kicked out of him.

At this point, I don't care what these people want. I don't give the tiniest fuck about their grievances. I am going to ruin their day.

Jonas must sense my rage, because he puts a hand on my shoulder, squeezing tight. Against all odds, it clears my mind a little. I can't charge in there angry, even with my PK. Not if I don't want this situation to go super sideways. I bite my lower lip, trying to run through the best way to approach this.

Dyson says something to the woman, who pulls out her phone, and holds it up. She turns it sideways, the way people do when they're filming something. And before I can process this, Dyson grabs Weiss by the collar, and starts dragging him towards the railing at the edge of the roof.

THIRTY-ONE

Annie

Nic's car is parked further up the hill from Wilcox's mansion, in the shade of a tall eucalyptus. Annie sits in the passenger seat, eyes closed, letting the AC's icy blast wash over her. Somehow, the Coke that Nic put in her hand is still cold. She drains the last sip, even though it hurts to tilt her head back.

"Wow." Nic says. He holds out his own soda. "You want mine? Looks like you—"

Annie burps. It just pops out of her. She lies back against the headrest, feeling bloated and stiff. But at the very least, she doesn't feel like she's going to pass out. The cold air and cold Coke aren't as good as three weeks of bed-rest, which is what she really needs, but at least she doesn't feel like she's about to pass out again.

"How did I not sssssss-see you on the ridge?" she croaks. "There was nobody else up there."

"I saw you go up, but I didn't follow. I kind of had . . . I sort of didn't really know what I was doing. Not quite like a panic attack, nothing like that, but like . . . I had too many options. I kept thinking maybe I should go get someone, but I didn't know who. And then I saw you pop out and I thought, fuck it, OK, maybe she listens this time."

"You an idiot, you know that?"

"Come on, man. If I hadn't tailed you—"

"Not what I mean. A b-b-b-black dude and a brown girl sitting in a parked car in Laurel Canyon in the middle of the day. How long you think it's gonna be before 5-0 come by?"

"So tell me what's going on. Give us a reason to not sit here."

When she still doesn't speak, he turns in his seat. Leans closer. "I know Teagan's in trouble," he says quietly. "Let me help. Let me at least do *something*."

"You *can* do something. Get as f-f-f-far away as possible. Be there for when we get Teagan back."

It's the wrong thing to say. Nic stares straight ahead, chewing on his lip. Slowly, he starts to shake his head.

"Nic, you gotta und—"

Abruptly, he pops his door, clambers out. Begins pacing back and forth, hands laced behind his head. Annie watches as he moves around to the front of the car, rests his palms on the hood. The metal is scorching-hot, and he pulls back with a yelp. He kicks the car's bumper, hard. Does it again.

"God's sake," Annie murmurs. What a fucking drama queen. She's about to yell at him to quit it, but she has zero energy. She lies in the waft of the AC as Nic paces around the car, muttering to himself.

After a few minutes, he climbs back in. Shuts the door. Not looking at her.

"Done?" she asks.

He puts his hands on the steering wheel, drums his fingers. "Look. I get it."

"Good." Maybe he'll listen to her now.

"I'm a civilian, I don't have clearance, blah-de-blah. No,

no, no, don't try talk over me. I *understand*. Here's you guys, hardcore superpowered secret government agents doing some next level shit, saving the world and whatnot, and here's me. Two parents, two cars in the garage growing up, law school, District Attorney's office, suit and tie. At least until I started doing earthquake relief. I got a CrossFit membership and I drive a damn Corolla that I'm still paying off, with whatever money I'm *not* putting into my 401K." He smacks the steering wheel. "I'm normal. I'm boring. I'm not about that life."

"Jesus, stop fucking *whining*."

"Whining?" He twists in his seat to look at her. "You think this is whining? No. You see, I'm *fine* with my boring-ass existence. I worked hard for it. But just because I'm boring does not mean that I'm useless. It doesn't mean I'ma sit at home like a, like a, a good little boy and wait for you to handle your shit."

"Nic—"

"And more importantly, I'm not gonna sit at home while someone I care about is AWOL, and the person looking for her just came out of a coma and can barely string two words together. You think that shit is smart, Annie? Or do you wanna keep going, doing your own thing, because the one guy trying to help you is *boring*? Give me a fucking break."

He slaps the steering wheel again, stares out the window.

For two whole minutes, they sit in silence.

"You really wanna know?" Annie says.

He doesn't reply, just turns to look at her.

Slowly, haltingly, she tells him. When he hears about Teagan's abduction from the hospital, he swears quietly. After she's finished, the silence returns.

"Fuck," he breathes, after a few seconds.

"Yeah."

"*Fuck.*"

"So now you know. Happy?"

He doesn't respond, scratching his stubble. Annie has never noticed his hands before, and are surprised at how big they are, rough and calloused.

"So you think Teagan is inside that house."

"Maybe. I dunno. But I'm pretty sure C-Chloe and Adam are."

"Yeah, but OK, hold up. We know Teagan got arrested, right? That means she *can't* be with her brother and sister. For all we know, she might still be locked up."

"Then why ain't the rest of the crew answering their phones? Why is n-n-n-n-nobody picking up?"

He spreads his hands. "I have no idea. But—"

"Maybe China Shop tried to hit Chloe and Adam." She jerks her chin in the direction of the house. "Maybe the guys're in there rrrrrright now."

"But we don't *know.*" Nic drums his fingers on the steering wheel. "Annie, I just … If you're going to risk yourself going in there, you gotta do it for the right reasons. Otherwise there's—"

"Those people fucked with me and mine." Annie is surprised at how clearly the words come now, her confusion and dizziness abandoning her for a short moment. "Yeah, OK, I don't *where* Teagan is. I don't know if she's in jail, or in that house, or what. And I can't do anything about that. You know what I can do? Confirm that it's her brother and sister. Maybe fuck their shit up, if I can. They don't just get to sit in that fancy house and sip fucking mai thais by the pool. Not after everything they've done."

"Can't we just call the cops?" He sees her expression, and spreads his hands. "Why not? What's the risk?"

"They might skip town. And we don't know if the cops w-w-w-would find anything anyway."

His head drops. "Shit, OK. Yeah."

Another long pause.

"This Chloe chick can see infrared," Nic says, his tone thoughtful. "So even if you got a way to get inside, all she has to do is look in your direction, and it's over. Right?"

"Mm-hmm."

"So look: you know I left the DA's office?"

Annie nods. Ever since the quake, Nic has been volunteering with the people clearing rubble from damaged areas. She glances down at his calloused hands.

"I felt good about it, you know? After the quake . . . it was a way I could get my hands dirty. Help out. But there's so much damage out there, and half the time you're just chipping away at the same building for weeks. So I started looking into what else I could do."

Annie's mouth twitches. "Thought you said your life was boring."

He gives her a look that says, *Don't push your luck.* "And I found out – no, for real, listen – I found out you could get trained for hazardous zones. Spots where there's a risk of fire, or gas leak, shit like that, so if you gotta shift debris or whatever, you can be safe. They're so desperate for manpower that they train you for free. You don't have to pay for any of the turnout gear at all. They haven't sent me in to one of those spots yet, but—"

"Is there a point to this?"

"Yup. I think it's gonna help us get inside."

"How you fffff-figure that?"

Nic tells her.

THIRTY-TWO

Teagan

Weiss fights. He throws wild punches, twisting his body, lashing out with his feet. But he is seventy-plus, fighting men in their thirties and forties.

Dyson pushes Weiss against the railing, open blue sky behind him. The thin-faced woman holds up the phone, filming it. A horrible moment, frozen in time. The hostage-taker from the bar stands off to one side, smirking, rifle held at port arms.

OK. No. There is no way in hell that I'm going to let this happen. Not ever. I am not going to stand by while they murder a senator, and capture it on film for the world to see.

Dyson is talking to the senator. There's a long moment as they go back and forth where I don't know what to do. I don't know if my PK is strong enough to keep the senator on the roof if Dyson decides to pitch him over the edge. And if we rush them now . . .

I squeeze my eyes shut. *Idiot.* Of course we can rush them. We just have to lockdown those assault rifles. I don't know how that's going to stop Dyson launching the senator up and over as soon as we show ourselves, but first things first.

As Dyson and Weiss go back and forth, I send out my PK, hunting for the guns, zeroing in on their safety catches. Jonas tenses beside me, unsure what to do. I put out my hand, touching his chest, in case he gets any ideas. I don't really know how this is going to go, but it's going to be a lot easier if I don't have to worry about him.

My PK finds three safeties. Closes around them.

"*Drop it!*"

Burr, dagger eyes visible over the top of a rifle, is just coming out of the bar. Behind him is Moira Tanner. She looks even more of a mess than she did in the hotel room, and there's a crust of blood on her upper lip. But her own gun is up, pistol held tight, pointed right at Dyson.

Weiss collapses onto all fours, his whole body shaking. Dyson and the thin-faced woman take aim at Tanner and Burr, while the third guy whose name I don't know keeps his gun pointed at Weiss.

Burr comes to a halt a few feet away from them, barking at them again to lower their weapons. He may as well be telling them to make their fingernails grow faster for all the good it does.

A slow smile creeps across my face. This situation – this stand-off – is absolutely *perfect*.

Yeah, I know. I just described a situation involving an armed stand-off, with a senator in mortal danger, as perfect. But that's the thing: it is. I can shut down the safeties on the bad guys' guns, locking them in place. It doesn't even matter if I'm not at full-strength with my PK yet; it's the tiniest thing in the world. It requires almost no energy.

I don't even have to let anyone know I'm here yet, because sooner or later, one of these three clowns is going to try squeeze off a shot, and be completely befuddled when his gun doesn't work. Then the other two will have the same reaction, and Tanner and Burr will suddenly realise that they have the upper hand.

Once they've beaten the crap out of the three of them – Burr could probably do it just by himself – I'll swagger up, preferably just as the senator is getting to his feet. *Hey, you're welcome, it was nothing. Why yes, I did just save your life. All of your lives. Why yes, Tanner, I still do have my ability, and it's working fine, thank you very much. How about we go downstairs, save the day, then shake hands and peace out so I can go and chase my psychotic brother and sister? And get a burger and a beer. I'd really like a burger and a beer. I've earned them.*

And yes: it may be ever so slightly selfish to be thinking about a situation like this in terms of me and my ability. Don't care.

I catch sight of Africa, peeking out from behind an AC unit on the opposite side of the roof. I can't see Kanehara, but she must be there too. Amazingly, it doesn't look like anybody involved in the stand-off has noticed them, or us. Even better. These guys can get their asses kicked by six people instead of two.

I always wanted to be the cavalry.

"Teagan," Jonas says urgently. "What do we do?"

I wink at him. "I got this."

Pulling down the safety catches is something I've done so many times in the past that I've lost count. Mostly, the people holding the guns don't actually notice. They are so focused on their target that they don't register that the catch has clicked back down until they try pull the trigger and end up with a stupid, dumbfounded look on their face. It's a simple manoeuvre, with a completely predictable outcome. Like asking an NBA player to dribble the ball through his legs a few times. There is absolutely no chance of it not working out as I expect it to.

Which is why what happens next takes me completely by surprise.

All three guns get pulled downwards, as if the floor is a huge magnet, slamming hard onto the concrete surface. Dyson manages to keep a grip on his, which means he goes down too, yanked forward onto his face. My mouth falls open, my brain trying to catch up with what the hell just happened.

There's another frozen moment as Tanner and Burr stare in confusion. And then the guns leap off the ground, twisting upwards through the air. Dyson's gun almost brains him, and one of the other rifles slams into Tanner, knocking her backwards. Her own gun goes off, the bullet burying itself in the helipad.

OK – I did *not* mean to do that.

And right then, a huge, staggering, invisible wave of energy explodes out from my mind.

I've had my ability my whole life, and I have a pretty fine-grained sense of how much energy I'm putting out at a given time. And right now, it's like I've plugged myself into a nuclear power plant.

I usually have control of what I grab onto with my PK, but that goes completely out the window. Suddenly I'm locked onto all the guns. Then the metal railing around the helipad. The AC units. The chairs on the patio, the glasses and bottles behind the bar, The cell phone in Jonas's pocket. And before I can even suck in a breath, everything starts to move.

Fast.

The rooftop becomes a whirling hell storm of flying, bouncing, smashing metal and glass and concrete. Pistols and assault rifles whirl through the air, crashing off metal chairs, slamming into anything that gets in the way. Glass shatters, deadly shards glittering in the sunlight. With a crunch, a door comes flipping out of the bar, bounces down the apron, as if blown by a strong wind. The AC units creak and bend, metal panels and rivets snapping.

And it's all me. This titanic, enormous, uncontrolled energy is all coming from me. I've turned the rooftop into a god-damn tornado.

Let go. Let. Go!

But I can't.

Jonas yanks me down, right before a chunk of metal takes my head off. I can't let go. It's as if pulling the safety catches down – moving objects with my mind – started a cascade, a small crack in a dam suddenly bursting open. And here I am, trying to stop the flow by standing in front of it.

The senator, screaming. Burr, yelling my name. A sudden burst of gunfire. I can't see any of it, because I am down on the concrete, face pressed against the surface, still trying to let go of everything. This can't be happening. There is no possible way I can go from absolute zero to ... whatever the hell this is.

What did Chloe and Adam do to me? To my ability?

I force myself up to my knees, desperately trying to bring my PK energy back to me. Instead, amazingly, it gets worse. Because that's when my PK starts latching onto organic objects. And by organic objects, I mean people. And by people, I mean Kanehara and Africa.

When I'm in fight-or-flight mode, when adrenaline is flooding my body, I can sometimes move very small organic objects alongside the usual inorganic ones. After I snorted meth, during our little adventure in the storm drain, I was able to control organic matter easily, even water. It's how I stopped the flash flood. This is different. I've lost all control. The two other members of our little raiding party trace a low parabola across the apron, arms whirling, screaming. Africa takes out Tanner at the knees, while Kanehara bounces sickeningly off the concrete.

Jonas grabbed my shoulder. "Stop. Teagan, stop this."

He knows I'm doing this. Oh, that is going to come back to haunt me.

Dyson comes hurtling past the AC unit. Suit shredded, a huge bruise blooming on his cheekbone. He crashes into a heap on the concrete, not more than four feet from us.

Amazingly, he is still conscious. Not just conscious: alert, focused. For a split-second, his eyes meet mine.

Confusion. Then recognition. Then anger. He reaches inside his jacket, pulls out a combat knife.

No, since you ask, I have no idea why my PK has not sensed or grabbed hold of his damn knife. It's like it's grabbing hold of objects at random, completely uncontrolled, unable to focus.

He slashes at me, and it's only Jonas jerking me backwards that stops the knife slicing into my gut. The two of us take off running, staying low, heading for the bar, trying not to get brained by the insane whirlwind of *stuff* flying through the air directly above our heads. The noise is insane: a creaking, grinding, crashing nightmare. Gunshots echo off the concrete.

And still, I try as hard as I can to rein it in. Even to just focus it on a single object. But I can't. It's like a jammed accelerator in a car, one I can't pull back.

At any second, I'm expecting a knife between my shoulder blades. I can only hope that my PK has grabbed hold of either Dyson or his weapon. I really have no idea. At all.

What if I can't stop it?

I thought the loss of my ability was bad. But what if the

opposite happens? What if it goes full tilt, and I can't shut it off? In that case, there are really only two solutions. Knock me out . . . or kill me.

It's at that moment that I spot Tanner.

We're past the helipad now, running for the bar. Tanner is on her back at the far end of the roof, desperately holding at the remains of a metal railing as my PK tries to pull her away. Our eyes meet, and at that moment, it's like she doesn't even know who I am.

"*I'm really sorry!*" I yell.

Looking over at Tanner was a bad idea, because it means I'm not looking at the ground any more. My feet tangle up, and I almost trip, stumbling against Jonas. The move turns me nearly one-eighty. There is no one behind me, no hostage-taker running up. Off to one side, the senator is crawling towards the bar.

The oddest thought: *It worked.* I wanted to save the senator with my PK, and I did. I just might get everyone else killed in the process.

Right then, something hits me in the left shoulder. Hard.

I go down, skidding across the apron. My left arm is numb – I must've landed on it, squashed it underneath me. And whatever the hell has hit me, I can't stop moving. I've got to get away, get somewhere quiet, or quiet*er* anyway, figure out how to shut this PK off.

I push myself up. Only, my arm won't support my weight. There's a weird tingling in my fingers, and Jonas is staring at me in horror.

No: not at me. At my shoulder.

I look down. It takes a really long time.

There's a hole in my shirt. A big one. But it isn't as big as the hole in my left bicep. It's an enormous, ragged divot, purple red flesh glistening over a hint of bright bone. Blood soaks my arm.

The guns. They never stopped shooting. They—

I blink. "Oh. OK."

Then I sort of lose track of things.

THIRTY-THREE

Annie

Annie thought she knew what it meant to be hot. She's from California, after all, the land of wildfires and climate change summers. But she has never, not once, been as hot as she is now: wrapped in a fireproof Nomex suit, hunkered under a tarp in the back of a pickup truck, surrounded on all sides by tools and equipment that has spent the past few hours baking in the sun.

The suit – which Nic had in his trunk – is made of thermally resistant fabric. It's the most scratchy and uncomfortable garment Annie's ever worn – but, in theory, it should block her body heat, making her invisible to Chloe. But it also keeps all of that heat inside. Annie could swear the sweat is boiling on her skin.

Should have let Nic do this.

He certainly tried to stop her. When he suggested the fire suit that he'd been using for his earthquake relief duties, he'd meant that *he* could somehow use it to get inside Wilcox's property. Annie wouldn't let him. There was no way in hell she was putting him in danger, no matter how much he protested. He didn't like that one bit, but Annie wouldn't be moved.

"You wanna help?" she asked. "Get up onto the hillside. Gimme a birds' eye view of the house. Let me know if there's anything coming my way."

The pickup truck comes to a halt, wheels crunching on gravel. In the Bluetooth bud in her ear, Nic says, "You're at the gate. Guard coming out."

There's the sound of a window rolling down, muffled rap music becoming clear. Annie is suddenly irrationally jealous of Jah, sitting up there in the air-conditioned cab. Her line repairman contact – the one who she spoke to at her mom's place – had taken a lot of convincing to do what he's about to do. Annie had to remind him of services rendered, and even then, it had taken longer than she'd hoped.

Her skin itches from the rough Nomex fabric. She's dizzy. How the hell can she be dizzy when she's lying down?

"What it do?" Jah calls, turning down the music.

The guard at the gate has a faintly Slavic accent. "Can I help you, sir?"

"Yeah, uh, we got a call about possible downed line on this property?"

"I am sorry, but there must be a mistake."

"OK, but—"

"There are no power lines on this property. It's all underground."

"That's what our paperwork says too. But state law mandates we have to check out every report."

"Who reported it? Who says this?"

"Beats me, man. I just wear the uniform. Hold on, here's the call-out order."

Silence. Hot. Scratchy.

"I'm sorry," the guard says. "You cannot just show up and come onto the grounds like this. I do not know who you are."

"Look, my dude, you want to send me out of here, that's fine. I'll log it. Refused entry, no problem. But then you have the City coming with an enforcement order, it gets kicked up the chain, maybe your boss has to make a court appearance explaining why he – or she! I ain't sexist – refused entry to a qualified tech when the public is in danger, and, you know . . ."

"But there are no power lines on the property!"

"You know that, I know that, my system tells me that. It's probably nothing. But all I need to do is make a circuit of the house, do a visual confirmation, you know, the whole deal. Take me five minutes. Then I'm out of your life."

"Who made this call?" Irritation seeps into the guard's voice. "That there was a problem?"

"I dunno. I just got told by my supervisor to come down here."

"Fine. I will talk to your supervisor."

Goddammit, Jah, hurry the fuck up.

"Look, man," the tech says, dropping his voice. "We don't have to do that, aight?"

"What are you talking about?"

"My supervisor? She's a real hard-ass, man. Always on me for every little thing. I'm due for a promotion, put in my application and everything, and she'll need to sign off on it. And she hates it when people call her. People who aren't employees, I mean. One time, this woman out in Century City made me put her through, and I got all my overtime cancelled, do you believe that? So why don't we just keep this between us? We both know there's no downed power line in there, but the regs say I have to check it out. In and out, five minutes. Just you and me. What do you say?"

The guard says nothing.

"Come on, man. Don't do this to me. I just work this job, OK? I—"

"I want to talk to her."

"But if we just—"

"Now."

"... Aight. Let me get the number for you ..."

"Stop. No. I will look it up on your website. Just tell me the extension."

Copeland does so, and the guard heads off, ordering him to wait.

"Annie," Nic says, tinny and quiet in her ear. "This is a bad idea. If you drop out the truck now, I don't think they'll see you. We can find another way."

"Negative," Annie murmurs.

"Come on, just—"

"I said, nnnnnn-negative."

A minute ticks by. Another. The Nomex suit is baggy on Annie's slim frame, but right now it feels like it's tightening, constricting, crushing the life out of her. She makes herself breathe, long and slow.

By now, the guard will have found the number for the Los Angeles Department of Water and Power. He'll have found his way to an irritated woman named Cynthia Reyes, who will confirm that, yes, technician Elijah Copeland works for them, yes, they received a report of a downed power line, and yes, the property owners are legally obliged to admit them for inspection. At least, that's what'll happen if Cynthia plays her part as Annie instructed.

After what seems like an eternity, during which Annie

concentrates very hard on not passing out, she hears footsteps on gravel.

"Five minutes," the guard says. "And I will go with you."

"You see what I mean? And your ass just had to deal with her for a phone call. I got her for the rest of the week. Or like, for ever, probably."

"Drive." There's the sound of the truck door opening, the guard clambering in. The door slams shut, and there's a creaking groan of metal as the gates open. The truck vibrates beneath Annie as Jah puts it in motion.

"OK," Nic says in her ear. From where he is on the ridge-line, he should have a clear view of the truck's path. "He's going around the side of the house, on that little access road. I don't see anybody around. Get ready."

She is going to have to move fast. And she's going to have to do it in this goddamn fire suit. It might – *might* – prevent Chloe from detecting her body heat, but it's going to make climbing out of the truck's bed ridiculously hard.

"Hold," Nic says. "Wait for it . . ."

The sunlight on the tarp above her head vanishes, the truck in the shadow of the house.

"Go. Now."

Annie launches herself upwards, like she's doing a push-up. The Nomex suit fights her. And she is weak, so goddamn weak, her strength sapped by the heat and the horrible pound-ing in her temples.

Somehow, she manages to get a leg underneath her. Somehow, she manages to push up the loose corner of the tarp, worm her way through it, blood pounding in her ears, sure that at any moment there's going to be a startled shout from the cab, the truck coming to a screeching halt as the guard clambers out to stop her.

And then she's out, over the tailgate, landing hard and rolling in the dust. Adrenaline pumping, she scrambles to her feet, throwing herself at the bushes hugging the house, not even caring whether anybody spots her. There's only one thought in her mind: to get out of the fire suit. She doesn't even care about Chloe spotting her any more. If she doesn't get this thing off her, she's going to boil alive.

Nic is in her ear, but she barely hears him. The second she's in the bushes, she rips the suit jacket off, throwing it aside, dancing as she does the same with the pants.

Nic, harsh and tinny in her ear. "The fuck are you doing? Put the suit back on!"

Air. Real air. It's hot and muggy, but it's like the caress of silk sheets on her skin. She collapses against the side of the house, soaking in it, wallowing in it, taking long breaths through her nose. Willing her pounding heart to slow down, willing the headache behind her temples to even out. Neither of those things happen. In her head, all she can hear as her father: *You can't aim that fastball, you didn't practise enough, you can't aim that fastball.*

She shakes her head, which doesn't quite dislodge him. Dead for almost two decades now, and the abusive motherfucker won't leave her alone. She spent a long time getting him out of her head, and it's as if the lightning strike and the coma opened up a door for him to get back in. Or perhaps he was there the entire time, and she just managed to block him out all these years.

"Annie?" Nic says, frantic. "Tell me you're OK."

Through a dry, sour mouth, she says, "I'm good."

"Holy shit. All right. Holy shit. Put the goddamn suit back on."

She makes a noise that might be a laugh. There is no way in

hell she's wearing that again. And in any case, even if Chloe *can* see her body heat now, she won't automatically suspect an intruder. This place has plenty of staff, after all. She just has to be careful.

Her gaze tracks right, to an open ground floor window. "I'm going in."

THIRTY-FOUR

Teagan

I've never been shot before.

I've been shot *at*, more than once. There are quite a few people who want me dead for one reason or another. And yet I have never taken a bullet. Until today.

Can confirm: getting shot sucks.

There's no pain until I actually see the wound – the horrible, gaping hole in my flesh. Then there's a whole lot of it. As if my brain goes *oh, hey, that looks nasty. Here, have some agony to enhance the experience.*

It's like someone poured kerosene on my bicep and set it on fire. It's the kind of pain that doesn't actually let you scream, because it locks your throat up tight. All I can do is make this weird little hissing sound, forcing its way between my clenched teeth. And holy crap, that's a lot of blood. Are there arteries in the bicep? How long do I have before . . . before I . . .

I don't know if I black out, not really. It sure feels like it. When I come back, Jonas has his hands under my arms, and every time he pulls, my left shoulder flares in unspeakable pain.

I have no idea what's happening with my PK. There's

nothing in my ears but a high-pitched ringing. *Shock. I'm going into shock*. The thought forces itself to the surface of my mind. Sugar water. Isn't that what you're supposed to do with shock? Someone should get me some sugar water . . .

Blink. Burr is crouching over me, his expression grim. There's a metal chair behind him, and a shattered glass window behind the chair. "Put pressure here," Burr tells someone. "Whatever you do, don't—?"

And then more gunshots split the air. Burr returns fire, up on one knee, squeezing off precise bursts. Jonas shouts something, and at that moment, there's an instant of clarity where I *am* aware of my PK. It's still completely out of my control. Behind me, it grabs hold of glass bottles, popping them like balloons, sending the shattered pieces whickering through the air.

Bottles. We must be in the bar. How did I even get here?

I roll onto my right side, as if it'll help me escape the pain. Tears squeeze out from between my eyelids. I get a doubled glimpse of Tanner, on her knees underneath the bar, her back to me, messing with something. A shotgun, maybe? Don't they keep those under bars? Isn't that a Hollywood thing?

Tanner's tugging at the floor, bracing herself and pulling at . . .

A trapdoor.

Why in the hell is there a trapdoor here?

It pops up, a slab of wood grinding on rusty hinges. "Quickly," Tanner snaps at . . . Burr? Jonas? Africa?

Oh God. Africa and Kanehara. Are they OK? Are they here? Are—?

Kanehara saw. She saw everything.

I don't have time to process this. There's movement behind me, hands slipping under my arms. I know what's coming, try to twist away from it. They lift me, and when it happens, a shriek bursts out of me. This time, I really do black out.

What I get next are little flashes. Maybe a few seconds each. Ceiling lights, dim and dusty.

My shoulder bumping against something, more agony screaming through me, driving up into my jaw and down into my stomach. Jonas saying "Is she—?"

Gone.

A few hours or years later, I'm moving down a flight of stairs. They're covered in frayed, faded carpet the colour of old red wine. Peeling wallpaper strips hang in the dusty air.

Jonas: "My Instagram! I'm getting all my—"

Burr: "Schmidt, now is *not* the time."

"You don't understand. It's—"

Skip forward. I'm being helped through a door, one with a tarnished golden handle. It's so small that they have to duck me through it, and when I bend my head, my shoulder wakes up again. Screaming.

When I next come back, everything is quiet. And I'm staring at a naked woman.

She's looking right at me. Breasts the size and shape of beachballs, left index finger just touching her perfectly-shaved pussy. Flowing hair the colour of sand, and a look on her face that says she wants me, yes, me.

At least I know I'm not dead yet. Your life is supposed to flash before your eyes, and I'm almost certain that I've never had a naked lady look at me like that. I'd remember.

Everything is quiet. Nothing but muffled voices, off to my right. I turn my head, which sets my shoulder off again, dialling the pain back up to ... well, not quite eleven, but definitely an eight or nine. I squeeze my eyes shut, a moan slipping out of me. I both want to hold my shoulder very tight, and also not touch it ever again.

When I open my eyes, the woman is still looking at me. She's on a poster, which should have been obvious from the get-go. In my defence, I've been through quite a lot today.

The oddest thought: *You should give yourself a rap middle name. If Eric Wright can be Eazy-E, why can't you be Eazy-T? Teagan Eazy-T Frost.*

Slowly, very slowly, I roll onto my good side.

I'm lying on a threadbare couch, the porn poster six feet above my head, stuck to the low ceiling with yellowing tape. The room itself is an office of some kind. There's a dusty desk, with a curved, rolling top – the kind you see in *Downton Abbey*. There's nothing on it but an ancient MacBook and a coffee cup displaying the words ALBUQUERQUE ISOTOPES. The battered rolling chair beside the desk is missing one of its armrests, and it's currently occupied by Jonas. His elbows rest on his knees, his arms laced around the back of his lowered head. Tanner and Burr are over by the door, arms folded, talking in low voices.

The animal currently gnawing at my shoulder bites deep again, and I grunt. Three pairs of eyes turn to look at me. I'm surprised by the look of concern on Tanner's face, the brow furrowed with worry.

"There she is." Burr crosses over to the couch, squats. "Lemme see that shoulder."

"Hurts."

"Yeah, a seven–six–two'll do that."

"A . . . what?"

"7.62 mm. It's what AK-47s fire."

The sensation of the impact comes back to me, the sudden, startling numbness. Automatically, I turn my head, trying to get a look at my left shoulder. It sets off another explosion of pain, digging deep into my jaw.

"Easy," Burr says. His voice is surprisingly gentle. "Stand down, Frost. Let me take it from here."

"Don't touch it." The thought of him doing that makes me want to throw up.

He half smiles. "That train's long since left the station. Take a look."

Somehow, I manage to turn my head. My bicep is bound tightly in gauze, blood leaking through the wrapping.

"Kind of amazing they had a first aid kit down here," Burr says. "Disinfectant expired ten years ago, but it'll do for now. I think we managed to stop the bleeding, but you're going to need a trip to the hospital before long. I could only clean out the wound so much."

He leans over me. "You're all kinds of lucky, you know that? The bullet went in and out. Didn't hit the subclavian or brachial veins, and no broken bones. Half an inch to the left, and it's just a graze. To the right . . . "

That does it. I dry heave, my throat contracting, squeezing to a pinhole.

"Easy," Burr says again. "You're going to feel woozy for a while. Don't worry, happens to everybody. Me included."

He lifts his right arm, unbuttons his cuff. There's a pucker mark on the inside of his wrist. It looks like a crater on the moon, seen from a distance.

"Guatemala," he says, tapping the scar. "First posting after basic. Kid with a nine-mil . . . To this day, I don't know where he pulled it from. Point-blank range. Thought I was going to lose my hand." He flexes his fingers. I'd never noticed before, but he can't actually make a full fist with them.

Somehow, I find my voice. "Is this the part . . . the part

where you tell me that our scars are what make us? Some shit like that?"

He smirks. "Nope. I hate getting shot. Zero out of ten, would not recommend."

I can't help but laugh, even though it hurts.

Burr pats my cheek, a gesture which is less condescending than I expect. "But they do make fun stories. Assuming you live to tell them." He must see the expression on my face. "Relax. You're gonna be fine."

"Where . . . ?" I cough. "Where are we?"

"Sub-basement."

"Yeah, but how did we get down here? We were on the roof."

"Secret passage."

"I'm sorry, what?"

Then it all comes back.

Tanner's comment, on the car ride over here. How . . . who was it, Greta Garbo? How she used to sneak her side-piece in.

"You found it," I say to Tanner.

The barest flicker of a smile. The edges of her mouth *juuuust* twitching. It makes her look fractionally less evil.

"I suppose we did," she says.

"But, like, how? How did you even—"

"The staff sergeant and I explored the basement levels, and I used what I knew about the hotel to make a deduction." She glances around the room. "From the looks of things, the staff here knew all about it, although they certainly kept it out of the press. It also appears that the exit to the hotel grounds was walled off long ago. At any rate, from here, it was easy to get to the roof."

"And the bad guys didn't follow us? After we came back down?"

"I don't believe so. I think we managed to enter the passage without them seeing – the trap door doesn't really rise above the level of the bar. And if they were coming after us by now, we would have heard them." The smile is gone now, the familiar ice-cold stare replacing it.

"That's awesome," I say. "The passage, I mean. Good for you. Did you ever think you'd find it? Or like, actually come down here? It must feel really good."

I'm rambling, but I want to see that ghost of a smile again. And not just because I want her to actually acknowledge how cool it is that she just got us out of there through a secret freaking passage. I want to know there's a human being in there I can talk to: an actual person who will see my side of what happened on the rooftop.

Because, shit: my PK just went completely nutso in front of a bunch of witnesses, including a journalist. A journalist who probably filmed it all, and who will no doubt reach the entirely logical conclusion that the short, black-haired person in the storm drain video is the same short, black-haired person who just made a bunch of shit move in front of her.

Holy crap. Bigger problem. "Africa . . . where's Africa? And there was a journalist, the one from before, with Jonas—"

"We don't know," Jonas says quietly. "We lost track of them."

They're alive. Africa would have found a hiding place, and there's no way he would have let Kanehara see. He would have . . .

Oh.

Forget Kanehara. You know who *also* saw my little display? Jonas Schmidt. Billionaire playboy entrepreneur.

Christ, my throat is dry.

"Anyway, we're good," Burr says. "The FBI is on the way."

"Wait, what? What did you do? Send up a smoke signal?"

"Jammer's destroyed. Thank you for that, by the way." He makes a finger gun, points it at me.

"Are you saying that I . . . ?"

"Yup."

"The jammer was . . . ?"

"Yup. It was in the bar. You sort of threw it around a bit."

"You saw this happen? The jammer getting wrecked?"

"*Nein*," Jonas says. "We were only aware when my phone reconnected to the hotel Wi-Fi on the way down the stairs. All my notifications and emails began to come in. Many of my followers wondering why I haven't posted."

Burr holds up his phone. "We talked to the FBI twenty minutes ago. They're on their way."

Well, shit. For the first time in what feels like years, I actually did something right, even if I did it by accident. Whatever, I don't care, I'm claiming it.

"Feds're going to set up a perimeter," says Burr. "See if they can start negotiations."

"And let me guess: they want you to be their inside man? Take out the bad guys from within?"

He gives me a strange look. "This isn't a movie, sweetheart. They want us to stay the hell out of the way, and not get killed."

"Smart. Wait, holy crap – I forgot to tell you! In Phan's room! The Vietnamese lady! We found—"

"I have told them," Jonas says.

"She had a photo of me." It seems very important to get this out. "She knew I was going to be here. She knew about the whole hostage thing before it happened."

Tanner nods. "So it seems. We've communicated this to the FBI."

"How did she know about me? I'm top-level classified!" I

also stopped a flash flood in front of witnesses and I recently just blew up a rooftop, but I don't want us to get distracted.

"Unknown," Tanner says. "A problem for later."

"I guess. Hey: what is this place?"

Burr looks around. "Someone's office, below the basement. I'm not quite sure." His eyes flick up, towards the naked woman. "Pretty sure they didn't do much work down here, though. Sorry about putting you on the couch by the way. It was either that or the floor."

It takes me a second to catch his meaning. "Ew."

"Like I said, you'll live." He produces a bottle of water – I have no idea where he got it from – and a pill bottle. "Here. All the kit had was Tylenol, which probably won't make a single bit of difference to the pain, but what the hell. Take the max dose, see if it works."

The pills are bitter, but the water goes down beautifully. I shift on the couch, trying to find a position that doesn't make my shoulder scream.

"That was quite a performance, Ms Frost," Tanner says softly. No smile this time.

I don't say anything. I have no idea what to say. On the one hand, I unquestionably saved the senator's life. On the other . . .

"You continue to disobey my orders," Tanner says. "I specifically told you to stay where you were, and once again, you—"

Jonas interrupts. "Actually, it was me who brought us to the roof."

"I'm sorry?"

"I was the one who decided to leave the hotel room. To find the jammer." He clears his throat. "Teagan and the others tried to stop me. She managed to pursue me all the way to the top

floor, and she was telling me to go back to the room up until
the very moment we spotted you on the roof."

Tanner inhales a long breath through her nose. "I see."

Boy. It's nice to have someone else take the bullet, for once.
Ugh. Could there be a worse metaphor at this point?

"That was a grave mistake, Mr Schmidt," Tanner is saying.

"I hardly think—"

"You are a guest in our country – I presume on a business visa? When this is over, you should know that I will
be recommending to immigration services that said visa be
examined closely."

"Is this *really* the time?" I ask.

"And you," says Tanner. "Regardless of how or why you
left the room, that doesn't explain your performance on the
hotel roof. You put everyone in danger."

"Ma'am." Burr says. "I don't think that's a fair assessment of—"

"I was under the impression your ability had vanished. It's
disappointing that you didn't tell me that it had returned,
and that you thought the best way to utilise it was to
wreak havoc."

Maybe the Tylenol really is making a difference, because
suddenly my shoulder isn't bothering me as much. "OK,
number one, fuck you."

"I beg your pardon?"

"Two, it only came back about five minutes before we got
to the roof, and I thought it was normal again. And three,
I was trying to close the safeties on their guns. That's it. It's
something I've done a million times before."

"Then why did you end up—?"

"Going full-tilt boogie? I have no idea. It was like ... " I
lick my lips. "It was like my PK went into overdrive. Like
I was suddenly hooked up to ... I don't know, an F1 car or

something. Where you touch the accelerator a little bit, and you're suddenly going a thousand miles an hour."

"Then you shouldn't have used your ability in the first place."

"*I didn't know it was going to go insane!*"

"You should have stayed hidden. Staff Sergeant Burr and I had the situation under control."

"Ma'am." Burr's voice has changed. I hadn't really noticed until now. There's a core of steel in it, the kind of steel you only get from leading soldiers into battle. For a moment, it doesn't matter that he technically works under Tanner. "If I might speak freely?"

Tanner sighs. Nods. All at once, she looks very tired.

"I understand you and Frost have worked closely together for a while, and you know her better than I do. But she made the right call."

My mouth falls open, just a little. Burr? Defending me? To *Tanner*?

"When Jonas here didn't feel like following orders," he continues, "Frost tried to get him in line. And when she encountered the situation on the roof, she made a solid decision. If I'd been with her, and I had the same information she did, I would have advised her to proceed too."

"Her actions put the senator's life in danger."

"It was already in danger." He shrugs, as if he and his boss are having a casual conversation about the Lakers' chances of going to the Finals this year. "I would also point out that perhaps criticising your employees can wait until the debrief."

Tanner folds her arms. "I'm sorry that you don't think I'm being fair, staff sergeant," she says, not sounding the least bit sorry.

"Ma'am, it isn't about being fair, it's about morale, and what's tactically—"

"The signal jammer was destroyed." No glance over at me, not a hint of acknowledgement that I was the one who did it. "The FBI are here, and the situation will be resolved shortly. All we need to do is wait."

"What about the asset, ma'am?"

"What asset?" I ask.

He doesn't appear to hear me. "Schmidt?"

"I have already told you," Jonas says. "I am a hardware person, not software. I do not spend my time cracking things open."

"Is somebody going to tell me what the fuck you people are talking about?" I say.

"Your friend wants me to decrypt a phone," Jonas says, not looking away from Burr.

"What phone?" If they don't start speaking sense, I swear . . .

"We retrieved a phone from one of the terrorists," Tanner says. She's looking at Burr now, and it's not a friendly look.

"No shit, really? How did you pull that off?"

"We didn't," Jonas says. "It was one of the objects you . . . I mean to say, it was part of what happened. On the roof."

I almost deny it. Just flat out say: that wasn't me. But what's the point?

He holds up the phone, the screen cracked and spider-webbed. It looks like a truck ran over it, but when he hits the power button, the screen flickers to life. The clock reads 15:02.

"So you can't get in?" Burr says.

"For the thousandth time: no."

"Yeah, but we know who can though," I croak.

All three of them turn to look at me.

I snap my fingers – the ones on my right hand, because occasionally, even I can be smart. "Right, sorry, Jonas, I forget you're not actually part of China Shop. We have this woman named Reggie – Regina. You met her once, back during the whole earthquake thing. She's bad-ass when it comes to hacking and stuff."

"Out of the question," Tanner says.

I gape at her. "Seriously?"

"Miss McCormick is no longer part of our operation. She doesn't have her security clearance, and I am not about to—"

"Oh my God." I come very close to shouting the words, dry throat be damned. "I don't give a shit about clearance. I really don't. *Or* whether she's part of the team any more. There are people being held at gunpoint right now, including a United States senator. Do you not think that *maybe* we should be doing everything we can to fuck with the people holding the guns?" I jab a finger at Tanner. "Call her. Grovel, if you have to. But she is going to open that phone."

Moira Tanner looks around her. Burr stares back, impassive. Jonas raises an eyebrow, the phone still clutched in his hand.

Why on earth was I ever scared of this woman?

Ever since she walked into that room in Waco and told me that it was either working under her or ending up on a dissection table, she's terrified me. Sure, I've pushed back over the years, but she's still been this looming presence who could shut my life down at any point. An angry god, in Brooks Brothers tailoring.

And when she's playing politics in Washington, she *is* a god. She can end lives with a word, make decisions that save thousands without her heart rate jumping even a little bit. But it's been a long, long time since she was in the field. She's let that part of her stiffen, petrify, grow hard as old wood. And it means that in a crisis situation, like this one, she is going to end up getting people killed.

"If you don't want to talk to her," I say, "then I'll do it. But one way or another, that call is getting made."

For a moment, Moira Tanner stands completely still, eyes locked on mine. Then she pulls her phone out of her jacket pocket, shoves it at Burr and stalks from the room.

THIRTY-FIVE

Annie

Moving real damn carefully, Annie heads to the open ground-floor window. Crouches next to it, still on edge. She's deep in shadow now, as hidden as she is ever going to be. The Nomex suit lies crumpled behind the bushes. Above her, the window is open, just a little. Scarcely daring to breathe, Annie peaks over the sill.

It's a guest bedroom, as sterile and anonymous as a hotel room. Two neatly made twin beds, a desk, an expensive-looking office chair. Hideous art on the walls, the kind of abstract crap that Reggie, who knows a little about art, would turn her nose up at. The lights are off, the room in shadow, but the door is open. Through it, just visible, is the edge of the couch. A lampshade. The living room – or *a* living room.

Well, what the hell was she expecting to see? An evil lair? Hooded henchmen scuttling around?

For the thousandth time, she hears Reggie in her head, telling her to observe *only*. For the thousandth time, she pushes it away. She still hasn't seen anybody but the staff. If she leaves now, she leaves with precisely nothing. Is she really going to do that? After risking so much already?

"The fuck I am," she mutters.

"Say again?" Nic asks.

"Never mind."

And when you think about it, where she is now is the perfect entry spot. The guest bedroom is hardly what you'd call a high-traffic area. It's spotless, so household staff won't be around to clean anytime soon. At this particular point, there's no reason for anyone to be here. She can get in, get a closer look at the main living area, go from there. As for getting out . . .

One problem at a time.

Moving quickly and quietly, she gets one leg over the sill, then the other. In seconds she's crouched behind one of the beds, listening hard. Still nothing. Without looking, she fumbles her mom's phone out of her pocket. "I'm going to video," she says.

"Got it."

"You can rrrrrr-record it?"

"Yeah yeah, video capture app is up."

Annie holds the phone to her chest as she moves in a crouch towards the door.

The headache hits just as she reaches it. A thunderclap, booming outwards from the base of her skull. It forces her to her knees, head to the floor.

"Annie!" Nic sounds frantic. "Are you OK?"

Amazingly, she manages to stay silent as she rides the head-ache out. It takes a long time, almost a full minute, before it edges back. "Fine," she whispers. "Just . . . I'm f-f-f-f-fine."

The edges of her vision are grey and floaty as she slowly moves to peek out the guest bedroom door. As she thought, it's a living area, and it's absolutely enormous. Bigger than her apartment. Gigantic windows look out over the garden, shafts of sunlight slicing across chocolate brown leather couches, arranged in a horseshoe around an enormous open fireplace. A crystal chandelier hangs from the ceiling, and just at the edge of Annie's view, there's an oak dining table with high back chairs. At one end of the living area is another set of couches, these surrounding a flat-screen TV that must be ten feet on the diagonal.

"Nice spot," Nic says.

"Yeah. Listen, I'm going silent."

Annie raises the phone a little, capturing the room. Still nothing she can use. She didn't come all this way just to film some douchebag's living room, so—

A voice. Close by. Whoever it is starts talking a second or two before they come through the wooden door on the left of the TV area. Annie retreats a little, ducking back into the shadows.

" ... said that wouldn't be a problem." It's Wilcox, on the phone, looking identical to his online photos. He's a short man, oversized blue New Era fitted cap on his head, green polo shirt untucked over cargo shorts. He has the face of an entitled baby, spoiled by the peach fuzz he's clearly trying to sculpt into a manly beard.

His voice is high-pitched, slightly nasal. It makes her think of Nic Delacourt and his broken nose.

Just before the door behind him shuts, she catches sight of what's beyond it: a laptop, open on a desk, bathed in more liquid sunshine.

"I don't understand why I wasn't brought into the loop about this," Wilcox says. He paces back and forth for a minute, listening intently to whoever is on the other end of the line. "Look, the facility can't stay as it is," he says eventually. "You already know what we need here. I shouldn't have to babysit every single aspect of this fucking operation." He glances upwards, to something Annie can't see. "I've already got enough of my own problems. I . . . No, *you* listen. I'm fed up with this shit, OK? Just make it work."

He hangs up, jams the phone into his pocket, then stalks out of sight. A moment later, somewhere Annie can't see, another door slams.

Annie lowers the phone for a moment, looking across to the door Wilcox came out of. For the first time, she might have caught a real break. That's Wilcox's office back there, has to be. And from the way he came out and closed the door behind him, the chances are good that it's empty.

Very slowly, Annie eases her head out of the guest bedroom door. More of the living area reveals itself. A kitchen, just visible beyond the dining room, all gleaming steel and marble surfaces; the kind of space that would make Teagan squeal with delight. To her left, there's an imposing staircase, made of the same hardwood as a dining table. The mezzanine above it is empty, lit from above by skylights.

When she's sure there's no one else around, Annie stands up and heads into the living room. It's a lot messier than she thought it was, with empty beer bottles and half-full whiskey tumblers clustered on glass end-tables.

She pauses at the office door, listening for the telltale, shifting-fabric sounds of someone inside. Nothing.

Inside, there's a lacquered, wooden desk that looks like it came from the captain's cabin of a sailing ship. A second one sits off to one side, covered with memorabilia: photos, trophies, a signed football. An expensive-looking stereo system opposite, with speakers taller than Annie is. In her ear, Nic whistles, long and low.

Behind the desk, the entire back wall is glass. Double doors lead to a wide balcony, dotted with metal chairs, that looks over Hollywood to the west. Annie films it all, stepping around to the other side of the desk.

"Jah just left the property," Nic says. "So far, nobody else in sight."

Which is good. Exiting the property should be a hell of a lot easier than getting in; the gardeners, wherever they are now, were using a ladder earlier to work on the fruit trees. She's pretty sure she can track it down, scale the wall, make her escape.

There's plenty of paperwork on the desk, but nothing that immediately leaps out at her. Building permits, it looks like, a few bank letters, a contract. The laptop sits on the edge of the desk, screen dark. Annie swipes a finger across the touchpad, and it springs to life, showing a login screen.

Annie's breath catches in her throat. The login screen shows a photo, and in that photo . . .

Chloe Jameson.

A younger version, to be sure, but it's definitely her. The resemblance to Teagan is unquestionable.

Unlike Teagan, she's blonde, her long hair pulled back in a ponytail. Wearing a thick North Face jacket and grey scarf, arm around Wilcox. They're both grinning at the camera. Behind them is a mountain of some kind, sticking up from scrubby earth against a blue sky studded with clouds.

"Oh shit," Nic says.

"Got you, bitch," Annie murmurs, raising her phone to film the screen. That truck outside definitely belongs to Chloe and Adam, and if they aren't here now, they definitely were. This is proof. It definitively links Wilcox to Chloe, and even if Chloe vanishes again, he won't. Not easily, anyway. They can bring him in, question him.

She should just take the laptop. Oh, how sweet it would be

to crack it wide open. Bring it back to Reggie. Can she risk that? What will happen if Wilcox raises the alarm? Will Chloe and Adam—?

Voices reach her from the living area. Annie's head snaps up, and she freezes, goes dead still for half a second. Two speakers: male and female, although she can't make out the words.

"I heard something," Nic says. "What's going on?"

Annie moves without thinking. She slips through the glass door, out onto the balcony, closing it gently behind her. There is a section of concrete wall to her left, with just enough space to hide her from anyone in the room. She flattens herself against it, head down, trying not to breathe. Behind her, the voices enter the office. They're closer now, but a gust of wind rolls around Annie, muffling the words.

This isn't good. They can't see her from the office, sure, but if either of them come out onto the balcony, they'll spot her immediately.

The office is technically on the mansion's ground floor – she didn't go up a flight of stairs to get to it – but the building is on a slope, and the balcony she's on is some way above the ground. She peeks over the railing to her left, and immediately regrets it. It's not far, perhaps twelve or thirteen feet to the ground, but it's enough to make her gorge rise. When she's standing on solid footing, heights of that nature aren't a problem. But having to climb over the edge, somehow figure out how to drop down . . .

Wilcox's muffled voice reaches her. " . . . can't go down there. Have you lost your mind?"

There's no question who the second speaker is. Annie knows that voice. The last time she heard it, she was in a coma, completely helpless.

"We should have heard something by now," Chloe Jameson says. "It's taking too long."

All Annie can do is hope like hell that Chloe doesn't see her body heat. Maybe, just maybe, the concrete wall will be enough to block it. Not that she has a choice; for the first time, she regrets ditching the Nomex suit. She should have stuck it out, lived with the heat.

"So what, you're just gonna go down there?" Wilcox says. "Just barge into the Del Rio in the middle of all that? Even if you had your brother as backup, you'd get cut to pieces."

The Del Rio? That ridiculous hotel on the hilltop? The one Annie saw from the ridgeline? Why the hell does Chloe want to go there?

"I should have told her." Chloe sounds as if she's talking to herself more than Wilcox. "I thought if I could get her out of that hospital, I could . . . I should have just told her straight out. I thought, if I could get her away . . ."

"You should never have made contact in the first place. You risked everything."

"You think I don't know that?" Chloe snaps. "Goddammit, she should be here with me. I should never have let her get dragged into that conference. It should never have gotten that far."

She. Annie's eyes widen. Is she talking about Teagan? Is she at the Del Rio Hotel? What in God's name for? In her ear, Nic is silent, listening.

Wilcox cuts in. "The whole thing was your idea, from the beginning. *You* laid it all out. If you'd just stuck to it, we'd be fine."

"Excuse me?"

"The risk is too—"

"If you were scared of risk, you should never have gotten involved. I've been completely straight with you, at every step of the process."

"Except when you decide to throw the plan out the window so you can *maybe* bring your sister over to your side, which was never going to happen. I just think you're opening yourself up to—"

"To what?" She laughs, a surprisingly delicate sound, like a fine, thin crystal champagne flute one doesn't dare touch. "You act like a group of operators is about to bust through your office window."

"They *know* about us."

"They know nothing. Fragments. They are fumbling in the dark, trying to deal with something they've never encountered before."

"Are you fucking with me? Chloe, this *School* of yours is now on every federal radar. And for what? For what? All that work, all that experimentation, and you got, what, four kids?"

"More than we need." Chloe's voice has gone very cold.

"And one of them won't help you! This Leo kid *hates* you, or did you forget that? How are you going to power your little project without him? Because you're sure as hell not going to hook it up to the National Grid."

"He'll come round. In any case, the School doesn't exist any more. You know that."

"Please. Just because you've taken the lab down doesn't mean it doesn't exist. Don't fuck with me, Chloe. Without me, you got nothing."

"If you think—" Abruptly, Chloe stops talking.

"That's not what I'm—" Wilcox goes silent too.

Annie holds her breath. They can't have spotted her, there's no way they can see her from inside. Did she leave evidence? A dirty footprint or something?

She shivers, the wind suddenly cold against her skin. The only way out is over that balcony railing, and even the thought of it makes her want to retch. She won't be able to climb down slowly and carefully; she'll have to jump. And if she lands wrong, if she twists an ankle . . .

The shivering isn't stopping. Her whole body is starting to shake, and her fingers and toes are going numb. She looks down at her hands, uncomprehending. Her skin is pale, as if the blood is draining away. *What the hell?*

"Annie," Nic murmurs. "Are they still there?"

Her ears burn, her legs starting to turn to jelly. She clutches herself, hugging her chest tight, unable to stop the movement. Is this some side effect from the coma? Did the lightning strike throw her internal temperature gauge out of whack? But why is it happening now?

"Annie?"

She has to jump. There's no choice. But as she turns, her legs give way underneath her. The railing slides away from her in slow motion. She lunges, the tips of her fingers brushing it, and feels nothing. Her entire body is shaking uncontrollably now, drowsiness tugging at the back of her eyes, the urge to go to sleep almost unbearable.

Move. Run!

But she can't. Desperately, she tries to speak. Tries to tell Nic to get out of there.

But she's lost all control. Even her thoughts are sluggish now. *"Annie!"*

Footsteps. Slow and casual. And then a face, swimming into view above hers.

"You." Chloe Jameson sounds almost disappointed. The word seems to stretch and elongate, filling Annie's ears like water. The water breaches the inside of her head, pulling her under.

THIRTY-SIX

Teagan

"Hello?" Reggie says. "Moira?"

"Think shorter, and better-looking," I say.

Silence.

"Oh come on. It's not that ha—"

"*Teagan!*"

"Miss me?" I was a little worried that the pain would make it hard to hold a conversation. But hearing Reggie's voice, that sing-song Louisiana accent, is better than any painkiller.

"Teagan, where are on earth are you folks? Nobody was answering at the office, and Africa—"

"I'll give you the short version."

"You're hurt." It's not a question. Goddammit. She must have heard it in my voice.

"It's nothing."

"Honey, you have a knack for injuring yourself. Don't you *it's nothing* me."

"... Gunshot grazed my shoulder. I'll live, I promise."

"*Grazed* your shoulder?"

"Fine, I got shot, and it hurts like hell. Happy?"

"Ecstatic. At least you don't sound like you're bleeding to death."

"We found a first aid kit. And Burr's here. He knows his way around gunshot wounds."

The man in question flips me a lazy salute. I surprise myself by smiling back.

Quietly, Reggie says, "How bad is it? Really?"

"Dug a chunk out my shoulder. It sucks, but it'll heal. Besides, chicks dig scars."

"This chick doesn't. Are you safe? Are you—?"

"I'm safe. I'm here with Tanner and Burr ... wait, I mentioned him already didn't I? And Jonas Schmidt's here, too."

"Schmidt?" For the first time, she sounds genuinely confused. "The German guy? The one who we—?"

"Bingo. And listen, Reggie, we don't have a lot of time here. We need your help."

As quickly as I can, I explain what's happened in the past few hours. Tell her what we want to do. When I finish, there's crackly silence for a few seconds. Then she says: "Is this you asking, or is it Moira?"

"Are you kidding?" I look over at the door, which is slightly ajar, Tanner just visible beyond. I can't tell if she's listening in or not. "I basically had to throw something at her to get the phone. You know what she's like."

A mirthless laugh. "Yes, I suppose I do."

I'm about to say something when there's another voice on Reggie's end of the phone, someone in the same room as her. "Regina, who you calling?"

"It's Teagan," Reggie says, her voice muffled, as if turning away from the phone.

"Teagan? My Annie's friend? The one who likes to cook?"

"Reggie," I ask. "Who is that?"

"Doesn't matter. Now listen—"

"Is that Annie's mom? Where are you?"

"We're in Watts."

"Watts . . . oh my God." I sit up before I can remind myself not to, sending another jagged stab of pain through my shoulder. "Reggie, did something happen to Annie? Did the hospital call?"

"Annie's OK. She woke up this morning, about eight-thirty or so."

"She *what*?"

The whole room feels like it tilts on its axis. Like I'm about to slide right off the couch. I clutch the phone with both hands, words spilling out of me, urgent, blurring into each other. "Jesus, fuck, is she OK? Was there any damage? I mean, of course there was, but was it permanent? Can she speak? Is she still under, like, observation? Reggie, if—"

"Hey." She says it softly, almost kindly, and it brings me to a halt faster than any shout would have. "She's conscious. She's talking. Walking, even. And she's lucid. It's unusual, but not unheard of. We don't know if there's any permanent damage, but she checked herself out of the hospital this morning."

"Well shit, can I talk to her? Is she there?"

Talking to Annie right now would be amazing. Even with everything we said to each other before she landed in hospital. Just to know that she's OK . . .

Something tugs at the edge of my mind – something Reggie just said that's important. Before I can figure out what it is, she says, "Annie's not here right now."

"Well, where is she?"

Reggie takes a deep breath, harsh over the compressed phone line. "Don't worry about it."

"Yes, because that's guaranteed to make me completely relax and never think about this again. Come on."

"She ... she went looking for the people who took Leo. Your, uh ... your brother and sister."

I'm clutching the phone so hard that my fingers hurt. "Please tell me that's a joke."

"'Fraid not."

"And you *let her*? Don't you understand what these people can do? And after she just got out the hospital?"

Annie's mom says something ugly sounding, which Reggie ignores. "The Great Wall of China couldn't have stopped her. I've never seen her like this. She's ... not herself."

"Have you heard from her, at least? Since she left?"

Reggie clears her throat. "Not for a while now."

I close my eyes.

In a way, it would have been better not to know. It would have been better if I never had cause to call Reggie. Because thinking about Annie chasing after Chloe and Adam, trying to stop them, is no fun at all.

She's smart. She can take care of herself. But can she? The last time she tangled with somebody who had abilities, she ended up getting struck by lightning, blasted into a coma. You can't fight Adam and Chloe with street smarts. An extensive contact list is not going to help you. And the fact that Reggie can't get hold of her ...

At that moment, it's Jonas I happened to be looking at. He nods gently, as if he understands what Reggie and I are talking about, despite only hearing one side of it. "There's nothing you can do now," he says quietly.

I swallow hard, and nod. "OK, Reggie, um. We need you to ... to get into this phone for us."

"Sure, but I can't access it unless there's a computer nearby, one already connected to a local network. If—"

"Funny you should say that." I glance over at the office desk, the old-school MacBook on top of it.

She picks up what I'm putting down. "Do you have access to it? Is it password-protected?"

"Dunno. Burr, Can you boot up the—?"

"On it," he says, stepping around Jonas and popping open the laptop lid. I'm so prepared for a password screen that when one doesn't appear, it actually takes me a second or two to process it.

"Well?" Reggie says.

"Um, yep. No problem. We are definitely in."

"It's porn isn't it?"

"So much porn." I glance at the poster on the ceiling. I should definitely have seen that one coming. And I should definitely not use the word *coming* again today.

Burr tilts his head. "One of the better sites, actually. Motherfucker's got good taste."

"Thanks, Kyle. I could have gone the rest of my life without hearing that."

"OK," says Reggie in my ear. "So what I'm going to need you to do is hook the phone up to the laptop."

"Hold on. How do we connect the phone to the laptop? Would Bluetooth—?"

"Not for what I need to do. Use a cable."

"We don't have a cable."

"Sure we do." Burr digs in his jacket pocket, frowns, digs deeper. His face lights up, and he yanks out a short phone charging cable. "Assuming it's USB-C . . ." he mutters, picking up the phone.

I close my eyes. Surely the universe can't be so cruel as to have this ruined because Burr packed the wrong charging cable this morning.

"Ha! Got you."

He's slotted the cable. It's the right one.

"Reggie," I say. "I love you. You know that right? I love you. And not just because you—"

"I know, honey." A soft chuckle. "Love you too. Now let's get to work."

THIRTY-SEVEN

Annie

Zip ties, securing her wrists to the back of the chair. Two more at her ankles, one to each wooden leg. Simple, but effective.

Annie's neck and shoulders and hips ache. She is desperately thirsty, utterly exhausted. Her head hangs, her breath coming in shallow gulps. Her side is a raging forest fire.

She's stopped shivering. That's something at least, although it's going to be a long time before she can feel her fingers again. Her hands are numb blocks of lead at the ends of her bound arms.

She is vaguely aware of where they've put her. She is not in a cellar somewhere, or an abandoned warehouse. She's in a garden shed. A big one to be fair, a couple of hundred square feet at least, but still a garden shed.

Under better circumstances, it might be funny.

Late afternoon sunlight arcs through the high, grimy windows, illuminating walls neatly lined with hanging tools. Shears and shovels and secateurs. Lawnmowers and sacks of fertiliser.

They must have sent the garden crew home. Somehow, Annie doubts their loyalty to their scumbag boss would include ignoring a prisoner in their shed. It's impossible to tell how long she's been in here. The sunlight coming through the windows hints at late afternoon, but she can't be sure. Her body is a wasteland of aches and pains. Every so often, she gives a weak cough, like an invalid.

At some point, she looks up, and Chloe is standing in front of her.

The woman is dressed simply, in jeans and a sleeveless, black polo-necked sweater, anonymous running shoes on her feet. Bare, stick-thin arms. Blonde hair pulled back in a neat ponytail. A woman who has utterly wrecked Los Angeles, hit it with earthquakes and lightning strikes, caused the deaths of however many thousands of people. And yet she looks like a law school sophomore on her way to a lecture on torts.

For a moment, Annie doubts herself: could a woman this young have done all that? But then the thought hardens, calcifies, and with it comes a welcome burst of anger. She opens her mouth, tries to speak, but her numb tongue won't respond.

Chloe stands casually, left hand on her hip, studying Annie. "Careful. You don't have hypothermia or anything, but you're going to be feeling it for a while."

"Y . . . you . . . "

"You're lucky, in a way. It takes a lot for me to change someone's body temperature, and I can't hold it for very long. I've got stronger over the years, but I'm still a work in progress." She gives Annie a small, patient smile. "I've gotten so used to tuning out the body heat of others . . . guess my sister is probably the same. You can't let all those stimuli in, or you'll lose your mind. You learn to selectively pay attention." A wince. "Guess that's why I didn't notice you at first. Well, that and where you were hiding. It's harder for me to sense heat if there's something in the way."

Chloe looks around, as if she's never been in here before – which, to be fair, she probably hasn't. She wanders over to a stack of fertiliser bags, leans against them.

"I'm impressed, I'll admit," she says. "Not a lot of people could come out of a coma and do what you did. My sister's made some interesting friends."

"Ffff . . . fuck. *You.*"

Her earpiece is gone. Shit – *Nic.* They don't have him too, do they? Annie is desperate to know, but she doesn't dare ask. If they haven't found him, the last thing she wants to do is alert them to his presence.

Chloe looks away, then back at Annie, piercing blue eyes boring into her. And the most amazing, incredible thing happens.

Annie stops hurting.

The electric bolts running up and down her arms slow, then stop. The headache clawing its way through her brain fades to nothing. And her side . . . the tightness is still there, the burned skin parched and dry. But the pain has almost vanished.

Her mouth falls open. It's a long time before she speaks, and when she does, she can't believe how much strength has come back into her voice. "How did you do that?"

There's a sheen of sweat on Chloe's brow that wasn't there before, but her demeanour hasn't changed. She gives a small shrug. "I never used to be able to do it. The older we get – people like me and my brother, my sister – the more our powers evolve. I can raise and lower body temperature, and somewhere along the way, I figured out I could control nerve signals. Up to a point, anyway." Another one of those small, self-satisfied smiles.

Annie's amazement has faded away, replaced with cold fear. She tries not to let her voice shake. "And let me guess: if

I don't answer your questions, you turn all those nerves back on. Overcharge them. Make me scream."

For the first time, Chloe looks angry. Her face tightens, hollows forming in her cheeks.

"This ain't the first time I've been in a chair like this, bitch. I had MS-13 pull me off the streets, work me over some. Maybe you don't know them Salvadoreans, but they don't play."

"And yet, you don't remember the pain, do you? You know you were hurt, you can see the evidence in your body, but you can't remember what you went through. It's a self-defence mechanism. Your mind simply won't let you relive it." Chloe looks away. "But when you *cause* pain, when you see someone suffering, and it's because of something you're doing at that moment, you never forget. The scars that leaves are far worse than anything you can imagine."

"Seriously? You were the one who sent a little psychopath to set off a bunch of earthquakes here. Everybody who died is on you. All that pain? On *you*." The hatred that seeps into her voice gives her strength. "The kid you sent? He killed my ... my Paul. One of the only people who ever made sense to me. You wanna talk about pain? You don't know the first goddamn thing."

"It was necessary," Chloe says simply.

"*Necessary?*"

"Perhaps not this Paul person specifically, and I am truly for your loss, by the way. I am. But yes: necessary. The earthquakes were the only way. I simply could not afford the government any opportunity to pay attention to what I'm doing. I needed them distracted, and that was the most efficient way. If there had been another option, one which didn't involve anybody dying, I would have taken it. There simply wasn't." She begins to pace, slowly and deliberately. Moving with a dancer's grace. "I don't expect you to understand that."

"Talk all you want, bitch. Make yourself feel better. I know how this goes. You'll start asking me questions, and when I don't give you the answers you want, you'll hurt me. That shit never works, by the way." Voicing it like that makes it real. Annie clenches her fists behind her back, trying to stop them shaking. *Here we go.*

"You haven't heard a single thing I've said, have you?" Chloe stops pacing, crouches down in front of Annie, studying her. "I don't like to cause unnecessary pain. And right now, it's not necessary for you to suffer. Physically, at least. In fact, physical pain might get in the way."

"Get in the way of . . . what?"

Chloe continues speaking as if Annie hadn't. "You think I came down here to explain myself to you? Tell you my plans? I came down here to minimise your suffering. You should be thanking me."

"Kiss my ass. Where's Teagan? What's happening at the Del Rio?"

"Hm. I guess you heard that." Chloe sighs. "Just a bad idea that I should never have been a part of. Not that it matters. Chances are, Teagan is fine – she always did have a knack for survival. For now, let's talk about *you*." She raises her voice. "Adam, will you come in here please?"

A beat, and then Teagan's brother enters the room.

Chloe's twin is enormous, well over six feet, with mountainous shoulders. Even with the scraggly beard, Annie can see the resemblance. The last time Annie saw him, his hair hung around his face in greasy, unkempt strands; this time, the strands are tied back in a ponytail, like his sister.

Teagan has told Annie about her brother before. It was him who killed their parents, burned down their ranch. He was genetically engineered to never need sleep, and it drove him utterly insane. Even if Annie didn't know these things, it only takes one look into Adam's eyes to understand how far gone he is. His eyes aren't empty, like those of an asylum patient. Instead, they hide a horrid, burning intensity, a bright, dancing spark of madness. He towers over her, gazing down, not moving a muscle.

Adam's powers have evolved, just like his siblings. He's gained the ability to project visions into his victims' minds, visions pulled straight from their worst nightmares. Annie got hit with a taste of this before, when she first encountered him on the LA River with Teagan and Nic. He made her see Teagan dead, body sprawled across the cracked concrete. Even now, seeing him again brings a ghost of the vision back, turns her blood to icy slush in her veins.

All the same, she finds her voice. "So that's how it is. That's how you're wiggling out of this. You all up on your high horse because you're not causing me actual pain, but you're gonna turn your psycho brother loose on me anyway. Make me see things."

She laughs. At the back of her mind, she is aware that she's not just laughing at Chloe; she's laughing because if she doesn't, she'll start screaming. "You're stupider than I thought. Torture's torture, no matter what you use. And by the time you finish checking whether my info is accurate, I'll have either gotten out of here, or Tanner is gonna roll up in a Black Hawk helicopter to smoke your ass."

"Oh, I'm not going to ask questions yet," Chloe says. "You're right about torture; it never really produces the desired result. But I think you'll find that my brother has a way of . . . clarifying things."

"Yeah, we've met," Annie spits. She tries to make herself meet Adam's eyes again, can't do it. "If that's the best you've got, you'll be waiting a long time for those answers."

Adam shifts in place, ever so slightly. It's a tiny movement, barely noticeable, but Chloe's head snaps towards her brother. "Rhetoric. Parallel. Window. Prospect." Her voice is urgent. "Triangle. Altitude. Zigzag. Zigzag. Zigzag."

Adam stills.

"Trigger words," Annie says. "Cute trick. You know that kid Leo? The one your brother chased us up and down the LA River for?" She jerks her chin at Adam. "He called him the Zigzag Man."

Another half-smile from Chloe. "Leo always did have a big imagination."

"Fuck you. If you've hurt him . . ."

"He's fine. Sedated, ready for transport." Something in her expression changes, a look of what might be disappointment creeping in. "You really didn't listen when I talked about necessary pain. You think I would harm a child? A little boy? God. I just don't want him hurting *us*, that's all."

"Good for you."

"When you met my brother on the LA River, you were exposed to his ability for a very short period of time. But the longer you spend in his world, the harder it gets to leave."

The zip ties behind Annie's back won't give, not even an inch. She flexes her ankles, desperate. If she can get one of them loose, then maybe . . .

"After a while, you'll tell us everything we want to know. You simply won't have a choice. And the longer he works on you, the more suggestible you'll become. You'll be able to return to Teagan and Tanner and your little outfit, and then you can start telling us what they're doing."

"The fuck I will."

"It's not a pleasant process, I'm afraid. I wish there was an alternative, but as I said, I never cause pain unnecessarily."

A sudden flash of inspiration. "Rhetoric. Parallel. Window! Prospect! Uh ... Altitude. Zigzag. Zigzag! Zigzag!"

This time, Chloe's smile is very slightly mocking. "It doesn't quite work like that, I'm afraid. The trigger words have to be in *my* voice. And anyway, you missed one."

With that, she turns, and heads for the door. Just before she gets there, she turns back. "I'm sorry you have to go through this. If you'd stayed away, it would never have happened."

Then she's gone, leaving Annie alone with the monster.

THIRTY-EIGHT

Teagan

As Burr starts work at the computer, I let my head sink back into the couch cushion. A wave of profound exhaustion sweeps over me. It's all I can do not to go to sleep right there.

My PK is still present, kind of, the shapes and locations of objects clear in my mind. This might be the first time I'm actually scared of it. I don't dare use it, not when it could cause the entire environment to explode around me.

"So. You can move things without touching them, hm?"

I open one eye. Jonas is crouched down next to me.

"I'd heard of you, of course," he says. With an effort, he turns himself around until he's sitting on the floor, leaning against the couch, talking to me over his shoulder. "I had heard rumours about the facility in Texas. And then when the video from your storm drains here came out, I knew it had something to do with that. But I never imagined . . . I never thought it would be *you*."

"Surprise."

"I have so many questions. Are you able to—?"

"Yeah, Jonas? I'm not really in the mood."

"But—"

"Seriously."

He nods. "I'm sorry. You're right. There are times and places. Do you need anything? Is there anything I can get you now?"

"Steak sandwich, curly fries, choc shake. Big-ass bubble bath."

He raises his eyes to the ceiling. "Well, we are in a luxury hotel. When this is all over, perhaps we should get a room. I mean, if you want to. And I don't mean getting a room as in ... well, you know. Getting a room. I mean just for the sandwich. And so you can have that bath. When you—"

"You should quit while you're ahead."

"*Ja.*"

It's weird. Even a few hours ago, this kind of innuendo would have bought a blush to my face, sending heat surging through my cheeks. Now, it barely bumps the needle. I just don't have the energy to think about my feelings for Jonas right now.

I can't help but picture Nic. God, I hope he's okay. At the very least, he's probably somewhere safe. Recuperating from his broken nose, feet up, Netflix on. Very far away from any and all China Shop bullshit.

"It was a good idea, calling your friend. Reggie, I think." Jonas moves his legs underneath him to sit cross-legged. I kind of want him to leave me alone, while at the same time hoping that he won't. "If she is as good as you say she is, we should at least be able to gain some extra information."

"Assuming our fearless leader doesn't stick her nose in," I mutter.

He glances towards the door. "Perhaps you should not be so quick to judge her."

"*I* shouldn't be so quick to judge *her*?"

"She does not have an easy position. Not everything she decides to do will be popular."

"You sound like Africa. He's got a real hard-on for Tanner. In a non-porno way, I mean." Is that even true any more? If anything, Africa is just as frustrated at what Tanner is doing. Frustrated at the decisions she's made since she arrived in LA.

"Without her," he says, "we would never have found the passage. We would not be in the safe position we are in now."

"Yeah, well, without her, I wouldn't even be in this hotel."

"How many jobs have you had, Teagan?"

The abrupt change of direction rattles me a little. "Just this one. Well, technically I work as a removals person too. That's our legit cover."

"But you've never been in a leadership role before?"

"If you are about to say *you can't possibly understand*, I'm going to slap you."

"You know," he says, after a few beats, "when I first founded my company, I tried to do everything. I was working out of a basement in Bern with three employees, and I insisted on being involved in every single thing we did. I did not understand that there were some things that were better left to others. It ended up almost bankrupting the company, and I lost all three of those original employees."

"What's your point?"

"My name was on the door, so it was all on me. But I did not understand until it was too late that this was no way to run a business."

"Still not hearing a point here. Unless it's *don't act like a dick, or your co-workers will hate you?*"

"True. But not quite the point I'm making. When the last of my employees left, I could not at first understand how I had gone so wrong. My product was good. The demand was there. Of course, I had some idea of how I had ... confused things by getting involved in every aspect of the business, but I had no idea *why*. What was the reason behind my actions?"

He looks at me, as if expecting me to provide the answer. It's a very irritating look, and I'm about to tell him so when he says, "Pride."

"Oh, my dude. You have got this ass backwards. Tanner is a lot of things, but she's not proud of China Shop. She spends half her time telling us how we fucked up."

"That is not what I mean. She is proud of having built something. Something of her own."

He sighs. "I know a little of what it is like to work in the halls of power, as she does. I have not done it myself, but I am in those circles. And everywhere, it is the same. Everything a compromise, everything a negotiation. You have to scrap and claw for every single inch of ground."

His words come fast, like he's been waiting to get this out for a long time. "She controls your team. It belongs to her. It is the most she can hope for because, let us be frank, she is never going to hold high public office. No one is going to elect her president. So she has built this house for herself, brick by brick, and she will fight hard to make sure that no one takes it away. That's the pride I am talking about.

"You wish to know why she is so harsh with you? Why she cannot tolerate insubordination? Because it threatens the one thing she values above all else. And when that threat comes from the people who live inside the house she has built, she is even less able to tolerate it."

He scratches the back of his neck, a scratch that turns to a distracted rubbing, as if there's an itch he can't quite get to. "I feel for her. It is a lonely place to be in."

"Nice speech."

He raises an eyebrow. "*Danke.*"

"But there's one thing you haven't thought of."

"And what is that?"

"The house she built is kind of janky. And the people who live in it – me and Africa and Reggie and Annie – we have to hold it up. We have to make all these little repairs and unclog the toilets and figure out how the fuse box works."

"I think you may be taking my metaphor a little too far."

"You started it. The point is, we're the ones putting in the work, and all she's doing is yelling at us because she thinks she knows better. She built the house, but she doesn't have to live in it – we do. We know it way better than she does, and yet she's still wandering around getting pissed at us. It's kind of hard to care about her pride when I'm trying to keep the roof from falling in."

The nerves in my shoulder choose that moment to really wake up. "And when I'm the one lying here with a fricking bullet lodged in me."

"Actually, the bullet passed straight thr—"

"You know what I mean."

At the desk, Burr makes a triumphant noise. He's been working hard on the PC, not paying attention to us, and he's obviously gotten somewhere. White text on a black background fills the screen, too small for me to read. I can just hear Reggie's voice over the phone, her words inaudible. That makes me even more annoyed at Jonas's little speech about pride and houses. It's really hard to sympathise with Tanner's wounded pride when someone as awesome as Reggie gets shoved out the front door into the cold.

"All I'm saying is," Jonas continues, "I understand why her management style and her orders can sometimes be a little . . . what is the word? Rigid. I sometimes move in similar circles to the ones she moves in, and—"

"Jonas, could we just stop? Please? I really don't wanna hear about the *circles* you move in. I don't care about rich people stuff right now."

It's hard not to remember how Jonas has been acting this whole time. On the one hand, I feel bad about Gerhard, his bodyguard – that must have hurt. But so many little moments keep popping up. The way he spoke to Africa, how he looked me up and down later on, almost automatically.

You know what these things remind me of, actually? How the crowd in the lobby looked at me, before the shit hit the fan in the ballroom. It's the way Phan Duc Hong looked at me in the parking garage. A kind of knee-jerk contempt.

And there's more. The way he spoke to Kanehara when she was just doing her job – I might have been mad at the time, but if I was a journalist, I would have kept filming too. And of course, it's impossible not to think of how he charged out of the suite to go find the jammer, ignoring the rest of us, acting like he was the only one who could save the damn day.

Jonas is the last person I expected to look at people like that. He's done so much good – during the earthquake, he put his life on the line to help others. When he talks to you, one-on-one, it really seems like he listens. But he's *still a billionaire*. Someone who is wired differently to everyone else, and not in a good way. When he's prevented from doing exactly what he wants to do – like saving the day – it comes out, and it comes out bad. Maybe he was like this the whole time; maybe my little crush blinded me to what was happening.

Jonas isn't a bad guy. I think he genuinely wants to help people, and do the right thing. But he does *not* like being told no.

I close my eyes, shifting my position for the millionth time. Maybe I can distract myself. *Finely dice an onion and sauté. Cube*

*two pounds of chuck, toss in flour, then sear. Deglaze pan with red
wine, and add two cans of tomatoes.*

"I did not start out rich," he says. "I know more than anyone
what it's like to be outside."

I open one eye. "Want to give that sentence another try?"

He has the good grace to wince. "I take your point. But
what I am trying to say is, I know what it is like to have almost
nothing. And I would do anything to stop myself from going
back to that."

"Stop dancing around it. Just say what you mean."

"I'm almost bankrupt, Teagan."

Said as casually as a remark on the weather.

"Um," I say. "No, you're not."

"Sadly, that isn't true. My reserves of capital are almost
exhausted."

"But you're ..." I want to say, *you're Jonas Schmidt.
International billionaire playboy and philanthropist. Instagram hottie.
The man who moves further and shakes harder than anyone else.* It's
a good thing those thoughts stay in my head, because they
would be kind of stupid when said out loud.

He doesn't appear to hear me. "It's been happening for some
time. Several ventures I invested heavily in did not pan out.
They did not even make it to the proof-of-concept stage. My
investments have performed poorly. What is the expression in
America? This –" He gestures above him, to the hotel. " – was
my last throw of the dice."

"... OK?"

"I have a new product, with military applications. Advanced
control systems for fighter aircraft. I was planning to talk to
as many people as possible during the conference, Phan Duc
Hong among them. If I could just make a few contacts, get
one or two commitments ..."

When is a hostage situation not a hostage situation?

That same thought, playing at the edge of my mind.

"It was not supposed to turn out like this." Jonas's voice turns dark. "I had my whole plan for this conference mapped out. But then these bastards. They ruined it all."

That must be why he lost it in Phan's suite. Why he smashed that glass.

"I have so much work to do," he continues. "So many things left unfinished. Projects that could truly benefit humanity. And I cannot do it if I no longer have the resources. I cannot do it if I have nothing."

"Just your stunning good looks, your private jet and your massive network of contacts."

"I had to sell the jet."

"What?"

"We flew commercial."

"I liked that jet."

"*Ja.* So did I."

He wipes his mouth with the back of his hand, looks away. "I am . . . I'm sorry for not listening to you, and your friend Africa. When you told me that we needed to stay in the hotel room. I just . . . these *Arschlöcher Terroristen.*"

" . . . Asshole terrorists?"

He makes a noise that might be a distant cousin of a laugh. "*Ja.* Exactly. I was so angry. I was not myself, and for that I apologise."

But how true is that? This isn't just some new quirk of his personality that popped up today. Again, that thought: has he always been like this?

"It's OK," I say, even though it kind of isn't. "Just—"

Burr slaps the table, making me jump. "*Yes,*" he snarls.

"Are we in?" Jonas asks.

"Kind of. Almost. I'm not really sure." He still has the phone to his ear, and pauses as Reggie asks him something. "Yeah, I see it. No, it's there, I'm telling you. It worked this time." He picks up the phone he's trying to unlock, frowning down at it. "Yeah, OK. We have to wait for that to run, I guess."

As Reggie speaks in his ear, he rolls his eyes at us, then makes a talking motion with his hand, tapping his thumb against the tips of his fingers.

"Let it go," Jonas murmurs, when he sees me about to get angry.

"I guess. And hey, who cares about the jet when you got the girl, right?"

"The girl? Which girl?"

"The reporter, dumbass. Kanehara."

Even now, saying her name causes a little pang of jealousy. It shouldn't. Jonas and Kanehara clearly aren't fans of each other any more . . . and to be honest, I'm not sure I'm a fan of Jonas.

So why am I still jealous? Why does it still hurt thinking about him and Kanehara together?

"Michiko?" Jones shakes his head. "I am sorry, Teagan, it has been a difficult day . . . What exactly are you saying?"

"What do you mean, what am I saying? You got the girl."

"So you keep telling me, but I do not understand what you think Michiko and I—"

"I know you slept with her, dude. You don't have to keep pretending."

He goggles at me. "I did not sleep with her."

"Sure."

"Why do you say these things? Our relationship is strictly professional. She was doing a profile on me. For the *New Yorker*."

"But she . . . "

I want to tell him to stop bullshitting me. But if he is, he's one of the greatest actors I've ever seen. I've completely blindsided him.

"Teagan," he says slowly. "I do not know her that well. I only met her for the first time today. Surely you can't believe that I would . . . that I would *seduce* her?"

"I didn't say you *seduced* her. She was probably hot for you the moment she laid eyes on you. No seduction necessary."

"This is absurd. I don't know why you think these things, but I can assure you—"

And at that moment, the important thing Reggie said, the one that bothered me, suddenly snaps into focus. The thing she said about Annie.

She woke up this morning, about eight-thirty or so.

At eight-thirty this morning, I was being let out of jail by Burr, and Tanner was getting told that she had to spend the entire day babysitting a senator.

At eight-thirty this morning, Tanner still had full communications. Eight-thirty this morning was at least two hours before the jammer in the Del Rio blocked off all calls.

Two hours where Moira Tanner would have been able to get an update on Annie's condition.

"Teagan, what is it?" Jonas asks.

I don't answer, replaying those two hours in my head. The office. The drive to the hotel. The senator's suite. And didn't . . . didn't Tanner get a phone call while we were in there? She didn't say who it was, but . . .

She would have left some sort of order with the hospital to call her if Annie woke up. She must have done. Which means this whole time, she knew. She knew my friend was awake, that she was OK, and she didn't tell me.

"Son of a bitch," I murmur.

"Teagan—"

"*Tanner!* Get your fucking ass in here now!"

The anger, the *fury* chases away the pain, as well as any respect I might have had for our fearless leader. How dare she? How dare she keep this from me?

Tanner comes back into the room, looking grim. And just as I'm gathering a breath to really unload on her, she snaps at Burr. "Hostiles."

He's instantly alert. "How many?"

"Unknown. I'm hearing footsteps, and voices."

I lie there with my mouth hanging open, the verbal salvo I was about to fire at Tanner stuck in its launch tube. "Shit," I say.

"Is it them?" Jonas asks. "How did they find us?"

Tanner ignores him, looking around the office, her head snapping left and right. I get a feeling I'm thinking the same thing she is: no way out. There is exactly one entrance and exit to this little wank-den, and precisely zero hiding places inside it.

I can hear the voices now, angry and clipped, along with thundering footsteps. Burr catches Tanner's eye, and the look between them tells me all I need to know.

Burr reaches down, scooping up the laptop and the phone. "Coming through," he mutters, lifting the couch cushion my legs are on and shoving the electronics underneath it. I'm so surprised that I barely notice the bolt of pain through my shoulder. I'll admit, I don't really know why he's bothering to hide them, but right now, it doesn't seem important.

He straightens up, and for a second, I know in my bones that every one of us is thinking the same thing: what now?

But as we look at each other, the answer is obvious. There's nothing now. There's nowhere to hide, not even a convenient closet. There is space for maybe one of us under the desk.

OK. This sucks. But I still have my PK, sort of. If I could just . . .

Just what? Shut down their gun safeties again? It'll be like before, with everything going completely haywire, control ripped away from me. Only this time, it's going to happen in an enclosed space. If those guns go off, there's no telling who they might hit.

Tanner picks up on what I'm thinking. She shoots a look at me, gives a quick shake of her head.

Fuck that. There has to be a way. I reach out, sending my PK as far as it will go, only just picking up the approaching hostage-takers. I count six weapons, closing quickly on our position. Maybe sixty feet down the passage. If I activate my PK now, and it goes haywire, we should be able to hunker down.

And . . . now.

But it doesn't happen.

It's not that I can't. I can feel the weapons perfectly, feel the hard edges of the safety catches. But I keep seeing Tanner's little shake of the head.

Fifty feet. Forty.

You know this feels like? This hesitation to use my PK? It's like I've inhaled poison gas, and I have to stab myself in the heart with a giant syringe to live. Yes, exactly like Nicolas Cage in *The Rock*. I know I have to do it, I know I have no choice . . . but all the same, I hesitate. Because that's one mighty big needle.

Thirty feet. Burr raises his weapon. Holy smokestacks, it's going to be a firefight anyway. And we are all going to get shot to pieces.

Jonas gets in front of me, shields me with his body. He's breathing way too fast, his eyes wide. Thundering footsteps now, getting closer to the door. "I saw movement," someone says. "In there."

Do something!

Tanner lowers her weapon. Her shoulders slump, and she says, very quietly, "I'm sorry, everyone."

Then, much louder: "Don't shoot. We're coming out."

The footsteps outside the door stop suddenly. The whole world holds its breath.

"Ma'am," Burr hisses.

"I'm sorry, staff sergeant. It's over."

THIRTY-NINE

Annie

Adam hasn't moved.

It's been five minutes since Chloe left, and he hasn't so much as shifted position. Just stared down at Annie with those wild, livid eyes.

Every muscle in her body is tense, every nerve ending wired. She's already tried the trigger words again, correctly this time, remembering the missing word (*Triangle, it was Triangle*). Adam hasn't budged, and after a couple of attempts, Annie gave up.

Eventually, Adam's silence gets too much. "So . . . are we gonna dance? Or are you just gonna stand there and stare me to death?"

The door behind Adam opens. Chloe, she guesses, returning to check on things.

Only, it isn't Chloe; it's a man. Annie can't get a good look at him, with Adam partially blocking her view.

The man walks towards her slowly. He's tall and lanky, with pipe-cleaner arms and a torso that seems far too small for his legs. Bald on top, middle aged, with a wispy moustache and hangdog eyes surrounded by wrinkles. He wears a faded work shirt, sleeves rolled up, over a dirty white T and jeans. Annie remembers that work shirt.

It was what he was wearing on the day he died.

"*Hola, mi hija,*" her father says.

Adam has vanished. Dimly, Annie is aware that what she's seeing isn't real. But she can't look away from Martin Cruz, standing right there, in front of her, big as life.

"You look well," he says. He always spoke quickly, in a hushed monotone, and that hasn't changed. "You've grown into a very fine woman. I've been watching you, you know, watching you grow up, and the things you have done are amazing."

"You're not real," she croaks.

Annie can't believe the look in his eyes. Paternal, understanding. Almost kind. "Real is what you perceive, *si*? You are in a house with many rooms, and yet you think yours is the only one that exists."

"You're. Not. Real." She twists her body away as much as she can, refusing to look at him.

"You know," he says, "I never meant to hurt your mother."

"Shut up. *Shut up.*"

"I couldn't control it, and every time, afterwards, I say to myself: Martin, what have you done?" He wrings his hands in front of him, as if squeezing out a washcloth. "I would walk and I would walk. I would promise to do better, promise *myself* that I would do better."

Despite herself, Annie looks at him. She doesn't want to, but there's a sick fascination that makes her.

"You could have been great." He holds his hands out to her. "The way you played baseball ... you could have beaten anybody, if you were pushed. But your mother would not let me push you; she would never be quiet and let me guide you the way you needed to be guided. I had to stop her, do you understand? No, I can see that you don't. Even now, even when I finally have a chance to explain myself, a chance you never gave me, you won't listen."

Annie slowly shakes her head. She's surprised to find she's actually disappointed.

"Is that the best you can do?" she says to the room. "For real? You want me to ... " She clears her throat, spits. "You want me to feel bad? You think this is going to drive me insane?"

To her father: "Let's get one thing straight here, *pendejo*. You beat my mom. You broke her arm, smashed her head against the wall. She was in hospital for a week. And you want to come tell me that it was because she didn't agree with the way you coached me for fucking *baseball*?"

"Annie ... "

"All the pain you caused, everything you did, and that's your excuse? That Mom didn't agree with how you wanted to train me? That's pathetic. *You're* pathetic. You hit her because you wanted to hit her, because you were a shitty husband and a worse dad and you were a drunk. Get the fuck out of my face with your excuses. And you," she says, addressing the room, and the hulking monster she can no longer see. "Try harder, asshole."

His paternal smile hasn't changed. Annie would like more than anything to wipe it off his face, preferably with a punch of her own. "Maybe I was all those things. But tell me this: did I deserve to die?"

Dust motes dance in the afternoon light.

"Did I deserve to have my own daughter kill me?"

Annie starts to shake her head, as if she's about to deny it. Then all at once, she stops. Takes a long, hard look at the thing pretending to be her father.

"No point denying it, is there?" she says. Speaking to Adam, even though she can't see him. "You looked inside my head, so you know already. What, you assume I never thought about this? You think I didn't spend every single day after it happened beating myself up? That I just boxed this up and put it away and never dealt with it?" Her voice turns venomous. "You pull this out of my head to break me? You're seeing it for the first time. I've lived with it for *years*."

"I just want to know why," her father says.

"You know why." This time, she's not sure if she is talking to Adam, or her father.

He doesn't reply. Just waits.

"You deserved to be in prison," she says slowly. "But Mom wouldn't report you, and the cops wouldn't listen to me. So I knew what had to be done. And yeah, I could have done it myself. But I was ten. I was a lot smaller than you, and I couldn't risk fucking it up."

"So you asked your friends." He shakes his head sadly.

It was how she'd first met Marathon. The dealer she ended up working for. He wasn't a boss then; just another foot soldier. Asking for his help terrified Annie. What she didn't know then was that Marathon came from an abusive home, too. One that, by all accounts, was a lot worse than anything Annie had suffered.

So he looked her in the eyes and told her what he was going to do. How he was going to make it look like an accident. He knew how to run a car off the road at just the right spot, make a clean getaway. No witnesses, no collateral damage. All Annie had to do was keep her and her mom out of the car for a while.

And in return? Marathon had smiled when Annie asked what he wanted, and replied, "When you get a little older, you come find me again."

"San Pedro," Martin says, eyes never leaving her. "23 January 2003. You took matters into your own hands." He seems perversely pleased. "Clearly you learned something from me."

"All you gave me were some anger issues, *Martin*. Everything important, I learned from Mom. And you wanna know something? She figured out what I did."

Annie isn't surprised to find that she is crying again, tears tracking down her cheeks. But these tears are welcome. Cleansing. "Because she's smart – a lot smarter than you ever gave her credit for. I don't know how she knew, but she knew."

"That's cold."

"Got it from you, Pops. I thought Mom hated me for it, and I guess part of her did. But by the time we actually talked about it, you'd been gone for years. And you know something? They were good years. Not perfect, but *good*. Mom saw what life was like without you in it. So we got through it, and even though . . . even though it's never been the same between us, it's still better than anything you ever brought to the table."

There's no pleasure to his expression now. Just a blankness, as cold and desolate as the Arctic. "So you're glad that you killed me?"

"What's done is done, and you're nothing but a ghost. Get the fuck outta here."

"But are you *glad* that you killed me?"

It occurs to Annie that Chloe might be recording all of this. An attempt to blackmail her. It's a laughable idea: all she'll have is a one-sided conversation that makes absolutely no sense. And even if it does, even if there are consequences, these people must be stupid if they think she can't wriggle out of them.

No: that's not what's happening here. A blackmail recording is too crude, and there's no way they could have known about this until Adam pulled it out of her head. The simplest explanation is the best: it's an attempt to break her, nothing more, nothing less. And it has failed miserably.

Her dad can't hurt her any more. And if this is the best Adam has to offer, he can't either. So she sucks in a huge gulp of air, and bellows an answer to her father's question.

"*Fuckin' right I am.*"

"Annie?" says a woman's voice.

And all at once, she's back in the China Shop office.

It happens instantly, her father vanishing, the shed too, her restraints, all of it. She's lying on the office couch, body stiff, blinking gritty sleep from her eyes. She's on her side, staring across at Reggie, who is looking at her with something like horror.

"Dozed off," she says, propping herself up on her elbows and rubbing at her face. Christ, was she dreaming all that? She must have been. It's rare that she gets nightmares that vivid, but they do happen. Coming back into the real world always feels like a shock, but it's not unfamiliar.

She's OK. Just a bad dream. "How long was I out?" she says.

It takes Reggie a few seconds to reply. Her eyes never leave Annie. "You were talking in your sleep."

"I ... what?"

Reggie tilts her head to one side, and slightly away, like she's worried Annie is going to strike her. "You killed your father."

Annie's heart starts to beat faster, a skittering beat, like a fluttering moth banging against her ribcage. "What do you mean?"

"You were speaking to him," Reggie says slowly. "Like he was still alive. You said you were glad you killed him."

"It was a dream. That's all." The words are shaky, almost a whisper.

"No, it wasn't." Now a note of anger creeps into Reggie's

voice. "Annie, how could you? How could you do that? Your own father."

Annie pushes herself up to a sitting position, trying to control her breathing. "I didn't."

"You're lying, honey. I always know when you're lying. Did you think we wouldn't find out?"

Annie stands, tottering on shaky, sleep-drugged feet. "Reggie ..."

"*Get away from me.*" Reggie moves her chair backwards. "Africa!"

And all at once, the big man is there. Getting between Annie and Reggie. Huge hands balled into fists. "We trusted you. All of us, we trusted you with our lives, and you think it is OK to kill your own family?"

"That's not what—"

"*Stop lying!*" His voice is so loud that it set her ears ringing. Africa's voice changes, goes low and steady. "I always knew there was something wrong. Something you are not telling us. I think to myself, hey, she has problems, and maybe one day she will tell us, huh? But something like this ..."

Annie's mouth is very dry, the lights in the room way too bright. There's a part of her that insists this isn't real. It's just a dream, like her dad was a dream, like Adam and the mansion and the coma and the lightning strike and all of it was a dream. She can wake up, any time she wants. And yet: this doesn't feel like a dream. This feels as solid and real as a slap to the face. There's no question that she's here, standing in the office. "You don't understand."

"Oh, we understand perfectly," Reggie says from behind Africa. "You thought you could just keep this under wraps, didn't you? Keep it between you and your mother, and everything would be fine."

"Please. I can explain." Annie takes a step towards the two of them, raising her hands.

A piece of broken glass snaps through the air to hover in front of her face.

She stares at its quivering point. "No ..."

"I'm gonna need you to take a step back," Teagan says.

She's off to one side, arms folded. And she's not looking at Annie.

"Teagan. Baby girl, you know me. You *know* me. I would never—"

"But you did, didn't you?" The girl looks up at the ceiling, slowly shaking her head. "You give me all that shit about how I'm your only friend, how I'm the only one who cares, just loading me up with guilt. And the whole time, you're hiding something like this. What kind of fucking friend does that?"

This can't be real. There's no way that those words are coming out of Teagan's mouth. "I was trying to protect my mom."

"Then why keep it a secret at all? Why not tell us?"

"Because she knew how wrong it was," Reggie says.

"Do you think her Army knew?" says Africa. "Her what-what, her *connections?*"

"Nah," Teagan replies. "Or hey, maybe they did. Maybe she used it to scare the ones who wouldn't do what she wanted. Like, 'I killed my own dad, you think I won't kill you if you fuck with me?'"

"He was a monster," Annie says. "He—"

The trashcan comes out of nowhere, flying through the air, spewing bottles and paper and sauce-slicked takeout boxes. Annie ducks. The can crashes against the wall, denting the plaster. The air fills with the stench of decomposing food and cracked styrofoam.

"*My* dad changed my fucking genetic code!" Teagan yells.

"He messed up my whole life before I was even born. You think that would give me the right to have him killed? If he were still around? That's sick. It's disgusting."

This can't be real. There's no way. But deep inside, Annie understands this *is* real. She has screwed up in the worst, most indefensible way possible: talking in her damn sleep.

She wants to shout at them, *scream* at them the truth: that she didn't tell them because she knew this was how they'd react. But that would make it worse. It would confirm to them that she really is a monster. And the thought of Teagan believing that is almost too much to take. She is the kindest person Annie knows, and if *she* thinks . . .

"We were always going to find out," Reggie says. "Did you think this was just going to stay buried for ever?"

"Of course she did."

The voice comes from the door of the office. Slowly, very slowly, Annie raises her head to look.

Paul Marino is exactly how Annie remembers him on the night he died. Same neat button-down shirt, open at the collar. Same gleaming bald head. Same warm, rough hands at his sides. Hands that held her, caressed her, pulled her close.

"No," she tells him. "You died. I know you did."

"You sure that wasn't part of your dream too?" he says.

"It wasn't . . . "

But was it? Isn't that just the kind of thing she would dream up? A dream where the only man she's ever really loved suffers a horrible death? Where she can't save him?

At that moment, the relief she feels is overwhelming. Historic. "Paul," she says, stumbling past Africa and Reggie, pushing past Teagan, arms outstretched.

He holds up a hand, stopping her in her tracks. "I don't think that's a good idea."

Somehow, those seven words are worse than the shard of glass, the thrown trashcan that nearly took her head off. She stands gaping at him, the bright lights searing into her.

He steps aside, jerking his chin at the office door. "You need to leave."

"Paul . . ."

"You're not welcome here," says Reggie from behind her.

"*Yah*," Africa spits.

She can't take her eyes off her lover. "Please talk to me. Please."

"I loved you," Paul tells her. "I don't know if you can even understand that. You were everything to me."

"I still am." She puts a hand on his cheek. "Paul, *listen*."

Gently, almost pityingly, he pushes her hand down. "I won't ask again."

The burning white lights in the ceiling blind her. She opens her mouth, but her words are stuck, frozen solid in her throat. She's going to throw up, the nausea burrowing a hollow in her stomach.

"You deaf?" Teagan snarls from behind her. "Get the fuck out. We don't want you."

The lights in the ceiling are growing, the white glow hanging in the air. The word *baseball* floats through her mind, followed by the whisper in her ear, the whisper she now knows she'll never escape, not ever. *You haven't practised enough.*

"Out. Now."

"Leave!"

"Go, before we call the cops."

"You're not part of this team any more."

"I thought you loved me, Annie."

She starts to scream.

FORTY

Annie

There's something scratchy rubbing against her cheek.

She tries to open her eyes, but dry tears have glued them shut. Her throat is raw razor blades, but somehow she is still screaming. No: not screaming. It's worse than that. It's an animal sound, almost a bark. Rough and ugly. Again and again and again.

Slowly, very slowly, she forces her right eye open.

She is no longer in the China Shop office. The room she's in is a shed, familiar somehow. Shafts of dusty sunlight and dirty gardening tools. She has no idea where the shed is, or why she is here, just that she's been here before.

She's tied to a chair, zip ties cutting into her wrists and ankles. At some point, the chair tipped over, or she tipped it over. She is lying on her side on the grimy floorboards, the wood soaked with her tears and sweat. She is alone. The shed door is very slightly open, and from somewhere in the distance, there are angry shouts.

None of this is real. She's dreaming again, trapped in an endless maze of nightmares, a maze she will never escape. But slowly, she starts to remember. The office, Teagan and Reggie

and Africa and . . . and Paul. They weren't real. They were all
in her head.

A sick dread settles over her. Because with that relief comes
understanding. It's an understanding born deep in the primal
parts of her mind, the parts that sense more than her conscious
world lets on.

There is a part of her that almost snapped in two, like a
bundle of twigs. If she'd stayed in that unreal version of the
China Shop office any longer, if she'd had to look at those
searing lights, hear those voices, then she would never have
come back. And she was close, so very close, maybe seconds
away . . .

He'll be back soon.

Annie thought she knew fear. She had no idea. Because now
she knows what's waiting for her when Adam returns, and he
will return, there's no doubt about that. She has seen what's on
the other side of that particular door, and it's worse than she
could ever have imagined.

She has to escape, and she has to do it now. But she is
so damn tired, her limbs made of lead; she can barely even
lick her lips.

She tenses the muscles in her arms, relaxes them. Does it
again. Hoping for just a tiny bit of give in the zip ties. Twisting
back and forth, and getting precisely nowhere. "Come on, you
stupid bitch," she says. "*Vamonos*, come on, *come on.*"

The door creaks open, a figure entering the shed with the
light behind him, and the last bit of Annie's hope snuffs out.

"Fuck – Annie!"

There's too much light coming in through the door, sil-
houetting the figure as he rushes over, feet pounding on the
boards. But then he gets close, crouches down, and Annie can
finally make out his face.

"N . . . Nic." Annie's voice is barely audible. Her throat is a black wasteland. Somehow, the son of a bitch got inside, he—

No. No, no, no, this isn't happening, not really, she's still locked in Adam's dream world. The Nic Delacourt she's seeing isn't real.

"Are you OK?" His hands hover over Annie, as if he's not sure what to do next. "Are you going to be able to walk? Shit . . . zip ties. Hold on." He springs up from his crouch, stepping around her and out of her line of sight. There is the sound of rummaging, of tools lifted and then dropped, and then he murmurs, "Got you."

Cold metal against the inside of Annie's wrist. A moment after that, and she's free. Her ankles are next, and she slumps over, trembling on the hard floor.

"OK, let's get you up," Nic says, dropping the secateurs he used to cut her bonds. "We don't have a lot of time left."

Annie pulls herself into a foetal position, tucking in her head. Her hands and feet are numb and burning, but the sensation seems to be coming from a very long way away.

"Annie, come on." He tries to get his hands under her armpits, which only makes her curl into herself more.

"You're not real." She's not sure if she says the words, or only thinks them.

The hands under her armpits go still. Nic mutters something that sounds like "Fucking Zigzag Man." He moves around in front of Annie, putting his face next to hers. "That son of a bitch got in your head, didn't he?"

"You're . . . not . . . real."

"Annie, they are going to come back any second; please, *please* listen to me. I'm real. I'm here, and we need to go."

Annie tries to push him away, her weak arms barely budging him.

He rubs at his chin, looking around in desperation, as if there's something nearby that will help convince her. From somewhere outside another angry shout reaches them, the words inaudible.

"Fuck this shit," he snarls. In a burst of strength, he gets his arms under Annie, and pulls her to her feet. She almost goes over straightaway, and he has to brace himself to hold her up. But she's too weak to resist him. For a few seconds, they stand, wobbling, and then Nic starts to steer her towards the door. "I did not climb up here and bust my ass into this rich dude's property ... *hmmrf* ... just so you can tell me – *ha*, you're heavy – that I'm a figment of your imagination. We are getting the fuck out here whether you like it or not."

As they reach the door, terror grips Annie, wrapping scaly fingers around her. It gives her enough strength to tear away from Nic. She crashes to her knees, then collapses onto her side, trembling uncontrollably.

"Jesus." He kneels next to her, tries to pull her back up. She resists him, this time with more success. "Annie, please, we don't have much time. We have to go *now*."

It's a lie, this is all a lie, just another mind game. Adam getting into her head, making her see things.

Except ...

She was about to break. This is the one true thing she knows, the one part of all of this she doesn't doubt. She was seconds away from snapping, becoming a willing tool of Adam and Chloe. The China Shop office and the people inside it might not have been real, but it felt real. And it reached deep inside her and began to crush her.

So why change things? Why would Adam abandon that particular dream world in favour of this one? To break her further? What would be the point? She turns her head to look at her rescuer, as if seeing him for the first time.

"He could have kept me there," she rasps softly.

"What?"

Annie is exhausted, traumatised, in agony. But there is a tiny part of her mind that is still working, the part that has been conditioned to keep her alive, the one that kept her safe for all those years on the streets. It says: *You need to go.*

It seems to take an age to swing her arm up. To grasp Nic's wrist. Startled, he pulls her up, helping her stand. Her breaths are ragged, but she manages to croak out, "Let's go."

"Teagan — is she here too? Have they got her somewhere else?"

"I don't ... I don't think so." The words *Del Rio* flicker through her mind, although she can't remember what they mean.

He absorbs this, nods. "OK. Let's get out of here."

The sunlight nearly blinds Annie as they push out of the shed, Nic supporting her, the two of them moving in an awkward shuffle. There's no sign of Chloe, or Adam; no sign of anyone. Cicadas chirp from the bushes, unseen. The sky is bird's egg blue, without a single cloud ... unless you count the oily plume of smoke issuing from somewhere around the front of the mansion, on the driveway side.

"How ... ?" Annie breathes. "How did you ... ?"

"Long story."

"You followed me."

"No shit."

"How are you ... how are you here? What—?"

"Annie, if we get out of here, I'll buy you a drink and tell you the whole story. Christ, where the *fuck* is that ladder?" They are moving in the direction of the hillside Annie surveyed the house from, limping through a line of neatly manicured shrubs. "It was right here, I swear to God."

Ladder. The word sticks out, flaring briefly inside her mind. She saw one recently, she knows she did . . . but where?

There's a distant bang from the other side of the house, something exploding. What the hell is happening back there? What did Nic *do*?

He's breathing hard from holding her up, his head snapping left and right. "Shit. OK. We don't have time for this. I don't know what they did with the ladder, but it isn't here any more. Time for Plan B."

Abruptly, he changes direction, pulling Annie down towards the bottom of the garden. They navigate a stone path through a grove of monkey flowers, swaying in a gentle breeze. It's all Annie can do to keep her feet underneath her. "Plan B?"

"Way too much action around the front, so we gotta go out the same way I came in."

There's something in his voice, something that expresses more worry than just the risk of getting caught. Annie doesn't have time to dwell on it. The simple act of staying awake and focused is taking almost everything she has.

Ahead of them, the ground slopes downwards, grass turning to rocky soil. And a few feet beyond that . . .

The cliff at the edge of the property.

It looks to the south-west, over Beverley Grove and Century City, all the way to Santa Monica, the ocean just visible through the smoggy afternoon. There's a waist-high fence along the edge made of sturdy metal drilled right into the rock. Wilcox and his guests can lean on the fence, or sit at the wrought-iron chairs and table set a few feet back from the edge. On either side, where the property walls meet the cliff, there is a flurry of barbed wire to stop people clambering around the side of the walls.

"It's only about fifty feet down," Nic says. Annie didn't notice before, but he's grimy and sweaty as hell, dirt smeared on his cheeks and arms and forehead. "I've been climbing my whole life, and trust me when I say this one isn't that bad. You can follow me all the way down. I'll point out all the handholds and footholds you need. My car's at the bottom – there's this access road. If we go over right there, where the fence meets that rock . . ."

She freezes in place, feet welded to the ground. She can't even shake her head, can do nothing but gape. The idea of going over the edge, with nothing securing her to the rock but her own hands, fifty feet of empty air beneath her, is an impossible concept.

Nic is still talking. "I know it's crazy, but it's the only way out. Any minute now, these assholes are going to come looking for us, and I really don't wanna be here when they do. Annie? Annie, look at me."

He actually has to pull her chin towards him, pin down her roving eyes. "You're going to be fine. We'll do this together, you feel me? One step at a time."

There has to be something that can help her avoid this, some reason for them not to climb over the fence and into the open air. And as if summoned by the thought, she has it. "She can see body heat."

"I know, you told me!"

"It doesn't matter if we go over the . . . over there. Down the rocks. She'll know where we've gone."

He thinks for a moment. "Can she see through rock?"

"I don't . . . I was hiding behind a wall. A concrete wall. So yes. Maybe."

"So she couldn't see you at all?"

Annie forces herself to remember what Chloe told her. "She said it was *harder* to sense my heat, because I was hiding behind the concrete."

He half laughs. Points at the rock leading up to the cliff's edge. "That's a lot thicker than a little concrete wall. And it's a chance we have to take, because if we stay up here they'll find us for sure."

"They can look right over the railings if they want. They'll see us, and then Chloe will—"

"They won't see us."

"How can you be sure?"

He points, finger trembling. "The top of the cliff juts out over the edge. There's like a lip. It was hell on the way up, but it should be a lot easier on the way down. There are a ton of handholds. If we can get below it, they won't be able to spot us from up here."

"I *can't*." Annie almost sobs the words. And even as she says them, she can't stop herself from looking at the edge. There's a perverse urge to take a step towards it, as if it's exerting a magnetic pull on her. *Come closer, Annie. Take a good look.*

There's no trauma in her past to explain her fear of heights. It's as close to baked-in as you can get, a phobia that she's had since she was a little girl. Maybe if they'd had the money for psychologists when she was growing up, she could have dealt with it. Then again, the thought of going near the edge and not wanting to throw up is so foreign to her, so utterly alien, that she can't wrap her head around it at all.

"Yes you can. Annie: *look at me.* You can do this."

That moment, she almost rejects where she is. There is no possible way this is real. It's Adam, still forcing her to face her worst fears.

But on the heels of that thought comes another one. If this *is* real, then everyone she cares about – her mom, Teagan, Reggie, Africa – is out there waiting for her. And if she stays up here, if she falls back into Adam's clutches, she'll never see them again. Even if they turn her loose, it won't be *her*. The Annie that emerges will be broken, a shell of her former self.

Compared to that, slipping and falling doesn't seem nearly as bad.

Even then, it takes her a few more moments to start approaching the edge. It's like she's trying to walk with lead weights tied to her legs.

"That's it," Nic says. "Listen, I'm gonna go down first. I'll spot you from below, tell you what handholds to grab."

He hops the fence with almost contemptuous ease, vanishing out of sight.

Slowly, her aching body protesting, Annie manages to get one leg over the fence. Then another, turning as she does so. She's now facing back towards the house, the metal rough under her palms as she leans herself out, very purposefully not looking down. Her heart is going to hammer its way right out of her ribcage.

"All right," Nic says. "Now what I want you to do is slowly lower your left foot down. I'm going to take hold of it and guide it to a foothold. From there, you're going to lean down to your left. There's this big root right about where your left foot is now. If you hang onto that, we can get you moving."

Annie closes her eyes.

"Take it slow," he says. "You have all the time in the world."

Little by little, Nic coaxes her down the first few feet of the cliff. He was right about there being a lip, an awkward ledge that juts out from the fence, with nothing underneath it. But it's smaller than she thought it was, and there's no question that there are plenty of handholds. At some point in the past, someone cut back the vegetation on the rocky cliff. Wilcox has clearly neglected it, banking on the height and his existing security to deter anyone trying to get in. The rock surface is sandstone, offering plenty of friction.

After a few minutes, Annie and Nic are below the lip, out of sight from anybody peering over the railing above. Annie stops for a moment, balanced with both feet on a thick stub of a branch. She's drenched in sweat, her legs and arms aching, and she still hasn't given herself permission to look down. A flicker of a memory: Nic's hands, calloused and rough, scratching his stubble as they sat in his car outside the gates. She thought the callouses were from clearing earthquake debris, but it's not just that. Like Nic said, he's been a climber his entire life. And maybe, just maybe, he knows what he's doing.

Nic is just off to her side, slightly below her. "OK," he says, putting a hand on her shoulder. "We don't have much further to go. There are still tons of handholds, so just keep focusing on my voice."

Another lie. They can't have gone more than six or seven feet down, which means there's another forty or fifty to go before they hit solid ground.

"You can move your left hand down to your waist, then out a bit," Nic murmurs. "There's a nice branch for you there."

Annie does so, grabs hold of the branch, puts her weight on it. Nic's voice comes again. "Right foot. Down and in a little. There. That's it. Thaaaat's—"

The branch in Annie's left hand creaks, very slightly — then snaps.

She drops. Her left arm and leg flail, and in that moment, and she nearly goes mad with terror. She can't speak, can't even scream. Even her breath has stopped.

Nic's strong fingers wrap around her upper arm. "Got you." With his right foot, he guides her left one to another hold, then finds one for her free hand. "Christ, you're shaking. Let's just chill here for a second, OK? You're good. Just relax."

"Can you see her?"

Chloe's voice comes from above, shockingly close. Neither of them heard her approach. With a sharp intake of breath, Nic flattens himself against the cliff, his arm in the middle of Annie's back, pushing her to do the same.

She risks a glance upwards. They are below the lip. Chloe must be leaning out over it; the top of her head is just visible, a flick of blonde hair against the sky. All the same, Annie doesn't know if she can spot them.

Chloe doesn't wait for whoever she's addressing to answer. "How the hell did she get out? I checked those zip ties myself. Did she have help?"

Wilcox's voice floats down to them. "I'll have to check the cameras."

"You said this property was secure."

"It *is* secure."

Annie doesn't catch Chloe's next words, but they sound ugly as hell. A beat, then: "Jim, you and I are gonna go down into that valley. She can't have gone far."

"Why can't you see them? I thought your range was—"

"Don't you *dare* start questioning what I can do. You know there are limits. If I could see her, we'd have found her and she'd already be dead, which means she's figured out a way to hide. If—"

"I can feel them."

Adam.

Annie has heard his voice before, on the LA River. For a big man, his voice is surprisingly high, almost childlike.

"Where?" Chloe says. And then: "*Them?* There's more than one? Do you know where they are?"

"No."

"But if you can feel them . . ."

"They are in my house. The walls know them."

Annie meets Nic's eyes. *Shit.* Both of them flatten themselves against the rock even more, scarcely daring to breathe.

There's a creaking sound from above as Chloe leans out further over the railing. Annie braces herself, knowing what's coming. The sudden cold, the drop in temperature turning her blood to ice. Or maybe Chloe will go the opposite way, overheating them in moments. If that happens, she won't be able to hold on.

Seconds tick by. Up on the cliff edge, Chloe has gone silent, as have Adam and Wilcox. Annie keeps waiting for her fingers to go numb, to lose their grip. There are very faint sounds coming from just above them. Footsteps. Something that might be a hushed whisper.

Nothing happens. Chloe can't see them, can't sense their heat signatures, which hopefully means she can't touch them. Maybe—

The woman's voice reaches them from above, hard and contemptuous. "You shouldn't have run, Annie. It would have been easier."

I have to warn Nic. Warn him about Adam.

But then, faster than she can blink, she is back in the China Shop Offices. Reggie, Africa and Teagan staring at her in horror and rage.

FORTY-ONE

Teagan

Jonas might be into bondage, but I'm not. I don't like having my hands tied. I especially don't like having them tied when I have a bullet wound in my shoulder, because fucking *ow*.

The secret passage winds through the bowels of the hotel, our footsteps echoing off the barren concrete walls and stairwells. Most of it is unfamiliar, but that's hardly surprising, given that I was barely conscious the first time round.

I'm worried they're going to march us all the way to the roof. But after the second flight of stairs, they lead us down a short dog-leg, and then out through a slim door set into the wall.

Guess old Greta Garbo decided she needed a second exit. Maybe that's how these assholes found us.

The door leads out into a storage room, big metal racks of linen and cleaning supplies running up to the low ceiling. The storage room leads out into the main lobby. After the dimness of the corridors, it's so bright that it makes my eyes water – and that's before I glance up at the enormous, gleaming chandelier.

The place is deserted, the main doors secured with that blast block, sealed across the glass. And beyond them, keeping a very

wise distance: the cops. And the FBI, probably. Lots of black
SUVs and flashing lights and dark suits. Patrolmen and women,
doing that thing where they take cover behind open car doors
while aiming a gun. Tracking our movements. From somewhere out of sight, there's the sound of a hovering helicopter.

No paparazzi at least. None that I can see, anyway. So, yeah,
there's that.

For the thousandth time, I weigh up whether or not to use
my PK. Bust us free, get us out of here. We're in an open space
now, or more open anyway, so maybe . . .

But can I risk it? What if I can't control it? What if somebody I care about gets hurt?

We head through the doors to the ballroom. I guess I always
knew we'd end up back here, one way or another.

The first thing I notice is the body. One of the hostages, a
man, hands zip-tied like ours, lying on his stomach. Right by
the door. A massive blood pool underneath him. A hostage-
taker steps over him, like he isn't even there.

The rest of the hostages are huddled in small groups, each
one presided over by a dickhead with a gun. A hundred eyes
looking in our direction, desperately hoping for rescue, knowing that we aren't it. Behind the podium, the glistening, red
Rorschach blot of DiSantos's blood.

There's a gasp. It's Africa, off to my left. Sitting with his
legs splayed out in front of him, his hands bound. His face is
a bloody mess, swollen with bruises. Kanehara next to him,
restrained in the same way, but unhurt. There's a hostage-taker
standing behind them. It's Brandon Evans – I recognise him
from the file photo in Phan's room. He does not look happy.

"Teggan!" Africa shouts.

"Dude!" I yell back earning me a shove from the person
marching me forward. "Are you OK?"

"Ya ya, fine." He spots my shoulder, a thunderous look crossing his face. "What did you do to her, you bloody—?"

Evans hits him in the upper back with his rifle. Africa grunts in pain, collapses. At that moment, I almost lose control, let my PK slip the leash and take out whoever it wants. I pull it back at the very last second. There are way, way too many people here.

Just be cool. Don't save the day. Ride it out. The cops already know what's going on, and pretty soon they'll . . .

What? Storm the place? How many casualties will there be then? It's hard not to picture the body by the door, blood spreading out from underneath him.

Another of the hostage-takers in Africa's vicinity locks eyes with me, and it takes a second to remember why he looks so familiar. Shane DuBois, that was his name. From Phan's photos. I recognise a couple of the others, too. *Just one big happy family.*

Someone starts slow clapping.

It's such a bizarre sound that it actually stops me in my tracks. It's coming from someone seated on the dais, legs dangling. Rifle slung over his shoulder, an easy smile on his face.

Dyson.

"Not bad," he says, raising his voice over the tense murmur of the hostages. "Not bad at all."

He looks rough. Actually, scratch that: he looks awful. A world away from the smooth, confident, quote-slinging douchebag I saw this morning. There's a sizeable bruise on his left cheekbone. His red tie is pulled down, and he has his jacket off, sleeves rolled up.

"We were never introduced," he says, sliding off the dais. Still languid, despite looking like ass. "The name's Dyson."

"Thought they called you the Reverend."

It pops out of me before I can stop it. Dyson's face flickers with annoyance, then rearranges itself into that smooth smile.

He gestures to our armed escort. They walk us off to one side, past the dais itself, a little way away from the other hostages. As we get there, our captors shove us to our knees. By now, the pain in my shoulder is a living thing, breathing down my neck and digging its claws into my flesh.

"Look." It's Weiss – I hadn't even realised he was here. He's on his knees too, off to one side ... but he's OK. Thank fuck. "If we could just—"

"Sorry, senator," Dyson says crisply, not looking at him. "I don't have time for any more of your shit today."

He nods to one of the others, a nondescript dude with thinning red hair. He looks as exhausted as Dyson, but moves quickly, grabbing the senator and hustling him away. There are a hundred eyes on us, everybody in the ballroom staring, hostages and hostage-takers alike. I hadn't noticed it before, but every single one of the hostage-takers looks on edge. Maybe not as dishevelled as Dyson, but still looking like they badly need a cigarette and a stiff drink.

Like this wasn't where they expected things to end up.

When is a hostage situation not a hostage situation?

"Give me a minute with them," Dyson tells them. Our escorts nod and head off, leaving us with him and two others. There's the older woman from the rooftop, the one who helped Dyson bring the senator out. Up close, her face is thin and hawk-like, her eyes sharp as flint. Next to her is a younger guy, slightly pudgy, desperately trying to grow a goatee and failing miserably.

They're different from their pals, and it takes me a second to put my finger on exactly how. The other people with guns move ... I guess you'd call it *efficiently*. Like trained soldiers. Shane, Brandon, the others: they've all got the same way of walking and standing. As exhausted and stressed as they look, they hold themselves carefully, coiled springs ready to pop. These two, and Dyson, aren't quite as polished. And there's an arrogance to them. Like they're used to giving orders – although Randi Metzger, the woman Africa shot, was different. She moved like ex-military too.

The Children of Solomon. Or the ones who are on this little mission, anyway. Which means the rest of the hostage-takers must be hired guns.

I lock eyes with Dyson. "Randi says hi."

At the mention of the hostage-taker who tried to drown me in the hotel pool, the kid with stupid goatee steps towards me, his eyes widen. "You're gonna regret—"

Dyson puts a hand on his chest. "Aaron. Enough."

"But she—"

"I said *enough*. Randi forgot what she was supposed to be doing, she went too far, she got herself killed. That's all."

Where the hell is Phan? I have a few things I'd like to say to her, of the four-letter variety. I scan the room, but I can't see her.

Aaron backs off, even if he still looks like he wants to murder all of us. Dyson squats in front of me. For a long moment, he says nothing.

After about ten seconds, it gets too weird. "Can I help you?"

"You know," he says. "It's funny. When we figured out where you'd gone, we were expecting a lot more resistance. My team and I, we've been in plenty of bad situations, but I think this is the first time we've met somebody like you. Feels a little strange that you just came quietly." He nods to my bullet wound. "What's the matter? You all tapped out?"

"I don't know what you're talking about."

"After the little display on the roof? Come on." He gives me an easy, almost gentle smile.

I shrug. "Wasn't me. I was surprised as anybody."

He laughs, pulls out his phone. Taps it for a few seconds, then glances up at me, mouthing the word *sorry*. As if he's struggling to find something.

"There we go," he says, and hold the phone up. There's a video playing. It's the one circulating online of me stopping the flash flood in the storm drain.

Ah. Shit. I'd forgotten about that.

"Come on now, don't be modest," he says. "I know the video isn't very good, but it's not hard to make the connection here."

I say nothing.

"You can do all that," he says, pointing a finger to the ceiling – referring, I guess, to what happened on the roof. "All that, and you just let my guys bring you up here. How does it work? Can you only do it once, and then you have to recharge?"

I'm not about to confirm or deny. And the truth is, if I really concentrated, I could have my PK ruin his day right now. The problem is, there are lots of other people around whose day it would ruin, too.

Can I take that risk? Can I have their deaths on my conscience?

He grips my chin, turns my head left and right, studying me. "To think God would give someone like you such a gift," he murmurs.

"God had nothing to do with it."

"Ms Frost," Tanner spits. "That's enough."

"Seriously?" I try to look over my shoulder, which hurts, and I can't see her anyway. "The horse has left the stable. OK? Stop trying to bolt the door."

I can practically hear the tendons in Tanner's jaw creaking as she grits her teeth.

"And it's not a gift," I tell Dyson.

"Really?"

"Nope. It's not a gift, or a power, or a talent. It's an *ability*. It's something I can do. You have the ability to pick up a gun and take a bunch of scared people hostage. I have the ability to move things without using my hands. It doesn't make either of us particularly special."

"*Au contraire.* It makes you very special indeed. And where did you get such a magnificent *gift*, if not from the Lord?"

"I was born like this."

"Then I suppose you have your mother and father to thank, yes? And does it not say in Proverbs, verse one, chapter eight: *Hear your father's instruction, and forsake not your mother's teaching, for they are a graceful garland for your head and pendants for your neck?*" An edge creeps into his voice. "You dishonour your parents."

"Look, man." I lick my lips. "I've had a very long day. Actually, I've had a very long week. I do not have the energy and time to deal with your Bible shit today, so—"

He slaps me.

It's not a soft slap. It's a thumping backhand that snaps my head sideways and sends me reeling, collapsing to the ground. Dyson leans down, grabs me, hauls me back up. That does wonders for the pain in my shoulder, as you can imagine. I stare at him through a fuzzy veil of glinting, grey dots. Blood in my mouth. Somewhere distant, Africa is roaring my name.

"Don't take the Holy Word in vain," Dyson says quietly, the same maddening smile still on his face.

Somehow, I find my voice. "What. The hell. Do you *want*?"

He's actually chuckling to himself now, slowly shaking his head. It is the single most irritating thing I've ever seen.

"Come on, man," I say. "I've been stumbling around for

hours now, and *none* of this makes any sense. Please, please, just so there's one less thing I have to think about today. Tell me what you're trying to get out of all this."

He looks amused. "Money."

"Really?"

"It's not that much of a surprise, surely?"

"What, your congregation not dropping enough in the collection plate? Or are you just tired of writing sermons and you want to go buy an island and drink daiquiris for the rest of your life?" A flash of inspiration: "Doesn't Jesus have that whole thing about rich people not being able to go through the eye of the needle to get into heaven, or some shit?"

He shrugs. "The money isn't for me."

"Right. It's for your sick grandma."

"All I want is to spread the word of our Lord," he says.

"Suuuuure."

"It's all I ever wanted. But it's becoming harder and harder. Even with social media, with more news sources than ever before, people turn away from the Gospels. I just want to help them."

The crazy thing is, he actually sounds serious. "So, what, you're gonna start some kind of megachurch?"

He lifts a hand, seesaws it back and forth. "I want to create the kind of world our Lord envisioned. A just world. Preaching can't do that, not any more, not when there are so many distractions. So many perversions. But money . . . it can change things. Influence policy, pass laws, hire lobbyists."

"But *how*? You never called the cops. You blocked all calls in and out of the hotel. Who were you planning to get this money from?" Suddenly, it's all spilling out of me. "None of this shit makes any sense. You *obviously* knew who I was, you *obviously* knew what I could do. And if I'd been myself this morning, I could have stopped you idiots cold. No hostage situation, which means no money. Right? What am I missing here? *Where are you getting this magical money from?*"

The puzzle pieces are all jumbled together. Phan Duc Hong, Dyson, the lack of police until now, the jammer, the ridiculous ratio of bad guys to hostages ... none of it makes any sense.

Dyson nods. "You're right. You could have stopped us cold. I think it's time you did that."

" ... I'm sorry, what?"

Dyson hauls me to my feet, drags me up onto the dais. He has me by the collar, and holds me out, as if presenting me to the room. Africa yells my name, and the panicked whispering of the hostages rises to fever pitch.

"Here's what I want you to do," Dyson says. "I want you to stop us."

"You're going to have to run that by me again."

"Use your gift. In front of everyone else, right here. You must be able to, right? What's stopping you?" He shakes me, suddenly angry, yelling in my ear. "Take our guns away. Snap your zip ties. Don't just stand there and tell me there's nothing you can do."

Wait – is he really telling me to take out his buddies?

It's such a bizarre request that for a moment, all I can do is gape at him. Has he lost his mind?

He thinks I don't have enough juice right now – he said so himself. So is he dragging me up here to expose me as ... what, a fraud? To reassert his power after I wrecked him and his crew on the roof? But he can't know that I'm out of juice, not for sure. Which means he's accepting the fact that I could take out this entire team in one go. How does that benefit him?

"Come on then," he growls in my ear. "Give us a show."

"I . . . I don't under—"

"Dyson."

It's Shane DuBois. The rifle he's holding isn't pointed anywhere nasty yet, but it's not exactly pointed at the ground,
either. "What are we doing here?"

Dyson ignores him, continuing to hiss in my ear. "Ephesians
chapter two, verse ten. *For we are his workmanship, created in
Christ Jesus for good works, which God prepared beforehand, that we
should walk in them.* You were put on Earth to do this, so do it."

"You're saying she's the person from the roof?" Shane says,
looking between me and Dyson. "You out of your mind? We
should shoot her!"

"Not another word," Dyson says, snapping a finger at him
without turning his way. His face inches from mine, his breath
smelling sharply of peppermint. As if he freshened it just for
the occasion.

"Everybody stand down," Tanner says from behind me.
Nobody pays any attention to her.

"Take them out," Dyson whispers. "I know you've got the
power. Do it. Do it and end this."

"Listen to him!"

The voice comes from the back of the room, from a woman
getting unsteadily to her feet.

Phan Duc Hong. The biggest arms dealer in Asia. The one
who had photos of me, and Tanner, and Dyson, and Shane
and Randi and Brandon and everybody else. She's restrained
in the same way we all are, which makes no sense at all. But
somehow, she still manages to look in control. "Whatever you
do, Frost, do it now."

I don't get a chance to ask any of the zillion questions bouncing around my mind. Brandon Evans, off to my right, speaks
first. His waiter's bow tie has turned straight up, making him

look absurdly like a clown. It's an effect spoiled by the gigantic pistol he swings to point at me. "Not a fucking chance."

Dyson moves quick as a snake. From out of nowhere, a pistol of his own appears in his hand, and he levels it at Evans.

Someone in the room screams, and it's like a starting gun. Suddenly, the rest of the hostage-takers are pointing their weapons at me and Dyson. Dyson, along with Aaron and the hawk-faced woman whose name I don't know, are pointing theirs right back at them. Children of Solomon versus the mercs they hired. *Oh, excellent.*

It takes every atom of self-control I have not to throw myself off the dais and out of the line of fire. The only thing that stops me is the thought that making any sudden moves right now would be a very, very bad idea.

"Y'all need to think very carefully about what you're going to do next," Dyson says, addressing Evans, but raising his voice so the entire room can hear him.

"*Mein Gott,*" Jonas murmurs from behind me

"What we're going to do next?" says DuBois. "What, you mean, get killed by the fucking cops?"

"You said you had that under control," Evans adjusts his stance, seating the gun better in his hands. "Where were they before? Why'd they only get here now?"

"The FBI is here!" someone else yells.

"Frost!" shouts Phan Duc Hong. "You need to do what he says."

This is a nightmare.

If the shooting starts now, then I die. It's that simple. I'm directly in the line of fire. That's without talking about Jonas and Tanner, who are behind me. And who knows how many stray bullets there'll be, how many hostages will die. Including Africa. Kanehara.

Senator Weiss.

But if I use my PK, if I actually do what Dyson says, I can't guarantee the same thing won't happen. There's going to be so much flying debris that it's bound to land in the wrong place.

The sound in the room is horrible. A mix of screams and panicked shouts and horrified whispers as every hostage crouches down to the carpet, trying to get as low as possible. Africa, bellowing incoherently. Violence hangs in the air, ready to drop.

Slowly, I turn my head to look at Tanner. I don't know what I'm hoping for. Maybe some instructions, an order from our fearless leader. Whatever beef I have with her, however angry at her I am for not telling me about Annie, it doesn't matter now. She's the head of China Shop, and *I want her to tell me what to do.*

"Last chance," Dyson hisses in my ear.

Tanner's eyes meet mine. They are the colour of old ice. Deep and dark and cold.

The room vanishes. So does Dyson. The hostage-takers. Jonas, Africa, Kanehara, the cops, the FBI, the whole world. There's no one else but me and my boss

Everything Moira Tanner does, absolutely everything, is about saving lives. Always has been. Reggie once told me something about her – and maybe it's the adrenaline thundering around my system, but in that moment, I remember her words perfectly. *If your goal is to save as many lives as possible and to protect the interests of this country, then how does it help you to get wrapped up in the details of those lives? Look at them as numbers, and you'll never hesitate when you're making any decision. As long as the number saved is larger than the number lost, you've won. I'm not saying I agree with it, but it's worked out pretty well for her so far. Her, and a lot of other people who will never, ever know her name.*

Through that lens, everything she does make sense. Even not telling me that Annie had woken up. In Tanner's view, it would distract me, get me thinking about my friend when my job was to think about the situation in front of me – which, at that time, was protecting Senator Weiss.

And as I look into those cold eyes, I know what I have to do.

I cannot save everybody here. There is nothing I can do that will keep all the good guys safe.

If I do nothing, then I lose control of the situation. I won't be able to dictate how many people live or die. But if I *make* a choice, if I decide to do something instead of nothing, then I can save more people than I lose. The numbers will balance out.

The weight of that decision is . . . indescribable. It's almost too much to take. And yet somehow, Moira Tanner has found a way to bear it. Not just once, or twice, but endlessly. Year, after year, after year. She's welcomed the weight, let it sink onto her shoulders. No matter how much people hate her for it.

I might hate her. But for the first time, I understand what it's like to be her.

And in that moment, I make my decision.

"Hey, Dyson?" I say.

His eyes flick my way.

"There's one part of the Bible I always enjoyed. Want me to tell you how it goes?"

And I reach out with my PK. As far as it'll go. Out the doors of the ballroom, into the lobby. Outwards and upwards. Wrapping it around the gigantic chandelier. Wrapping it around the bulbs and the wiring and the metal frame and the shaped shards of crystal.

"*Let there be light.*"

And with that, I tighten my grip on the chandelier, and *pull*.

FORTY-TWO

Teagan

It's a gamble.

A big one.

There's always a chance that one of these assholes is on too tight a hair trigger – that they'll fire at the first loud noise, and then everybody else will, and then we'll all die.

Using my PK is different this time. Back on the roof, I was just trying to do something small. I wanted to activate the safety catches on a bunch of guns. A little movement: one which resulted in a massive, uncontrolled burst of power. Like a dam giving way.

This time? I go for broke.

And the chandelier in the lobby ... *explodes.*

The crystals shatter into a million pieces, with a sound like radio static turned up to eleven. The metal frame bends and splits and twists, screaming and groaning. The lightbulbs pop, the filaments slicing through their glass prisons. Wires stretch and fray, ripping loose in showers of sparks. Plaster in the ceiling above vaporises. Wood and mortar and metal rivets rip loose, spinning through the air.

It's not just the chandelier. It's the whole goddamn lobby. I wasn't even focusing on it. I put every ounce of PK energy I had into the chandelier, but whatever my ability has morphed into, it's gone beyond my control. It's a wild, raging beast that has broken out of its cage. The energy reaches to every corner of the hotel lobby, and rips it apart. The air fills with a roaring mass of objects: chunks of marble and crystal, computer screens, tables, chairs. Everything not nailed down goes flying, hurled away by my PK.

No one in the ballroom sees this, of course. But they can hear it all right. Dyson glances at me, then in the direction of the lobby, then back at me. Amazingly, he doesn't fire. Neither does anyone else.

It buys us a moment. A single, frozen moment.

Which is all I need.

"Everybody – *get down!*" I yell. And then I hurl myself off the dais.

And that's when somebody – one of the mercs, I don't see who – pulls their trigger.

I hit the deck hard as the air erupts with gunfire, curling myself into the tiniest ball I can. I'm face-down on the carpet, and I can't tell if every person *not* holding a gun is doing the same thing. I hope to hell they are. The gunshots are impossibly loud, a slick of what must be blood splattering the back of my neck, the stench of cordite searing my nostrils, a thousand panicked screams and yells erupting into the space around me.

And somehow, my PK in the lobby is still going. It's like holding onto a charging horse, being dragged behind it as it thunders towards the horizon. It's all I can do to direct my PK into the lobby, because if I let it loose in here . . .

There's a distant explosion. A bang that somehow manages to blot all the other noise out for a split-second. The blast block, ripping off the front doors? The cops somehow making an entrance? I have no idea.

I raise my head, just a fraction – and slam it back down as something very fast and very loud whips by my scalp, like an angry insect.

Holy hell, my PK ... I've never felt anything like this. It's like I've plugged directly into some gigantic mainline, like I'm channelling a billion watts of power. I'm sensing a thousand objects at once, sensing and moving them in the same instant. Latching onto an object and letting go immediately, grabbing a dozen more.

Enough is enough. I have to stop this, before anyone else gets hurt. I try to bring my PK back, force it to let go, the kind of thing that has become second nature by now.

It doesn't work. It doesn't even come close to working. It's like a muscle that can't unclench, a cramp that won't release no matter how much you plead with it and massage it and stretch it. It's taken on a life of its own: an invisible hydra, tearing through the lobby of the Del Rio Hotel.

What if you can't get it back? What if the energy never runs out? What if it just keeps going and going until—?

I don't get a chance to finish that thought. Because right then, someone kicks me in the stomach.

If it's possible to curl into a tighter ball than I was in already, I manage it. Through slitted eyes, I look up.

Dyson is a mess. Red spatters his white shirt, although there's no bullet wound visible. He leers at me, a mad grin. The pistol is still in his hand, and as I blink stupidly at him, he slowly lifts it to aim right at my head.

Time slows right the fuck down.

Dyson has his back to the lobby doors, which have popped wide open. Beyond, the lobby is a whirling, crashing nightmare. A tornado, no, a *hurricane* of glass, marble, crystal. There's no end to it.

Something is trying to force its way through the doors.

The chandelier.

It's a wreck. A jagged mess of metal and glass and wires. It's too big to fit through the door, so it slams into the frame again and again. Like it heard that all the action is in here, and wants a part of it.

"Behind you, fuckface," I tell Dyson.

I don't know if he hears me. He takes careful aim, relishing the moment. Whatever his plan with me was, whatever all this was about, it's over. Which means he's going to take pleasure in putting me down.

With a grinding crunch, the chandelier breaks free of the door. It thunders into the room: a whirling, roaring Catherine wheel of metal and glass.

Finally, Dyson turns to look.

Tries to dive to the side.

Not fast enough.

I can't describe the noise it makes when it hits him. It's halfway between a *sCRONch* and a *shBANG,* with a little bit of *sPRSH* thrown in for good measure. One second, he's standing above me. The next, he's gone.

I have to stop this.

I have to control my PK. Grey is starting to creep in at the edges of my vision, and my thoughts are getting harder to track. What's next? Coma? Death? And how many people are going to die before we get there?

The fight with Chloe and Adam made my ability retreat, go dormant – but the whole time, it was only building its strength. Now it's escaped, bursting out of me, tearing through everything and everyone.

And I don't know if I can stop it.

The problem is, there's nobody else who can.

I drop my head. Take a deep breath. Push past the pain, and the exhaustion, and the fear, and the raw insanity of this day. I channel myself into every strand of PK energy I can feel . . .

And ask it to stop.

Ask it to let go.

It doesn't want to. It holds on, snarling, roaring, like a beast I'm trying to ride. My ability has never felt like this; it's always been something I control, as much a part of me as my own hands. I've never had to negotiate with it. Never had to force it to do what I want.

And I pay for it. Boy, do I pay for it. The headache starts at the base of my skull, and grows in seconds to spread through my whole head. I crash to the ground, whimpering, clutching at my temples.

Tanner, hands still bound, has gotten her way over to the senator, shielding him with her body. Africa is nowhere to be seen. Somebody yells my name: Jonas, trying to get to me.

Somehow, I manage to hold on. Somehow, I claw back control.

It comes in inches. Tiny fractions, like an unclenching fist. More than once, I lose some of that control, the energy roaring out of me again. Gritting my teeth so hard that it's a wonder they don't snap, knots burning in my shoulders. *Come on. Come on, you piece of shit. I never asked for you, I never wanted you, but we're stuck together, so how about you stop fighting me?*

Slowly, the whirling objects begin to settle.

The tornado starts to wind down. Chunks of marble crash to the floor, crystal shards tinkle as they bounce off the walls. The roaring, crashing chaos subsides, replaced by sobbing, panicked shouts. Inch by inch, I bring it back under my control. Until only a few broken objects hover in the air, barely moving. One of them is an assault rifle, the housing cracked and dented. Like a reminder of everything that has happened today.

I lie there, curled into a ball, as the world fills with thundering feet. And as it does, someone reaches down, and scoops me up off the floor.

Africa. Bruises livid on his dark skin. Bleeding from a cut on his lip, the blood soaking his chin and neck. But he scoops me up as firmly and as gently as he would a child, pulls me close to his chest. Hold me in his arms, and carries me towards the flashing lights.

FORTY-THREE

Annie

"We trusted you," Teagan says slowly. "We thought you were one of us."

Annie's guilt comes rushing back, the anguish at seeing her friends look at her this way. The scaffolding of her mind begins to strain and bend. Her fingers hurt. Why do her fingers hurt? She tries to look down at them, but she can't tear her gaze away from her friends.

"I *am* one of you," Annie pleads.

"Not another word," Reggie tells her. "I want you out of here right now."

"Go back to your mom," says Teagan. "She knows what you did, doesn't she? What kind of mom lets her own daughter kill her husband?"

Christ, her fingers are on *fire*. But that doesn't make sense. She's not holding anything.

Your fingers hurt because you're trying not to fall.

But fall from . . . where?

Images flicker in Annie's mind. A house, shielding an enormous green garden. Iron railings. Iron chairs. The deep blue sky. A cliff.

Teagan is shorter than Annie, but in that moment, it's as if the girl towers over her. Her face twists in the ugliest expression Annie has ever seen. There is something awful behind her skin, something insane.

"Time to let go," the thing pretending to be Teagan says. "You don't belong in our house."

And it would be so easy, wouldn't it? Teagan's right. She isn't worthy of this. Someone like her doesn't belong where she is.

Except . . .

When she was in her coma, lying in that hospital bed, Annie couldn't move or see or speak. But sometimes, she could hear. Teagan was in the room with her, talking to her, cursing her out for leaving her at the homeless camp. She was going to leave, walk out and never come back.

But Teagan hadn't left. Instead, she'd said: *I don't want you to go. Please. Stay with me.*

She needed Annie. And Annie needed her. And Teagan would never, ever turn Annie away, not even over what she did to her father.

The thing pretending to be Teagan stares down at her. "I said: *let go.*"

"No," Annie replies. She focuses on her howling fingers, embracing the pain. "This is where I'm supposed to be."

"You're a liar." All four of them are yelling now, their voices blending into a horrifying tidal wave of sound. "We hate you. *Leave!*"

"And I . . . said . . . *no!*"

She screams the last word, throwing it back in their faces. And then, with a sensation like a speeding car throwing on the brakes, Annie slams back into the real world. Pressed against the cliff face, face jammed against the rough sandstone.

She gasps for air, sucks in huge lungfuls of it. Looks around frantically, expecting the nightmare version of Teagan bearing down on her. But it's just her and Nic, clinging to the cliff. He's shaking, twitching, still hanging on but lost in a dream world, just like she was.

Annie doesn't know exactly how she managed to break out of Adam's grip. Is he aware? Does he know she's slipped his grasp? He must do. Even now, he must be trying to regain control.

Slowly, she turns her head upwards. Taking in the handholds, the little ledges in the rock. The edge of the cliff, the blue sky beyond it. She's aware of the massive drop beneath her, the wind pulling on her back ... but somehow, it's become background noise.

There's no way they are getting down this cliff. Annie isn't sure of Adam's range, but what she *is* sure of is that given time, he'll find a way to get back into her mind. She has to go up. Bring the fight to him.

The problem is Nic. She might have been able to bust out of Adam's dream prison, but whatever he's going through, he's still there. And if she can't break him out ...

Breathing through her nose, Annie stretches out a hand. Grabs Nic's arm. Squeezes as hard as she can. "Come on, motherfucker, wake up. I'm right here. Listen to my voice."

He doesn't respond. Instead, his right arm slips free of its grip. Annie yelps, grabbing at his wrist, slamming it back onto the surface of the cliff. "*Nic!* It's not real. None of it is real. Whatever you're seeing isn't there."

He whimpers, like a trapped animal. Above them, Adam is ... chanting? Yes, chanting, that deep voice murmuring a blurred stream of words.

Listen to me, says Teagan, at the back of Annie's mind.

"Fuck off," Annie growls. "Nic. Hey, *Nic.*"

There must be something in her voice, some note that gets through. Nic turns to look at her, blinking in confusion. "What . . . ?"

He lets go of the cliff.

It's like a reflex action, like he's trying to get away from the pain in his hands. For a horrible second, he's suspended, in defiance of gravity. His eyes go wide. "*Ohshitohshitohshitfuckfuckshit—*"

Annie reaches over, grabs his collar, grimaces as his weight nearly pulls her off the cliff. The terror threatens to come rushing back, and she grits her teeth as she fights it off. "Got you."

From above them, Adam roars.

"You with me?" Annie has to repeat it twice before he hears it. Even now, Adam's visions claw at her mind.

"I'm here," Nic gasps, clinging to the cliff.

Annie takes a breath. She's done all she can.

She lifts her head. Gaze locked on a stubby branch above her. With a thin, wheezing groan, she swings her right arm up, and starts to climb.

When you're trapped on a cliff, a dream demon pulling at the edges of your sanity, you have very few options. You can go down, you can stay put, or you can go up. That's it. And when the first two aren't going to happen, you really only have one choice.

There's a chance that Chloe is waiting at the top, gun in hand, or simply waiting for the opportunity to get close so she can turn Annie's internal organs to ice. But somehow, Annie doesn't think so.

She has an idea that Chloe does not trust her brother.

He's insane, a man with horrifying powers who lives in a world of his own. Chloe has to control him through those trigger words. But even then, even when she should have complete control of his actions, Annie has a feeling she expects her brother to fail. Why else would she have intervened on the LA River?

No, she's not up there. Plan A is to have her brother mess with their heads, make them lose their grip and fall. But Plan B? She'd get in a position where she could take them down herself. She'd go to the valley below, perhaps with a rifle.

Did Chloe leave Wilcox with her brother? Is he up there right now — maybe with a gun of his own? Annie squeezes her eyes shut. There are things she can control, and things she can't. And if she and Nic stay hanging off this cliff, the things she *can* control are going to get taken away from them.

Hand over hand, she climbs. With each breath, she makes herself move. Focusing only on the next handhold. Hands scraped and raw, forearms and shoulders and hips aching. And the fear is still very much there, hammering at the door along with Adam's visions. But somehow, in a way she doesn't fully understand, she can tune it all out.

She is dimly aware of Nic climbing the cliff to her left, but she doesn't dare look over at him to check his progress. Even when she reaches the lip, when the cliff juts outwards overhead, she doesn't falter. She finds the handholds, finds the little spots in the rock that she can push her toes against.

As she climbs, as she carefully adjusts each finger on every hold, the fear vanishes. There's simply no room for it. There is nothing but total focus. The world around her slips away, her vision shrinking down to a tiny, bright spot of clarity. The next hold. Then the one after that. Then the one after that. Adam's chanting has reached fever pitch.

And as she finally, finally swings her arm over the top of the cliff, gets her hand around the iron railing, she hears something that freezes her heart in her chest.

"Aight, motherfucker, let's go! You and me!"

Nic is a faster climber than she is. Even now, when both of them are run ragged by Adam's visions, he has muscle memory and upper body strength on his side. So while she's still on the other side of the fence, he's already over it. Annie pulls herself above the edge of the cliff just in time to see him rush the hulking figure of Adam.

"Nic, don't!" she cries.

Teagan's brother is alone – there's no Wilcox waiting with a loaded weapon. Adam is down on one knee, head bowed. As Annie watches, he rises to meet Nic, gigantic body unfolding. Nic cocks his arm back on the run, fury etched on his face, using every ounce of power he has to drive a targeted hay-maker right at Adam's temple.

Adam doesn't flinch. He jerks his head out the way, then steps sideway, letting Nic's own momentum work against him. As Nic tries to bring himself to a halt, correct his strike, Adam lunges. He grabs Nic around the right arm and under the left shoulder, twisting his body and hurling Nic through the air.

Somehow, Nic recovers. He gains his footing, almost falling but catching himself with an outstretched palm. When he looks up, there's a manic gleam in his eyes.

With a grunt, Annie pulls herself up and over the railing. She crashes to the ground as Nic and Adam throw themselves at each other, a whirlwind of fists and elbows. Coughing, she tries to get to her feet, but it's at this point that her body finally decides that it can't go on. There's no strength left in her limbs. None.

Adam puts Nic down with a gigantic right hook, then climbs on top of him and wraps those huge hands around his throat. Nic tries to push him away, but he's on his stomach, and simply can't get enough leverage to shove his attacker off.

Adam glances over at Annie, those insane eyes falling on hers. He starts to laugh. And inside her mind, the monster punches a claw through the door she built to keep it out. The monster is her father, the monster is Teagan, Reggie, Africa, the monster is what she did. The monster is her.

"Fuck. *You*," she hisses through gritted teeth. Gets her elbow underneath her, then another. On all fours now. Then one knee up. Then two.

In her head, Annie hears her father. It's not even something Adam is doing. It's the presence that's been inside her since she was a little girl, the one she's never been able to get rid of. *You can't aim your fastball. You haven't practised enough.*

She doesn't even realise she's picked up the rock until it's in her right hand. The ground leading up to the cliff is clean and neat, the dirt surface mostly free of debris. Except, there are still stones here and there, half embedded in the earth, and now one of them is in her hand.

It's bigger than a baseball, and certainly isn't spherical. There are no seams to guide her fingers, and there's no telling what it will do once it leaves her hand. But when you're a pitcher, when you're good at it, you *know* when you're holding a ball the right way. It never leaves you. You've either got it or you don't. And Annie has always had it, a talent she was born with, a talent that could have changed her life if she hadn't come from Watts, if she hadn't had Martin Cruz for a father, if she hadn't decided to stop him hurting her mother.

If, if, if.

As she rocks back, lifting her left leg and pivoting on her heel, Annie stops thinking about the *ifs*. There is only her, and the ball, and her target.

She grips the rock very lightly with three fingers and her thumb, her pinkie cocked underneath. She raises her left knee almost to her chest, then lunges forward into her stride. Her weight moves from her back leg to her front, left hip leading. Her spine is perfectly vertical, stacked exactly over her pelvis. She has no glove, no comforting oiled leather to grip, but her left hand pulls in tight to her chest anyway. Elbow tucked, out of the way of what's coming.

As her left foot hits the ground in front of her, she swings her pitching arm down and back, letting it lag very slightly so she can get maximum thrust from her body before she lets it go, like revving an engine before a green light. Eyes locked on Adam's head. And as she starts to bring it up, swinging it around and over her shoulder, she thinks: *My aim is fine, pendejo.*

It always was.

Her right arm crests the line of her shoulder, and she accelerates it, violently whipping it up and out. Her body following through, torso turning to generate even more thrust. The rotation is perfectly timed, neither too early nor too late. And at the very last instant, when every ounce of energy she has is screaming towards the four fingertips wrapped around the rock, Annie lets go.

A talented pitcher can send a fastball at home plate at a speed of around ninety miles an hour, more if they're in the majors. Annie – sore, exhausted, on uneven ground – doesn't get anywhere near that fast. And the rock is not a baseball. It does not fly through the air with the same grace, and certainly not the same speed.

But her aim is true.

Her target is a lot closer than home plate.

And a rock to the head is still a rock to the head.

It thuds into the base of Adam's skull, just to the right of that ridiculous ponytail. He's looking down when the rock hits, so it bounces upwards and away. The sound is almost hollow, like a heavy-gauge steel pipe dropped from height.

Annie's follow-through makes her lose her balance, and she and Adam fall at the same time. He slumps to the earth, his body twitching. The rock bounces into a distant bush, sending a roosting bird whirling into the blue sky.

And there is silence.

Annie can't look away from the monster, sure that at any moment he is going to rise up, shaking off the hit like it never happened. She is still not completely convinced that all of this isn't a dream.

But Adam doesn't rise up. Doesn't move. Dead, maybe, and Annie is surprised to find that she doesn't give a shit.

Somewhere, below them, there is the sound of a car coming to a halt. Nic coughs, rolls over, hacking and spitting into the dirt. He tries to get up on all fours, can't quite make it.

We need to get out of here.

Instead, she forces herself to get up, stumble over to the railing. The old fear of heights rises up inside her, but compared to what she just went through, she barely notices it.

In the valley below, perhaps three hundred yards from the base of the cliff, Chloe is getting out of the passenger side of a blue pickup truck, a rifle in her hand. Someone else is driving – Wilcox, perhaps. He's parked a few feet from Nic's black Corolla.

Chloe tilts her head upwards, scanning the cliff. Annie gives her the finger. It would be nice to imagine Chloe's eyes going wide with surprise, although of course, Annie can't tell from this distance.

The woman drops to one knee, bringing the rifle up. Annie steps away from the railing, out of Chloe's view. She stumbles over to Nic and somehow manages to pull him upright. The two of them stand for a moment, leaning on each other, not speaking. And at that moment, Annie sees the most wonderful and frustrating thing in the world.

There's a manicured grove of apple trees close to the south wall of the property. And there, almost completely hidden, just caught by the sun . . .

A ladder. Propped behind one of the trunks. It might be the one Annie saw earlier; right now, she doesn't know, and she doesn't care.

"Come on," Annie says eventually, pulling Nic in the direction of the grove. Even now, Chloe will be making her way back. If they encounter her, it's over. There's no way they have the strength to take on a second person with abilities.

"We can't." His voice is that of a fifty-year-old, pack-a-day smoker. "There's . . ."

He erupts in coughing, clutching at his throat. If Annie hadn't been holding him up, he would have crashed to the ground.

"Security guards," he says. "Armed. Front gate."

For the first time, Annie smiles. "Ladder."

"I don't . . ."

"Nic. *Ladder*."

"What? Where?"

"Apple trees."

He huffs an exhausted laugh. "So that's where they put the damn thing."

FORTY-FOUR

Teagan

Cops everywhere.

In my line of work, that's usually a bad thing. I've been in more than one police chase in my life, although for the record, none of them were my fault, and they started it. And of course, I've been arrested. Hard to believe that that was no more than a couple of days ago. Feels like a couple of years.

This time, though? I have never been so happy to see the LAPD. Or the FBI. Let them handle this. Let them figure it out. Let them dance naked through the crime scene if they like, I don't care. I just murdered someone with a chandelier.

I'm outside the hotel now, in the syrupy afternoon sunlight. It's almost four o'clock. I'm weirded out that it's still daytime – it feels like I've been in that hotel for much, much longer. I sit on the bumper of an ambulance, getting checked over by a paramedic. He has the most amazing tattoo: this geometric pattern, thousands of dots all the way up his arm, vanishing under his sleeve. Maybe I should get one like it as a celebration. And in the middle, I can have the words: I SURVIVED THE DEL RIO.

And *survive* is the operative word. If I turn my head to the left, I can see the body bags. I happened to be glancing that way when a cop asked to take a look, and saw that one of them was Phan Duc Tran. Her throat was a red mess, her eyes still open. Sightless.

I decided not to look that way again.

Six people dead in the ballroom. Four hostage-takers, including Dyson. Two civilians – Phan, plus a French businessman who was in the wrong place at the wrong time when the chandelier made its entrance. A few others from elsewhere in the hotel, including Gerhard. That's to add to the twenty injured, eight seriously. At least the surviving hostage-takers are all in custody.

Africa killed one person, and it nearly destroyed him. I'm now responsible for six – and that's just today. What does it say about me that I'm completely numb?

I keep wondering if I could have saved more. If there was another option open. But whatever the hell was going on today, in this weird hostage situation that wasn't a hostage situation, I did the best I could. I think.

All the same, it's hard not to picture Phan Duc Tran's face, pleading with me to do what Dyson said.

We still have no idea how she was involved in all of this, although I assume Tanner – someone, anyway – has grabbed the evidence from her hotel room. Come to that, we still have no idea what *this* is. Or how Dyson even knew about me. I'd never seen him before. I'm not amazing with faces, or names – I once called Annie *Angela* – but I feel like I'd remember a Bible-quoting lunatic preacher. And why did he want me to use my ability on his buddies? Because *they* sure as hell didn't know what I could do. And what—?

I can't right now. I'm sorry. My brain is mush.

I don't really know when the ambulance showed up, or

how I ended up here. I vaguely remember Africa carrying me, remember him talking to ... someone. Cop? Doctor? Al Pacino? I have no idea. I am somewhere past the point of exhaustion. Several times, I have considered just slumping down on a stretcher and passing out. The only reason I haven't is because I'm pretty sure that someone – Tanner, probably, who has been in earnest discussions with a bunch of FBI agents – would stop me. When I do finally go to sleep, I don't want to wake up for a thousand years.

Also: I want a fucking sandwich. And time to enjoy it. That's not too much to ask, right?

There's a stab of pain in my shoulder, and I pull away, hissing. It doesn't faze the paramedic. He's cut through the bloody bandage, inspecting the stitches. "This is good work," he says. "Who patched you up?"

The words *Burr* and *staff sergeant* wander through my brain, and what comes out is, "Staff Burr Sarge."

He raises an eyebrow, starts to rebandage my shoulder with fresh strapping.

He's just tying it off when someone taps him on the shoulder: a middle-aged man in a rumpled suit, jowls hanging down over his shirt collar and loosened tie. He looks so much like classic detective stereotype that I almost laugh out loud.

"She good?" he asks the paramedic, who waggles his hand back and forth, wincing. "Can she answer questions?"

"I'm right here, bud," I say.

The paramedic shrugs. "Have at it. Doesn't look like she's going to bleed out any time soon." He steps away, begins packing up his medical bag.

"Agent James Foley," the classic detective says to me. "FBI." He flashes me a badge. "I'd like to talk to you about what happened in there."

It takes a lot of effort to stop my shoulders slumping. Here it comes. This is where I start getting grilled about the little PK tornado I caused. This is where it all comes out.

I don't even know if I care any more.

Over the past few days, I've left a trail a mile wide. Between the lobby, the rooftop, the hospital and the storm drain, it's a damn miracle the whole of LA doesn't know about my PK. And if they don't yet, they will soon, thanks to Michiko Kanehara getting a front row seat to both of my little outbursts today. I haven't seen her since back in the ballroom. Most probably, she's already phoning her editors, telling them to get the front page ready. Or whatever the internet equivalent of a front page is.

So fuck it. If Tanner and her boss can figure out a way to hang me high for exposing my ability, if they genuinely want to put me back in Waco for what happened today, let them. There's only so much I can do.

Then again, I suppose I have to at least *try* and deny it all.

"Not sure I can help," I tell Foley, sounding about as convincing as a teenager lying about buying whiskey and smokes off the school janitor.

"I'm just trying to get a picture of your role in all of this. We've already questioned plenty of folks, but I'm a little hazy on what you were doing in there." He pulls out a battered notepad, digs inside his jacket for a pen. "Let's start with your name."

"Don't I get a lawyer or something?"

He frowns, suspicion clouding his face. "Like I said, I'm just trying to get a picture here. So could you tell me—?"

"*Eh.* You."

I don't even see where Africa comes from. All at once, he's just there, looming over Agent Foley, looking murderous.

"She is hurt. You can save your bloody questions for another time, huh?"

Foley flashes Africa his badge, along with a sour smile. "Sir, I'm gonna need you to step back."

"I am not stepping back for you, not for anyone. What she do in there, she is a hero, and you were not even there, so don't come and try pretend that you know things."

"It's OK, dude," I tell Africa. "You don't have to—"

"Sir." There's no smile from Foley this time, not even a sour one. "Step away. *Now.*"

"May I ask what you think you're doing, agent?" Moira Tanner's cut-glass voice makes me jump. She's standing off to my right, fixing Foley with a look that reminds me of someone pinning a butterfly to a board.

It doesn't quite work like it's supposed to. Foley is starting to get angry. "FBI, ma'am, step back please."

"Mrs Tanner," Africa says. "This man is trying to talk to Teggan. Ask questions."

"Guys, it's OK," I mumble.

Foley jerks a thumb at Africa. "I need both of you to vacate the area. Immediately."

"On the contrary," Tanner says slowly. "This is above your pay grade. She is a government employee, and she was here on official business."

"My man, you want to be very careful here." It's Burr, gently but firmly stepping between Tanner and Foley. Christ, I didn't see him either. My general awareness is shot to shit. I have a vague urge to just get up, walk away, go somewhere quiet.

"That's it." Foley snaps his fingers at a couple of uniformed cops. "Get these people out of here. If they resist, book 'em for obstruction."

Tanner's eyes flash. Which is where my general awareness, clearly embarrassed that it's been dropping the ball up until this point, spots Arthur Weiss. The senator is coming up behind Tanner and Burr, looking dishevelled and exhausted, but very much alive. He holds out a hand to the approaching officers, but speaks directly to Foley. "Thank you, agent. That will be all."

"And just who are you?" Foley says. He's exasperated, but there's a hint of wariness in his voice now. Like this particular puddle is a lot deeper than he thought it was.

"My name," the senator says, and I swear his voice drops an octave, "is Arthur Weiss. *Senator* Arthur Weiss."

From the look on Foley's face, he's suddenly remembering the last time he saw this person on TV.

"These people are on my staff," Weiss continues, "and if you wish to interview them, you can make an appointment through my office."

"Senator." Foley clears his throat. "This is an active crime scene, and I have to ask you to—"

"*That will be all*, agent. Or do I need to call the bureau director and ask why you are harassing my employees?" He gestures at us. "All of us were held hostage in there. It's a damn miracle we survived. Damn miracle. Now: what's it going to be?"

There's a moment where Foley looks like he's going to try his luck. Then he gives the barest nod and stalks away, waving back the uniformed officers.

"Thanks," I tell Weiss, my voice barely more than a whisper.

"Quite all right. How are you holding up?" He reaches out to grasp my shoulder, then pulls back just in time when he realises it's the injured one. "Sorry."

"Senator," Africa says. "You all OK? Not hurt?"

"No, thank God."

"On the roof, when you were ... I do not think Teggan

planned for it to be so . . . " Africa rolls his hands around each other, like he's calling a travel in a basketball game. "So *waaah*. You know?"

Everyone looks at me, but it's Burr who I focus on. He's got the strangest expression on his face as he stares back at me. Almost embarrassed.

The senator nods slowly, although he doesn't look quite as pleased as he probably should. Which I guess is understandable, given the clusterfuck this day turned out to be. I stare at him, spent, waiting for the axe to fall.

"I owe you thanks," he says slowly. "I think we all do. That was a very difficult situation you faced. I'm not sure what I would have done if I were wearing your shoes. But . . . " He rubs his chin. "I am a little curious. Why weren't you able to stop this *before* it all went to hell? What happened to your ability? Even in my room, before . . . well, you didn't seem to—"

"Yeah . . . I didn't really have my PK at all then." I probably shouldn't be telling him this, but at this point, it doesn't feel like it matters.

"Senator," Tanner says. "I can assure you that I was unaware of this before we met in your hotel suite. You can trust that we will have a formal debrief, where we will consider the future of—"

"Ma'am." Burr steps in. "Maybe we should think about how we approach this."

Tanner glares at him. "Where we will consider the future of Frost's existing situation,' she finishes. "I'll be conducting a full investigation, and then I will have a much more coherent response for you and the committee."

"Please, ma'am, let's at least have this discussion behind closed doors."

"Teggan?"

"Ms Frost, I don't understand. When did you lose your ability? How long has this been going on for?"

"*Teggan.*"

Their voices press in on me, like physical barriers pushing me back against the ambulance, crushing the breath out of me. If I don't get out now, I'm going to do something I might regret.

"'Scuse me," I mumble, getting shakily to my feet. I don't even bother listening to what they're saying any more. I put my head down, and walk as fast as I can around the side of the ambulance. Ignoring the outstretched hands, the puzzled and angry voices. *Just a minute. Please, just give me a minute. Just so I can catch my breath, please . . .*

My walk turns into a stumbling jog, which would turn into a run if I had the coordination for it. I squeeze past the cop cars parked bumper-to-bumper, and find myself on the edge of the driveway, next to a sweeping flowerbed that runs down the hillside. I can see all the way to the bottom of the driveway, to the streets and beyond. The view from here isn't as spectacular as it was from the roof, but it's enough to calm me. Just a little.

I hang my head. Five minutes. I'll just take five minutes, take a few deep breaths, get my head in gear. Figure out what the hell I'm going to do next.

And what, exactly, is that going to be? I have so many problems that need solving, so many different things in play, that I haven't got the faintest clue where to start. Hell, even getting something to eat is a mountain I have no idea how to climb.

"What a day, huh?" says a voice next to me.

Slowly, I raise my head to find Michiko Kanehara looking back at me.

FORTY-FIVE

Teagan

The elegant, put-together journalist from before is gone. The Kanehara standing next to me looks like she's aged a decade. Her hair is a mess, plastered to her forehead with sweat. Her mascara has started to run, and there's a crust of dried blood on her rolled-up sleeve.

"Are ... you OK?" I point to her sleeve.

She stares down at it, like she's never seen it before. "Would you believe I actually forgot about that?" She pulls the sleeve up to show me a small gash. "It hurts, but I'll live. I got off lucky, I think."

For a long moment, the two of us just stand there, looking out at Hollywood. There's a part of me that thinks, maybe if I don't say anything, she won't bring up the fact that she saw me use my ability on the roof, and then again in the ballroom. She won't ask me for comment, or an interview. She'll just let me go on my way, and we can pretend we never met each other.

I've tried to avoid thinking about it, but standing here, next to a respected journalist who has a massive readership and who just saw me use my ability – twice – makes it really freaking difficult. What is Tanner going to do if, all of a sudden, I'm splashed across the cover of the *New Yorker*? Blast into orbit, probably. And when she comes down, she'll land right on top of me.

I have to say something. I have to at least try and steer away from this colossal fucking iceberg.

"So." I clear my throat, wincing as a jab of dull pain shoots through my shoulder. "About what happened. On the roof. And, you know, in the ballroom."

"Quite a situation," Kanehara says, continuing to look out on the city.

"Yeah. I just—"

"Wish I'd seen more of it."

"I didn't really intend to do what I did; it just kind of happened and . . . what?"

She shrugs. "I was behind the AC vent on the roof. My camera didn't really get much. And then in the ballroom, they took my phone away, and I got flat on the floor as soon as the noise started. Didn't see a thing."

What is she talking about? I know she saw, she was *right there*, she looked right at me and—

Oh.

Huh.

I see.

"It was pretty crazy," I say carefully.

"I bet." Another uncomfortable silence. "It'd be quite a story, if the people involved ever decided to speak up."

" . . . It might not be up to them."

She turns to look at me. It must crick something in her neck, because she gives a soft grunt, massages the base of her skull. "No, I imagine it wouldn't. But if they ever do decide to tell the story, I'd be . . . *disappointed* if they didn't come to me first. You know, after not seeing what happened, even though I was right there."

"OK, actually, I don't really have the evens for the cloak and dagger stuff right now. Sorry. Say what you mean."

A flicker of a smile. "Fair enough. I want the exclusive. As and when you decide to go public, I want you to come to me. On-the-record interview. Nothing off-limits."

It's like I'm standing on a frozen lake that has just started to crack. "It might never happen. You understand that, right?"

"I'll take the risk."

"But why? You can write about what happened today for real, and be on the front page of every paper from here to ... to ... "

Michiko says nothing.

And I think I get it.

What's more powerful? An eyewitness account that a million people can pick holes in? That Tanner herself will probably try to discredit? Or an exclusive interview with me, with an on-camera demonstration of my ability? For someone like Michiko Kanehara, it's one hell of a long-term investment.

And it's not one I'm a fan of. Because it's a chip she could call in at any time. Who's to say that six months or a year or two years down the track, she gets tired of waiting? Decides to put her career on the fast track? Even if I don't cooperate, she has more than enough ammunition already.

The problem is, there's not a single thing I can do about it.

"You know who my boss is, right?" I murmur. "Scary lady back there? You think she'll be cool with this?"

"Maybe. Maybe not. I assume she'll want to talk to me at some point, browbeat me with some *classified* nonsense. But I covered wars for a long time, and plenty of governments. You'd be amazed at how quickly priorities can shift, and how fast personnel can change."

It's hard not to think of the senator. The boss of my boss. The one who could decide to rip my entire life apart if the mood took him . . . or simply replace Tanner.

"I could go to another journalist," I say carefully. "Go public with someone else." Frankly, the idea of going public *at all* gives me the screaming heebie-jeebies, but it's a fair question.

She tilts her palm back and forth. "I can't stop you. But let's just say that my subsequent story – and there *would* be a subsequent story – might not paint in you a very flattering light. And just so we're on the same page: yes, I have video of what happened on the roof."

"You mean video of me saving the senator's life?"

"Things can be spun. Looked at differently."

"Thought reporters were supposed to be objective."

She gives me a look that says *oh, you sweet, naive summer child.*

"You can go to someone else," she says, "and risk that my story will the muddy the waters . . . or you can give me the exclusive at some point in the future. Your call."

"Looks like you got a deal," I murmur. "I just hope you know what you signed up for."

"And what about you? What's next?"

Boy. How do I tell her that what I have to do next is track down my psychotic brother and sister and stop them from doing even more heinous shit? The answer, obviously, is that I don't tell her at all.

"There are a couple of people I need to see," I say, thinking of Annie and Nic. "I could—"

"Teagan. Teagan!"

And then Jonas Schmidt has his arms wrapped around me, pulling me close to him.

I'm so unprepared for the hug that I almost pull away, but at the last instant, I stop. He smells of sweat, and gunpowder, and the barest hint of cologne. It's a weirdly comforting mix of smells, and for just a second, I allow myself to relax into his embrace, even though I didn't give my permission.

After a good few seconds, he lets me go. "Are you hurt?"

"Dude, you know I'm hurt. You were there when I got shot."

"Yes, yes, but is there anything else?" He's trying to look everywhere at once.

"You're right, I totally forgot about the other three bullet wounds. Also, I think there might be an axe lodged in the back of my head." I bend forward. "Can you check?"

"Do not even joke about these things, Teagan." It's then that I realise how wired he is. There's a haunted look in his eyes. A wild look.

"Hey," I say. "I'm good. OK? I made. We made it."

He nods, more to himself than to me. "Michiko? *Mein Gott* – the blood. Are you . . . ?"

She glares at him . . . but then, the glare softens. Just a little. "I'm all right," she says.

He opens his mouth, then closes it again.

"I wanted—" Jonas says.

"Could you—?" Kanehara says at the same time.

They stop, embarrassed.

"You go," says Jonas.

"No, please."

He clears his throat. "Michiko . . . would you give me a minute with Teagan?"

She raises an eyebrow. "You realise we never actually finished our interview?"

He looks confused for a second, before it hits him. "Ah. Yes, of course. Are we still doing that? I would have thought—"

"Am I still writing the first profile to feature the subject in the middle of an active hostage situation? The profile that is going to win me a Pulitzer? Why yes, I am." She happens to glance at me as she says it, and there's no mistaking what she really means: *My first Pulitzer. You, Teagan, are going to win me my second.*

"Would you mind if we . . . if I did have that moment alone with Teagan first?"

A flicker of annoyance on her face, gone in an instant. "Sure. I'll give you a call in a day or two."

And then she limps away, leaving me alone with Jonas.

"You are sure you are all right?" he asks.

"Like I said, I'm fine. I—"

"Would you like to leave with me today? Right now?"

OK. Was *not* expecting that.

"Um." I blink at him. "What do you mean?"

"There's an island I go to sometimes, in the Fijian archipelago. A friend of mine owns it. I don't think it's ever seen a day without sun. If we leave now, we could be there by tomorrow morning."

He sees my confusion. "And you must not worry. There will be all the medical attention you require."

"Jonas . . ."

"And if you are going to recuperate anywhere on earth, then why not have it be somewhere with white beaches and blue water? Surely your bosses would not begrudge you this, after what you have been through today."

"Jonas, are you asking me out on a date?"

"Yes," he says simply. Then his eyes widen. "But I wish to be absolutely clear. There is no commitment here, and I would never ask you to do anything you do not wish to do. I'm simply asking you to spend time with me."

"On an island."

"Why not? I have the means, I have the access – my friend will not hesitate to offer if I ask. He may even lend us his plane to get there." He spreads his hands. "I am giving you the chance to recover in perhaps the most beautiful place on earth. What is the point of having this if I cannot share it with anyone?"

He pauses for a moment, rubbing his chin. "Even before I knew about your powers, I found you fascinating. I wanted to know more about you. But we moved in different worlds, and I was aware that as an intelligence agent, it was not in your interest to get too close to me. For me, it was a fantasy. Nothing more."

It's hard not to think of the times I spent dreaming about him, wondering where he was, what he was doing. Stalking him on Instagram, reading news reports about him and his work. And at the same time, my crush had a crush on me, which is . . . wow.

"And then, all at once, life throws us back together!" He's really getting going now, an almost feverish quality to his voice. "What is that, if not fate? And that is why am asking you: come with me."

I've run out of words. I don't have anything left to express the thousands of things I'm feeling.

"I don't expect you to fall at my feet," he says. "I don't expect anything. Instead, I am simply asking you to take a chance. Come with me. We will eat, drink, swim, lie in the sun. We will talk. We will get to know one another, as people, away from . . . from all of this. And if you decide that we should not be together, then we will part as friends. But my hope is . . . my hope is that you will come to see me as something more."

This is how it's supposed to go, isn't it?

The hostage situation ends, the bad guys go down and the

hot guy walks up to the leading lady and asks her to go on a date with him. It's the kind of thing that almost never happens in real life, until you're standing outside a swanky hotel after an insane adventure, and it actually does.

In the movies, the girl always says something witty. Raises a perfectly manicured eyebrow. Consents, after some light banter, to explore the relationship a little further.

I don't say anything witty. I don't say anything at all. I just stare at Jonas, my mouth open.

Say yes.

But I don't.

It's not just the fact that Tanner won't let me, or the need to chase after my brother and sister, the need to find out just what the hell happened today. If I really wanted to, I could get past all of those. I could tell Tanner that I was taking a damn vacation. I could let Burr be the one who gets to chase after my siblings, put his special forces training to good use.

But here's the thing about Jonas. Like every billionaire ever, he's successful because he bet on himself. It's the belief that led him to land his private plane in the middle of a disaster zone so he could offer help to those who needed it.

There's a flipside to that belief. Arrogance. It showed itself a few hours ago, when he charged out of the hotel room, acting like a spoiled, entitled asshole, talking down to me and Africa and Kanehara. He acted exactly like you'd expect a self-made billionaire to act: like he was invincible. Like he knew better than everyone around him. He may have been one of the good guys in this little escapade, but that doesn't change the fact that he considered himself above us.

In his own mind, he's a hero.

And when you get down to it, that's why he wants to be with me. He thinks I'm a hero too.

Because it works both ways, doesn't it? He has an idea of me, just as I have one of him. And as far as he's concerned, I'm a secret agent with superpowers. He doesn't know the truth: that I'm terrible at my job, that I would much rather not have my ability at all, that I'm no good at being a hero. How long would it be before he figured that out? Would he still want to be with me when he did? Or would he move on, casting me aside? Would he look at me the way he looked at Africa? Or Michiko? Would he decide I'm more trouble than I'm worth? Would he get bored of me? And how long would that take? Three months? Six?

I don't know any of the answers to these questions. But it doesn't matter what he thinks I am, because this isn't just about him.

There's a lot about my life that I don't get to decide. Where I work, who I work for, the missions I go on, what people expect of me. But I do get to decide who I spend my time with, and I don't want to spend my time with someone who thinks I'm something I'm not, or who will get bored of me when he realises the truth. I want to be with someone who accepts all of me. Good stuff, and bad. Who knows that I might – no, that I *will* fuck up, probably over and over again.

And that someone is Nic Delacourt.

Someone who *has* fucked up, over and over again. Who has, on occasion, acted like an asshole. Who is just as messy and complicated and occasionally as stupid as me.

I live the weirdest, wildest life imaginable. My fantasies are *all* about being normal, about having a normal life with a normal job. It's something I'll never get. Even after I lost my ability, it was never going to happen, and I think the Del Rio proved it. But Nic will be there no matter how crazy things get. He is someone who knows what I'm like at my worst ...

And who knows what it takes for me to be my best.

"So?" Jonas spreads his hands. "What do you say?"

And still, there's a moment where I almost say yes.

Almost.

I lean forward, standing on tiptoe, and give him a peck on the cheek.

"Thanks, Mister Germany. Maybe another time."

Then, before he – or I – can say anything else, I squeeze his shoulder, and walk away.

FORTY-SIX

Teagan

If we lived in a just and fair world, this is the part where I'd find a friendly cop to take me home, where I would sleep for a billion years.

But we do not live in a just and fair world, so all I can do is hang around while Tanner and the senator talk to various agents and cops. I rest my ass on the hood of a squad car, wondering if whoever owns it will shout at me. They don't. Africa flashes me a thumbs-up, raises a questioning eyebrow from his bruised face. He gets the first real smile I've given out in hours.

Jonas, wisely, doesn't follow me. I spot him talking on his cell phone, walking off down the sloped driveway.

I last exactly five minutes before I've had enough. It's too bright here, too loud. Maybe Tanner'll let me use one of the empty bedrooms, which means I can sleep. Fine, that'll never happen, but maybe—

My eyes go wide. Despite my exhaustion, I've just had a brilliant idea.

I limp over to Tanner, still deep in conversation with the senator. She looks up as I approach.

"Sorry I ran off like that," I say, before she can speak. "It just . . . got too much, you know?"

"Quite understandable," says Weiss. "You're feeling all right?"

"I'm good, thank you." I turn to Tanner. "Did anybody grab the phone?"

The senator frowns. "What phone?"

"We took it from one of the hostiles on the roof, sir," Tanner says, looking back towards the hotel entrance.

Weiss's eyes go wide. "Oh. Yes, I think I know the one you mean."

"Reggie was helping us crack it," I say, ignoring the angry flash in Tanner's eyes. "Regina McCormick? Our hacker?"

"I'm familiar," Weiss says. "She's good."

"Very. Look, did anybody go back down there and get the phone? It might be evidence, and I don't know if these cops know about Greta Garbo's little secret passage or whatever."

Now the senator looks even more confused. "I'm sorry, did you say Greta Garbo?"

"Yup. She had this stairway built so she could have her sidepiece come visit." I point. "Comes out in a storage room off the lobby. We used it to get down to the basement."

"I see."

Tanner looks down her nose at me. "I'm not sure I want you wandering around. I was going to retrieve the phone after—"

"Please." I step in closer. "I . . . I just want to be useful. I don't want to sit around and do nothing."

"I don't think that's necessary," Weiss says. "I'll have one of the patrolmen pick it up. You take a load off."

"It's OK. I don't mind."

Tanner pauses for a few moments, then nods. "All right. But come straight back here."

"Thank you," I sing, waving to Weiss as I skip off.
Well, limp off.

Truth be told, the phone is secondary. It's the room I'm
interested in – the porn room. It's quiet. It's empty. And it has
a couch I can lie on for a while.

I wind my way through cop cars and patrolmen and FBI
agents. Back through the gigantic doors into the hotel lobby.
I'm expecting one of the cops to stop me. At its most basic
level, this is an active crime scene, and I'm probably not
allowed to wander around inside.

But there are so many people here now that nobody really
pays attention to me. I glide through them, and there's barely a
glance in my direction. I walk back behind the check-in desk,
past the blood stains and cracked marble, into the storage room
and back into Greta Garbo's secret passage. Again, I get a little
flicker of amazement that nobody stops me, gets in front of me
and demands to know what the hell I think I'm doing.

After a long time – or what feels like a long time – I
reach the sub-basement, the hidden office with the poster of
the naked lady on the ceiling above the couch. I give her a
secret smile as I come in, then think, what the hell, and tip
her a wink.

The room is the same as it was we left: same battered desk,
same threadbare couch with a little patch of my blood drying
on the crusty upholstery. Same dusty, faintly sweet smell.
And it is mercifully, brilliantly, beautifully quiet. But I am
not inclined to listen hard. I bathe in the quiet, wallow in it,
filling only it with the longest, deepest exhale I can manage.
The breath doesn't unkink the knots in my neck or lower the
pain in my shoulder, but it helps.

A yawn rises out of me: the kind of yawn that forces you to
stretch your jaw as wide as it will go. The kind of yawn only

given by someone who is perhaps ten seconds away from just passing out.

"Fuck me, what a day," I say to the porn star on the ceiling. She doesn't reply, just keeps smiling that coquettish smile.

My wandering feet take me over to the couch. I jam my hand under the cushion, half wondering if the phone and laptop will even be there. Maybe one of the cops *did* make it down here. But then my fingers close over plastic and metal, and I yank them out. Mission accomplished. Guess I'll head back upstairs and report to El Capitan Tanner. Oh wait, no – in fact, I think I'll take a well-deserved nap.

I put the laptop and phone on the floor, then fall onto the couch. Lord almighty, that feels good. I drop my head, breathe deep. Then slowly, with much grunting and wheezing, I lie back on the cushions and close my eyes.

Ten seconds pass. My eyes open, and without looking, I reach for the phone.

There is a large part of me that just wants to go, *fuck it*. Close my eyes again, blot out the world for a bit. After all, the bad guys are either dead or in handcuffs. So what difference does it make what's on this phone? Ultimately, it's just evidence in a case that I will never participate in. Tanner would rather shoot herself than have one of her people take the stand in a court of law.

But that doesn't stop the same damn question turning over and over in my mind: *When is a hostage situation not a hostage situation?*

I expect there to still be a password lock; even if Reggie cracked the phone and downloaded the contents. But to my surprise, the phone opens immediately. Displays a bank of apps: contacts, email, photos. *Candy Crush Saga*. I grimace at that last one, unable to picture one of Dyson's goons whiling away the time between jobs shuffling around brightly coloured candy shapes.

There's another app, too, one I recognise: Telegram. An encrypted messaging app. Makes sense – it's probably how they all communicated before the job. I tap it, not expecting much, and get a password screen. I don't even bother trying to open it. Reggie's probably got it handled already. God, I still can't believe Tanner fired her. What a stupid, stupid thing to do. *Hey, here's an idea, let's get rid of one of the most qualified hackers in the country, it'll be great for team morale.*

The little spark of anger towards Tanner quickly grows into a blaze. Jonas might have been right about her pride, but that doesn't change the fact that she made some very dumb decisions today. She might not think she's the hero, but she still believes that her way is the only way.

Forget her. You've still got Africa. And Annie. And Nic.

I can't wait to see them. Hug them. Hell, Annie is probably going to give me endless shit, and I'm even looking forward to that. God, I hope she's OK.

Ah, fuck this. If there's anything on the phone, the owner will have encrypted it. I'm on the verge of putting it down, getting my shut-eye. But that's the thing about smartphones: there's always something else to distract you. Without really intending to, I navigate to the photos app. Mildly curious, I guess: what kind of photos does a psychotic religious nutjob even have?

The first thing I see is a video. And on the thumbnail image: Senator Arthur Weiss.

Up against the railing, anger and fear on his face.

Frowning, I play the video. Not sure I really want to, but unable to stop my thumb tapping it.

The footage. For a moment, the view is all cockeyed, blue sky and lens flares, a hint of grey concrete at the bottom corner. As if the phone's owner hit record before positioning the camera. The sound, tinny through the phone speakers, is all wind noise.

The angle stabilises. The camera blurs for a second, then focuses on the senator. He looks terrified, his mouth moving, the wind obscuring his words. Dyson holding him, the railing pushed against the small of his back, his top half stretching out over the drop.

The wind noise drops. "You getting this?" Dyson says.

"Yeah yeah," the woman holding the phone replies.

"I don't know what you think you're going to achieve," the senator says. "If you kill me—"

"What?" Dyson sounds relaxed, almost languid. "What's going to happen, that won't happen already? Will Elise and I –" He gestures to the camera, or at least, to the woman holding it. "– not get arrested? Not get our money? Tell me, senator, what exactly does keeping you alive get me? I'm curious."

Weiss's face is the colour of old paper. "This is a mistake."

"I don't make mistakes. But apparently, you do. Elise, are you getting this?"

"I already said I was."

"Good. I want a record." No more languid tone now. Just cold, hard steel. "If I'm going down, I'm not having you making it out smelling like roses."

"Please . . ."

"Time to choose, senator. You die, and Elise and I go to jail, along with those poor saps we roped into this. Or you live. The only way you get to that second choice is if you give me my insurance."

He shakes the senator, who lets out a choked gasp. "So let's hear it. Why did the Frost girl not do her thing? Where the hell was she?"

What the fuck am I watching? What is this?

"I don't know."

"Come now, senator."

"*I don't know!*" Flecks of white spit flicker in the sunlight, grainy on the footage.

Dyson smiles.

"Let's start from the beginning," he says. That relaxed tone is back in his voice, which is somehow scarier than when he was angry. "Let's start with you hiring us to crash your little party here today."

FORTY-SEVEN

Teagan

I've lived through actual earthquakes. I have been in situations where the ground was literally shifting underneath my feet, the whole world tilting and shaking. I think I felt more stable then than I do now, sitting on this perfectly steady couch in this crappy little office, staring down at the phone. The whole room feels like it's slowly tilting sideways.

The senator's head sags. He raises his eyes to the camera. "You don't have the faintest idea what's going on here," he says. "If you're smart, you'll—"

"*Drop it!*" Burr's voice, offscreen. More jerkiness, more wind noises.

A few moments later, the camera goes haywire, a whirling mass of sky and people and ground and guns, flipping end over end. My PK, getting in on the action. The video keeps filming, but whatever happens to the phone, it comes to a stop face down. The screen goes black, the audio nothing but crashes and bangs and terrified shouting.

There is no freaking way I just heard what I heard.

It takes me more than one try to rewind the video. My

fingers are shaking too much. Once again, I hear Dyson say, "Let's start with you hiring us."

It's a trick. Another part of Dyson's game plan. Or Phan's. It has to be.

I stop the video on Weiss's face, when he looks back up at the camera. Stare at it. Trying to decipher the look in his eyes. I'm expecting to find surprise, shock, outrage even. But that's not what I'm seeing. There's a cold look on his face: cold, and determined.

You can't see shit. You're imagining things.

But that isn't true is it?

"You have got to be fucking kidding me," I say to the empty room.

I watch it again. Then once more. Each time, I'm convinced I'm going to see or hear something different. No dice.

OK. OK, think. If Reggie cracked the phone, then she probably downloaded the contents. She may or may not have seen the video, and she may or may not appreciate what it means. She may or may not have reached out to Tanner already, but either way, it doesn't matter. Because I've got to show Tanner this, right fucking now.

It's starting to sink in now, really sink in. Why the hell would the senator hire Dyson? Why take hostages? Why disrupt an event that would benefit him if it ran smoothly? And how was Phan involved?

Enough. Get it to Tanner.

And that's when I hear footsteps. Coming down the passage towards the office.

Tanner, or Africa, or even Jonas. Someone who knows about this place, anyway. This time, I do push myself off the couch, the phone clutched tight in my left hand. The vacant, weary feeling has gone, my brain fizzing, like a Coke poured too quickly into a glass.

"In here!" I say, as the footsteps reach the door. "Holy crap, you are not gonna believe th—"

Senator Arthur Weiss pushes through the door.

For a few seconds, we just stare at each other. There's a quizzical, almost pleased little smile on his face.

He's not alone. There is another man with him, a broad-shouldered, middle-aged dude with a chest-length, greying beard. He has a sunburn and an ID badge in a lanyard around his neck.

I don't know what expression is on my face. Really, I haven't the faintest clue. Do I tough it out? Pretend I was just leaving? He can't know that I have the phone, right? I mean, fine, it's in my hand, but he can't know that I have *the* phone. Then again, there's nothing he can do to hurt me, not a single thing, and the hostage situation is over, so . . .

"Teagan," he says, as if we just bumped into each other on the street. "You weren't kidding. That is one well-hidden passage."

What am I supposed to do here? Attack him? Push past him? Run like hell? Then again, I don't know if I can get past the scary-looking guy with the beard. Who is he? I haven't seen him before.

"After everything that happened," he says, "I wanted a chance to talk. Just you and me."

"I . . ."

"I asked my pilot to come pick us up." He gestures to the other man, who gives me a guarded nod. "My chopper is on the roof right now. How about you and I take a quick ride? Of course, I can't drop you at your apartment." His smile gets wider. "But my plane is at Van Nuys, and I'd be happy to arrange a car for . . ."

His voice trails off as he looks down at the phone in my hand. For a long moment, the three of us are silent.

Do something.

But my poor, exhausted brain is still trying to process what I saw on the video. It's trying to match the friendly, calm face in front of me, the face belonging to a man who almost got thrown off a roof, with the idea that he may be into some seriously bad shit. It's not quite deer-in-headlights, but it's close.

The senator's smile reappears. He shakes his head, digging in his pocket. "You know," he says. "None of this had to happen."

Too late, my PK picks up the shape of the object in his hand. Right before he pulls it out and aims at me.

His Taser.

The one he showed us before, back in his hotel room a million years ago.

There is perhaps half a second between me noticing it and him aiming it at me and pulling the trigger. Half a second when I could have grabbed it with my PK, ripped out of his hand. What stops me is the knowledge that I won't be able to control the energy, that in this close space, I could end up hurting all three of us.

The hesitation is the polar opposite of what I should do. But that's the thing about dangerous situations: you can go through a bunch of them, one after the other, and when a new one comes along you still freeze.

I should have learned kung-fu.

And then the barbs embed themselves in my chest.

FORTY-EIGHT

Teagan

Tasers are not just my kryptonite – they are everyone's kryptonite. There isn't a single person on the planet, abilities or not, who can withstand fifty thousand volts delivered directly to the chest.

God, it hurts. Imagine the gnarliest cramp you've ever had, multiplied by your entire body, only a million bees are attacking you at the same time and they've gotten inside your skull. But that's not even the worst part. The worst part is that you cannot express this pain, on account of your entire body going rigid and everything up to and including your voice box freezing solid.

I go down hard, back arching as the electricity rips through me. It is impossible to use my PK. Impossible to do anything but lie there and absorb the agony.

The senator bends down, plucking the barbs from my chest, which somehow makes the pain even worse. "Daniel," he says. "Bring her." The pilot scoops me into his arms. I'm barely aware of it, locked in my private world of pain.

The last time someone used a Taser on me, my PK went into overdrive. But it didn't happen right away; it took a good minute or two. Until that happened, my ability was completely walled off. Plus, the first time, I only got hit with one barb. It's both this time, and it hurts exponentially more.

I'm dimly aware of moving down the passage, then of the three of us stepping into an elevator. I have no idea where the elevator is in relation to the secret passage or the porn poster room. I'm desperately hoping that someone spots us, but it doesn't happen.

As the elevator rises, the pain fades a little. I latch onto the sensation; I still can't move, not really, but maybe if I can hold onto this, I'll be able to use my PK. If I can do that, then—

"Think you need to hit her again, boss."

"Yes, I see that."

No, d—

The pilot puts me down, on the floor of the elevator. A second later, the senator pulls the trigger.

Ow.

Out of the elevator. More passages. Stairs. sunlight. Footsteps heavy on concrete. Helicopter rotor blades, silhouetted against an open blue sky. The sound of a sliding door. The pilot grunting as he heaves me inside.

Come on, you motherfucker. Come on!

No dice. My PK is there, I can feel it, but it simply isn't responding.

Surely someone will have come looking for me by now. Africa or Tanner. Where are they? Why are they letting this asshole kidnap me? What the fuck is happening?

The door slams. I'm lying on the floor of the chopper, and as I watch, still twitching uncontrollably, a pair of gleaming leather shoes slide into view. The senator, making himself comfortable. A moment later, the helicopter's engine starts. This being a luxury chopper, the cabin has sound insulation, so the noise of the rotor blades is just a distant roar.

My stomach lurches as we lift off, the world rolling around me as the chopper banks.

The senator puts a hand on my head, turns me up to look at him. He still has that maddening smile. And the Taser is still in his hand.

"If I see anything," he says, "anything untoward, I will hit you again. There are still one or two charges left in this thing. I don't think it's caused any permanent damage so far, but my dear, that might change if you get another dose. And believe me, you're going to need your strength."

He pats my cheek. "So how about you just lie there quietly, like a good girl? Soon, you won't have to worry about a thing."

What. The fuck.

I try to speak, but my lips are burning-numb, and all I end up doing is drooling on the carpet. The senator notices. He pulls a handkerchief out of his jacket pocket and dabs at my face, almost kindly. Up close, I can just see the letters AW monogrammed on one edge in red stitching.

The senator straightens up, nods to himself, then pockets the handkerchief. He reaches over to somewhere I can't see. "How long is the flight time?"

Daniel's gravelly voice crackles through the cabin. "A half-hour, sir. The team is already on the ground."

I replay the entire day, everything from the moment we met the senator. Trying to understand why he betrayed me. Trying to figure out why on earth he would hire Dyson and his friends.

The sheer number of hostage-takers. The lack of police. Phan's photos. The Children of Solomon. The fact that Dyson seemed to know me, zeroed in on me before everything went to shit. The way he turned on the mercs he hired, all but ordering me to take them out. And the video on the phone.

My face reflects off Weiss's polished leather shoes. It distorts my features, twists them almost beyond recognition. And deep inside my mind, the final puzzle piece clicks into place.

When is a hostage situation not a hostage situation?

All at once, the answer is there.

When it's an audition.

"I beg your pardon?" says Weiss.

I must have spoken the words out loud. Amazingly, I manage to raise myself up one elbow, slowly lifting my head to look at the senator. It hurts like hell, but the pain seems unimportant now.

"I was supposed to stop it before it started," I slur. "Wasn't I?"

He tilts his head, as if seeing me for the first time.

"Not bad," he murmurs. "You're smarter than you look."

My strength fails me, and I crash back down to the floor, breathing in thick, heavy gasps. But oh, it's all coming together now, all the little pieces. Weiss didn't hire me to protect him. He hired me to protect *everyone*. Everyone in that ballroom. He hired Dyson to stage the whole attack, with the expectation that I would stop it before it could get going. Because that's what I do, isn't it? That's how my PK works. If I'd been in tip-top shape, I'd have sensed the guns long before they were ever fired. I would have handled shit.

"Phan Duc Hong," I say. "She was a . . . buyer. Wasn't she?"

"Hm? Oh. Yes," he says, speaking absently, looking out the window. "Her, and a few others. Geoff Williams from ArmCo. Ted Krzynski and Mia Horvitz from Steiner Group. The three people DynaCore sent over. Shame about Phan, although Ted and Mia will probably waste no time moving in on her interests."

Almost everyone in that ballroom believed what has happening in front of them. The mercs holding the guns believed it too. They had no idea who I was. They had no idea that seven of the hostages, plus Weiss, plus Dyson and his fellow religious wack jobs, were there for a show.

My show. *The Teagan Show.*

They were there to watch me up close, to witness me stop an attack. A live demo of my ability. Where I would take out eighteen bad guys in one go. It's a huge number for this kind of hostage situation, but that was the point. It wouldn't have been enough for me to *just* take out the armed waiters, if they attacked. Weiss wanted to show that I could handle large groups, no problem.

It wouldn't even have had to be dramatic. No flying objects required, no need to reveal my abilities to others. It would be the *absence* of guns that would confirm my ability. Well, that and a whole bunch of waiters getting arrested and/or getting the shit kicked out of them. *Well then, there you go, folks. Isn't she something? The saviour of the storm drain, up close and personal. Now, bidding starts at two hundred billion. Do I have two hundred billion?*

And of course, Weiss knew what I could do. He trusted that if I was specifically on the alert for people with bad intentions, I'd be able to find them and shut them down. That's probably how he sold it to these assholes. Yes, there'd be an element of danger, but it would be as close to battlefield conditions as you could get. Hell, maybe he even pitched it scientifically. A blind test.

And he protected himself. He didn't just go out and hire a bunch of mercenaries. He hired the Children of Solomon, an insane religious group that badly wanted money to be insane and religious in front of as many people as possible. *They* hired the mercenaries. A bunch of suckers who would take the fall. Brandon Evans, Shane DuBois and the rest of them. They weren't the bad guys – not really. The real bad guys were seven hostages, sitting there tied up with the rest. Wondering how it all went so wrong.

Weiss probably already had a plan in place to spring Dyson from jail afterwards. Maybe even the other Children of Solomon would come along for the ride. Everybody else takes the fall, Dyson and the senator ride off into the sunset, and I get forced to work for a bunch of multinational corporations.

My voice is barely there. "Why?"

His sigh is weary, as if he's too old for this shit. "I would have thought you'd have figured that out too."

I'm expecting him to leave it there, but he doesn't. He bends down, elbows on his knees, eyes bright and alive. The Taser still pointed right at my midsection.

"Come on, Ms Frost. You're not unintelligent, as much as you seem to enjoy presenting yourself that way. You must have known how wasted you were in Los Angeles. All the small little jobs Moira had you doing? You were meant for bigger things."

"Like what?"

"Every year, there are dozens of geopolitical situations across the world where the United States needs to get involved. Insurgents, rebels, demonstrators. Rogue elements. Having someone like you address these problems—"

"Oh, and your arms dealer buddies were just there for funsies?"

"It's how the world works, Ms Frost. If you think we manage to carry out operations overseas without the assistance of multinationals, you're more naive than I thought."

"And you just told me your evil plan, like a fucking Bond villain. Who's naive now?"

It's a dumb comment. But the look on his face is worth it.

Confusion, followed by realisation, followed by deep irritation, all in the space of about two seconds. But it's quickly
replaced by an amused expression, and he leans back in his seat,
hands folded in his laps. "Perhaps I just decided you deserved
to know the truth."

"Sure you did. And tell me, these . . . " I cough. "Insurgents.
Rebels, whatever. They wouldn't happen to be causing problems for these *multinationals*?"

"Ms Frost—"

"You wanted to pimp me out." I'm too weary to even
be that disgusted. Somehow, I manage to get up to a sitting
position, arms wrapped around my knees. "Shit. It makes
so much more sense now. I even said to Burr, why are they
holding this big-time conference in LA? Why not at a ranch
or up a mountain or somewhere secluded? But you had to hold
it here, *because I was here.* You've probably been planning this
for months."

What was it that Tanner said to me? In that prison cell in
Hollywood? *Do you know there is a company that has offered the
government five billion dollars for your hippocampus?* Weiss was
probably down . . . but I'm guessing the other two members
of the committee weren't. They, and Tanner, wanted to keep
me exactly where I was.

And Weiss couldn't have that. So he needed to create a situation where so much money was on the table that the other
members of the committee would come round. He needed to
stage a live demonstration that would get seven of the biggest
multinationals in the world to pledge billions and billions.
A *gigantic* payday. One that would wipe out any scruples the
committee had. And the corporations wouldn't just fork over
money without a live test, one they could witness first-hand.

"You couldn't just do it at, like, a little private demonstration could you?" I tell him. "That would be too suspicious. The other people on your little committee wouldn't allow it. It had to be a big event, where an attempt on your life would make a lot more sense."

I lower my head, laughing softly. "But it all went wrong, didn't it? You didn't take into account me losing my ability in the same week."

"You can't plan for everything. There'll always be an element of luck."

The whole day is replaying in my head. Dyson and the other wackos in his group would obviously have known something was wrong, even if the other hostage-takers didn't. That's why he took Weiss up to the roof, so he could threaten him, get a little insurance in case things went really wrong. And when he captured me, he knew he had to get me to save the day. He didn't give the tiniest fuck about his colleagues.

"And DiSantos?" I ask. "The guy Dyson shot, onstage? Was *he* part of the plan?"

A shrug. "Omelettes and eggs. And he's been a thorn in my side for years."

Without asking his permission, I clamber up onto the leather couch opposite him. Out the window, Los Angeles gleams in the sunshine, a winding mess of streets and freeways and dollhouse-size buildings. We're heading south, over Beverly Hills and Culver City, skirting LAX airspace.

Here's the weird thing. I'm actually impressed. This whole scheme, this little live demo, solves a lot of problems for Weiss. He couldn't just film me using my abilities – no way the buyers would accept that. Maybe – *maybe* – the footage from the storm drain would have done it, the video of me stopping the flash flood in its tracks, but that came too close to the conference.

And Dyson's attack happening in a public space would mean that I'd be careful not to expose my ability. I'd be subtle. I'd demonstrate what I could do, without outing myself to the people attending the conference. Stop the guns being drawn, lock the safeties down, the triggers.

Would it have been enough for the buyers? Or would they have thought Weiss was trying to con them – maybe by hiring actors? Where would the ironclad proof be?

Except: he had no incentive to pull the wool over their eyes. He *knew* how powerful I'd gotten. He *knew* that a bunch of guns would pose zero problem. Why con people when you can offer the real thing and get away clean? Even if that wasn't true I can't see him conning seven of the most powerful arms dealers on the planet. Not if he wanted to live past next week.

"Tanner would never have let you," I say.

"Oh?"

"She'd never have let you whore me out to your corporate buddies."

But that's not true, is it? Convince the other two members of the committee, and it won't matter what Tanner wants. They can just reassign her. They can break up China Shop. Oh, I bet she'd fight like hell, but it wouldn't matter.

Like she said, she's just a civil servant.

We're heading out over the ocean now, a beach visible out of the right-hand window. The chopper starts to climb as we fly out over the water. The sea is a wide expanse of deep blue, almost calming. But it can't stop my mind from going into overdrive, the thoughts racing around my brain as I connect the dots.

"What are we doing here, man?" I ask.

He raises an eyebrow.

"You're fucked, you know that? This whole grand plan

of yours is in the toilet. And even if you do get some people to give you money for me and my ability, there's no way you're going to get to spend it. That video? The one they took on the roof? My team has it. They'll figure you out. You're toast."

But even as I'm saying it, I'm wondering: he must know this too.

So why has he kidnapped me? Why didn't he just run?

As if sensing my thoughts, he gives me a kindly smile. "There are certain countries where extradition is challenging. And many of those countries have surprisingly advanced medical facilities."

The helicopter banks slightly, causing me to shift in my seat. *I really should have a belt on.*

"Tell me, have you ever been to San Clemente Island?" he says. When I don't respond, he shakes his head. "You don't even know where it is, do you? Amazing to me. You spend all these years in Los Angeles, and you're completely ignorant."

"OK, Number one, kiss my ass. Number two—"

"A small island off the city's coast." He gestures to the window. "Not much to recommend it. Lots of rocks, mainly. A few naval facilities. And a private airstrip, very isolated."

He looks out the window, almost pensive. "You'll be sedated, of course. And there are certain drugs that can be used to make you more pliable over the long term. They take some time to build up in the system, but you'll be kept in relative comfort. As long as you cooperate, of course."

The temperature in the cabin is perfectly pleasant, but right now, it feels like it drops about ten degrees.

"And what about my brother and sister? The kids they've made? There are other people out there. Christ, do you not understand where the earthquakes came from? Without me—"

He scoffs. "The very *idea* that you could stop someone like your sister."

"Um, hello? Were you not briefed on that little fight I had with them at the hospital? I took on my sister *and* my brother, and they end up running away."

Another flash of irritation. "The only reason they ran is because your sister miscalculated. Going to the hospital was a foolish decision. But she got cold feet, and she decided to take matters into her own hands."

"Cold feet? What the fuck are you talking about?"

He says nothing. Studying me.

I grit my teeth. "Cold feet from what?"

Weiss rolls his tongue around his cheeks, looking away from me and out the window. "Well, I suppose it doesn't matter now, one way or the other," he says, more to himself than to me.

"What does that m—?"

"You want to know what she got cold feet from? Our entire operation today. You can't handle your sister because she thinks twenty steps ahead. She had a plan for you, a plan to take you off the board." He smirks. "Everything at the Del Rio Hotel today was her idea."

FORTY-NINE

Teagan

For the first time since I got dragged onboard, the helicopter cabin is completely silent.

I stare at Weiss, open-mouthed. "Bullshit," I say, so softly that it's almost inaudible.

He spreads his hands. "That's the problem with getting the villain to reveal his evil plan, Ms Frost. Sometimes you hear things you'd rather not know."

"Bullshit."

"Your sister contacted me months ago, although it took a lot of negotiation for us to come to an agreement." He lifts a finger, leaning forward, as if making a key point in an argument. "You know what sold it for me? She didn't want any of the profits. Not a red cent. In fact, she paid for the privilege. I could keep any income we made from hiring out your services, *and* she offered me a very healthy signing bonus. Even if everything went wrong, as it did today, I'd still make it out in the black."

He smiles – the same warm, beaming smile he gave me when I first walked into his hotel suite. "Somebody always wins, Teagan. Somebody always makes a little money."

"You . . . " The air has gone from my lungs. I don't believe it. No way. There is absolutely no way my sister would—

Do what? Sell you out? Is it really that surprising? For seven years, she's been alive, and hasn't once made contact. She's sent nothing but destruction your way. You being brainwashed, pimped out to these multinationals, sent overseas . . . wouldn't that play right into her hands? Wouldn't it remove one of the biggest obstacles to whatever she's planning? If I wasn't here, if I couldn't stop her . . .

I shake my head, find my voice. "No. That isn't right. She . . . she was at the hospital two days ago. She was trying to take me with her."

"As I said. Cold feet. I must admit, I was disappointed in her."

I'm already replaying that clusterfuck at the hospital in my head, over and over. Remembering the things Chloe said to me.

Teagan, you're in danger. You need to come with us. Right now. Once we're somewhere safe, I'll tell you everything, I promise. Just hold on for me.

It doesn't make sense. If she really did have cold feet, if she really was trying to stop me going to the Del Rio, then why didn't she tell me? Why didn't she let me know what was going to happen when Senator Arthur Weiss rolled into town?

The answer comes almost immediately: there's no way I would have believed her. What on earth was she going to say? *Hey, Teagan, good to see you; yes, I'm alive and have been for the past seven years; also, don't go anywhere near the Del Rio Hotel this week, K?*

She probably thought she'd have time to explain after she got me out. Hell, she totally believed she'd be able to take me with her, so she might have figured she wouldn't need to explain the Del Rio thing at all.

But couldn't she have come for me? Before we got stuck

in the hotel? Then again, what was she supposed to do? I was
locked in a police station for two days, which is a lot tougher
to break into than a hospital. When Tanner sprung me, I more
or less went straight to the hotel. Chloe simply didn't have
the chance.

All along, she had a plan to take me off the board. Maybe
she convinced herself it was necessary. That it was the only
way. But I'm still her only sister and, like Weiss said; she got
cold feet. She decided I didn't deserve it. That she couldn't
leave me to these people. After seven years, she finally realised
that she wanted her sister back.

I have no idea how to feel about that.

And there are more important issues on the table. I have to
get out of here.

Right fucking now.

Maybe I could try to escape when we get to San Clemente
Island, and *maybe* I might succeed. But I'm wounded, and
everything in that situation is flashing *bad idea* in neon lights.
There are just too many things that can go wrong. Besides,
Weiss will keep that Taser close.

And I have a better idea. It's risky as hell . . .

But I'm not sure I have a choice.

A while ago, China Shop got into in a police chase across
LA. They thought we'd murdered someone, and they sent a
helicopter to track us. Reggie was in the car, and as a former
pilot, she knew exactly how we could bring the helicopter
down without killing everyone on board. We had to force it
into a manoeuvre known as auto rotation, where the engine
cuts out but the blades keep spinning. If that happens, the pilot
can bring the chopper into land – a bumpy landing, sure, but
one they will survive.

My PK wasn't as strong then as it is now, but I managed to

grab hold of the chopper's engine. The fuel pump specifically, just below the rotor. Crunch that, and it's game over.

Having to make an emergency landing is dangerous, sure. But even that puts me in a much better situation than I would be in if I was on some private airstrip, surrounded by Weiss's goons. It's a risk I'm prepared to take. In any case, we're super high up, which will give us more than enough room to make it back to land.

It's going to take every ounce of focus I have. I can't let my PK get out of control. If I do that, it'll tear this chopper apart.

I close my eyes. Slow my breathing. Send my PK out, dive deep into the rotor assembly above my head. Find the fuel pump, feel it, the metal and the oil and the bearings and the joints. Focus just on that, nothing else. Block out the world. Everything that's happened to me today, everything that's happened to me in my entire life. There's nothing but my PK, and this tiny little engine part.

Please, I ask my ability. *Listen to me. Just this once.*

Weiss must have picked up on what I'm doing. When he speaks, there's an urgent note in his voice. "Think very carefully about what you do next."

I let out a low breath. I think I have it. I've wrapped my PK around the fuel pump and only the fuel pump, and this time, it's going to do what I ask. I'm sure of it.

"You stupid little girl," he says. "Look at me."

I do.

He opens his mouth, but I get there first. "Enough with this *little girl* shit. I have a name. It's Teagan. Teagan *Fuck You* Frost."

Look at that. I finally found a middle name I like.

Weiss's eyes go wide. He jerks the Taser at me, at the exact same moment that I crunch the fuel pump with my PK.

It goes hilariously wrong.

I understand that the second I use my PK on the helicopter's fuel pump. I don't have nearly the amount of control I need. Instead of simply crushing the pump, I manage to tear it clean out of the rotor assembly. Along with just about every other piece of machinery in there.

Shit.

Weiss fires the Taser. He does so at the exact moment the helicopter lurches sideways with a squeal of cockpit alarms, and the barbs embed themselves in the leather to my right. The senator flies off his seat, barrels into me. The impact pushes my head sideways, and I get a glimpse of the cockpit. The pilot fighting with the controls. And the ocean, far below us, filling the entire view out the windshield. The world spinning wildly as the chopper plummets out of the sky.

Weiss screams. I can barely hear it over the insane ringing in my ears, but I feel it, feel the furious energy in it. He pushes off me, not even bothering with the Taser any more, just cocking back his arm to throw a punch right into my face. He doesn't know what he's doing any more. I don't even think he knows where he is. At that moment, he just wants me dead.

Unfortunately for him, the chopper dips even further. It sends me sideways, rolling away from him. Unfortunately for *me*, I land right on the helicopter's side door.

It takes my weight, the metal creaking. But between that, and the forces from the spinning chopper, it's too much.

Pop.

The lock snaps, the door swinging wide. And in the next instant, I'm tumbling backwards into open air.

FIFTY

Teagan

There's a part of me that doesn't believe this is happening. That doesn't believe I'm actually falling out of a helicopter, twenty thousand feet above the Pacific.

That lasts right up until the rotor blades almost take my head off.

The chopper is still tilting as I fall, and the blades pass no more than a couple of inches from my nose as I drop past them. I actually feel them part the air in front of my face. Then the rushing air whips me away, sends me tumbling, sea and sky and land and clouds whirling around me.

That's when I start to scream.

I whirl my arms, kick my legs frantically. My shirt and pants flutter like mad, my hair flying in a crazy mass around my forehead and eyes. It's freezing cold, a cold that drives right into my heart and stomach and lungs. I can't breathe – the rushing air forces its way up my nose, scours my sinuses.

In desperation, I throw out what's left of my PK, looking for something, anything I can use. I'll take the smallest thing. The smallest object that I can hold onto, that I can lift, that I can use to slow my fall. The door! What if I grab the door, rip it off the chopper—?

But I can't reach it. I don't know whether I've fallen too far, or if my PK has finally run out. I can't breathe, even when I force myself to stop screaming. The noise is unbelievable. Sky, sea, sky, sea. I get a glimpse of the helicopter, turned completely on its side, dropping even faster than I am towards the Pacific.

Do something!

My clothes. I can use them, can't I? If I can put enough PK into them, I *might* be able to get them to support me, get them to slow me down just enough so that the impact doesn't kill me. And then I can . . .

Do what? Swim to shore? Through miles of freezing ocean?

I try anyway. For a half-second, I get the barest little sensation of grip . . . but of course, I know what'll happen if I try. My clothes will shred themselves, tear right off my body.

I push past the panic and picture a skydiver. Arms and legs out, knees and elbows bent. But when I try, I start to tumble in the opposite direction, somersaulting backwards, over and over.

"Come on!" I howl, throwing my limbs out as far as they'll go, desperately trying to keep myself steady. There's an instant where I've got it . . . then it's gone, the tumble starting again. The panic has me now, gripping me in its claws. Squeezing.

How long have I been falling? Ten seconds? Fifteen? How long before I hit? What will it feel like? Will it hurt? What if it leaves me alive, body smashed to pieces, drowning as I sink into the ocean?

And all at once, the panic is gone.

It's over.

There's nothing more to do. No more tricks to try. Nothing I can grab onto, no one coming to save me. This may be the first time in my entire life that there is not a single thing I can do. And as I realise that, it's as if the worry and the fear just drain out of me.

Seconds left. I'm not going to spend them scared. I'm not going to spend them trying to fight something inevitable. Instead, I picture the people I love. The people I wish I could spend just a few moments more with.

And in my mind, I speak to them.

To Reggie, I say: *You made it all work. No matter how bad the job got, you were always there.*

To Africa: *I never gave you the respect you deserve. You earned it.*

To Nic: *I'm sorry I'm going to miss our date. And I'm so, so sorry I never told you that I love you. I shouldn't have been so scared.*

And to Annie . . .

I wish we had more time.

And then, amazingly, I picture my own brother and sister. Chloe and Adam.

I never got to talk to them.

Despite everything else, despite the heinous shit they're involved in, that's what I want more than anything else right now. I want my brother and sister back. I want it to be like it was before, when we could talk for hours and tell stupid jokes and beat each other up with zero consequences.

There are so many questions I never got to ask them. For the past seven years, I've been on my own with my ability. I've had to figure all of it out by myself. What would it have been like if I had Chloe and Adam with me, going through the same things I was? Our abilities getting stronger and stronger? Changing? Even just to have one of them to talk to . . .

I don't have long now. The ocean is so, so close, rushing up to meet me. My mind has never been this clear. This calm.

And into that calmness, comes a single thought.

An idea.

Clean and clear and complete.

I never actually lost my ability.

When you break a bone, it's almost impossible to use it properly. Your body won't let you. The muscles swell and constrict, refusing to take any weight without staggering pain. It happens so that the bone can knit together. Heal. And when it does, the limb comes back stronger than before.

I thought Chloe and Adam altered my brain chemistry, removing my ability completely. But what if . . . what if they just hurt it in some way? What if my ability just needed time to heal? And what if, when it did heal, it came back stronger than before? So strong that I needed much less effort than before to use it?

No way. My ability isn't a broken bone. And yet I can't help thinking about the rooftop, when I tried to shut down those guns. The same amount of energy I'd normally use for the task brought me a much more potent result, and I simply wasn't prepared for it. I lost control.

Wait . . .

In all the years I've had my ability, there's one thing I've never used it on. In all this time, I have never tried to lift myself.

My own body.

Not once.

Back when my parents were still testing me in their lab, it simply wasn't an option. Not only could I not move organic matter, at all, but I simply wasn't strong enough. Ditto for when I was in the facility, in Waco. And when I got to LA, when I started working for Tanner, I had absolutely zero interest in using my ability beyond what was strictly necessary. I was much happier pretending that it was just a tool.

Give it a shot.

The thought is blazing hot, dazzling terrifying. Impacting the ocean is one thing. I'd die instantly, snap to black. No pain; just "good night, Teagan". But if I turn my supercharged ability on my own body, I might rip myself apart. Just plain vaporise in mid-air.

But do I know that for sure? Or is that just the part of me that hates my ability, that wishes I could be normal? The part of me that wants to pretend my PK doesn't exist?

The ocean is very close now. The water so dark, it's almost black.

Just let go. There's nothing you can do now.

And then, another part of me speaks in my mind. It's a part of me that is behind every rash decision, every screw-up, every poor choice. It's the part of me that loves trying strange food, and rapping along badly to songs I love in public, and making dumb jokes. It's the part of me that loves. That feels. That shouts.

And right now, it's shouting: *Fuck that noise.*

Before I can stop it, before I can get in its way or out-think it, my ability turns inwards. I send my PK energy deep into my core.

Imagine you're walking down the street, and someone tackles you from behind. You are absolutely not braced for impact, so you go flying, all the wind knocked out of you, every cell in your body going nuts.

That's me. My direction changes in an instant. I go from falling straight down to falling at a forty-five degree angle in half a second. Winded, gasping for breath, eyes bulging out of my skull. I've lost my PK's grip, but for a second there, it was as if I'd grabbed an electric wire. An incredible, unbelievable jolt of raw energy.

It didn't vaporise me or completely stop my fall. It just

changed my direction, as if I really *was* tackled sideways in mid-air. I have no idea how close I am to impact now, and the momentum from that little forty-five degree sideways kick is already gone.

So I do the only thing I can think of, and pull that PK inwards again.

Again, the enormous kick in the midsection. I think I actually black out for a fraction of a second. My entire body is going through the worst pins and needles I've ever felt, as if every blood cell has frozen in place.

I'm flying sideways through the air. Maybe two hundred feet above the ocean.

That kind of sudden movement, that transition of momentum, should have vaporised my organs. But it didn't. Whatever I've tapped into, it dissipated the energy. It kept my body together. It pushed me sideways . . . and for a split-second, it held on.

I start to tumble again, the sideways movement turning into a drop, the PK grip gone. The ocean roars up to meet me, opening its jaws wide.

Terror claws at me. I push past it, going in for the third time. There's the same insane, nuclear-level kick, and unconsciousness flickers at the edges of my mind. But this time, I don't let go. I let the energy flow through me, channelling into every single cell in my body.

I open my eyes.

The water is ten feet below me . . . and it's moving. No, not just moving: rushing past. As if . . .

I'm flying.

Rocketing above the water, all the speed I built up in my drop transferred into this insane sideways flight. And my PK . . .

It's holding on to me.

When I grab something with my psychokinesis, I can feel its texture and its position in space. Exactly the same as you would when you reach across a table to pick up a water glass. That's what's happening here, too. I can feel every single atom in my body. I can feel the texture of my skin, the hardness of my bones, the soft resilience of my internal organs. It should be a horrifying sensation, but it isn't. I have never felt so in control. It's as if every single time I used my PK up until this point was just a hint of what I was capable of. Now, I've tapped into something . . . more.

I am fucking *flying*.

I can't describe the sensation, the sheer wonder of it. It's like every good dream I've ever had, all happening at once. The exhaustion? The fear? The pain? All gone. Blown away by this *feeling*.

In that instant, I lose control. I start to roll, falling slowly towards the pounding sea, and grab hold of myself again. This time, there's no black-out kick. Just a lift, a little hitch in my stomach. A momentary catch before I'm back up, flying again.

Something catches the edge of my vision. There's a pillar of black smoke rising from the ocean half a mile from me, flaming wreckage just visible at the base. The helicopter. And with it: Senator Arthur Weiss.

I don't like it when people die. Even him. But right now? I'm too wrapped up in what's happening to care.

The California coastline rushes past to my right, two or three miles away. Without really understanding what I'm doing, I bend in its direction, dropping my right shoulder and flaring my arms, not really knowing if it's going to work.

It does. I turn in mid-air, slowly at first, then tighter. Instinctively, I tuck my arms back in, and the turn halts. Now

I'm rocketing towards the beach. Sun on the back of my neck, warm and clean.

At any second, I'm expecting whatever energy I've tapped into to fade, to drop me back into the ocean. It doesn't happen. It just keeps coming and coming and coming. I am dimly aware that the muscles in my back and sides are protesting, as if they're having to work extra hard to hold me up, and are going to make me pay for it later. Don't care. Don't give a shit. Grinning, I do a barrel roll, because I freaking can. It gives me the same drop in my stomach that you get from going over the hill on a rollercoaster.

I nearly lose it coming out of the roll. Just because I have the basics down doesn't mean I've got full control yet, and it sends me tumbling. With an effort, I stop myself, slowing down just a little and telling myself to take it easy. All the same, I'm still giggling. This is *wild*.

Was this hiding in me the whole time? Could I have taken off whatever I wanted?

That's when I almost lose control for real. The grip slackens, and suddenly I'm dropping towards the surface of the ocean again. I yelp, windmilling my arms, as if that can somehow make a difference, doing everything I can to grab hold of my core again. I only just manage it, bouncing upwards with a lurch that sends me tumbling, a second before I hit the waves.

And despite it all, I'm *laughing*. Cruising above the ocean in a barely controlled, swooping glide, laughing my ass off. I'm maybe half a mile from shore, the beach rising up to a strand of Los Angeles coastal forest ahead of me. Christ, what if there are people around? Surfers or sunbathers or . . .

But as far as I can tell, the beach is deserted, and there are no surfboards in the gaps between the waves. And even if I did see somebody, what the hell am I going to do about it?

I'm tired now, the drained feeling starting to come back. Whatever energy source I've tapped into is still going, but I'm losing my ability to handle it. It's getting harder and harder. I'm slowly dropping, getting closer and closer to the water. *Come on, just a few hundred feet. You can do it.*

I come over the top of the nearest wave, cresting it – and then all at once, I lose my grip.

There's a half-second where I think I can get it back, but I'm way too close to the surface. Before I can do anything, before I can even suck in a breath, I go into another tumble. An instant later, I slam into the water, freezing cold, air knocked out of me.

I have no idea which way is up. I can't see a damn thing. I kick hard, pistoning my legs – and break the surface. My eyes sting with the salt, blinking in the sunlight. My shoulder is screaming at me, which I guess is what will happen if you introduce a bullet wound to salt water.

I barely have any energy left at all. I can barely move. But somehow, I find the strength to grip my core one more time. To turn myself around in the water, lift my body very slightly out of it, point myself towards the shore. Position myself just right so the waves can scoop me up and push me towards the sand.

FIFTY-ONE

Teagan

The sheer number of bad things that have happened to me in my life is actually kind of staggering.

I'm not saying this to complain, I'm saying it as a stone-cold fact. I have been shot, buried alive, almost burned to death, nearly drowned in a flash flood. I've been Tasered, punched, choked. I have seen friends die. I have come very close to spending the rest of my short life in a government black site where masked surgeons are waiting to cut me open, and I have come close more than once. Quite recently, I fell out of a helicopter above the ocean. The universe has consistently and repeatedly taken gigantic dumps on my head.

And yet, amazingly, I do not spend all my time sobbing in the corner, rocking back and forth. Which, I think, would be an entirely understandable and acceptable response to even half the stuff I've been through.

I used to think I just didn't know how to deal with trauma. I was half convinced that one day, it was all going to crash down on me like a tidal wave. And yet lately, I'm starting to suspect that I simply don't process things in the way an average human being does. I'm built different.

And now, I have proof. Because I just took a dip in the freezing cold Pacific Ocean, and I *liked it.*

Seriously: the Pacific Ocean sucks. Everybody thinks that because California is all sunny and has beaches and shit that swimming is a big thing here. Fuck no. The sea here is as cold as Baba Yaga's left titty. Even hardcore surfers rock wetsuits.

And yet here I am, dripping, shivering, aching, sitting on the sand and staring out to sea, in the kind of state that would make most people absolutely miserable ... and I can't keep a smile off my face.

I sit cross-legged like a buddha, hands resting on my knees. My shoulder is on fire. So is my left knee. My entire body is one massive ache. I am pretty sure one of my teeth is loose – God knows how *that* happened. Sand covers just about every inch of my body, and yes, I am still freezing cold.

But for the thousandth time, I have survived something that should have killed me. I am still alive, and I'm sitting in the sun on a beautiful Californian beach – our ocean sucks, but our beaches are world-class. And despite my shivering, aching, wounded body, the energy I tapped into is still there.

I thought my connection to it would vanish. In the past, whenever my ability has gotten stronger and I've fully unleashed it, it's left me completely wiped out. It's always taken me days to recover, which I've only managed to do by mainlining Netflix, snacks and whiskey.

This time, it's different. It's still there. The energy.

I'm not using it right now. I'm not sure what would happen if I did – if I'd have the control to make it do what I want. But I can sense it, just below the surface. It's like I've unlocked something – something that was there all along, which I simply didn't have access to.

There's that old saying about humans only using ten per cent of their brains. It's trash, obviously. That's not how brains work. But I can't help feeling that something along those lines is happening here. Like a whole bunch of synaptic connections just got turned on. Brains and neural tissue are plastic; they change. In a regular human, it takes a long time, years, for the changes to take effect. In me . . .

I don't know.

I find myself reaching out and touching the energy inside me. Concentrating as hard as my exhausted brain will allow. Because I have to know, you see. Even after everything that happened to me, even after the fact that I just took fucking *flight* . . .

I need to be sure.

Ahead of me, a small section of a breaking wave stops cold. The rest of the wave continues, leaving an uneven, spherical blob of water hanging in the air. It's the size of a basketball.

I make a sound that is half cough, half gasp, and the water drops, splashing back into the sea.

"Woah," I murmur, which is when I realise that some of the grains of sand around me are floating.

More than that. I'm surrounded by concentric rings of hovering sand. Like the beach is a pond, and I'm a stone that just landed in it – only each ripple floats two feet off the ground. They remind me of an asteroid belt, seen from a distance. There are perhaps five or six rings, rippling out from my body. "*Woah.*"

Holy fuck. Is that me?

Stupid question. Of course it's me. Even if I have no clue how I'm doing it.

I blink, and the sand falls, silently pattering onto the ground. With an almost physical effort, I let go of my ability.

It sits there inside me, impossibly huge. Beyond anything I've ever experienced.

Chloe and Adam changed the synapses and neurons that control my ability, in a way I could never have predicted. In a way *nobody* could have predicted. Maybe the broken bone analogy from before wasn't quite right, but whatever happened, it first stopped my ability working, and then supercharged it.

Is this going to last? Will it fade away over the next few hours, or days? I don't know if I can take that. To be able to do what I just did, to fly, to experience that unbelievable, euphoric control, and then to have it snatched away ...

That's out of my control. The only thing that is in my control is what I do next.

I want to find my friends. I want Annie and Nic. Africa and Reggie. I don't have a phone to call them on, and I have no idea how to find one, but I guess I'll have to do that soon. I want to find them, and hug them, and tell them that I'm OK. That I love them.

And then, I want to get after Chloe and Adam.

But right now ...

Right now, I just want to sit.

Sit in the Californian sunshine, on the most beautiful beach I've ever been on, and just be by myself for a little while.

And that's exactly what I do.

By the time the surfer arrives, the salt water on my skin and clothes has dried to a crust, and the sun is low in the sky.

"Yo," the man says. I jump a little at his voice. He's a Latinx guy with a neat goatee, shirtless, his wetsuit tied around his waist. Carrying a board with a giant spider logo on it, leash dragging in the sand.

"Yo yourself," I say. They are the first words that I've spoken in a while, and my voice is all crackly.

"You been swimming?" he says, frowning at my damp shirt and pants.

"Yep. These days I don't even bother taking my clothes off. It saves time."

"What?"

"Never mind."

"You oughta be careful. This spot is locals only." He gestures out at the waves. Them Lunada Bad Boys don't play.

"Cute. Where is this spot, exactly?"

"Huh?"

"Where are we? What is this beach?"

He gives me a sideways look. "You OK? You look kinda—"

"Dude."

"Um, I mean . . . Malaga Cove? Palos Verdes?"

I know the last part, anyway. It's to the west of San Pedro and Long Beach. That gives me a starting point at least.

He starts to walk towards the water. "Like I said," he tells me over his shoulder. "You don't live around here, you probably shouldn't be paddling out. Not unless you want your tyres slashed."

"I don't have any tyres. Or a car, actually."

"Whatever." He bends down, starts to strap his leash to his ankle.

"Hey, can I use your phone?"

This time, the look is a lot longer, and a lot more searching. I hold his gaze. After everything I've been through today, an obnoxious little surfer boy is easy.

After a few moments, he shrugs, then digs in his wetsuit and pulls out a plastic pouch. He unzips it, and tosses me an iPhone. "Make it quick. The wind is good, but it won't last."

"Ain't that the truth," I murmur.

I memorised Reggie's number a long time ago. And I'm

relieved to find that whatever changes my brain has gone through, it's still there, popping to the front of my mind.

I may be Teagan Version 2.0 now. Or 3.0. Or 4.1, or ... whatever. But the point is: I'm still Teagan Frost.

I'm still me.

FIFTY-TWO

Annie

Climbing the wall is the easy part.

Annie and Nic have to stick to the trees, staying away from the roads for as long as they can. Solid rock might defeat Chloe's ability, but distance will prove no problem. They can't do anything about that, beyond making it as difficult as possible for her to track them. Even then, Annie has a sense that the danger is past. For now.

Eventually, they step out onto a quiet stretch of hillside road, winding through a grove of jacaranda trees, no traffic, no houses visible. By then, Annie has dropped into what feels like a living death. The kind of exhaustion where the body goes on autopilot, capable of nothing more than putting one foot in front of the other.

She sits on the side of the road, head hanging, while Nic calls an Uber. There is no other option; his car is at the base of the cliff, and there's no way they're going back there.

The sun has dropped low in the sky. Annie has no idea what time it is, but it feels like five or five-thirty. *Golden hour.* When the hills of Hollywood and Beverley Grove and Laurel Canyon glow with liquid, luminous light from the setting sun.

It's one of the best things about this part of town, and she's always loved being here when it happens. Not today though. Today, she cannot wait to get the fuck out.

The driver who picks them up is the same one who dropped Annie off earlier. The same taciturn Sikh. Annie stares at him for a moment after she gets into his neat Prius, wonders if she should say something. But she just doesn't have the energy. Getting the same Uber driver twice in a few hours is nowhere close to the weirdest thing that has happened to her today.

A yawn rolls out of her as she climbs into the car seat. *Gotta stay awake.*

The next thing she knows, someone is shaking her by the shoulder. Nic leans over, popping her door, then clambers out himself. She follows, groggy with sleep.

They're at the corner of a busy intersection, cars and buses and trucks whizzing past. It's an industrial area, grimy office blocks and loading bays, bus stops and fire hydrants, cracked sidewalk baking in the late afternoon sun. Behind them is a gas station, the forecourt busy with a long line of dusty cars and vans with the logos of plumbers, construction companies, exterminators. Annie prides herself on her knowledge of LA, her ability to pick out the differences between areas. But right now, they could be anywhere.

Nic walks her over to a nearby bus stop bench, sits her down on it. "Back in a minute," he tells her.

She wants to ask him where they are, but she doesn't have the energy. She just sits, staring dully out at the traffic. A bus pulls up, the door briefly hissing open, the driver giving her an irritated glance. When she doesn't move, he closes the door and trundles away.

"Here." Nic is back, and he's holding something out to her. A bottle of Gatorade, bright red. Plus a bag of potato chips.

Bought from the gas station store, no doubt. Dumbly, Annie takes the bag and bottle. "Thought we could use something to eat," Nic says, sitting next to her.

The Gatorade is warm, sickly sweet, but it doesn't matter. She drinks and drinks and drinks, draining the bottle in about ten seconds. It's just enough to take the edge off, to bring her a little closer to reality.

"Where are we?" she says, wiping her mouth.

"Century City. Thought about taking us to Sawtelle – my apartment's there. But I couldn't shake the idea of that psycho bitch coming after us. I wanted somewhere public." He takes a slug of his own Gatorade, gestures around him. "Maybe she's not so ready to start shit here, you know what I mean?"

It's smart, Annie has to give him that. God knows where they go next, however. Back to Watts, possibly, but even so—

Watts. Her mom. Reggie! She has to get hold of Reggie. But even trying to figure out how to do that is too big, too much right now.

"How the hell," she says, settling for a simpler question, "did you get inside? How did you find me?"

Nic leans back. His Gatorade is neon-blue, and he takes a long swig. The ghost of a smile plays around his lips.

"So I'm on the ridge when you drop out of contact," he says. "And I'm bugging. Freaking out. But I stay there, because what the fuck else am I gonna do? And like ten minutes later, I see you getting dragged into that shed by those two superpowered motherfuckers."

"And you ... what, you climbed the wall? How did you even—?"

"Oh yeah, sure, I'm just gonna jump a twelve-foot-high wall with cameras and laser alarms and shit. Also—"

A burst of hooting from one of the cars at the pumps

obliterates his words. Someone getting in the way of someone else. They wait for it to resolve, and then Nic continues.
"Anyway, I end up calling the cops. Yo, don't look at me like
that, you know it was the smart thing to do. It's the first thing
we should have done before we even tried to get inside. I
called them, told them I'd seen someone being kidnapped at
such and such address, hung up. I figured you being arrested
for breaking in was better than you being dead."

"I don't understand. Didn't they show up?"

"Oh, they showed up all right. Two black and whites. Came
right into the property, guns out, clean sweep. I saw it all from
the ridge. And when they went into that shed thing, I figure,
OK, job done."

He lets out an exhausted laugh. "But then they come out,
and you ain't with them, and they ain't pointing their guns any
more. They're just talking to that Chloe bitch."

For a moment, it doesn't make sense. Then the realisation
hits. "Adam," Annie says.

"I guess. He probably got inside their minds like he did
with us, made them see an empty shed. So they figured it was
a prank call, someone with a grudge against the rich dude who
owned the place, apologies all round, see you later alligator.
Bye, 5-0."

"Fuck."

"Yeah. So anyway, at that point I'm freaking out again,
because right now I am the only one who knows you're in
there. And I don't know what they're doing to you, so I don't
know how much time I got. I'm looking for a way in ...
there was this access road I saw earlier, so I drive around to
the bottom of it, and it goes right past the base of that cliff."
He rubs his chin. "It looked pretty doable. Like I said, I do
a lot of rock climbing, and I've done way more challenging

ones than that, so no biggie." A flash of anger in his eyes. "By the way, maybe next time *tell* me about that cliff? You realise me climbing up there was a much, *much* better plan than that bullshit with your line repairman buddy?"

Annie waves this away. "But you weren't climbing up there without a distraction."

"Right. I didn't know if there was an alarm at the top, and I wouldn't be able to see if there was anybody around before I actually got there. And I didn't want to bust into the shed when there might be who knows what going on in there."

"What did you do, put a bag of dogshit outside the gate and set it on fire?"

Nic doesn't laugh.

"You can't be serious."

"I mean, it wasn't *dogshit* necessarily, but ... "

"What the hell did you *do*?"

He chews his chips for a moment, as if trying to decide how best to describe it. "OK, so I go back around the front of the property, thinking maybe I can talk to the guard or something. But he gave me the evil eye as soon as I rolled up, so I got back in my car. I needed to think. And I don't know if you remember the front gate, but it's directly opposite this big hill – this really steep road that goes all the way up."

" ... Kind of?"

"I'm driving up this road, and I'm like: maybe if I let my car roll down the hill and crash into the gate, it would cause a big enough distraction. The problem is that it wrecks my car, and I sort of need my car."

"I'm busy getting tortured, and you're worried about crashing your car?"

He ignores her. "Anyway, right then, I look over at one of the houses at the top of the hill and it has this gigantic metal dumpster outside it. You know the kind I mean? The ones on wheels?"

She gapes at him. "You didn't."

"Plenty of flammable shit in there. Paper and cardboard. Nobody around, nobody looking at me ... and I *did* have a lighter in my glove box."

"You *didn't*."

He rubs the back of his head. "Made one mother*fucker* of a bang when it hit the gate. Flaming trash everywhere. Pretty much all the neighbours came out to see, and I think just about everybody on the property came too. I get back in my car, hit the access road, start climbing, and then—"

Annie starts laughing.

Just a chuckle at first, which becomes an uncontrollable fit of giggles, and ends up as the kind of laughter that makes her belly and her cheeks ache with delicious pain. She doubles over on the bench, clutching her stomach, tears running down her face. Every time she thinks she's got it under control, she hears the phrase *Flaming trash everywhere*, and it starts again. Before long, Nic is laughing too.

"Ain't that some shit," she manages to croak out, a few minutes later.

"It's something."

"The neighbours gonna be talking about that for years. You know that, right?"

He grins. "They can put it in their newsletter."

"Laurel Canyon Residents group chat blowing up."

"Brunch at the country club is gonna be very interesting for a while."

"Goddamn kids." ·

Their laughter slowly fades, and for a minute or two, neither of them speak.

"How you like your new non-boring-ass life?" Annie says.
He smiles, see-saws a hand back and forth.

"You want to know the worst part of all this?" she says.

"You mean, beside the fact that we almost died?"

"Everything we went through. Me breaking into the house,
all of it. You know what I got?" She puts her thumb and fore-
finger together. "A big fat nothing."

"Really?"

"Yep."

"I don't get it. You must have found *something* out in there.
Did you at least figure out who owns the house?"

"Oh yeah. But I had that even before I busted in. I got into
this office, and I was filming a bunch of stuff, but there was
nothing I could use. If I had more time maybe ... I mean,
we can dig into the guy who owns the property, Wilcox or
whatever his name is, and *maybe* we get something, but ... "

"But they'll skip town."

"Uh-huh. Boom, gone. And we're back to square one."

Nic leans his head back, cracks his neck. "They'll leave
some evidence behind, something we can use." But he doesn't
sound sure.

"I should have waited," Annie says, more to herself than to
him. "I just thought ... I thought Teagan and the crew might
be in there, and if I didn't do something ... "

Carefully, Nic says, "You know Teagan can take care of
herself, right?"

"No, she can't." Annie surprises herself by the depth of
feeling in her voice. "She's a little kid with a gun, and she has
no idea how to use it. She think she's way more capable than
she is, she constantly gets herself into these insane situations,
and the rest of us have to pick up the—"

Nic spreads his hands. "Are we talking about the same

person? Do I have to remind you that she saved all those people back at the storm drains? Pretty much by herself?"

"It doesn't matter, don't you get it? One of these days she's going to get herself in too deep, and if she's by herself, she won't be able to get back out."

"Annie, *stop*." Nic slumps on the bench, the exhaustion finally starting to show. "Look. I'm the first to admit that Teags has done some dumb shit in the past. No argument there. But Annie, people *change*. If you try to tell me that she's the same person she was when we first met her, then I don't know if we can have this conversation. She doesn't need protecting any more."

"I just—"

"No, listen for a sec. She cares about you, Annie, and I'm pretty sure you care about her. So stop acting like she's a *little kid with a gun*. She doesn't need saving all the time."

It's her anger at Nic that finally makes Annie understand. It's an automatic anger, a reflex, an emotion she reaches for and finds instantly. But in the moment before she grasps it, she thinks: *Why?*

Why is she still angry at Teagan? The girl keeps landing up in dangerous situations, sure, keeps putting herself in danger. But how is that any different to what Annie did back at Laurel Canyon? An insane, dangerous mission that yielded absolutely nothing, and almost got her to turn traitor on her friends. How is that any less stupid than facing down a flash flood in a storm drain?

Ever since her dad, she's approached every situation with anger. With raw fury. She's done it that way because it worked. It got things done.

And it isn't going to work any more. Not with the enemy they're facing. Not when that enemy can weaponise that anger to completely destroy you.

Nic is still going. "She's a better person than you think she is. She can be annoying as hell sometimes, but . . . "

"Wait, hold up." A thought occurs to Annie. "Didn't you guys have a fight?"

" – And she . . . what?"

"Yeah. On the river. She was mad racist towards you or something, wasn't she?"

"She wasn't *mad racist*. She was just an idiot."

"And you guys made up? Wait . . . are you dating her?" A smile quirks Annie's lips. "Shit, you are, aren't you? Man. You should have said something. It makes much more sense now."

"I'm not dating her yet. We're going to go *on* a date. Or we were, before everything else happened."

"I should have known you were in love with her."

"Jesus, I'm not in love with her. I don't know that yet. I just . . . like her, OK? We're gonna take it further. See what happens."

"Shit." Annie shakes her head, still smiling. Then she glances at Nic, and the smile drops away. "You break her heart, I'll break your neck."

He raises an eyebrow. "Did you just quote Vin Diesel at me?"

"Who?"

"Vin Diesel. *Fast and the Furious*. Paul Walker is dating his sister."

"Never seen it."

"Stop it. You totally quoted him."

They fall silent for a few moments.

"Thanks," Annie finally murmurs.

"What was that?"

"For following me. Thanks. I owe you one."

"So you admit I can handle myself?"

Annie looks away, but Nic presses. "Come on, you can say it. I can handle myself."

"Fine. Yes."

"No more *don't follow me* bullshit, aight? And next time you tell somebody to shoot me if I move, we're gonna have words."

"What, Candice? Stop being a little bitch, she didn't shoot you."

"Yeah, but she was talking about it. That's one of the scariest people I've ever met. I think I'd rather hang out with that Chloe woman."

The exhaustion has crept back. Annie is about to ask Nic where they should go next, possibly suggest somewhere with dark rooms and warm beds, when his phone rings, making them both jump.

He fumbles it out of his pocket, frowns. "Huh. Unknown number."

For some reason, Annie wants to tell him not to answer it. She has the strangest feeling that it's Chloe herself. That she's tracked them down, is coming for them right at this moment. Before she can say anything, Nic answers. "Hello?"

His face lights up. "Reggie! Oh, shit, it's good to hear from you."

"What?" Annie sits bolt upright. "Give it here. Let me talk to her."

"Wait, Reggie, hold up a second ... I'm sorry, Teagan is *where*?"

FIFTY-THREE

Teagan

There's a bar.

It's a little way inland from Malaga Cove, a good twenty-minute walk up the winding road. Cars nearly cream me more than once, but I make it. I'm still flying high, pun definitely intended.

I don't know the bar's name. It probably doesn't need one. It's the kind of place you only know about if you're a local, a place so familiar that you don't need to name it when meeting friends there. It has a dim interior, a scuzzy, sand-swept patio with battered plastic chairs and wobbly tables. Nautical bric-a-brac everywhere, nets and old life preservers and those fish that sing if you push a button. Neon signs, either turned off or not working. The smell of old booze and cigarette smoke and weed, mingled with the stench of rancid grease from a kitchen you'd only ever order from if you'd drunk enough to numb your taste buds.

But the beer is cold. The patio is quiet. The waitress gave me a free bowl of peanuts, which was nice. My friends are on their way. And for the first time since this morning, nobody is trying to kill me.

It's enough.

It's times like these when you contemplate what you've been through, the kind of person the events have made you. These are times to re-evaluate yourself, to acknowledge how you can do better. To reassess your place in the universe. That's what normally happens when you finally get to sit down and drink a beer at the end of a very long, very unusual day.

But right now, I am absolutely incapable of self-reflection. I mean, more than I normally am. All I have the energy to do right now is sit here and drink my beer and be very still.

I don't actually know who's on the way to pick me up. Reggie said she would send whoever she could find, whoever would pick up their phone first. And obviously I don't have a phone on me any more – I couldn't exactly steal the surfer's. So for the time being, it feels like I've stepped outside reality. Like I'm adrift in my own little world, utterly undisturbed.

I really do want to get back to the others, to see Annie and Nic. Reggie and Africa. Hell, I'd even be happy to see Tanner at this point, if you can believe it. At the same time, sitting here doing nothing, sipping a beer, is just . . .

Man.

Maaaaaaaaan.

I'm not really paying attention to the parking lot, even though I probably should. I'm too zoned out, lost in my own head. I'm at the bottom of my second beer and just contemplating how I'm going to pay for it when I hear someone shout my name.

And then Nic is there, coming through onto the patio, striding towards me. I get up so fast that I knock my chair over, spill the rest of my beer. I stumble across to him, and he sweeps me into his arms, wrapping me in a gigantic bear hug.

We rock back and forth for a moment, my face buried in

his chest. This is where I want to be. Nowhere else. Was I really jealous when I saw Jonas with Kanehara? Really? It feels like something that happened to someone else. There is no way, ever, that Jonas could give me what Nic does. There is no way he could know me as deeply or as completely as this man, right here.

Nic touches my cheek, very gently. Tilts my face upwards.

The last time we kissed, he backed off. Told me he wasn't ready. But that was a long time ago, years, decades, aeons. We have covered a lot of ground since then, and this time, he holds the kiss. My lips on his, soft and yielding, tongue tips just touching. He moves a little deeper, and I accept, my hand around the back of his head, his on mine, fingers wrapped in my hair. Holding on.

Even though we have yet to go on our first official, actual date, this feels right.

Eventually, we pull apart. I hug him again, my face in his chest, his chin resting on top of my head. I'm not quite crying, but I'm very close.

"Hey," I murmur.

"Hey yourself."

He's filthy, his clothes smeared with dirt and dust. "What happened to you?"

He puffs out his cheeks. "Man, that's a long story."

I must've truly been in my own world not to notice his state. "Jesus, is that *blood*? Who the hell did this to you?"

"Look, I promise I'll tell you everything. But before that—"

"Well, shit, now is good." I gesture to my table. "Lemme buy you a beer. Well, I say that, but I'm kind of short at the moment, so you might have to pick up the tab."

"In a minute. There's someone you need to see first."

"What? Who?"

Even before I'm finished saying the words, I spot her.

Standing at the edge of the parking lot, arms folded, like the temperature is much colder than it is. Looking down at the ground. Not in a coma. Standing there, awake and alive and real.

Annie.

FIFTY-FOUR

Annie

She saw Teagan on the patio before their Uber even came to a stop. Nic had hopped out without thanking the driver, gesturing her to hurry.

Annie made it as far as climbing out the car, but couldn't take another step. Couldn't even look at the figure behind the grimy patio glass.

What if she doesn't want to see me? What if she hates me?

Nic had turned back when he realised Annie wasn't following. "What are you doing? Come on."

"I just need a minute." She was barely aware of speaking the words.

Now, as she stares down at the packed dirt of the parking lot, she gets the strangest feeling. The feeling that if she looks up, the entire world will crumble. Like she's trapped in one of Adam's nightmares.

She doesn't know this part of town well. For whatever reason, very few of the people in her Army hang out here. But Torrance and Carson are nearby, areas she knows in her bones. If she leaves, right now, she can vanish. Disappear into the swell and sprawl of Los Angeles. Draw a line under this part of her life, completely forget that it ever happened. She never has to see Teagan again.

Being feared or hated has never fazed Annie Cruz. You can't operate on the streets if you do. But the thought of Teagan doing it . . .

She is on the verge of turning and running, perhaps a second away, and then Teagan is there.

The girl looks like she got hit by a truck. Her shoes are gone, along with one of her socks. Damp sand crusts her jeans. There's a bandage around her shoulder, dotted with blood. Her spiky black hair is even messier than usual, strands sticking up in all directions.

And yet, Annie can't help but notice something else. Something deeper.

It has always seemed to Annie that Teagan was constantly vibrating: a twitchy ball of nervous energy, even when she was standing still. But it's different now. There's a calmness that wasn't there before. A stillness.

Her expression is unreadable. Her face a perfect blank.

For a long moment, she and Annie just stare each other. Nic stands off to one side, arms folded, looking uncomfortable.

There is so much she has to say. So many things she has to tell Teagan. But the words freeze in her throat, refusing to come. The urge to turn tail and run is there again, powerful, screaming at her.

Eventually, she manages to speak. Her voice choked and broken. "I'm so sor—"

Teagan crosses the space between them instantly, as if she's developed teleportation to go with her telekinesis. She hugs Annie so hard that it squeezes the breath out of her, makes her gasp. The two of them stumble, almost fall, but at the last second Annie hugs her back. They keep their footing.

Annie lowers her head, drops it into the hollow between Teagan's neck and shoulder. The girl is a lot shorter than she is, and bending her head that far hurts, but she doesn't care. She never wants to leave the circle of her friend's arms. This girl – this insane, talented, infuriating, brilliant girl – has caused Annie more grief than just about anyone she has ever met.

And Annie is never going to let her go.

FIFTY-FIVE

Teagan

"The oversight committee has been dissolved," Tanner says. "There are multiple investigations at the highest levels, and I am assured they will be full and thorough. I expect it will take some time to get to the bottom of what Senator Weiss was ultimately planning, and how Chloe Jameson initiated contact, but we will get there."

She's standing in the middle of the China Shop office, arms folded. Her suit today is even darker than usual.

It's two days since the events at the Del Rio Hotel, and at the house in Laurel Canyon. Two days since I got shot, then fell out of a helicopter over the Pacific Ocean. Two days since Annie came out of her coma. Two days since a sitting US senator survived a hostage situation, then died in a mysterious chopper crash. That's exactly how much time she gave us before she called a team meeting.

I'm sitting on the couch, dressed in my favourite Jurassic 5 hoodie. Annie sits next to me, arms folded. We've talked a lot in the past couple of days, said a lot of things that we probably should have said a long time ago. She told me a little bit more about her childhood, although I couldn't help feeling that she was holding something back. I didn't push. If she wants to tell me, she'll tell me.

Africa leans against the kitchen counter. When I arrived this morning, I expected him to be in his customary Scarface suit, but he was wearing his garish purple and gold Lakers jacket. He gave me a huge hug, which felt fantastic.

He always has given the best hugs.

Burr's here too, sitting off to one side on the arm of a couch, back ramrod-straight. He hasn't said a word to me, although he gave me a guarded nod when I came in.

It's a beautiful day outside. Blue sky, temperature in the seventies. The mid-morning sun glides through the windows, making the office almost cosy.

Tanner continues. "The role of overseeing my activities with this team has fallen to the vice president, although the president himself is in the loop. It won't stay that way for long. The higher-ups don't like to have black budget projects operating on their own, as I'm sure you can imagine. But for now, the executive branch seems content for me to handle the day-to-day operations without too much oversight, as long as we continue to operate as before."

"What about Teggan's brother? And her sister?" Africa says.

I glance at him, then back at Tanner. I was about to ask the same question.

She looks at all of us, as if choosing her words. "Tracking them down is high priority, as you can imagine. Especially now that we have some idea of where they were based. Staff Sergeant Burr, with a hand-picked special forces team and the assistance of the LAPD, executed a full raid on the house of James Wilcox in Laurel Canyon. It was scrubbed clean. Almost sterile. Wilcox and his . . . *guests* . . . have dropped off the map. We are questioning all household and security staff we can track down, as well as everyone arrested at the Del Rio. Rest assured: we will find Adam and Chloe Jameson."

"We?" I say.

"There are dedicated sections of our intelligence apparatus who are out looking for them now. I know you probably want to get after them yourselves, especially given what happened, but that is not a good idea. This is going to take a coordinated, multi-agency search operation, and China Shop is simply not equipped for that."

She is clearly expecting an outburst. Instead, she's met with stony silence.

"We will continue to execute operations here in Los Angeles. There are still several threats the city faces, and we have a lot of work to do. Having said that: Ms Cruz, I'm grateful that you came today, and I'm delighted that you're on the mend, but I'm placing you on medical leave."

Annie says nothing.

"Your recovery has been remarkable, no question, but I want you checked out by the doctors at Cedars Sinai. We need you in top shape, and I'm not prepared to risk that." She clears her throat. "That will be all for now. There's nothing immediately urgent on our radar, and I think given the circumstances, we can all take a day or two more to decompress. Keep your phones on you, and be ready to get back to work soon. Ms Frost, I'd like a word in private."

"Nope."

"Excuse me?"

"Whatever you have to say, you say to me in front of everybody."

"It wasn't a request. It was a—"

She bites down on the words, snapping her mouth closed. Takes a very deep breath, as if trying to remind herself of something. Maybe the fact that even if she speaks to me privately, I'll share it with everybody else the second I'm out of there. "It concerns you specifically, Ms Frost. And your ability."

"I'm sure it does." I lean forward. "What you got?"

Another deep breath. Then, after a long moment, she says: "Your siblings' abilities clearly interacted with yours in ways we didn't anticipate."

"Ain't that the fucking truth," I mutter.

"There's no denying that you are significantly stronger than you used to be. And I would be lying if I said that wasn't making people in Washington very nervous indeed. It's no fault of your own, of course, but your increased strength added to the fact that there is no longer an oversight committee is going to cause problems. And it's going to happen sooner rather than later. That's not to mention your ... the incidents at the hotel, or the numerous witnesses. So far, we've managed to perform adequate damage control, but there may still be fallout. If the powers that be decide that you are too much of a liability to keep in the field, you are likely to be remanded to the custody of the US government."

God, the way she *speaks*. Does she talk this way at home? When she's in bed with someone? *I have become weary of the missionary position. I would like to make a request that we advance to doggy style as soon as is convenient.*

"Fortunately," Tanner says, "I know Washington. The way to keep things as they are is simply to prove yourself more useful inside the tent than out. We keep working, we stay the course, we keep making a real difference here on the ground. That's the way forward."

I hold her gaze for a long moment, then nod.

"If there's nothing else?" She looks around the room,

stony-faced, as if daring one of us to raise a hand. "Good. Dismissed."

Annie and I lift ourselves off the couch. Not going to lie, it takes some effort. My body is *not* happy with me. I'm pretty sure Annie's isn't either. We limp past Africa, who puts a hand on my shoulder, squeezes. I give him a nod, and he follows us out of the apartment. As we close the door, Tanner is in quiet conversation with Burr. Neither of them watch us leave.

We take the elevator down together. None of us say anything. There's nothing left to talk about.

The parking lot at the back of the building is in the shade, but it's a glorious morning. The kind of weather that makes you proud to live in California. There's a light breeze, carrying the scent of jasmine.

We cross the parking lot to where Africa's truck is waiting for us. It's a big Ford F-350 with a double cab. A metal shutter covers the back cargo well, and underneath it are our bags. Everything we'll need for the trip. Clothes, shoes. Warm jackets. And lots and lots of snacks. I made a very big batch of brownies, and my brownies are the fucking bomb.

Nic sees us coming. He's in the passenger seat, and leans across to pop the door for Africa. Reggie sits behind him, a small smile on her face.

Africa gets to the vehicle first, climbs behind the wheel. We all offered to take turns driving and he simply wouldn't allow it. "My car. My job. I am the driver for China Shop," he'd said.

Which I thought was cute. We have a long, long drive ahead of us, and if he thinks we're going to let him spend eight or ten hours at a time behind the wheel, he's lost his damn mind. I have no intention of dying in a car crash because our driver passes out from exhaustion. Not when I have so much work left to do.

When Annie broke into the mansion in Laurel Canyon, she thought she didn't get anything. She didn't have time to go through the papers on Wilcox's desk, or investigate the other rooms in the house. But the video she took uploaded to the cloud, and we did watch it. We weren't expecting to see anything that we didn't know already, but then the video caught the picture on the login screen of Wilcox's laptop.

The picture of him and Chloe. The picture of the two of them standing in front of a mountain.

That's when I told Reggie to freeze the video, and zoom in. She said it was actually really hard to zoom in on a video, and then there was an argument, and I told everyone to shut up because I knew that fucking mountain.

It's called the Boar's Tusk. It's the solidified remains of a volcano, and it's in the Green River Basin in southwestern Wyoming.

I know the mountain because I've been there. A long time ago, I took a trip with my family. When my mom and dad were still alive, and I was just Chloe and Adam's little sister. We stayed in the town of Rock Springs, twenty-six miles from the Tusk, in a beaten-up motel that smelled of cookies and incense. We took a day trip out to the mountain, went to the rodeo, had a picnic in a park.

And for some reason, Chloe went back there. Recently. With a billionaire who is, presumably, working with her. Something tells me they weren't out there to go to the damn rodeo.

What were you doing in Wyoming, Chloe? What's so important? What made that trip so memorable that Wilcox wanted to see it every time he turned on his laptop?

You probably think I'm crazy, reading this much into a photo on someone's login screen. But that's the thing. Chloe and Adam have been operating in the shadows, lobbing grenades at us, starting fires we have to put out. Splitting us up. Turning us against one another. This is the first time we've had anything close to a lead on them. I'm not going to stay bumbling around Los Angeles and let it go uninvestigated.

And I am not going to leave it to Moira Tanner.

She is one hell of an operator. A born intelligence agent. Someone who is perfectly built to navigate the corridors of power in Washington. And she is absolutely the wrong person for the war we are fighting.

With everything she said to us today, there was one thing that was missing: an apology. An admission that she could have handled herself better during the situation at the Del Rio Hotel, that she shouldn't have been so rigid. That she should have fucking told me my friend was awake and alive, the moment she got the call. I still haven't talked to her about it – I realised, in the hours and days following the chopper crash, that it simply wouldn't achieve anything.

She will never change. For her, no matter what the situation, her opinion is the only one that matters. She is so convinced that her way is the right way that she has completely lost sight of how to win this. All of us have direct experience of fighting Chloe and Adam, and she wants to keep us here while she plays power games with her superiors in Washington. She is so proud and protective of what she's built that it's blinded her. And the crazy thing is, she thinks she's doing us a favour.

Chloe and Adam are going to hurt a lot more people if we don't stop them. And we are not going to be able to do that if Moira Tanner is in charge.

It's going to complicate things. Actually, that's an understatement. The entire US government will be out looking for us. But at this point, we don't have a choice. We can't sit back and watch them try to handle something they are simply not equipped for. If we have to run, if we have to hide for a little while ... so the fuck be it. We're ready.

Annie climbs in the middle seat in the back, already fussing over Reggie. I put a foot on the edge of the door, ready to hoist myself up – the F-350 is big, and it's going to take a lot more effort than I would like – when a hand clamps on my shoulder.

"Going somewhere?" says Burr.

Shit.

That's the thing about special forces guys. You don't see them coming, or hear them.

"We're just getting a ride home," Annie says.

"Uh-huh. And if I looked in the back, I'm sure I'd just find Idriss's weed stash, right?"

"Now listen here, you bloody *toubab* ..."

Goddammit, what made him follow us? Was it something we said? Or didn't say?

Burr reaches over, grabs the door. "Just gonna have a little word with Frost over here."

Before the others can react, he shuts the door. Stands over me, arms folded. Studying me. After a long moment, he pushes his sunglasses up on his head.

"Look," I say. "This isn't—"

"You know, before I came here, I was down in San Diego." His tone is conversational, as if he's about to tell me a joke he heard the other day. "Working with the—"

"SEAL boys, yes, I know. You told me. So what?"

He raises an eyebrow, reproachful. "That's right. Out on Coronado Island. Now, the BUD/S course is one of the toughest in the world. Probably *the* toughest. I know those SAS boys like to think they're hardcore because they go dancing over a mountain in Wales or whatever, but—"

"Is there a point to this story?"

"Christ almighty, Frost, do you ever know when to shut up?"

He clears his throat. "As I was saying, it's a monster course. And the thing is, you can always tell who's going to pass, and who isn't. Some of the instructors might argue with me on this, but I think it's easy."

He pauses for a few seconds, as if deciding whether or not to tell me this. "It's the ones who don't drop their heads. You throw everything you can at them, and even if they fall behind, or fall down, they don't ever quit. And one of two things happen. Either they push themselves way beyond their capabilities and end up getting RTU'd for medical reasons, which is usually the case . . . or they make it."

"And you're telling me this because . . . "

"Because they are the ones you want on the battlefield. They're the ones who keep everyone going, even when they're exhausted and hurting."

I stare at him. Of all the people I expected to have my back, Staff Sergeant Kyle Burr was not one of them.

His voice drops, his words so quiet that I almost don't hear them. "I'll buy you as much time as I can. It's probably not going to be a lot. Make it count."

He doesn't offer his hand to shake. He doesn't need to. He gives me a short, curt nod, then walks away.

I have to replay what just happened in my head before I believe it. When Burr first met me, we hated each other. He genuinely wanted to put me back in a government facility and throw away the key. I broke his finger, for God's sake. And yet here he is, offering to run interference.

I wonder what I did to change his mind. Was it a single thing, or just pressure over time?

"Hey, Burr," I call after him.

"Yeah?" He doesn't turn around, doesn't stop walking.

"Are you saying I could become a Navy SEAL if I wanted to?"

That *does* make him turn. "Frost, don't even think about it. They would eat you alive."

"I don't know. Don't you spend half the course carrying big logs up and down the beach? I probably wouldn't even need anybody to help me—"

"Get the hell out of here before I change my mind."

I do.

I climb into the truck, shut the door. Africa turns the key, manoeuvres us out of the parking lot. Nobody asks what Burr and I talked about, although Reggie gives me a knowing look.

The streets are surprisingly busy this morning, full of traffic. It takes us a while to head north, first on the 605, then the big 210. Up through Compton, Downey, Pico Rivera, El Monte. Past trash, graffiti, glass, steel. Past houses and office buildings, taco trucks and limousines, low-riders and minivans, recording studios and movie sets, actors and screenwriters and lawyers and utility workers and chefs and dishwashers and soccer moms and gangsters and hustlers and bikers and homeless and millionaires and billionaires.

I stare out the window at Los Angeles, thinking about everything she's given me. Thinking about the people with me in this truck, and the ones we lost along the way.

At the Santa Fe Dam, the 210 dog-legs east, and at some point, we turn onto the Interstate 15. The city falls behind us, the skyscrapers vanishing into the haze.

This is the furthest I've been out of the city since I got here. That was the deal with Tanner: I was not to leave LA under any circumstances. I've only done so once, with her permission, when we were tracking down that earthquake kid up in Washington. Beyond that, this is the furthest I've been in four years.

If we keep driving, my arrangement with Tanner is null and void. I'll be on the run for good. I'll have to stay one step ahead of the federal government for the rest of my life. Everything I took for granted, every dream I ever had, will be gone.

The panic is suddenly there, hot and urgent. Sweat pops out on my forehead, my hands, my breath turning ragged. "Guys," I say, my voice choked. "Maybe this isn't such a good idea. Maybe we should think about this."

In response, Nic reaches back between the seats, grabs my hand. Turns to look at me, kind eyes on mine.

Next to me, Annie puts her hand on top of ours. Squeezes. "We got you, baby girl," she tells me. "Never doubt that."

"If you want to turn back, we will," says Reggie. "But . . . "

"You are where you need to be," Africa says simply.

And I am.

There is nowhere else I would rather be than right here, surrounded by my friends. Surrounded by *China Shop*. The greatest motherfucking black-ops crew in history. Reggie, Annie, Africa, Nic – who is as much a part of our outfit as any of us.

My brother and sister are out there. They've killed thousands, done everything they could to destabilise my city and my state and my country. They split China Shop apart, turned us against each other. They struck at the heart of every single one of us. They left us confused and bewildered and snapping at one another, jumping at shadows, unable to react.

Not any more.

We are not going to play defence any more.

I picture my brother and sister in my mind. Picture their

faces. I never wanted to be their enemy. But they started this fight, and now, we're going to finish it.

Chloe. Adam. I hope you're ready.

Because we're coming for you.

ACKNOWLEDGEMENTS

Hey. Teagan here.

Jackson Ford, for once, actually had a shot at writing his own acknowledgements. I found him passed out on his desk, next to a notepad with three things scribbled on it: *Celine Dion, vanilla ice cream* and *???editors???.* The thought process was obviously too much for the poor guy.

Here's who *really* needs to be thanked. To make this boring-ass task interesting for myself, I'm going to compare everyone to characters from classic movies set in Los Angeles. Comparisons are done irrespective of age, gender and race. For example, I myself am clearly Marsellus Wallace from *Pulp Fiction*, even though I'm the polar opposite of Ving Rhames in stature, skin colour, coolness, baldness and not-looking-like-a-bitch-ness.

Ed Wilson, Jackson's long-suffering agent, is very obviously The Dude from *The Big Lebowski*. He might not drink White Russians – he's more of a gin guy – but in almost every other aspect, he is Jeffrey Lebowski. The Dude abides. So does Ed.

Anna Jackson and Nadia Saward, the editors of this story, are Jules Winnfield and Vincent Vega from *Pulp Fiction*. Anna dances even better than Vincent (we've seen proof). And Nadia actually got a promotion while this book was being written, which was why, when Jackson turned in the manuscript late, again, she told him, "Normally, your ass would be dead as fucking fried chicken, but you happened to pull this shit while I'm in a transitional period. So I don't wanna kill you, I wanna help you." Just like my man Jules.

Sticking with the *Pulp Fiction* theme, Orbit's managing editor Joanna Kramer is totally Mr Wolf. Cool as hell, never flinches, expert at cleaning up others' messes. She did an incredible job with Jackson's. As always.

Bradley Englert, editor for Orbit US, is John McClane from *Die Hard*. Not because he looks great in a white vest, or knows how to tape a gun to his back. It's because he's a New Yorker, forced into wandering around Jackson's LA. He was most regularly found hunched over the manuscript muttering, "Fuckin' California . . . "

Madeleine Hall, Orbit's marketing guru, is Jack Traven out of *Speed*. This book is a chaotic, confused mess travelling at well upwards of fifty miles an hour, and only Maddy knows which direction to point it in.

Most people forget, but *Captain Marvel* is set in LA (and on an alien planet, which is functionally the same thing). Orbit publicity duo Nazia Khatun and Ellen Wright are clearly Nick Fury and Carol Danvers. They're both superheroes, and Nazia has an unhealthy obsession with cats that are probably horrifying monsters in disguise.

Sophie Harris, who designed the fabulous yellow monstrosity that is the cover, is Jake Hoyt out of *Training Day*: a skilled professional struggling to make things look good while everything around her is falling to pieces.

And then there's Saxon Bullock. Copy-editor, and Jackson's

nemesis. Saxon points out things that Jackson really, really should think about fixing. As such, he is both highly essential and highly infuriating, mostly because he's usually right. I had to think about this one, but he's the T-1000 from *Terminator 2: Judgement Day*. Jackson can squawk as much as he likes, but Saxon will just keep on coming. And a good thing, too, because otherwise this book would be an error-ridden hell-hole. It probably still is, but that's not Saxon's fault.

Alisha Grauso is Jackson's LA fact-checker. I'm going to go with Mr Miyagi here, from *The Karate Kid*. Just as Daniel-san is a clueless dipshit who knows nothing about karate, Jackson is a clueless dipshit who knows nothing about the city depicted in his books. Fortunately, Alisha is here to make sure he doesn't get his ass kicked by mean bullies. Wax on, wax off.

OK: if I keep doing these comparisons, then pretty soon I'm going to end up comparing someone to Hans Gruber from *Die Hard* or Vincent from *Collateral* (best ever LA movie IMHO) so I'm going to stop here before I get hit with a massive lawsuit. I do still have a few people to thank. Let's say they're the chorus from the opening number of *La La Land*. The whole thing falls down without them.

Nicole Simpson, George Kelly, Ida Horwitz, Werner Schutz, Mez Van Der Toorn, and Rayne Topham (Early readers – and in Werner's case, German language assistance). Prunella Barlow (Spanish language assistance). Emily Hayward-Whitlock and Fern McCauley (The Artists Partnership). Heather Kadin and Alex Kurtzman (CBS/Secret Hideout). The entire Hachette Audio division. The entire Hachette sales division. And of course, every blogger, bookstagrammer, booktokker, booktuber, bookseller, reviewer and reader. You guys are the real heroes here. Thanks for giving us another day of sun.

extras

orbit

meet the author

JACKSON FORD has never been to Los Angeles. The closest he's come is visiting Las Vegas for a Celine Dion concert, where he also got drunk and lost his advance money for this book at the Bellagio. That's what happens when you try to play roulette at the craps table. He is the creator of the Frost Files and the character of Teagan Frost – who, by the way, absolutely did not write this bio, and anybody who says she did is a liar.

Find out more about Jackson Ford and other Orbit authors by registering for the free monthly newsletter at orbitbooks.net.

if you enjoyed
A SH*TLOAD OF CRAZY POWERS

look out for

AUGUST KITKO AND THE MECHAS FROM SPACE

The Starmetal Symphony, Movement One

by

Alex White

When an army of giant robot AIs threatens to devastate Earth, a virtuoso pianist becomes humanity's last hope, in this bold, lightning-paced, Technicolor new space opera series from the author of A Big Ship at the Edge of the Universe.

Jazz pianist Gus Kitko expected to spend his final moments on Earth playing piano at the greatest goodbye party of all time, and

*maybe kissing rockstar Ardent Violet, before the last of humanity
is wiped out forever by the Vanguards—ultrapowerful robots
from the dark heart of space, hell-bent on destroying humanity
for reasons none can divine.*

*But when the Vanguards arrive, the unthinkable happens—the
mecha that should be killing Gus saves him instead. Suddenly,
Gus's swan song becomes humanity's encore, as he is chosen
to join a small group of traitorous Vanguards and their pilots
dedicated to saving humanity.*

CHAPTER ONE
OUR FINAL HOUR

August Kitko doesn't want to see the end of the world—which
should be any minute now.

He leans over the stone railing and gauges the distance to
the jutting pediment of the cliff face below. A couple of sharp
rocks poke up from beneath the choppy surf to say hi.

We're here for you, buddy, comfortable and quick.

Gus grimaces and waves back at them.

He stands at the very edge of Lord Elisa Yamazaki's estate,
one of a few dozen lucky guests brought in for this momentous
occasion. Behind Gus lies the famed Electric Orchard, full
of algae-spliced fruit trees: cherry luxes and pearshines. They
waver in the night like old diodes, dropping off in places when
the breeze rustles them too much. Over the course of hours,
their inner light will fade, and they'll lie upon the grass, gray as
a stone.

The taste is ultimately underwhelming. It's a glowing pear. It doesn't have to be good.

Gus was drawn to this place by the long stone wall with crystal lanterns, the cliffside overlook, and the patch of soft synth grass. This part of the estate has probably stood since the Middle Ages, though the lanterns are obviously new—concentrated vials of the spliced algae, *Plantus glowname*.

Gus missed the taxonomy twice when the lord gave everyone the tour, and was too embarrassed to ask for a third repetition.

As final resting places go, this one won't be so bad. The estate has a commanding view from the eastern rise, so he gets the best sunset he's ever experienced. Monaco's slice of the Mediterranean glitters in the moonlight like no other gem. The city is a thousand icicles jutting up from craggy mountainsides, lining the hills all the way down to the artificial land extensions in the harbor. The Nouvelle Causeway stretches seaward, a big tube atop massive struts, its iconic boxy apartments encrusting its underside like ancient pixels. The Casino de Monte Carlo's searchlights are on full blast in La Condamine district by the harbor—because of course there's a type of person who wants to spend this once-in-a-lifetime night gambling. Gus wonders: Why is anyone hanging around to take their money?

SuperPort Hercule, stretching between Monaco's two artificial mountains, is a relic of another era, when single-terrain vehicles were more common. Rich people still hang on to their water-based yachts, and rows of white boats nestle into slips like suckling piglets. Beyond these exotic antiques, a long expanse of water lily landing pads remains dark—the unused starport. Towering craft loom in the evening, engines cold.

The last ship from Earth launched three years prior. No one else dares—not with the Veil across the galaxy.

extras

Gus blinks at the waves. The fall is going to kill him either way, but for some reason, he'd rather hit the water than the rocks. It mostly comes down to a choice of who gets to eat him—the seagulls or the marine life.

And seagulls are assholes.

Gus needs to wrap things up; he doesn't want to be here when *they* arrive. He'd once been a bit more single-minded in his suicidal ideation, and he finds this last-minute attachment to survival annoying.

It seems unfair that life could get so fun right before the end. He's forgotten the taste of good times, and a dram of happiness has made him too exhausted to complete his morbid task.

If only Gus can make himself climb onto the railing, he knows he can take the next step.

Other "bon" vivants cavort nearby, drinks in hand, some clumsily pawing all over each other. Gus straightens up and stares wistfully at the sea. He can't be seen moping like he's about to jump. They might try to stop him, and then they'd all waste their last few minutes of life trying to calm him down.

Or maybe they'd actually let him do it.

Then he'd spend his final second offended with them.

Perhaps instead, Gus could go to his rock star lover, apologize to them, and pull them in close for the literal kiss to end all kisses—except Ardent Violet is on the veranda, holding court for their adoring public. People and holograms no doubt sit rapt before them, listening to some captivating speech. Ardent isn't about to even talk to Gus, much less peel themself away from a scintillating evening of compliments and basking.

Not after Gus screwed everything up.

The drunken revelers flop down on the nearby grass to step up their make-out game, hands going for buttons and clasps.

Another team of horny fools joins the fray, giggling and gasping. Maybe Gus's cold stare will shrivel their resolve.

They don't even slow down.

There must be somewhere Gus can find a blissful moment of peace. He thrusts his hands into his pockets and wanders back up the estate grounds toward the main house. The lonely path winds past botanical oddities and designer plants of all shapes and colors, vibrant like the coral reefs of old. Lord Yamazaki says she takes her inspiration from Dale Chihuly, but to Gus, she just seems like she's really into jellyfish.

La Maison Des Huit Étoiles rises out of the Electric Orchard like an enchanted castle, its eight glossy blue spires a stark contrast to the archaic walls surrounding the grounds. Atop each spire is a bright light, for the Yamazaki family members who...something. Again, Gus wasn't paying full attention during the tour of the place. He'd had his mind on other things, like being surrounded by the best musicians on Earth.

The bay breeze this evening is unbelievable, the kind of night best spent at an open window with a piano and a drink. The piano still exists, but the booze is all gone, guzzled by the revelers, the staff, and the talent. The staff can't be blamed; they've got their own partying to accomplish, and it's not like Gus is doing *his* job. Few people are—for any reason. Whole swathes of the world are going unwatched, on the verge of collapse, and it doesn't matter.

Gus Kitko, renowned jazz pianist, was flown here to play during the victory party, but they canceled that two days ago.

More accurately, his job was to play during the victory party after-party. His style doesn't exactly draw the millions required to headline, but he's a musician's musician. Some days, it's like his fans are all more famous than he is.

Gus has almost reached the sprawling manse when he detects Ardent's musical laughter. He doesn't want to look—he knows it'll stop his heart—but he glances out of pure masochism.

The rocker stands resplendent in a flowing robe, silks and textiLEDs luxed up like a bird of paradise. Their hair is an anodized red this evening, cut short with an edge like a knife. They've painted their exquisite face in jewel tones, pale skin traced into captivating shapes. Electric-blue lips remain quirked in a smile—until Ardent claps eyes on Gus in return.

They don't rage or scowl. They simply note him with a neutral expression and move on. Ardent Violet lives in another world of packed arenas and coliseums, of paparazzi and nightly jaunts to the most exclusive clubs out there. Gus will never run in their circle again after Monaco—they're above him.

But there is no "after Monaco." Every last person dies here tonight. Even the beautiful, fabulous Ardent Violet.

Yep. Looking was a bad choice.

As it turns out, Gus won't have to feel bad for much longer. A pale streak bisects the sky—a superluminal brake burn and the crackle of lightning. A flaming comet falls from the heavens, and the SuperPort's harbor erupts into a geyser in the wake of a towering splashdown. All eyes travel to the site of the crash, and even the raw magnetism of Ardent Violet can't continue to hold their attention.

A titanic exoskeleton rises from the waves, interlocking armor plates a sleek purple. It unfolds its long arms, each sheathed in an ivory gauntlet, and stands atop a pair of legs. It's humanoid, bilaterally symmetrical. A fission halo encircles its faceless head, spitting plasma sparks in all directions. A pair of silver handles jut from its rib cage like knives buried up to the hilt. It has no eyes, only a smooth purple dome, reflecting all around it.

This titanic disaster could have landed anywhere else on Earth. There was an entire planet of perfectly apocalyptic locations, and a huge pantheon of faiths to satisfy with a melodramatic entrance. But no, it had to show up at the exact spot where Gus was trying to get comfy for his own doom.

Juliette the Vanguard, destroyer of six colonies and two worlds. Soon three—counting Earth.

Two days prior, Gus had hope—tangible hope for the first time in five years. The remnants of the Sol Joint Defense Force had just deployed the unfortunately named *Dictum*, the "solution to the Vanguard Doom." It was a big fancy battle cruiser that could drag travelers out of hyperspace, yanking them into its firing line. That seemed to Gus like a meaningless achievement, but there was a sudden surge of hope among the populace.

The United Worlds leadership were eager to tout their coming success. The plan was to intercept any Vanguards and sucker punch them with the most powerful particle cannons in existence. With defense figured out, the Sol system—last bastion of the human species—could finally go on the offensive.

Gus had dropped his toast when he checked the news that first morning: "Ghosts Massing, Vanguard Incoming, *Dictum* Will Destroy in Sol System."

The harbinger of humanity's end was on its way, and the superweapon was going to stop it—foregone conclusion. Nothing in the news articles indicated this was an "attempt," or that it could fail. Every content outlet talked about the *Dictum* like it had already vaporized all fifteen Vanguards. Anything less spelled the destruction of Earth.

Gus reacted to this news in much the same fashion he handled all his problems: He sat down at his piano and began to play. The ivories calmed his nerves like a gentle rain, and he wrestled with the mortality that everyone on Earth faced. Young or old, they were all in the same boat, tomorrows potentially truncated.

Then came the holocall: General Landry and a cadre of USO coordinators, looking to put on a star-studded concert to celebrate their forthcoming first Vanguard kill. They offered Gus immediate passage to Monaco and accommodations at Lord Yamazaki's, asking him to be ready for the big party.

Gus agreed, and when he terminated the call, a swish Brio XR idled in front of his Montreal walk-up. Its swept nanoblack form absorbed all light, coppery windows and lines of chrome the only reflective surfaces on it. A team of smiling assistants hurried Gus from his house, promising to send anything he needed to Monaco. They even gave him a carte with a few thousand unicreds to load into his account, in case he wanted to relax ahead of time.

It was a hell of a lot nicer than government work was supposed to be.

A stratospheric jaunt later, he was brunching on the deck of a yacht with musical luminaries from the top of the charts. He had one piano song that had been sampled and remixed into a hit, so he felt a mild kinship with these gods. They'd all been summoned by their governments to boost morale, and they were excited to meet August Kitko, "the guy behind that one sample."

Everyone talked about the various battle watch parties they'd be attending that night. People spoke to Gus like he'd already been invited to one. He would've been glad to clear his busy schedule of clipping his toenails in his bedroom and staring wistfully out the window.

No invites were forthcoming, however, and Gus was too shy to ask. He could only hope that someone would take pity on him so he wouldn't spend the most stressful news broadcast of his life alone. The pundits figured the *Dictum*'s interdiction would come sometime in the next twenty hours, pegging the likelihood at eleven p.m.

Victory event details to follow.

To compensate for Gus's lack of friends, government handlers arranged activities and meetups. Every minute of the day leading up to the night was mind-blowing goodness. Champagne and croissants, wandering the casinos, staring into the seaside sunset from the little park at Point Hamilton.

Even though the greenway was just a couple of statues and a few bushes crammed between two luxury high-rise condos, the place had a peaceful air. Gus's hiking buddies, a pair of rockers from a town named Medicine Hat, said they wanted to call a friend to bring some wine. That friend turned out to be the multi-platinum-record-selling Ardent Violet, who showed up with a block party in tow. Food, liquor, and drugs followed, and Gus found himself ensnared by the wildest rave he'd ever attended in a public park.

When the throng became unbearable, Gus pushed out to the street for some fresh air. He wound down a few side alleys, trying to get a little space from Ardent's many admirers.

Instead, he ran into Ardent Violet themself.

They sported a forest-green pin-striped suit, its edges given careful folds like paper animals. A few fresh flowers bloomed on their wide-brimmed hat. The whole outfit looked like it cost a fortune, which was why Gus was surprised to find Ardent sitting on the old stone curb, flicking through the Ganglion UI on their bracelet.

Gus wasn't a fan, but he knew a member of the pop music royalty when he saw one. He was always wary of speaking to the big leaguers like them; half the time, they turned out to be nightmare humans with disturbing views.

"You okay?" Gus asked.

Ardent rose and brushed the dust from their butt. "Yeah. Just had to come up for air."

Gus glanced back the way he'd come, toward the party in the idyllic park. It was too much for him, a person whose scene was quiet piano bars, but surely Ardent could handle it. The rocker regularly flounced about circus-ring stages with all sorts of holograms, drones, strobes, tractor beams, and earth-shattering bass.

Gus frowned thoughtfully. "You *brought* the party."

"I always do." A bitter note flavored their voice.

"That sounds difficult." Gus sauntered over to a parked CAV and leaned against it. It squawked a warning at him, and Ardent jumped. Thank goodness, they both laughed.

"Uh, sorry about that..." Gus resettled himself against an aging wall near a historical marker dating it all the way back to the 2150s. The building's moneyed architecture bore the hallmarks of the Infinite Expansion—right down to the streamlined, printed flagstones flecked through with precious metals and gem shards.

"Gus Kitko." He raised a hand in a brief wave, then crossed his arms.

"Kitko," they repeated.

He pushed off the wall. "And I should go, because you said you were out here to come up for air."

"Aw, whatever."

"No, no! I shouldn't be taking up your time. Being Ardent Violet looks, uh..."

A raucous roar from the party wafted by on the breeze.

"Exhausting," he finished.

They fixed him with their gaze, and it was like staring into the sun. They'd tinted their irises an inhuman red to complement their dark green suit. What was going through their head? Had his comment been over the line?

When the silence grew too painful, Gus reached into his pocket and pulled out his battered old mint tin. Its contents jingled softly as he flipped it open. Ardent immediately perked up.

"What do those do?" they asked.

"Taste like mint," Gus replied. "Would you like one?"

"You're probably the only person here who carries candy instead of drugs."

"Then you need me around, for when you'd rather have things sweet and calm."

"Is that what you are?" Ardent asked, red eyes boring into him. They drew close and plucked a mint from the tin. "Sweet and calm?"

"My friends would say so."

Ardent cupped the candy in their gloved hand and keyed their Gang UI. They closed their fingers around it, and the glove flashed inside: a chemical analysis.

"No offense," Ardent said. "I'm a target for kidnappers."

"None taken. Sorry you have to deal with that stuff."

Ardent popped the mint into their mouth, and Gus took one of his own, savoring the evolving fizz of classical molecular gastronomy, the flowing of spearmint tendrils in his mouth.

Ardent let out a happy sigh, resting their hands on their hips to stare down the hill. "Pretty good mint."

"Straight from Old Town Montreal. Local delicacy."

"Really?"

"Nah. Bought them at Trudeau. What kind of a town would have a local delicacy like that?"

Ardent let out a short laugh. "You're proud of poutine."

"Well, where are you from?"

"Atlanta," they said, and he could *almost* pick out the accent.

"Ah, biscuits," Gus said. "So simple, yet so perfect."

Ardent cocked an eyebrow. "You need to get in the kitchen if you think biscuits are simple."

A few of the celebrants from the park made their way around the corner, screaming "Ardent!" the moment they saw their leader. Gus had fans, too, but they mostly held listening teleparties and talked about whether a seventh or a ninth was a more appropriate resolution to the end of Guy Keats's "Too Blue a Bird."

Teleparties were easily escaped. Real parties could hunt one down, as this crowd did to the unfortunate Ardent Violet.

"You're coming, right? To the prince's tonight?" Ardent asked. "Secret military watch party."

"I don't think I've got an invite."

"*I'm* your invite."

"Oh! I would love that. How will I get in if we're separated?"

"You won't. Better hang on to me, Kitty Kitko."

They gestured for Gus to follow, and—though he hated this sort of loud affair—he did.

if you enjoyed
A SH*TLOAD OF CRAZY POWERS

look out for

SHARDS OF EARTH

Book One of
The Final Architecture

by

Adrian Tchaikovsky

The Arthur C. Clarke Award–winning author of Children of Time *brings us an extraordinary space opera about humanity on the brink of extinction and how one man's discovery will save or destroy us all.*

The war is over. Its heroes forgotten.
Until one chance discovery....

Idris has neither aged nor slept since they remade him in the war. And one of humanity's heroes now scrapes by on a freelance salvage vessel to avoid the attention of greater powers.

After Earth was destroyed, mankind created a fighting elite to save their species, enhanced humans such as Idris. In the silence of space, they could communicate mind-to-mind with the enemy. Then their alien aggressors, the Architects, simply disappeared— and Idris and his kind became obsolete.

Now, fifty years later, Idris and his crew have discovered something strange abandoned in space. It's clearly the work of the Architects—but are they returning? And if so, why? Hunted by gangsters, cults, and governments, Idris and his crew race across the galaxy, hunting for answers. For they now possess something of incalculable value that many would kill to obtain.

PROLOGUE

In the seventy-eighth year of the war, an Architect came to Berlenhof.

The lights of human civilization across the galaxy had been going out, one by one, since its start. All those little mining worlds, the far-flung settlements, the homes people had made. The Colonies, as they were known: the great hollow Polyaspora of human expansion, exploding out from a vacant centre. Because the Architects had come for Earth first.

Berlenhof had become humanity's second heart. Even before Earth fell, it had been a prosperous, powerful world. In the war, it was the seat of military command and civilian governance, coordinating a civilization-scale refugee effort, as more and more humans were forced to flee their doomed worlds.

And because of that, when the Architect came, the Colonies turned and fought, and so did all the allies they had gathered there. It was to be the great stand against a galactic-level threat, every weapon deployed, every secret advantage exploited.

Solace remembered. She had been there. Basilisk Division, Heaven's Sword Sorority. Her first battle.

*

The Colonies had a secret weapon, that was the word. A human weapon. Solace had seen them at the war council. A cluster of awkward, damaged-looking men and women, nothing more. As the main fleet readied itself to defend Berlenhof, a handful of small ships were already carrying these "weapons" towards the Architect in the hope that this new trick would somehow postpone the inevitable.

Useless, surely. Might as well rely on thoughts and prayers.

On the *Heaven's Sword*, everyone off-shift was avidly watching the displays, wanting to believe this really *was* something. Even though all previous secret weapons had been nothing but hot air and hope. Solace stared as intently as the rest. The Architect was impossible to miss on screen, a vast polished mass the size of Earth's lost moon, throwing back every scan and probe sent its way. The defending fleet at Berlenhof was a swarm of pinpricks, so shrunk by the scale they were barely visible until she called for magnification. The heart of the Colonies had already been gathering its forces for dispatch elsewhere when the Architect had emerged from unspace at the edge of the system. Humanity was never going to get better odds than this.

extras

There were Castigar and Hanni vessels out there, alien trading partners who were lending their strength to their human allies because the Architects were everybody's problem. There was a vast and ragged fleet of human ships, and some of them were dedicated war vessels and others were just whatever could be thrown into space that wasn't any use for the evacuation. Orbiting Hiver factories were weaponizing their workers. There was even the brooding hulk of a Naeromathi Locust Ark out there, the largest craft in-system—save that it was still dwarfed by the Architect itself. And nobody knew what the Locusts wanted or thought about anything, save that even they would fight this enemy.

And there was the pride of the fleet, Solace's sisters: the Parthenon. Humans, for a given value of human. The engineered warrior women who had been the Colonies' shield ever since the fall of Earth. *Heaven's Sword*, *Ascending Mother* and *Cataphracta*, the most advanced warships humanity had ever designed, equipped with weapons that the pre-war days couldn't even have imagined.

As Solace craned to see, she spotted a tiny speckle of dots between the fleet and the Architect: the advance force. The tip of humanity's spear was composed of the Partheni's swiftest ships. Normally, their role would have been to buy time. But on this occasion, the *Pythoness*, the *Ocasio*, the *Ching Shi* and others were carrying their secret weapon to the enemy.

Solace didn't believe a word of it. The mass looms and the Zero Point fighters the *Heaven's Sword* was equipped with would turn the battle, or nothing would. Even as she told herself that, she heard the murmur of the other off-shift women around her. "Intermediaries," one said, a whisper as if talking about something taboo; and someone else, a girl barely old enough to be in service: "They say they cut their *brains*. That's how they make them."

"Telemetry incoming," said one of the officers, and the display focused in on those few dots. They were arrowing towards the Architect, as though planning to dash themselves against its mountainous sides. Solace felt her eyes strain, trying to wring more information from what she was seeing, to peer all the way in until she had an eye inside the ships themselves.

One of those dots winked out. The Architect had registered their presence and was patiently swatting at them. Solace had seen the aftermath of even a brush with an Architect's power: twisted, crumpled metal, curved and corkscrewed by intense gravitational pressures. A large and well-shielded ship might weather a glancing blow. With these little craft there would be no survivors.

"It's *useless*," she said. "*We* need to be out there. Us." Her fingers itched for the keys of the mass looms.

"Myrmidon Solace, do you think you know better than the Fleet Exemplars?" Her immediate superior, right at her shoulder of course.

"No, Mother."

"Then just watch and be ready." And a muttered afterthought: "Not that I don't agree with you." And even as her superior spoke, another of the tiny ships had been snuffed into darkness.

"Was that—?" someone cried, before being cut off. Then the officer was demanding, "Telemetry, update and confirm!"

"A marked deviation," someone agreed. The display was bringing up a review, a fan of lines showing the Architect's projected course and its current trajectory.

"So it altered its course. That changes nothing," someone spat, but the officer spoke over them. "They *turned* an Architect! Whatever they did, they *turned* it!"

Then they lost all data. After a tense second's silence, the displays blinked back, the handful of surviving ships fleeing the Architect's renewed approach towards Berlenhof. Whatever the secret weapon was, it seemed to have failed.

"*High alert*. All off-shift crews make ready to reinforce as needed. The fight's coming to us!" came the voice of the officer. Solace was still staring at the display, though. *Had* they accomplished nothing? Somehow, this secret Intermediary weapon had shifted the course of an Architect. Nobody had made them so much as flinch before.

Orders came through right on the heels of the thought. "Prepare to receive the *Pythoness*. Damage control, medical, escort." And she was the third of those, called up out of the off-shift pool along with her team.

The *Pythoness* had been a long, streamlined ship: its foresection bulked out by its gravitic drives and then tapering down its length to a segmented tail. That tail was gone, and the surviving two-thirds of the ship looked as though a hand had clenched about it, twisting every sleek line into a tortured curve. That the ship had made it back at all was a wonder. The moment the hatch was levered open, the surviving crew started carrying out the wounded. Solace knew from the ship's readouts that half its complement wouldn't be coming out at all.

"Myrmidon Solace!"

"Mother!" She saluted, waiting for her duties.

"Get this to the bridge!"

She blinked. *This* was a man. A Colonial human man. He was skinny and jug-eared and looked as though he'd already snapped under the trauma of the fight. His eyes were wide and his lips moved soundlessly. Twitches ran up and down his body like rats. She'd seen him before, at the council of war. One of the vaunted Intermediaries.

"Mother?"

"Take him to the bridge. Now, Myrmidon!" the officer snapped, and then she leant in and grabbed Solace's shoulder. "This is *it*, sister. This is the weapon. And if it's a weapon, we need to use it."

There were billions on Berlenhof: the local population as well as countless refugees from the other lost worlds. Nobody was going to get even a thousandth of those people off-world before the Architect destroyed it. But the more time they could buy for the evacuation effort, the more lives would be saved. This was what the Parthenon was spending its ships and lives for. That was what the Hivers would expend their artificial bodies for, and the alien mercenaries and partisans and ideologues would die for. Every lost ship was another freighter off Berlenhof packed out with civilians.

She got the man into a lift tube, aware of the wide-eyed looks he'd been receiving as she hauled him from the dock. He must be getting a far worse case of culture-shock; regular Colonials didn't mix with the Parthenon and before the war there'd been no love lost. Here he was on a ship full of women who all had close on the same face, the same compact frame. Human enough to be uncanny but, for most Colonials, not quite human *enough*.

He was saying something. For a moment she heard nonsense, but she'd learned enough Colvul to piece together the words. It was just a demand to wait. Except they were already in the lift, so he could wait all he wanted and they'd still get where they were needed. "Wait, I can't . . ."

"You're here . . . Menheer." It took a moment for her to remember the correct Colvul honorific. "My name is Myrmidon Solace. I am taking you to the bridge of the *Heaven's Sword*. You are going to fight with us."

He stared at her, shell-shocked. "They're *hurt*. My ship. We jumped . . ."

"This is your ship now, Menheer." And, because he was shaking again, she snapped at him. "*Name*, Menheer?"

He twitched. "Telemmier. Idris Telemmier. Intermediary. First class."

"They say you're a weapon. So now you have to fight."

He was shaking his head, but then she had him out of the lift and the officers were calling for him.

The battle displays formed a multicoloured array in the centre of the bridge, showing the vast fleet as it moved to confront the Architect. Solace saw that they were finally about to fire on it: to do what little damage they could with lasers and projectiles, suicide drones, explosives and gravitic torsion. But their goal was only to slow it. A victory against an Architect was when you made yourself enough of a nuisance that they had to swat you before they could murder the planet.

They got Idris in front of the display, though Solace had to hold him upright.

"What am I—?" he got out. Solace saw he didn't have the first clue what was going on.

"Whatever you can do, *do*," an officer snapped at him. Solace could see and feel that the *Heaven's Sword* was already on its attack run. She wanted desperately to be on-shift at the mass loom consoles, bringing that ersatz hammer against the shell of the Architect. She didn't believe in this Intermediary any more than she believed in wizards.

Still, when he turned his wan gaze her way, she mustered a smile and he seemed to take something from that. Something lit behind his eyes: madness or divine revelation.

Then their sister ship's mass loom fired and Solace followed the *Cataphracta*'s strike through the bridge readouts. It was a weapon developed through studying the Architects themselves, a hammerblow of pure gravitic torsion, aiming to tear a rift in their enemy's crystalline exterior. Operators read off the subsequent damage reports: fissuring minimal but present; target areas flagged up for a more concentrated assault. The *Heaven's Sword*'s Zero Point fighters were flocking out of its bays now and dispersing, a hundred gnats to divert the enemy's time and attention from the big guns.

The whole bridge sang like a choir for just a moment as their own mass loom spoke, resonating through the entire length of the ship. Solace felt like shouting out with it, as she always did. And kept her mouth shut, because here on the bridge that sort of thing would be frowned on.

Idris gasped then, arching backwards in her arms, and she saw blood on his face as he bit his tongue. His eyes were wider than seemed humanly possible, all the whites visible and a ring of red around each as well. He screamed, prompting concerned shouts from across the bridge, eclipsed when the Fleet Exultant in command called out that the Architect had faltered. Impossible that so much inexorable momentum could be diverted by anything short of an asteroid impact. But it had jolted in the very moment that Idris had yelled.

The mass loom sang again, and she saw the *Cataphracta* and the *Ascending Mother* firing too, all targeting the same fractures in the Architect's structure. Smaller ships were wheeling in swarms past the behemoth's jagged face, loosing every weapon they had, frantic to claim an iota of the thing's monstrous attention. She saw them being doused like candles, whole handfuls at a time. And then the Architect's invisible hands reached out and wrung the whole length of the *Cataphracta* and opened it out like a flower. A ship and all its souls turned into a tumbling metal sculpture and cast adrift into the void. And it would do exactly the same to Berlenhof when it reached the planet.

The Locust Ark was annihilated next, fraying into nothing as it tried to throw its disintegrating mass into the Architect's path. Then the *Sword*'s loom spoke, but the choir was in discord now, the very seams of the warship strained by the power of her own weaponry. Idris was clutching Solace's hands painfully, leaning into her and weeping. The Architect had halted, for the first time since it entered the system, no longer advancing on the planet. She felt Idris vibrate at that point, rigid as he did *something*; as he wrestled the universe for control over the apocalyptic engine that was the Architect. Her ears were full of the rapid, efficient patter of the bridge reports: stress fractures, targeting, the elegant physics of gravity as a bludgeoning weapon. Damage reports. So many damage reports. The Architect had already brushed them once and Solace had barely realized. Half the decks of the *Heaven's Sword* were evacuating.

"It's cracking!" someone was shouting. "It's cracking open!"

"Brace!" And Solace had to brace for herself and Idris too. Because his mind was somewhere else, doing battle on a field she couldn't even imagine.

*

There was a terrible impact and the screens briefly malfunctioned. Then in the chaos, as the *Heaven's Sword* died, the Fleet Exultant gave Solace her last orders. In response, she grabbed the Intermediary—the little Colonial man who might be their greatest weapon—and hustled him through the wreckage. She bundled him through the surviving sections of the ship to the life pods. She prioritized him even over her sisters because he'd been made her responsibility, but also because he was hope: the universe now had one destroyed Architect; before the Battle of Berlenhof that number had been zero.

extras

*

Later, in the vast medical camp planetside, Solace had been there holding Idris's hand when he awoke. They'd been surrounded by other casualties from the *Heaven's Sword*, all the other lucky ones who'd managed to escape with injuries rather than obliteration. Between the fight and its explosive end, half the fleet and a dozen orbitals had been crippled.

Idris had squeezed her hand, and she'd hugged him impulsively, just as she would have hugged a sister. There was more fighting to come, but right then they were just two comrades in arms. A pair who'd stood before the inevitable and still turned it aside, and the war owed them time to heal.

Six years later, the Intermediaries would finally end the war, though not by destroying or even defeating the enemy. The Architects, after almost a century of hounding humanity from world to world, would simply not be seen any more, vanished off into the endless space of the galaxy. Nobody could say where they had gone. And nobody knew when or if they might return.

Thirty-nine years after that, they woke Solace from cold storage one more time and said her warrior skills were needed. Not because the Architects were back, but because the Parthenon and the Colonies were on the brink of war.

Follow us:

/orbitbooksUS

/orbitbooks

/orbitbooks

Join our mailing list
to receive alerts on our
latest releases and deals.

orbitbooks.net

Enter our monthly
giveaway for the chance
to win some epic prizes.

orbitloot.com